About

Zena Barrie lives in Manchester and runs the Greater Manchester Fringe and the Camden Fringe. She ran the Kings Arms pub and Theatre in Salford for a while and also the Etcetera Theatre in Camden as well as working in a wide variety of roles at the Edinburgh Fringe. In the 90s she did a degree in Drama and Theatre Arts specialising in playwriting.

Up until recently she has been co-hosting the award-winning spoken-word night Verbose. This is her first novel.

Your Friend Forever

Zena Barrie

unbound

This edition first published in 2021

Unbound
6th Floor Mutual House, 70 Conduit Street, London W1S 2GF
www.unbound.com
All rights reserved

© Zena Barrie, 2021

The right of Zena Barrie to be identified as the author of this work has been asserted in accordance with Section 77 of the Copyright, Designs and Patents Act 1988. No part of this publication may be copied, reproduced, stored in a retrieval system, or transmitted, in any form or by any means without the prior permission of the publisher, nor be otherwise circulated in any form of binding or cover other than that in which it is published and without a similar condition being imposed on the subsequent purchaser.

This book is a work of fiction and, except in the case of historical fact, any resemblance to actual persons, living or dead, is purely coincidental.

ISBN (eBook): 978-1-78965-108-9
ISBN (Paperback): 978-1-78965-107-2

Cover design by Mecob

Printed and bound in Great Britain by Clays Ltd, Elcograf S.p.A.

Super Patrons

Rohan Acharya
Sonya Adams
Noor Ali
Samantha Allen-Turner
Rachael Allison
Angela Arbuckle
Craig Barrie
Richard Beck
Mick Booker
Jen Brister
Gus Brown
Phil Cass
Sarah Cassidy
Marina Castledine
Corin Christopher
Sue Clark
Carolyn Clewer
Andrew Collier
Stephen Colvil
Lisa Connor
Alice Cook

Caroline Cooke
Marie Crook
Tony Davey
Karen Dean
Silke Dykstra
Neil Edmond
Philip Ellis Mills
Steven Errington
Adam Farrer
Isabel Fay
Jose Ferran
Michelle Flower
Clare Foster
G.E. Gallas
Paco B. Garcia
Zoe Gardner
Nicola Gilchrist
Steve Hall
Rachel Halliday
Cheryl Hayes
Natalie Haynes
Sarah Holmes
Joanna Howard
Stuart Hudson
Robin Ince
Charlie Ivens
Alexander Kirk
Anna Kushlick
Simon Laird
Ari Levy
Chris Limb
Jeremy Limb
Geoff Lloyd

Caroline Mabey
James Mackenzie
Robert McCafferty
Dan Mersh
Faye Middleton-Duff
Stefanie Moore
Justin Moorhouse
Ed Morrish
Sarah Mosedale
Tiffany Murray
Nalini Naga
Clare Nightingale
Christopher Northen
Clare Northen
Cathy O'Donnell
Kate Orson
Libby Peryer
Jane Pinkerton
Agustin Piza
Paul Putner
Kathryn Ratzko
Stuart Reed
Angela Richmond
Claire Robinson
Laura Robinson
Lizzie Roper
Alasdair Satchel
Stephen Scott-Fawcett
James Seabright
Sandhya Sharma
Penny Sims
Rachel Smith
Tim Standish

Frog Stone
Nick Swift
Carbootymusic Tate
Lucy Titley
Andrea Todd
Piers Torday
Gareth Tunley
Susan Turnbull
Mike Wilson
Laura Woodroffe
Felicity Wren
James Wren

For Joanna, Claire & Lucy

Part One

January 1981

> For the attention of Mr Tom Harding
> Friends of Horsefly
> PO BOX 113
> London W2
> 8th January 1981

Maud Harrison
22 Slater Street
Hutton
Preston

Dear Mr Harding,

One's name is Maud Harrison and one is pleased to make your acquaintance. One is twelve years old, thirteen next week so one might as well say one is thirteen (a teenager). One lives in Preston, not in the centre where all the shops are, but in a place called Hutton. It's basically just lots of houses. There are some posh houses and some not posh houses. I live in one of the not posh houses. We do still have all our windows though (although the bathroom window is held in with chewing gum) so one mustn't complain about one's lot. One's mother called one's father a 'fucking fucker' when she realised he had fixed the window with Hubba Bubba and not special window putty from the do-it-yourself shop. Apparently it's 'not the same fucking thing'. One is a really big fan of your band (Horsefly) and of you in particular (as you are the songwriter and one gets a lot from the songs: life information, feelings, and most importantly inspiration for one's life). One read in Smash Hits that you collect thimbles since your Great Grandma left you some in her will. How did she die? (I hope it's not hereditary.) One has enclosed the thimble from one's Mum's sewing box. She doesn't use it (one has never seen her use it anyway). One hopes it fits. Your hands are probably bigger than Mum's. Do you have big hands? One has wrapped it in toilet roll (it's clean). Please could you send one your autograph and post it to one in the enclosed SAE (stamped addressed envelope)? One really likes the trousers you were wearing in Sounds magazine last month. They are quite unusual aren't they? You never see trousers like that in Preston. One only has one pair of trousers and they are flared and much too short so it can be quite embarrassing having to wear them. One has grown quite a lot recently, in length but not in width. One doesn't have any women's hips yet, you cannot pinch an inch anywhere. One is now the same height as a naturally short woman or a woman who has suffered stunted growth due to poor health.

Yours in anticipation of a favourable reply,
Miss Maud Harrison

P.S. How tall are you?

P.P.S. Are you married?

P.P.P.S. I hope you don't mind receiving unsolicited

correspondence (letters). I suppose it comes with the territory of being a very successful pop star.

P.P.P.P.S. It's not that I don't have any actual hip bones. I do, I can feel them. They're just still in line with my rib cage. I've been led to believe this will change after I have metamorphosed (changed) into a functional woman. How old were you when you changed into a functional man?

***

For the attention of Mr Tom Harding
Friends of Horsefly
PO BOX 113
London W2
14th January 1981

Maud Harrison
22 Slater Street
Hutton
Preston

Dear Tom (I do hope it's okay to call you that. I'm trying to be less formal but not overly familiar. Do please let me know at your earliest convenience if you'd prefer me to address you in a different or in a more inappropriate manner).

Hello, it's me, Maud Harrison, I've written to you before (last week). Did you get my letter? Firstly apologies if I confused you in my last letter by saying 'one' all the time. I read that that was the proper way to refer to yourself, but my English teacher took me aside the other day after I'd used it in some homework, an essay about what I'd done over Christmas (very little), and asked me if

I was the Queen and when I said no he told me to 'stop bloody referring to yourself as "one", then'. When I opened my exercise book he'd also put in the margin that he'd stopped reading after six pages because it was too long. So I'm very sorry if it was confusing, I'm quite new to writing letters. I've only really written one before that I can recall and it was to a girl in France called Marie who was supposed to be my pen pal. My teacher gave me her name and address. I didn't know and still don't know much French so it wouldn't have been a very good letter. Mostly just asking her directions really. She never wrote back. I'm not completely sure that my Mum posted it to be honest, French stamps are quite expensive.

I go to Hutton South Comprehensive, I'm in the second year, most of the people there (pupils and teachers) are dreadful and the lessons don't do much to inspire me. Every day we go through the motions of a normal day at high school, everyone is just waiting for their lunch and then waiting until the bell goes and we can all go home, no one actually wants to be there, it's a shame really when we're all supposed to be learning. The teachers all smell of coffee and fags apart from Mr Parkinson who Sarah (my best friend) says smells of whisky (and fags). I've never had a fag or drunk whisky and my Mum and Dad only drink tea, Dad did used to go to the pub but he hasn't for a long time. Sarah's Mum drinks coffee but I've never tried it. Sarah has had Mellow Bird's (sexy coffee).

I'd really like to play in a rock band when I grow up. At school when we do music the only instruments are recorders, xylophones, euphoniums and trumpets. The music teacher Mr Ward did say I could take a euphonium home and give it a try but Mum said I'm not allowed to learn that type of instrument because of my asthma, well she said 'good God no way', then she said because of my asthma. I hardly ever get asthma really, my brother has it worse than me. I told all this to my teacher and he just rolled his eyes. I'm not sure if he was rolling his eyes to my Mum or rolling his eyes at my asthma. What do you think? I'm not sure teachers should be allowed to roll their eyes at the pupils. It's not fair for them not to explain things properly. Do you think I should ask him to explain himself? I don't really like the noise of a euphonium anyway so I'm not too bothered. They don't have a euphonium in The Clash do they? You don't have a euphonium in Horsefly do you? It's only really good for Songs of Praise (when you can see all the people in their best clothes miming along to a hymn hoping to get talent spotted) or if you want the noise of an elephant or a rhino plodding through some woods or something, and that's not really music is it? More of a sound effect. My Dad has a record of sound effects, I'm not sure why. Lots of ones of taps running and the sound of rain and different doors opening and closing. It rains all the time in Preston so we don't really need a record of it. It's not like I ever miss the rain so much that I want to play it on a record. We can't play it any more anyway as the radiogram gives us an electric shock if we plug it in. Dad won't get rid of it though, even though it takes up half the front room. He doesn't like your music, he says he only likes Ska. He bought some two-tone shoes and Mum got really angry about them. She called him a 'fucking arse-hole'. I think it's because we don't have much money. Also I'm not sure where he'll wear them. I haven't seen him wear them yet, apart from sat in the front room but he did look really happy with them on, he kept looking down and smiling at them, I was watching him for ages, I watched him watching the telly in his new shoes. I could do with some new shoes. When did your feet stop growing? It would be really handy if mine would stop growing.

 I'm being shouted at so I have to go now.
 Your most humble servant,
 Maud Harrison

P.S. Mum was just shouting in general, it wasn't specifically at me, but when I went downstairs it became specifically at me so I've come upstairs again, I just seem to always be in the way.

P.P.S. I'm not sure if I am a humble servant really. I have quite a humble opinion about what I look like but I have quite a high opinion about my mind (I think it is better than most people's minds that I come into contact with). I think some of this is down to you. I read an interview in NME where you said you 'read everything you can get your hands on', and that you like reading poetry, in particular Keats and Browning. So I try to read everything that I can get my hands on too. Are you familiar with the poetic works of Pam Ayres?

P.P.P.S. Are you humble? You always look quite humble in your pictures, or maybe sad, certainly not proud which I think is the opposite of humble. I'm not a proud person even though I have a high opinion of my own brain, well maybe I'm secretly proud, although I am telling you about it so I think that just makes me a show off. I'll try to stop doing that.

P.P.P.P.S. I'm going to be a teenager next week. I'm not sure I'm prepared for it at all. I wish there was a book I could read that wasn't just about puberty. I know my body is going to change but I need to know all the other things. I suppose we are expected to find out for ourselves. I'd rather read a manual so I don't have to keep getting things wrong.

P.P.P.P.P.S. If you're wondering why I'm called Maud (an old woman's / witch's name) it's because I'm named after my Dad's auntie that he fancied. She died before I was born though and I've never seen a picture of her. It's probably a good job she's died because if my Dad had carried on with her instead of my

Mum I wouldn't exist, or I could have been an inbred (a human ass) and incapable of bearing children (if I ever wanted to).

***

For the attention of Mr Tom Harding
Friends of Horsefly
PO BOX 113
London W2
18th January 1981

Maud Harrison
22 Slater Street
Hutton
Preston

Dear Tom,

    I really want to play the guitar. I asked for an electrical guitar for Christmas, I didn't get one (I got some socks, tights, 7p in pennies, a writing pad, a packet of biros, one of my Mum's old jumpers and three tangerines) but my Dad says he'll look out for one in the pawn shop (it's a secondhand shop where people take things and sell them to the shopkeeper and then buy them back the next week if they can afford it and if they can't then someone else will buy them). I don't think he really will though because he's got no money and there's no one to teach me how to play it anyway. How did you learn to play the guitar? Did you have lessons? I've got no one to be in a band with anyway. Actually Sarah (my one true friend) might do it, but she can't play anything either, well we can both play Silent Night on the recorder, and Sarah said we could still be punk if we played Silent Night and then smashed them up. But if I smash mine up I won't be able to get another one, it's not mine anyway, it's the school's, it's about fifty years old, the top of it is all chewed. Also what if we wait until our first gig to try the smashing up and it turns out I can't smash it up properly. They're quite sturdy. And if I did manage to smash it at the gig it would mean no more gigs, and you can't just play one gig can you? I don't think we should do it anyway, it's not going to help matters.

I really like your song Shandy Hand. Sometimes we get a bottle of Bass shandy with chips on a Friday. I really like the taste of it. I don't think there is any alcohol in it though. My brother Simon always drinks it then pretends he's drunk. He's fourteen and a half. He's a real idiot, and I think he hates me because I'm (much) cleverer than him. It's stupid hating a person for being clever isn't it? I could help him with his homework and suggest some further reading for him if he wasn't so horrible.

Yours sincerely in anticipation of a favourable reply,
Maud Harrison

P.S. I can't understand why there is nothing inspiring or emotional about being at school. I am full of ideas and feelings all the time. I don't understand why everyone else isn't full of them. Or are they just hiding it? In which case I wish they wouldn't hide it. Is it just me having all these thoughts? I wonder if on the outside I look like a person without thoughts or feelings. Maybe I just look like a boring, pasty nearly thirteen year old. I suppose I am (but loads of interesting things are going on behind my face, sometimes too much, it's probably good that it's invisible, I could get arrested, I'm not sure if all of it is legal a hundred per cent of the time). Do you ever have illegal thoughts? I'd love to hear all about them.

February 1981

For the attention of Mr Tom Harding
Friends of Horsefly
PO BOX 113
London W2
14th February 1981

Maud Harrison
22 Slater Street
Hutton
Preston

Dear Tom,

Hello, it's Maud Harrison, I've written to you before, I don't know if you remember. Or if you got my letters.

It doesn't matter, I bet you're really busy anyway, writing songs, keeping up with the latest fashions or inventing them and doing that thing to your hair (which I would do if I had enough hair but I don't. Also I don't have any hair spray and I think I would get sent home from school if I did manage to achieve that look). It's just really nice to be able to write to someone who understands me. Things are a bit shit. (I hope you don't mind swearing, I have heard you use a wide variety of swear words in interviews so I thought you wouldn't mind, please let me know if it's offensive.)

I'm a teenager now, I have been one for three weeks. There's just nothing to do round here for us teenagers and I hate school. Me and Sarah, that's my teenage best friend, just hang out at break and lunchtime together. We've found this bit of the school where we can go behind a wall and no one knows we're there. We sit there every day, just two teenagers together. A few months ago I had a corned beef butty from the canteen that I just put in my coat pocket so I didn't have to sit in the dinner hall and eat it. The dinner hall is horrible. Every table has a battered water jug and in every water jug there is always a frog from someone's throat. I've never seen anyone do it but absolutely every jug has one. Maybe it's the dinner ladies. They always look as if they hate us. I'm not surprised. Think of the washing up. Oh and do you know if the food that goes in the pig swill bin actually goes to pigs? Or is it just put in a bin? I hope it does go to some pigs because otherwise it's such a waste. I'm not sure where the pigs are though. Maybe a farmer comes and collects it every day. He must get annoyed on the days when everyone likes their food and eats it all up so the pigs have to go hungry. It sort of means bacon is made of leftover school dinners and water with spit in it. It's enough to make me consider vegetarianism, though I suppose I am entirely made up of school dinners and water with my own spit in it so what's the difference. Oh and Mum's cooking too, mostly toast. I suppose I can never be fully vegetarian because I myself am made of meat. I wonder if I'm chickeny or beefy? I can't be porky because I feel certain I'd have smelt that.

Anyway, when I opened the corned beef butty from the canteen, it was horrible, there was loads of hard yellow fat in it. I didn't have a hanky so I rubbed the corned beef off onto the wall (and just ate the bread) and it's still there and it's been there for weeks. We call it the corned beef wall now and Sarah says if we ever start a band we should call the band Corned Beef Wall or maybe at least our first single. I'm not sure about the band having corned beef in the title though, and we think we might become vegetarian anyway. Sarah keeps trying to be a vegetarian but her Mum won't take any notice of her and just gives her meat pies anyway so she has to eat it but when she's old enough she's going to stop eating meat. I might, but I do really like meat when I have it and I don't have it that often anyway. Sometimes my Mum makes burger and chips but by the time it's defrosted and then cooked the burger is about the size of a 2p piece and that's including the bits of onion in it (I think it's onion, it might not be). You could probably make one without really killing the pig, just scrape a bit off its bum and then stick a plaster on it until next time. Though I'm sure that wouldn't be very nice for the pig, although surely better than dying? Anyway, beef burgers are supposed to be made out of cows. It would be harder to cut a bit off a cow's bum because of their thick skin. A pig looks like it's been skinned already. Don't you think?

Sorry about the pink envelope. It's from a writing set one of my Mum's friends got me when I was about seven. I don't have any other envelopes. The sticky bit doesn't work. I'll have to see if we've got any Sellotape. There might be a bit left over from Christmas.

Yours sincerely,

Maud (lead singer or maybe guitarist from Corned Beef Wall)

P.S. Happy Valentine's Day! What do you think of Valentine's Day? I'm not getting excited about it, as if anything will happen to me (I don't think I would want it to anyway, unless I could have a penis for the day).

P.P.S. Sarah just called and told me she's seen some Horsefly badges in the indoor market!

P.P.P.S. Although I've been a teenager for three weeks now nothing much has changed, actually nothing at all. Even my body looks the same, not a single hair anywhere. Well apart from on my head and the usual hair people have on their arms and legs (I'm not an albino) but no exciting grown up hair. How old were you when you got your first armpit hair / pubic hair?

P.P.P.P.S. Sorry about all the P.S.s, I know there are a lot of them, but Sarah said she overheard her Mum saying to her Dad 'keep that stiffy away from me'.

P.P.P.P.P.S. A stiffy is when a penis goes hard. I don't think it's the proper medical Latin name for it though. (We don't learn Latin at our school but I would like to learn it, well I'd like to learn Latin words for bits of the body, so I could sound knowledgeable. I know there are also Latin words for lots of flowers and to be honest, I couldn't be bothered to learn those. I'm just not particularly interested in horticulture.)

P.P.P.P.P.P.S. Mum opened a new box of tea bags today. There were two cards in the box. Usually there's just one. I was going to give the second one to Simon, but I don't think he's interested in them so I kept them both. One is about dandelion seeds and one is a magnified picture of human skin. Human skin is disgusting. Be thankful you wear glasses so you will never have to see it in great detail.

March 1981

For the attention of Mr Tom Harding
Friends of Horsefly
PO BOX 113
London W2
3rd March 1981

Maud Harrison
22 Slater Street
Hutton
Preston

Dear Tom,

How are you? I hope you're okay. I'm okay apart from being really fed up and I hate everyone at school (except Sarah). Hate is a strong word I know, but I'm not using it lightly.

My science teacher is a very odd man. He's called Mr Ranson. Sarah found out that he's actually called Geoffrey (Geoffrey Ranson) so she keeps asking him if he wants us to just call him Geoffrey. It's not even that funny but it really makes me laugh. I suppose we're lucky he hasn't given us a detention. He has a little walk-in cupboard just off the science room that he eats sandwiches in on his own at breaktime and dinnertime, he never goes into the staffroom and we asked him why and he said he doesn't like the smoke. Sarah says when he goes in that little room he's wanking. But I don't think he is all of the time. I don't know though. Is that what teachers do? Is that what men do? I'm not sure it is. Mrs Alderhay the history teacher also has a walk-in cupboard for all the books and I don't think she's wanking in there at breaktime, though maybe she is, if she has the time. Sarah is more worldly wise than me. Her parents give her much more freedom than I have, but she's more developed. I'm actually slightly older than her (by two days) but you'd never know it. She has proper hips and wears a bra and just looks more like a young woman than I do. I definitely still look like a girl, a girl that's a bit stretched and old looking. People keep telling Sarah she has 'childbearing hips'. Thin people can still have babies though can't they? Do they mean if your hips are wider that the baby will just come out really easily? Or are you more likely to get pregnant with the right kind of hips?

Are you going to release a new record soon? It's been ages. Sarah and I would like to come to one of your gigs. Do you have to be eighteen to get in? Can you be a bit younger and just not get drunk? Is it true that everyone spits at your gigs? Why do they do that? I really don't like people spitting. Maybe I'd stand at the back. Or maybe right at the front, unless you spit back at the audience. Sarah says she's been served at a bar before (Bacardi and Coke apparently) so maybe we could get in and get drunk, though I don't know if I like Bacardi. I hope that won't get you into trouble. I won't say you knew about it if we get caught. If I got spat at in the face I think I would die. I wouldn't be able to keep singing. You're such a professional.

I've no more thimbles but I found this other thing in my Mum's sewing kit. It's for unpicking. I hope you like it. I've wrapped it in toilet paper, it's very sharp so be careful not to stab yourself with it when you unwrap it. I hope you read the letter before you open the unpicker. Actually I'll pop a warning on the envelope so you don't hurt yourself.

Yours faithfully in anticipation of your favourable response,
Maud

P.S. Our band, Corned Beef Wall, is going okay.

P.P.S. We're not even a band really because we've no instruments but we've written some songs, well I have.

P.P.P.S. How do you write such brilliant songs? Next time I write I might send you some of my lyrics to see if you like them.

P.P.P.P.S. My brother is so annoying. He saw me using the His towel from Mum and Dad's His and Her towels and now he keeps saying I'm a man.

P.P.P.P.P.S. It took me ages but I have found out what the Latin is for stiffy. It's verpa. Libraries have some really filthy things in them don't they? I also looked up the meaning of the word 'rape'. It's a real shame for the beautiful yellow fields you see off trains that they have to be associated with unlawful penetration of the vagina (the Latin name for a lady's fanny) and / or anus.

***

ROCK CITY MAGAZINE

15th March 1981

We Take What We Want is both the title of Horsefly's new album and also a 'serious political point' from the band's resident-in-chief lyricist Tom Harding (twenty-one). But when Tom turns up late looking like a tramp, Sharon Michaels wonders whether we should take him as seriously as he takes himself...

Sharon: Why do you look so scruffy?

Tom: Erm, I didn't realise I did, this is just what I wear.

Sharon: But you look really really awful.

Tom: How kind of you to say so.

Sharon: Really really awful.

Tom: I'm very tired, we've been gigging a lot.

Sharon: Why is your album called We Take What We Want? Is it about shoplifting?

Tom: Not at all, it's political, it's a political point. It's about taking things or leaving things. Taking the bits you want, leaving the bits you don't want. Seeing through the shit, you know, and not accepting it all the time.

Sharon: Just accepting it some of the time.

Tom: Ideally no, take as little shit as possible. It's hard to see through the lies we get fed but once you notice it it's hard not to see it and then you have to do something about it.

Sharon: So you see yourself as an activist?

Tom: Not an activist, I'm a musician, but you know, an encourager of people to question stuff. Question the people wearing suits. Where are they getting their information from? You know, that sort of thing. Just because someone looks smart and is well spoken doesn't mean they are right, it doesn't mean they know what they are talking about, and it doesn't mean they know what's best for you or, you know, society. You have to, you know, have some faith in your own judgement.

Sharon: One of your songs is called High on Beauty. Is this written about any person in particular?

Tom: No one in particular… It's about inner beauty, you know, when you meet someone and you just really click with them and you can see them inside and out.

Sharon: 'The curl of your lips, the curve of your hips, I stand powerless in your gaze'. That kind of sounds like a person's outer beauty.

Tom: Sure, yeah you got me there, I'm not blind.

Sharon: Is it true that the whole of the band is vegetarian? Your tour bus must smell horrific.

Tom: It's not true. We all started off vegetarian in January and then there's only me still managing it. Warren, Ed and Martin lasted about a week. Actually I don't think Ed did it at all. I just think, why kill a cow if you don't have to? You know? Why not have a banana instead?

Sharon: Do you still eat chicken and fish though?

Tom: I eat fish and chicken sometimes. It's important to eat properly when you're on tour a lot otherwise you get ill. As you can see today, I'm not at peak health.

Sharon: Eggs?

Tom: Yeah, I like a nice boiled egg, it has to have a runny yolk.

Sharon: How do you feel about the way chickens are kept in battery farms?

Tom: Well obviously it's not ideal, but we all need to eat something don't we?

Sharon: In the song Corn Fed Me you make similarities between yourself and a duck being force fed for foie gras.

Tom: Yeah, it's about being fed shit, you know, people just feeding you shit, like the politicians and at school and everything.

Sharon: You feel like you've been filled with shit?

Tom: I feel like people try all the time, Thatcher, teachers…

Sharon: And did they succeed Tom:?

Tom: No, no they didn't, at least I don't think so.

Sharon: The Rise of the Drummer, what's that all about then? Because apart from the lyric 'the rise of the drummer' we are a little bit in the dark, no other words, just heavy guitar and a two- minute drum solo. Is it supposed to be a joke?

Tom: It's about the rise of the Third Reich.

Sharon: Really?

Tom: Yes.

Sharon: Right, and what about bacon?

Tom: What about bacon?

Sharon: Do you still eat bacon?

Tom: No, I don't eat pigs or cows. Pigs are really clever you know. Have you ever read Animal Farm?

Sharon: I haven't. Do you read a lot?

Tom: Yes, as much as I can. I think you have to keep educating yourself. For the sake of it, not for a certificate. Not just what they want you to learn, you know, you should learn for the sake of learning and expanding your mind.

Sharon: And the song Friday Night F**k**g. What's that all about then?

Tom: What do you think it's about?

Sharon: I have no idea.

Tom: Me neither.

Sharon: Quick-fire questions now. You have to answer them with one word as fast as you can. Here goes. What colour are your pants?

Tom: I don't wear any.

Sharon: I said one-word answers please.

Tom: Sorry, red.

Sharon: Name of your first pet.

Tom: Sidney.

Sharon: What do you collect?

Tom: Thimbles, cos of my great grandma.

Sharon: One-word answers please.

Tom: Thimbles—

Sharon: Favourite other band in the charts at the moment.

Tom: I don't know what's out at the moment I'm afraid, I've been so busy promoting the album.

Sharon: One-word answer please.

Tom: The—

Sharon: Weirdest town you've ever been to.

Tom: Bradford.

Sharon: If you were stuck on an island with your band for the next thirty years who would you eat first?

Tom: Ed, so he'd shut up.

Sharon: And who would you make babies with?

Tom: They're all blokes.

Sharon: Yeah but which one would you make babies with?

Tom: Martin I suppose, he'd be a good mum.

April 1981

For the attention of Mr Tom Harding
Friends of Horsefly
PO BOX 113
London W2
1st April 1981

Maud Harrison
22 Slater Street
Hutton
Preston
Pie Shop Central

Hi Tom,

This is Mrs Thatcher. I've been listening to your records and I'm writing to ask you if you'll be my special advisor at 10 Downing Street. Will you work in my office and come with me to the Houses of Parliament every day and tell me what to say? I can kick Denis out if you like and you can have his room (we don't share a bed because I'm up all night shuffling papers around and talking dirty to Ronald Reagan on the phone).

APRIL FOOL!

It's just me, Maud Harrison. I've been thinking a lot about

songwriting, and also about what you said in Rock City (they get it in the library but you're not allowed to cut bits out) about educating yourself. I think you're really right. I have to take matters into my own hands. I can't rely on what the people at school teach me. They're just teachers, they've done nothing with their lives so why should I listen to them? I've decided that I will do all my homework that they give me and pay attention at school but I'm also going to start educating myself. I'm going to start off with Animal Farm. It's loaned out at the moment but I've put my name down on the waiting list, hopefully I won't have to wait for too long. I must admit I'm not that interested in farming but if you found it an interesting book then I'm sure I will too. I think maybe because I don't have any hips I just can't picture myself as a farmer's wife.

I've written a new song, it's about my big brother Simon. I wrote most of it, but Sarah added in a few bits. I'm not sure about the bits she did to be honest but I'd feel bad cutting them out. The tune is sort of shouty / punky. It's definitely not meant to be sung. It's about my brother wearing a brace on his teeth which he clicks on and off all the time, I can't stand it. And he slurps too, when he's wearing it, and that makes me feel sick. And he leaves it by the sink sometimes and it's just disgusting. I tried to think of something horrible to put on it so he'd stop leaving it around but I could only think of salt, but he likes salt, or Jif but he'd spot that a mile off and give me a dead leg.

I was going to send you the lyrics with this letter but I've just had another read through them and I can't send them to you, sorry. I think there is a reason why people write songs about love and anger, it's what people want to hear about. People don't want to be reminded about braces. I could try and write about love but I don't know too much about that yet. People don't want to hear a song about a girl loving her Gran do they? And I bet no one would be interested in hearing my song about growing armpit hair for the first time and not wanting to shave it off because it proves that I've started puberty, but it's also disgusting, yet it took ages to grow it. So it's confusing what to do about it, also I don't have a razor so I'd have to cut the hairs off with scissors. Anyway, my armpits are still bald in case you're wondering, so it's all guess work. From what I've noticed though in PE, I've got armpit hair coming to me soon, probably before breasts. I'm not sure about pubes. Sarah has all three and she can't even remember what came first, she said she didn't really notice it happening, how can she not have noticed? I find it hard to think about anything else. Do you shave or trim your armpit hair? I'm not sure I could do it myself. I suppose I could ask Sarah to do it for me. I'm not really sure our scissors are sharp enough. They cut through bacon though so I suppose they'd do the job.

If only I could be in love I'd have so much more to write about. Or if I could at least meet someone that was in love or if I could meet someone that I could have feelings about. Or something, anything. So I won't be sending you lyrics for a while I'm afraid. When something happens though, I will. It's just Preston's fault that I can only think about braces and pubes.

Yours in faithfulness,

Miss / Ms Maud Harrison

P.S. If you think it's a bit mean, me writing about my brother's brace, it's really not. He keeps laughing at me because I don't wear a bra yet. He keeps saying I've got no knockers. There are quite a few girls in my class with no knockers (so I'm not worried yet).

P.P.S. I'm going to rip up the brace song and put it in the bin. It's not even something I could edit and improve and it didn't have a tune or anything. Hopefully Sarah will have forgotten about it.

P.P.P.S. I think you're the best songwriter in the world and not all of your songs are about love are they? The one you wrote called Youth Spit is not romantic at all. Luckily I can't really make out the words that well when I listen to it, which is good because the thought of spit makes me heave.

P.P.P.P.S. One good thing though, I don't need a brace, I've inherited my grandfather's teeth.

P.P.P.P.P.S. Not his actual teeth, just the same kind of straight teeth. I think my Gran does still have his teeth though. I suppose I might inherit them eventually.

P.P.P.P.P.P.S. I have enclosed a tape measure for your sewing collection. I found it in my Mum's tin, I've never seen her use it.

P.P.P.P.P.P.P.S. What do you think about Tristan Farnon being the new Doctor Who? He's certainly more handsome than the last one. I'm not sure I can sit near my brother through an entire episode though. I wonder if there will be more animals in it now or just the Daleks as usual.

P.P.P.P.P.P.P.P.S. I know that I'm the fool, because when you get this letter it will be after 12 o'clock and it won't even be 1st April any more. I don't really mind though. I'm used to it.

May 1981

MELODY MAKER

7th May 1981

I Hate Myself... Every Night I Die

Tom Harding, Warren Hamble, Ed Nailer and Martin O'Connell interviewed by Cindy McGee

I caught up with the band after their gig at Leeds Town and Country Club. Don't be fooled by the name, this was no country night...

Cindy McGee: Warren, it's Cindy McGee from Melody Maker, do you mind if I record this so I can transcribe later? It's pretty noisy in here so it would help.

Warren Hamble: Do what the fuck you want.

Cindy McGee: I'm backstage at Leeds T and C in conversation with Horsefly. Warren Hamble, did you enjoy the gig?

Warren Hamble: Did you fucking watch it? I fucking hate Leeds, they're all cunts. I'm never fucking coming here again.

Ed Nailer: Ignore him babe, he's just fucked off cos we beat him.

Warren Hamble: Only cos we was down to ten men.

Ed Nailer: Whose fucking fault was that?

Cindy McGee: Beat him?

Warren Hamble: Football. This cunt (*poking Ed Nailer*) supports Leeds.

Ed Nailer: I'm from fucking Leeds. Who else am I gonna support? Man U?

Warren Hamble: Bradford.

Ed Nailer: Fuck *off*. I'm not from fucking Bradford.

Cindy McGee: The gig was absolutely electrifying tonight, and equally terrifying in parts. Tom Harding, what did you make of the crowd tonight?

Tom Harding: Ah man, I want to stop this shit. It's just a shambles out there. The place is completely ruined. It's like we were playing in a zoo. Actually no, that's not fair on the animals.

Cindy McGee: You don't condone what happened?

Tom Harding: No, I don't condone it. Why can't people just listen and have a dance if they like it? They were all fucking punching each other and smashing glasses and jumping on the stage, it's horrible.

Cindy McGee: That's what we've come to expect at a Horsefly gig.

Tom Harding: I don't like it. For me, this isn't what music's about. I want to go home.

Ed Nailer: FUCK THATCHER! Make sure you get that in, all right?

Cindy McGee: Yeah, people were chanting that a lot throughout your gig. Do you see yourselves as a political band?

Tom Harding: I just want to write songs and play music.

Cindy McGee: So you don't want to *fuck Thatcher*?

Tom Harding: Yes, I want to *fuck Thatcher*... I mean, I wish she'd fuck off, I don't want to fuck her.

Ed Nailer: Tom wants to fuck Thatcher all night long, get that in, get that in won't you?

Tom Harding: I don't see us as a political band. I don't know enough about politics really. I just know about my life, what I've experienced so far. I try and write about what I see, what I hear.

Cindy McGee: But many of your songs are seen as a sort of bleak social commentary on how working-class life is under a Thatcher government.

Tom Harding: That might be how people perceive it, but I just write about my experiences. Most of the songs from the last album are shit, I didn't know what I was doing.

Cindy McGee: You don't like your own songs? People love them. Shandy Hand is an anthem.

Tom Harding: I hate playing it. It's embarrassing.

Cindy McGee: You did write it though.

Tom Harding: Yeah but only as a sort of joke that went too far. I didn't expect this. You wouldn't catch Simon and Garfunkel having a sing-along about a wank would you?

Cindy McGee: Is that who you aspire to? Simon and Garfunkel?

Tom Harding: I really like them, yes.

Cindy McGee: You're quite a long way from that at the moment aren't you?

Tom Harding: Yes, a long long way.

Ed Nailer: He wants Thatcher to sit on his face.

Warren Hamble: Ey love, have you finished with him? You wanna get out of here with me? Come on love. See that tin of Right Guard? That's how big my dick is.

Cindy McGee: So there's disquiet in the band?

Tom Harding: Of course there's disquiet... Look at them. I can't bear it.

Cindy McGee: Martin O'Connell, how did you find the gig tonight?

Martin O'Connell: Keep me out of it, I just turn up, I play, I go home.

Tom Harding: Martin's got the right idea. Ed! Put that fucking pen away, you'll get us all chucked out.

Ed Nailer: Keep yer knickers on yer soppy fuck.

Tom Harding: I might want to come back here at some point, without you lot.

Ed Nailer: Awww, Little Tom's going to be a singer-songwriter. Except he can't fucking sing. That's his problem. Get *that* in won't you?

Tom Harding: Thanks Cindy, and sorry about them, I really have to leave now. I can't stand this whole situation.

Cindy McGee: Am I looking at the end of Horsefly?

Tom Harding: How many gigs have we got left? About seven? I can't imagine ever wanting to see these people again. If I thought I had to I'd probably top myself. I don't know how I even got involved with them. Every night on stage I die a bit. I hate myself.

Cindy McGee: Were they always like this? Ed and Warren?

Tom Harding: No, no, I don't think so. I know I wasn't like this… I mean look at Warren, he's got actual shit all over his jeans and he still thought he was in with a chance with you. I can't bear it.

Cindy McGee: Why has he got shit on his jeans?

Tom Harding: He's a fucking lazy bastard who's had so many drugs his arse has fallen out.

Cindy McGee: Well, thank you Tom and good luck with the rest of the tour.

Tom Harding: Would you like to come home with me?

Cindy McGee: Yes.

Tom Harding: Yours or the van?

Cindy McGee: Where's the van?

***

> For the attention of Master Thomas Harding
> Friends of Horsefly
> PO BOX 113
> London W2
> 19th May 1981

Maud Harrison
22 Slater Street
Hutton
Forlorn
Preston

Dear Tom,

I'm just sat up in my bedroom while my Mum and Dad are shouting at each other so I thought I'd write you a letter. I know I write to you quite often, I hope you don't mind. It sort of really helps me to think about stuff and get things clear in my head. I know you're too busy to reply, it doesn't matter. I should really be doing maths homework and I've got English homework as well. Maths shouldn't take me too long, it's boring but I can do it, it's just lots of sums, long division, not too hard though, not like the ones you see on Open University. Do you ever watch that in the morning? Sometimes I wake up really, really early, and I go downstairs and put on the telly and I watch all the Open University programmes. I absolutely love them. I can't always understand what they're talking about, but most of the time I do, so long as it's not really long maths equations. I love listening to clever people talking, I find it quite soothing. It's good to know they are out there. I really hope I get to go to the real Open University one day so I can listen to clever people every day and hang around with them. I don't feel like my teachers at school are very clever. They've learnt some facts, but I don't think they are naturally clever people. Is that a horrible bigheaded thing to say? It probably is, they still know more than I do. At least they're not virgins, well I don't think they are. They all have wedding rings so I presume they have copulated, I'm not sure they've all bred, some of them really shouldn't.

Sometimes when I go to the library I pretend in my head that I'm going to the library at the Open University or sometimes I pretend (in my head) that I need to get books out for my Open University course. Maybe I will be able to go to the Open University in London. I think I'd like to live there eventually, although on the news there always looks like there's lots of trouble, we don't have that problem round here. I wish people didn't fight all the time so I could just go out whenever and wherever I wanted to without worrying about riots or strikes or petrol bombs or moors murders or Yorkshire rippers or being kidnapped. Do you know where the Open University is? Not Brixton I hope.

Zena Barrie

Mum and Dad are really going for it now. I've heard a plate smash, or it could have been a pottery horse I suppose, I'm surprised we've got anything left, they're always doing this and Mum has shouted something about the bookies. I don't know why, that's just this shop we go to and put bets on the Grand National. You get the paper and look at all the names of the horses and then you pick the one with the best name and then you have to listen on the radio and hope that your horse comes first, second or third and then you go back to the shop and he gives you your winnings. Dad really likes it. I'm not really that interested but I quite like looking at the names of the horses. My Mum does this thing called Spot the Ball. It's in the paper, have you ever done it? Do you even like football? You look at a picture of a footballer kicking a ball, but in the picture the ball isn't there, so you have to imagine where the ball would be. I always just look at where his foot is (usually up in the air) and then the ball must be a little bit away from his foot. So we put a cross where we think the ball is and then Mum puts on a few more crosses because you're allowed five chances. Then we send it off to the newspaper. She never wins anything. I don't know why because I'm sure my theory is right, the ball must be somewhere just a little bit away from his foot. I just heard Dad shout 'oh yeah, you've never spent a penny have you?' and I heard Mum shout something like 'fucking shoes'. I think Dad's new shoes have become political, maybe it's because they're two–tone. Could my Mum be a racist? It can't be my Dad that is, not in those shoes. The front door just slammed and I looked out of the window and it was Mum walking down the street. Usually it's Dad. I might go down and ask him what's going on when he's stopped swearing and slamming doors. The English homework is to write a story using lots of describing words.

> There was an old wizened lady with grey cascading tresses of matted stinking hair that lived in the furthest most point of our grey, windy and desperate estate. The wizened old lady had a

name, a name of beauty and wonder and corruption and that name was Eliza-bottle-black. Eliza was filled with sadness and despair, her handsome suave sophisticated and able lover had left one night, he'd gone to buy cigarettes as they had run out and they enjoyed smoking a cigarette together after passionately making love looking through the window at the willowy old peach tree. Her lover never returned. He got run over coming out of the off licence. After the police had broken the news to Eliza, she fell slowly to the floor, beating it with her slender whitish–blue hands (she could have been a hand model, it's a real thing). She wailed and cried at the wind, 'Why, why oh why oh why did you take him?' She screamed relentlessly. She closed her curtains and vowed never to look at the peach tree again, the peach tree whose boughs were heavy with fruit that no one picked. The fruit rotted on the branches and the stench pushed its way in through the dirty cracked windows and through the floorboards until the air was thick with repugnant peach. There was a knock on the door. There stood a man whose looks were utterly disarming. 'Excuse me madam, I hope you don't mind me knocking on your door, I couldn't help but notice your peach tree.' Within an hour they were making love.

Do you think that's a good start to the story? I think I'll start with that and go on from there. Maybe the old woman will fall in love with the stranger. Maybe he's an even more able lover than the last one. Do you know what 'able lover' means? I read the phrase in a romance book in a charity shop. I suppose he's a man that's a good all–rounder, like Daley Thompson. I bet he'd be classed as an able lover. I'm not sure if you would be. Are you any good at running or DIY (do it yourself)?

Yours truly,
Maud Harrison

P.S. I have enclosed for you three red buttons sewn onto a card. We've used two of them. So if you ever lose a button you can just sew one on, just cut it off the card, it's quite easy, I've done it before. Just don't try and use a bodkin even though they are easier to sew with, they won't go through the button's holes which are quite small. Mum says you have to use cotton the same colour as the button. I like using a different colour though, it's more punk, sorry I know you don't need me to tell you this. You have a terrific sense of style.

P.P.S. Sarah told me that sperm (a man's ejaculation) (from his penis) floats in the bath. Is this true? I wonder if it has to be poured onto the water or if it could float its way up from the bottom like a bad egg. I don't know why a scientist would get some and pour it into a bath to work this out. What do we gain from this knowledge? I'm not sure where Sarah got this information from, probably Tomorrow's World. I haven't watched the last couple of episodes because it's better to just stay upstairs out of the way.

***

For the urgent attention of Master Thomas Harding
Friends of Horsefly
PO BOX 113
London W2
21st May 1981

Maud Harrison
22 Slater Street
Hutton
Preston
The Land That Time Forgot

Dear Tom,

I told Sarah all about the Open University. I wish I hadn't now. She said she watched some and that she fancied the man with the beard. Why does she always have to fancy everybody? I hope she doesn't have a teenage pregnancy because of fancying just about every man on the planet. If she does that we won't be able to start our band up properly after we leave school. I'm not sure though if she really wants to go to the Open University, and what if we go to different ones? Maybe I'll have to make some new friends. I'm not very good at making friends, it's not that the other girls hate me, I don't really get picked on. It's just that they are so boring, so tedious. They are not interested in anything outside Preston or anything even outside school. It's like they think the whole world is inside the school gates. They should start thinking about the outside world though because they will be in it soon. I can't wait to be in it and do adult things. I should probably really try and get good 'O' levels so I've got options when I leave school. It's really hard when you know you're ready for the world but the world isn't ready for you to be in it. It's like I'm in suspended animation. That's what happens in space when you go to sleep for a couple of hundred years while your spaceship flies to another galaxy and then you can just wake up and you're still really young and still wearing the same space age clothes.

I wonder how you can go for two hundred years though without going to the toilet. You'd probably need to have a tube coming out of you and going into a toilet with some sort of automatic flush while you were asleep. Though I suppose if you kept going to the toilet for two hundred years without eating or drinking anything you'd just waste away. You'd be like a skeleton when you woke up. Maybe it's best that you don't go to the toilet when you're in suspended animation, though having all that excrement inside you wouldn't do your tummy any good. I wonder if bears go to the toilet when they're hibernating. I think they do because I've heard they are skinnier when they wake up. It wouldn't be very nice waking up and having six months of your own faecal matter stuck to your fur. I will have to ask one of my teachers.

Maybe one of the science ones but I'm not asking Mr Ranson just in case I accidentally catch him doing something unspeakable.

Yours,
Maud

P.S. Here is a brass button from my Mum's sewing box. There was only one of them. It might have been used during the war or something. It would look quite good sewn onto a lapel, just on one side. Not everything has to be symmetrical (the same on both sides) these days.

P.P.S. Mum hasn't come back yet. Dad has been giving us a lot of beans. She did phone up though and she says she'll be back on Tuesday. I think she's at Grandma's house because I could hear a budgie in the background. My Gran has quite a few budgies. She lets them out of their cages though so there's always bird excrement on the chairs and birdfood shells on the carpet. Her house is pretty smelly. She always says stuff like 'look at Bertie, he's really pleased to see you, look he's singing a song for you'. And Bertie is just sat there as usual attacking his reflection in the mirror. Budgies have no facial expressions at all, unless opening your mouth counts as an expression. I suppose it does.

P.P.P.S. I do quite like going to my Gran's house though. She has a blue rinse and a full set of Encyclopaedia Britannica. I wish we could have them at our house. I'm sure she doesn't ever look at them. Simon and I always look up the picture of the man with Elephantitis. Have you ever seen it? A poor man from Africa who has an elephant's leg. One normal leg and one elephant's leg. An actual thick grey elephant's leg. It must be really difficult for him to do anything. He wears a pair of shorts in the picture. It must be impossible for him to get anything to fit properly. It does make me feel quite thankful that I don't have that to contend with. It also makes me wonder what has gone on in his family in the past. Catherine the Great died from having sex with a horse, so these things do happen. Also donkeys and horses, humans and monkeys and all types of dogs get together. It's a shame that he's having to deal with the effects of something his great great grandmother or great great grandfather did, probably under the influence of a lot of Bacardi.

P.P.P.P.S. We learnt about symmetry at school today. I have discovered that I really don't have a symmetrical face. I will try and find a hand mirror to see if you have a symmetrical face. I'm sure you're not wonky like me. I've never noticed you looking wonky anyway.

***

MELODY MAKER

23rd May 1981

My Week in Music, By Valerie Sinclair

I've been spinning some radical tunes this week but some of them were not so palatable...

First up Horsefly with their new single Corn Fed Me, something to do with foie gras they think in the office... Never had it.

Tom Harding's lyrics are only made worse by Tom Harding's vocals. He sounds like he's been gargling with acid. Do us a favour someone please, and take him to the river and drown him before he can go solo and put us through more miserable years of listening to him wail about being raped in the dark by his own shadows.

> Shadows creeping up to kiss me or kill me,
> Holding me down, feeding me lies.
> Tastes so good I want to believe it,
> The silky feel of the shadows' thighs...

He's feeling up a shadow, right? Getting off with his own shadow? If you disagree, answers on a postcard.

Next, Electric Sky by Lady Punk: it doesn't matter what she's singing because it's happiness on the most beautiful of twelve inches. Buy, and turn it up as loud as you can. You'll feel better for it...

Your Friend Forever

***

For the attention of the major talent that is Mr Tom
Harding
Friends of Horsefly
PO BOX 113
London W2
29th May 1981

Maud Harrison
22 Slater Street
Hutton
Preston
The Forgotten Place at the End of the Earth

Dear Tom,

    I'm just looking at this picture of you that Sarah gave me out of her Dad's magazine, it's a hard rock magazine so neither of us ever read it. I don't really see you as a rocker, you don't have that long lank hair (thankfully), not that it matters what people look like. In the picture Sarah gave me you look really sad. Actually you all look really sad, even your drummer. Why do people in bands hardly ever smile? When you have your photo shoots does the photographer not tell you all to smile? You all look so miserable. Had something bad happened that day? In the picture I can see all your eyelashes, they are very long, like a giraffe's. Giraffes have the best eyes of anyone in the whole world. Giraffes and cows, which are quite similar animals really apart from the neck. I like cows, they're nice animals, it's a shame for them really that they're called 'cows' because they're not cows are they, I mean they're cows but they're not total cows, they just eat grass and moo and give us milk, they don't have any of the personality traits where you would end up saying something like 'Buttercup's milk is delicious but she's a right cow'.

It's the same with bitches, some female dogs are annoying I'm sure, but they're not really bitchy. Maybe they are if we could understand what their woofs mean. Though I'm not sure dogs are actually speaking another language. If they were we'd probably have worked it out by now. They're just either angry or sad or excited, they're certainly not slagging off each other's fur behind the other one's back. Wouldn't it be nice if sometimes we didn't have to think using words. We could just make a big noise if we were happy or sad. It would be quite freeing to be an animal. What sort would you be? I would be a meat eater of some sort because I like eating meat and I don't think I'd much like eating grass. I suppose it would be all right if I was in a zoo and we got lettuce and bananas and those types of food. Though I wouldn't want to be in a zoo. Even though I want to be a grown up it would also be nice to be a baby again and not have responsibility for anything. And I wouldn't be able to worry if I was a baby because I wouldn't have any words in my head. Imagine having feelings without words. It does explain why babies cry so much. Although sometimes I have a feeling that's like a worry but I don't know what it is I'm worried about. There are no words involved. It's more of an instinct, as if I'm a cavewoman and I have a feeling my husband has been killed while hunting.

I've just decided, I'd like to be a penguin.

Got to go Tom.

Love Maud

June 1981

MELODY MAKER

1st June 1981, Letter of the Week

Dear Melody Maker in particular Valerie Sinclair (I suspect it's not your real name)

I am writing to complain about your comments about Tom Harding in the May 23rd edition.

You said the following:

> 'Tom Harding's lyrics are only made worse by Tom Harding's vocals. He sounds like he's been gargling with acid. Do us a favour someone please, and take him to the river and drown him before he can go solo and put us through more miserable years of listening to him wail about being raped in the dark by his own shadows.'

Let me remind you.

You are supposed to be a newspaper about music.

I'd have thought because of that you would be the type of people that were supportive of musicians and artists and anyone creative.

It seems those who can't play an instrument write nasty articles about people who can.

Does it give you a semi? Does being mean give you a little semi?

Don't you think it is dangerous doing a call out for someone to be murdered? (It is very dangerous.) What if someone did it?

If he is drowned by someone who do you think will be responsible for his death? (You.)

Have you ever thought that maybe he has been raped by his own shadows and made love to a ghost?

You don't know what goes on behind closed doors.

Some people have a lot to deal with in their lives and it would be nice if you could show a little bit of compassion.

I hope someone takes you to the river and drowns you.

Could someone please do that soon?

Before we have to read more of your nasty words.

Actually maybe I'll be the one to do it.

Watch out.

Maud Harrison

Hey Maud,

You massive saddo.

Next time you send people threatening mail, which is an offence punishable by a jail sentence, don't put your address at the top of the letter, you absolute cretin.

We could, if we were bothered to, pass this threat on to the police.

However instead we've passed it round the office and all laughed at you.

***

Your Friend Forever

For the attention of his excellency Monsieur Thomas Harding
of London Town
Friends of Horsefly
PO BOX 113
London W2
18th June 1981

Maud Harrison
22 Slater Street
Hutton
Broken
Preston

Dear Tom,

    I've had a pretty good day today. My Mum let me just go out, which she doesn't often do, I think her and Dad were having a talk but their talks always end up with a screaming match and something broken. I'm glad to have missed it. I went into town and met Sarah. We met up at Winckley Square, it's this park that's like a kind of basin and you can see what's going on everywhere. We went into the newsagent and Sarah bought some Polo Mints and then asked for ten Regal Kingsize (a kind of cigarette). The shopkeeper just handed them over! He didn't even ask to see her bus pass or anything. She says you have to be dead confident and not look nervous and just say it like you've said it loads of times before (which she did really well). She had a packet of matches in her bag already so we didn't need to buy those though I reckon he'd have sold her some. Anyway, we went and sat on the grass and smoked. I was pretty good at it straight away, I thought I might cough or not do it properly but it's quite easy, I just inhaled like I'd done it before. Sarah thought I'd done it before when she saw me do it but I honestly haven't. The hardest bit was lighting the match in the wind, I used my parka hood to keep the draught away from the flame but I was quite worried about setting the fur on fire. Cigarettes don't taste that nice but there's something I like about smoking them and it changed the way I felt, it's hard to describe, I felt like I was someone else, someone much cooler than me. Like I was someone older and more confident, like Blondie, it made a nice change.

A gang of lads came up to us and I didn't even flinch (well maybe a tiny bit). I just sort of stared at them and kept smoking away. They asked us if we'd give them a fag. Sarah gave one of them one and also I saw her giving him her sexy pouty look which there is absolutely no point in me ever trying. Then the others asked if they could have one and she told them to fuck off and buy their own. I didn't actually say anything but I wasn't scared and I felt sort of cool. Like for the first time they weren't looking at me like some geek in a parka. The parka used to be my brother's but it doesn't fit him any more. It's dead warm and you can zip the hood up really well if it's cold which it always is. The hood never falls down. So many hoods are rubbish and only cover half your head. Why would you design a hood and not worry about it staying up? Although parka hoods are not great if you're talking to someone who is sat next to you or if you want to cross a road. You have to take the hood down to be safe. They are a bit like looking through a port hole. I liked the way I felt when I smoked. I've never felt like it before, I can't really stop thinking about it to be honest. We smoked three each and sat and talked on the grass and it felt good, like some of my problems had gone away. Then when I had to come home Sarah said she'd give me one of the fags that was left over but I was worried about my Mum finding it. She'd properly murder me so I didn't take it. I wish I had done now though, I'd love to just smoke one out of my bedroom window, I'd never dare though. I suppose maybe I could get away with it in the middle of the night, if I knew Mum and Dad were definitely asleep. Would the smell rise out of the window into the air or would it come back in my room? Sarah says she's smoked at home, she just uses joss sticks. I'm not sure what they are though and I felt stupid asking, sometimes I feel like I'm just asking questions all the time and never have any answers.

Sorry for going on about smoking. I know some people think it's bad for you and it's smelly and everyone does it so why am I going on about it? I just can't help it, it was such an incredible feeling. I wish I could feel like that all the time. It just felt like I was in a film or something, like we were going to run away and then get on a train to anywhere and meet a man on a train and have sex with him and then steal his money and get on another train and just carry on and on like that.

Anyway, now I'm back home in my bedroom, my Mum is banging around downstairs, Simon isn't home, I don't know where Dad is either. Back to being on my own in my bedroom with teddies in it. I could get rid of the teddies but I don't think that would make me feel better. Not being here would make me feel better, I don't know where else I could be though. I wish I was older and then I could just smoke every day. Do you think I might be addicted already? What happens if I'm addicted? Oh God I didn't think of that before. I can still smell the cigarettes on my fingers. Best wash my hands again. I'm going to seal this envelope up now. It would be terrible if my Mum read it and then found out I'd smoked. Though it would be awful if she read any of my letters. She'd scream her head off at me, she wouldn't understand any of it. She never tries to understand me one little bit. It feels like she doesn't really like me, there's nothing I do that doesn't seem to irritate her. That's why I keep out of the way as much as I can but sometimes I just have to speak to her. I'm not entirely sure why she had children, why have children if you're not at all interested in how they turn out? If I was my own Mum I'd give me a hug every day and say things like 'don't worry love, it's hard being a teenager, do you need any tampons?' I wish I could be my own Mum. You can't really hug yourself though, I mean you can but it doesn't make me feel any better. I always put these letters in the bottom of my school bag underneath all my books so my Mum will never see them. She never goes in my school bag, she never asks me what I'm doing at school, sometimes I tell her I've got homework to do but she doesn't seem interested, she doesn't know whether I'm clever, average or stupid. I think she has a lot on her mind but I'm not sure what. Maybe I won't smoke again, it's a bit too much to have to worry about the smell. I hope she won't be able to tell from my face that I've been smoking. Sarah says I worry too much but her parents are quite relaxed about what she does. They know she's nearly grown up. My Mum still thinks I'm a child and I'm not.

Okay, bye for now, I'm going to do some homework. It's biology (which I like) and physics (which I hate). What did you like doing at school? I bet you were good at music and English. I'm okay at English but no good at music, it's because there are no proper instruments though and I think if I had the chance I could do it. Who plays recorder in real life? You never see grown ups playing them. They must be one of the worst instruments. The noise they make is so unpleasant.

Why doesn't the school realise it's 1981 and not 1781? Why can't we write songs and play guitars and keyboards? Or sing? We never sing unless it's a hymn in assembly and then no one actually sings, everyone mimes or mutters. I think the school is making a big mistake. It's very shortsighted of them. I have come to expect this though from adults.

Love Maud

P.S. I've started thinking about cigarettes again. Is this addiction?

P.P.S. Blondie is so cool isn't she? She would look cool even without the cigarettes. I bet she would even look cool in my school uniform and parka.

P.P.P.S. I have enclosed a pin wheel from my Mum's sewing tin. Some of them are gone I'm afraid but there's still quite a few. I like the ones with the white round balls on the end. They are a bit easier to handle than ordinary pins but you have to be careful if you use them with a sewing machine. Best not to. If you use a sewing machine just use plain old pins.

P.P.P.P.S. Sarah told me that if you sit on your hand to make it numb and then stick it down your pants that's what it's like being fingered. I don't get it though. It's sort of put me off ever wanting that to happen. I don't want somebody's numb hand in my pants. I'll just carry on keeping myself to myself thank you very much.

P.P.P.P.P.S. On the way to school the other day I had to break a spider's web to get through the front gate. Simon told me off for doing it and said I should have climbed over the wall instead. He said the spider will have to make another web and that they're only supposed to make one web a day and that it'll go hungry. If you were a spider would you bother making another web or would you just think, never mind I've had two flies already, I'll just go out for the afternoon. It must be really boring spending your entire day sat in a web waiting for flies. Maybe the spider will be glad of the freedom. It's not going to starve if it doesn't eat for just one day is it?

Zena Barrie

***

For the consideration of legend Tom Harding
Friends of Horsefly
PO BOX 113
London W2
22nd June 1981

Maud Harrison
22 Slater Street
Hutton
Desolate
Preston

Dear Tom,

I have to have glasses like you. My eyes have been sore and things have been blurry unless I try really hard to focus on whatever it is I'm looking at, and it shouldn't be that hard should it. I went to the opticians with my Mum, I got a letter from school because she thought I was lying. The optician said I'm longsighted. I didn't even know that was a thing that you could be. Are you longsighted or shortsighted? I hope you're longsighted like me. Mum said I was only allowed to try on the free ones. I didn't mind because I like the chunky ones anyway, they are a tiny bit like yours. I don't like the ones with the little wings that sit on your nose, they make me feel a bit sick. I once saw a boy at school wearing those and he had a little yellow chunk attached to the nose–wing bit, I think it was from his eye, sort of eye snot, it's hard to get these pictures out of your head once you've seen them. Sometimes my imagination is a curse. Anyway you only get those nose wings on the expensive glasses. I chose some thick mottled brown plastic ones. I quite like them even though they're a bit big for my face. At least

I can see properly again. It was really horrible struggling to see everything. You might even notice an improvement in my handwriting.

There was a teenage boy in the opticians who came up behind me when I was trying all the glasses on. He whispered 'they look horrible' at me. I couldn't believe it. You have to try them on to see which ones fit. I never said I thought they looked good. Also, he was fat, and I hadn't asked his opinion. He, though, seemed to think that I wanted his opinion. I've been angry about it ever since. I keep imagining that I followed him and tripped him up so he fell into the gutter, and then I grabbed his straggly greasy hair and smashed his face into the pavement so his nose was broken so badly he wouldn't have a nose to put glasses on. I imagined pushing his pasty cheeks into pigeon excrement. I know this must sound very violent and over the top, but telling a stranger they look horrible is just too much. It was outrageous. I really hope some awful tragedy befalls him. I bet his life is shit anyway. I mean, mine is pretty shit but I know I can make it better. (Especially if I can move out and get some hair crimpers.) I bet he doesn't read. He'll be like all the other idiots at school that think everything is rubbish just because they don't understand it. When I listen to them talking sometimes I want to just bang my head against the desk. And you can't talk to them or explain anything to them because they don't listen, their minds are closed. They think it's cooler to laugh at everything than to think there might be something they don't know about. Do you know what I mean? Have you met people like that? I suppose in your world you get to meet lots of clever and interesting and artistic people all the time, why would you have to spend your time with fourteen-year-old girls that think it's cool to have anal sex in a park with a man called Nevil (like a girl in my class, she's called Lisa) and then tell everyone about it. Blondie wouldn't have anal sex in a park with a man called Nevil that's much too old for her. I'm almost certain of this.

I'm tired now, I need to sleep, I hope I can stop my mind from whirring. It's not even that late but I suppose I'm growing. I don't understand how people stay up really late for fun. Sarah told me that some night clubs don't even open until 10pm at night when everyone's in bed. It's amazing that anyone goes out at that time. They must have to sleep all day. Maybe they do.

Lots of love Tom, I hope you've had a happy day.

Maud Hazzerson (better than Harrison? No, it doesn't suit me at all. I don't really think I can carry off Hazzerson. You would understand if you saw the state of my school uniform, or my face for that matter)

P.S. I promise I won't really smash anyone's face in. I don't think I could.

P.P.S. I have enclosed three plain shirt buttons. They are good for when you lose a button from your shirt. You used to wear them a lot, not so much any more, but anyway if you feel like mending your old shirts you can, I'm sure I've seen you wearing ripped shirts on a number of occasions.

***

Your Friend Forever

F.T.A.O. Mr T. Harding Esq.
Friends of Horsefly
PO BOX 113
London W2
26th June 1981

Maud Harrison
22 Slater Street
Grim
Hutton
Preston

Dear Tom,

    Dad's gone. He pulled two big canvas bags out of the back of his and Mum's wardrobe and shoved loads of stuff in them and Mum was screaming at him 'just get out get out get out' and he was shouting back that he was 'fucking well going, let me pack my fucking bags, the fucking zip doesn't work'. Then Mum screamed at me to stop staring and go into my room so I did. Her face was all swollen looking and blotchy and her hair was everywhere. About ten minutes later I heard the front door go. I looked out of my bedroom window and Dad was shoving his bags through the back window of the car (the door hasn't opened for years) and then he just got in and drove off really fast, the car actually made a screeching noise like you only usually hear on the telly. I thought he'd have at least come into my room and explained to me what was happening and given me some words to hang onto, like they do in films, or handed me a note or a locket and told me I was beautiful. The only pictures of me are some old school photos and he hasn't taken any of them. You'd be able to see the outline on the wallpaper if one of them was gone. Me and Simon are quite young in all of them, she hasn't bought any of the new ones for about five years. Maybe he'd have taken one if there was a more recent picture. Or maybe he knows he'll be back tomorrow anyway. I suppose he'll be back when they've both calmed down. I was thinking of asking Simon what he thought about it all but I knocked on his door and he just shouted back 'go away'. So now I'm back in my room. There's a big black patch of mould on the wall over the top of the window. I might try and climb on the chest of drawers and see if I can reach it to wipe it off.

Sorry for writing to you about this. It's probably not very interesting for you is it, you don't even know my Dad. I need to try and do something to take my mind off it all, not homework, I can't concentrate on that. Maybe I'll read a book or just try and go to sleep. Sometimes if something awful happens I feel like I have to just go to sleep straight away so that my brain doesn't explode. Do you ever get that? I think I'll get in bed and read The Bell Jar. Hopefully Dad will just stay at his friend's house and get drunk and come back tomorrow a bit smelly. He looked really angry though. He storms out a lot but he doesn't usually take bags of clothes with him. It did seem more serious than usual. Do you ever get really angry? Who do you live with? If you live alone you can't really storm out on yourself can you, which must be a relief. I think I'd like to live alone. Imagine how nice that would be. I could have the radio on all the time and there would be no one to shout at me. I get shouted at so much, and I'm not a bad person, I'm sure I'd know if I was.

Yours,
Maud

P.S. Did your parents split up? Did it make you who you are today? Maybe this could be the making of me. I should try and write a poem while I'm in pain.

P.P.S. I'm not in that much pain really, I'm mostly just tired.

My Family

'Fuck off' cried Mum as she slammed the door,
'And don't you come back no more, no more.'
'Don't you worry' blasted Dad, as he picked up his bag,
'I can do without you, you drunken slag.
Go to your room Maud.'
I did, now I'm bored.
This is my family.
At least it's not bigamy.
My brother's name is Simon.
I have not yet broken my hymen.
I'd like to try using a Tampax.
Apparently they can make you climax.
I don't have pubic lice
But in our kitchen I've seen mice.
My Mother's crying tears.
I expect my Dad is drinking beers.
I'm going to go and read some Sylvia Plath
Then try to drown in my (very dirty) bath. (I'd clean it but we don't have anything to clean it with.)

P.P.P.S. Mum isn't a drunken slag but poems don't have to be real do they? You can make things up in poems. I'm pretty sure she's not a slag although I don't know much about her from her younger days, so she might be a recovered slag.

***

Private and confidential for Tom Harding only
Friends of Horsefly
PO BOX 113
London W2
30th June 1981

Maud Harrison
22 Slater Street
Hutton
Barren
Preston

Dear Tom,

  Simon came in my room tonight. He sat on my bed looking really sad. I asked him what was wrong and he started crying. He never cries. It made me cry because it was quite shocking. He said our Dad's never coming back, he spoke to him on the phone. He'd called to speak to Mum and Simon had answered. He said Dad said he was just really sorry but Mum didn't want him coming back and then he said he had to go, Simon thought he was calling from a phone box. I tried to sort of touch his arm a bit but we never do that and it was really awkward and he just got up and went out, he couldn't look at me. I think Dad has to come back though doesn't he. If you have kids you can't just get up and leave them can you. I know he's been gone for a few days but that's just while him and Mum sort things out. Sarah's Mum and Dad separated for a bit but he came back and Lisa the girl that looks like a hog and has anal sex, her parents have completely split up but she still sees her Dad every week. Maybe that would be better if we could just see him like that, every week, instead of him moving back in, just see him, without the shouting and the rows. If I had a kid (and I'm not sure I want any) I wouldn't be able to leave them forever because I think I'd love them. I feel as if I should talk to Simon about it a bit more but he looked really cross when he left my room so he'll probably just shout at me or ignore me.

We had a French test today at school and I got 12 out of 20 right. I was almost the worst in the class. I can't get my head around it. I can't do the accent and it's so confusing, it's my worst subject. Do you speak any other languages? I would like to be able to speak French, I do try, it's just so hard. Maybe I'll try to write to you in French next time. That might be a good way of practising. I hope you know some French so you'll understand the letter I send. It'll be mostly stuff to do with who I am (Maud) or asking for directions for the swimming pool (where is the la piscine?). Stuff like that, but you don't need to reply because I don't really need any directions, I know Preston like the back of my hand and it's shit.

Lots of love,
Mademoiselle (Miss) Maud
xxx

P.S. If you can't understand the letter and you want to decipher its meaning you could look up all the words in a book called Tricolore. They will probably stock it at your local library because it's quite a popular book.

July 1981

> For ze attention of Monsieur Harding
> Friends of Horsefly
> PO BOX 113
> London W2
> 7th July 1981

Maud Harrison
22 Le Slater Street
La Hutton
Avez–Vous Preston

Salutations Tom (hello)
    Je suis Maud. (I am Maud.)
    J'habite à Hutton près de Preston. (I live in Hutton near Preston.)
    J'ai 13 ans. Elle s'appelle la teen-ager. (I am 13, a teenager.)
    J'aime have a mon chat. (I have a cat.) (I don't actually have a cat.)
    Savez-vous où sont les piscines? Dois-je tourner à gauche? (I just copied this bit, something about going left to the swimming pool I think.)

Your Friend Forever

Avez-vous des animaux domestiques? (Do you have any domestic animals?)

J'ai un chat, j'aime promener mon chat. (A cat for example.)

Aimez-vous les sandwichs oh fromage. (I adore cheese sandwiches made by Les.)

J'adore les sandwichs oh fromage avec jambon. (I also like the ham sandwiches made by Les.)

J'aime le jambon. (I love jam.)

Oh j'ai mal à la tête. Je me sens malade. Pourrais-je avoir le projet de loi s'il vous plaît car je me sens malade. (Can I have the bill please because I'm going to be sick.)

Vous pouvez mettre votre sandwich au fromage en haut de votre fond. (Please stick your cheese sandwich up your bum.)

Oh revoir. (Bye.)

Tout mon amour pour toujours voulez-vous coucher avec moi ce soir?

Madame Maud xxxx

P.S. Do you like this French letter? I copied most of it out of my Tricolore book (my French isn't this good yet unfortunately). I got some of the words from Tricolore 3 in the library because Tricolore 1 doesn't have the word bottom (bum) in it.

P.P.S. Voulez-vous! I don't know what voulez-vous means. It sounds French doesn't it? But Abba are Swedish. I feel silly writing it now.

***

Zena Barrie

For the attention of the man known simply as Tom Harding
Friends of Horsefly
PO BOX 113
London W2
10th July 1981

Just Maud Harrison
22 Slater Street
Dire (Awful)
Hutton
Preston

Dear Tom,

It's Sunday today. I got up really early this morning and went for a walk. I had gone and come back before my Mum noticed which is a really good job because she'd have gone mad at me. I absolutely love it in the morning, before people start driving. It was quite chilly but everything is fresh and the air just tastes completely different. It's like getting up just as the world has been taken out of its box for the day and everything is the same but feels new. It's really quiet because everyone is still asleep. I sometimes have this dream, well it's not a dream because I think about it while I'm awake on purpose. I imagine I'm the only person left in the world. Everyone else has gone, but there aren't loads of bodies everywhere because that would be horrible after a while. I imagine I just get in someone's car and drive into town. It doesn't matter that I can't drive very well because the roads are clear, there's only me so I can't hurt anyone and so long as I go slowly I'll be fine. So I go into town and I go to live on this fountain. It's this concrete fountain. It's from the 1960s. Loads of different sized circles and levels. The fountain doesn't work any more. I've always wanted to live on it, I don't know why. It wouldn't provide any comfort or shelter but I just love it. My Mum would never let me climb on it when I was little because of the pigeon faeces. There were always loads of other kids playing on it and their parents weren't bothered about the pigeon faeces but then they probably had a washing machine. I think though, after a while, I would get fed up of being in the world on my own. I'd have to pick some people to stay behind with me. I'd keep Sarah of course, and you, and I'm reading Margaret Atwood at the moment. I'd like to keep her, perhaps she could be a mother to me. Or an auntie or a God Mother. I don't have a God Mother but I'd like one, I don't believe in God but I do like the idea of an extra mother. I'd also keep George Orwell and Bertrand Russell and Karl Marx, in my world they would be alive and well and they'd all be keen to chat with me all day long, and to chat to each other and let me listen to them and they'd be on hand to answer any questions. Like a living, handsome Encyclopaedia Britannica. I'd keep Blondie too, Ted Hughes and Sylvia Plath, and there are others.

Don't worry, I'd keep at least 500 people I'm sure. I just need a bit of time to think about the list. Let me know if there's anyone you think should go on it. I could put your family on, if you like. If you still like them. I'm not sure I'd put my brother on. It's a bit like Noah's Ark isn't it? Do you think it's a bit creepy? It's just a daydream. I'd definitely get rid of the piggy boy in the opticians who said the glasses I was trying on looked horrible. I mean, do we really need him in the world? I don't think he's going to suddenly become clever and nice. You're nice. Were you ever horrible to girls when you were younger? Were you ever really ignorant? And then suddenly you woke up one day and decided to start writing songs and being creative. Maybe I'm the ignorant one and maybe the glasses looked really horrible and he was trying to show me a great kindness by just quietly letting me know. Maybe I'm the ignorant one that didn't want to hear the painful truth. Maybe it's me that's awful. I'm the one that daydreams about getting rid of almost everyone in the world. That's like Hitler isn't it? God, no wonder I've only got one friend. Sorry about this letter. I might not send this one. I need to think about it.

I read it back and I think I will send it because I think you'll understand what I'm thinking about and you must think about all sorts of things when you write your songs. It's easy to accidentally think of something awful. I can't be the only person that does it. I've been looking at the lyrics to some of your songs and trying to imagine what you might have been thinking about when you wrote them. On We Take What We Want, in the song Corn Fed Me, when you wrote this bit –

> Let the darkness wrap itself around me,
> hold me down and whisper me to sleep.
> Darkness you can take me if you want I'm yours, I'm yours,
> just forgive me when I weep –

I think, that you're in bed alone and just really want a hug, and you feel like crying and you don't have anyone to cry to or hug you. Am I right? I feel exactly the same. I sometimes feel like I could cry forever about everything in the whole world but there's not much point crying on your own. It doesn't sort anything out and no one cares. You just get a red blobby face, mine swells up a bit and goes blotchy. Have you ever cried while watching yourself in the mirror? It's quite tricky because it stops you from crying because you can see your own face contorted and you just sort of stop it. Why do you get loads of snot when you cry? Not only are you feeling really upset but you've suddenly got a streaming cold. I wonder if crying could be a good way of losing weight. You'd have to cry so much that all your fat turned to snot and then ran out of your nose. I don't need to lose weight, I'm really skinny, you cannot pinch an inch anywhere, or even a centimetre. I hear lots of grown up women though always talking about losing weight. Why don't they just stop eating cakes for a bit? The answer is right in front of them and they can't see it. Sarah's skinny too, but she has wider hips than me and she has a bosom, her body is womanly. She eats toilet paper instead of school dinner though. She always has loads of toilet paper in her pocket and she just chews it all day. I tried it but it just tastes of nothing. She said that when she excretes she can see loads of pink toilet paper mixed up with the excrement. That's pretty horrible isn't it? But at least she doesn't have to buy dinner tickets. I think the school think she's on packed lunches.

This letter is really long so I will try and stop writing now, sorry it's so long and strange. I know you will understand and if you do ever need someone to hug and cry on and even snot all over I would happily wipe up your snot and hug you forever. Really tight.

Love Maud

P.S. Just looking at those lyrics again. Maybe it's not about hugging. Maybe you have / have had / want to have sexual intercourse with a ghost in the dark. Is that it? Sarah once told me she'd had sex with a ghost but I think it was just wishful thinking. She really wants to lose her virginity but I think it's best she doesn't do that with a ghost. What if they disappear in the middle of it? Or change shape? The ghost could start off as Elvis Presley and then you kiss him and close your eyes and then open them and you're kissing Hitler.

P.P.S. I don't think I believe in ghosts but there is that astro projection thing isn't there? I don't know too much about it yet. Sarah's mentioned it a few times. I will look into it and let you know if there's anything in it. Night night.

Zena Barrie

***

Tom Harding – Singer / Songwriter / Genius
Friends of Horsefly
PO BOX 113
London W2
12th July 1981

Maud Harrison – Schoolgirl / Not a Genius
(but at least I know it)
22 Slater Street
Derelict
Hutton
Preston

Dear Tom,

I had drama class today. There's just fifteen of us in the class. We had to get into groups of five and work out an improvisation based on a problem one of us had. I was with Claire and Sally and Michael and Christian. No one could decide on a problem for ages and then Michael said a man had showed him his penis at the back of a bus. So we pretended we were all sat on a bus. Christian pretended to be the man who got his penis out. But we decided not to actually do that because we weren't sure what Miss Bailey would think about that. So we all just sat on chairs facing forward and Christian pretended to get his penis out. We asked Michael what he did when it happened but he said he didn't do anything, he just looked at it once and then looked out of the window. Then we tried to work out why it was a problem and what he should have done. I thought he should have got up and moved and maybe told the bus driver. But bus drivers get really angry if you try and talk to them while they are driving. We performed it to the rest of the class but I don't think the rest of the class knew what was happening because we were all just sat on chairs facing forward and not speaking to each other.

What would you do if someone showed you their penis while you were sat on a bus? I've never been flashed at so far. Sarah said she saw her Dad's friend's penis when he slept on their couch one night. I don't think she did anything about that either. The other two groups didn't do much better. One of them did an improvisation about not wanting to do the washing up and the other group did one where they were just arguing about football. I wasn't sure what the problem was. Miss Bailey asked to speak to Michael after the class had left. I wonder what that was about. Maybe she told him to tell the bus driver next time he gets shown a penis on the bus, or to at least move seats. I would have moved seats. Unless it was George Orwell or Ted Hughes. Ted Hughes is very handsome for a poet isn't he. I saw a picture of him in the school library. George Orwell is not as handsome, but he's very interesting and not everything is about looks. Although I think I would think less of them as people if they were the kind of men to show their penis to girls on the bus. I don't think either of them would do that though. I plan to read everything by George Orwell. At the moment I am reading 1984. We are not far away from it now so it's good to be prepared for what might happen. They've already got a computer at school, it doesn't seem to do much though. I read Animal Farm too. It's not about animals. I mean it is about animals but it's not really a story about animals. It's about people and power. When you wrote the album Pigs were you influenced by Animal Farm? The pigs turn out to be really bad. I might read it again. It's only a short book so it won't take long and I think if I read it again having read the end I might understand the beginning a bit more. Do you think if you lived on animal farm you would try and grab the power? I don't think I'm power hungry but I do have a tendency to think I know better than everyone else so maybe I would end up being a pig.

After I've finished 1984 I'm going to read Down and Out in Paris and London, I've already reserved it at the library. I wish my French was better so I could be down and out in Paris. I'd love to live in Paris in a small room with ripped up wallpaper and shutters and all I would have in the room would be some wine and a bed. Just like Vincent van Gogh. I could speak French and smoke cigarettes and wear a sort of black sack dress. I know you've been to Paris because I saw your tour dates in Sounds magazine, I've never bought it but they have it in the library. What was Paris like? Did you go up the Eiffel Tower with the rest of the band? I've been to Blackpool Tower and it's rubbish. I went up it with Mum and Dad and Simon when I was really little, I thought we had to climb up the outside of the tower to get to the top. I was really scared. I didn't know there was a lift going up the middle. When you get to the top there's nothing there. It's just really windy and rainy. Then you get back in the lift and go down again. There is a ballroom there with this massive organ that goes up and down through the floor. There were some people dancing but we weren't allowed to go and dance and I wouldn't want to ballroom dance with my brother anyway. There is a circus underneath the tower. We went to it, they had a tiger, it was quite frightening and some clowns which were also quite frightening, and then at the end the whole circus ring filled up with water. Simon thought he'd seen one of the acrobats' vaginas (he didn't call it vagina though), it is possible he saw something as their outfits were really tiny. Basically glittery string. I don't know why they can't just wear a proper leotard. There was no way they had knickers on underneath what they were wearing. We were sat quite far away though so I think

Simon would have only seen a very fast moving outer labia (the outer bit of a lady's vagina). Circuses are pretty weird aren't they? I wouldn't mind if I never went to another one in my life. It's so strange isn't it, that people decide that they are on holiday so they should do the following things:

Go up in a lift to the top of a tower, get blown about and then come back down again.

See some men covered in makeup riding tiny bikes.

Watch a man holding a tiger at bay with a kitchen chair.

Ride on a bicycle with a cover on it up and down in the wind.

Eat more chips than usual.

Put a hanky on their heads and sit on a stripy chair doing nothing.

Put sand in a bucket and tip it over.

Eat rock in the shape of a penis.

Watch Ken Dodd / Roy Chubby Brown / Bernard Manning

Get burnt.

Also, on a beach you can lie around in your underwear, but only on the beach. If you cross over the road in your underwear you will get arrested or felt up. Sarah told me that when she went on holiday to Spain once there were lots of ladies on the beach with their breasts out. Can you imagine that? I suppose you can, you've been abroad. But they still don't cross the road with their breasts out. It's hard to believe that people do this. It wasn't a nudist beach like in Carry on Camping. It's just normal. Sarah said her Mum did it. Why are these things supposed to be fun? Why save up all year so you can watch someone ride a bike, and eat chips, and lie on wet sand with your breasts on show? If people like this stuff so much why don't they put a hanky on their head when they're at home, and why don't we put stripy covers over the top of bikes all year round? It rains so much it would make sense. I don't understand people. I have to go and do the washing up now so my Mum doesn't go nuts when she gets home. Simon won't do it so I might as well, just to keep the peace.

Yours faithfully,
Maud H or M Harrison

P.S. Which do you think sounds best?
P.P.S. Sarah's Dad has bought a Sinclair C5 and her Mum has gone mad about it. Have you seen them on the news? It's a sort of tiny electric car that only one person can get in and they don't go very far and they cost loads of money. It's like a cross between a go–cart and a remote control car. You can't put petrol in them.

P.P.P.S. I don't like Ken Dodd. I don't like his tickling stick.

P.P.P.P.S. I have enclosed some safety pins, they are useful when you are mending things. I kept a few of them because I have put some of them on an old T-shirt. It looks sort of cool I think. I just have to be a bit careful that none of them pop open when I'm wearing it, I don't want to stab myself. They would look good on a denim jacket but I don't have one. I think you do so hopefully you will get some good use out of them. I have also enclosed some royal blue cotton. I don't actually like the colour royal blue because I don't like the royals. I think they should be banned. If you hate royal blue too just throw it away, I hope you don't find it offensive. I'm sure you wouldn't actually wear royal blue. It looks okay on Superman I suppose. Anyway, it's just cotton.

***

Your Friend Forever

To be opened only by Dear Mr Thomas Harding
Friends of Horsefly
PO BOX 113
London W2
13th July 1981

Miss Maud Harrison
of
22 Slater Street
Hutton
Preston

Dear Tom,

I keep thinking about religion, there's a lot to think about really, there's so many different ones. I only really hear about people becoming born again Christians but can you become a born again Sikh? Or a born again Buddhist? Why was the Buddha so fat? He must have had to really eat like a pig to get like that. I know that's rude of me and I don't mean to be horrible about fat people, I'm sorry if you have a fat Mum but it doesn't seem very religious to me to sit around in your pants getting fatter and fatter. I'd like to believe in something though. It would make everything a bit easier I think, if I did believe. But I don't think I can believe in anything I can't see. Though I believe in other countries and I haven't seen them so maybe I'm being very shortsighted. Anyway I wrote this poem.

The Holy Holy Ghost (came in my bedroom)

Last night I saw the Holy Ghost
He asked me to call him Remy
I said I didn't know that was his real name
And that gave him a semi (a verpa)

Last night I saw the Holy Ghost

He gave me a Bible to read
And even though the stories are quite good (New Testament)
It didn't make me believe

Last night I saw the Holy Ghost
And I think he saw my Bum (the cheeks not the actual hole used for excretion)
I was just getting my pyjamas on
It made him get some pre-cum (clear fluid released when a man gets a semi)

Last night I saw the Holy Ghost
Or it could have been a demon
What was he doing in my room?
I refused to drink his semen (also known as sperm, spermatic fluid, ejaculate, see sperm whale)

Last night I saw the Holy Ghost
We ended up having sex
I hope I haven't caught anything
I will have to go (to the doctor's) for some checks

The Holy Ghost hasn't been back since then
Not for many weeks
But I think of him fondly from time to time
While I look at the stain he made on my sheets (from his semen).

Sarah told me all about stained sheets. She says she always knows if her parents have had sex because her Mum strips the bed and puts everything in the wash and they have navy blue sheets from the Littlewoods catalogue. Apparently semen (that comes out of your penis) really shows up on these. Her Mum was complaining that the sheets are bobbling already and she hasn't even finished paying for them. Have you ever bought anything on tick? I think we have quite a few things from Radio Rentals. Although our actual radio downstairs used to be my Grandma's so that's paid for. They don't just rent out radios. They rent televisions and hoovers and washing machines and stuff although we don't have one of those. I wish we did, the collars on my school shirts are always black round the edges and I have to make sure no one sees them when I'm getting changed for PE.

I wish I knew what you thought about all the religions of the world, there's so many to choose from. Maybe one of them would really suit me. It's odd that they teach religion in school though. Surely we should only be learning facts. If I was going to make up a religion I'd make up something much more interesting than Christianity.

Love Maud

P.S. Thank goodness it's the summer holidays soon so I can get on with actually educating myself.

P.P.S. What do you think of religion?

P.P.P.S. I really hope I haven't offended you, if you do have a religion which one is it and which book do they follow? You would suit being dressed as Jesus, not the long dress I mean the little leather pants and the crown of thorns.

P.P.P.P.S. At PE today when we were getting changed our PE teacher Mr McNamara saw Tracey that I don't speak to (ever) getting changed and he saw her knickers and said to her 'pink to make the boys wink'. I keep thinking about it. Why would you want boys to wink at you? It's really just shutting one eye and then opening it again really quickly. Also what did he mean by it? Did he mean that she was wearing her knickers specifically to make boys close and open their eyes at her? Why would they be looking at her knickers? Did he mean him? I couldn't see his face properly. I saw Tracey's face. She just went really red and then looked at the floor. I don't really think the teachers should be looking at our knickers or having an opinion on them. Knickers are not part of the uniform. It's presumed we'll be wearing them.

***

SOUNDS MAGAZINE

14th July 1981, In the Lounge with Tom Harding

Mandy Graham gets comfy with chart-topping Horsefly frontman Tom Harding and finds the twenty-two-year-old singer un-clad, un-impressed and un-satisfied. And why a bit of sunshine might be the cure for everything...

Mandy: Tom, thanks for dropping by. That's quite a look you're sporting.

Tom: It's the first stuff I picked up off the floor.

Mandy: Who are your influencers fashion-wise?

Tom: I try to just create my own style and not be influenced by anyone really. I like just putting on what feels comfortable.

Mandy: None of it looks comfortable. Don't those shoes kill your feet?

Tom: No, my feet are actually quite pointy anyway.

Mandy: And the jeans?

Tom: I'm naturally skinny so, you know...

Mandy: And it was a conscious decision to have a hole in your T-shirt where your nipple is?

Tom: Oh no, it just got ripped there.

Mandy: And yet you still put it on.

Tom: Sorry if it's distracting you.

Mandy: It's a bit pink. Like it's cold and wants to be covered up. Well thanks for being here. Can you tell us a little bit about your new album We Take What We Want?

Tom: Well, it's a bit more accessible I think than our last album.

Mandy: Yeah I thought that, it sounds like you've all learned how to play your instruments this time round.

Tom: Yeah, that's true, there's more melody but…

Mandy: Lyrically you still seem very angry.

Tom: Do I? Not so much angry as disappointed really.

Mandy: What are you disappointed with? You're a successful pop star, a pin up, you must be making good money now and you're only twenty-two. A lot of lads your age are on the dole.

Tom: It's not all about me though is it? Yes I'm okay but I look at the world around me and see so many people that aren't okay and I want to write about them, you know.

Mandy: So do you feel like you're still in touch with the common person?

Tom: Of course, I've only had money for a year, and you know, not that much. I'm not Freddie Mercury you know.

Mandy: You did arrive here in a taxi.

Tom: From my rented flat.

Mandy: You should buy somewhere.

Tom: Well I will when I have enough money.

Mandy: You don't have enough money to buy somewhere?

Tom: No, not yet, let's see how this record does.

Mandy: What sort of place would you buy?

Tom: I don't know, a little flat on a good bus route.

Mandy: Oh, so you still take the bus?

Tom: Yes.

Mandy: Don't you get mobbed?

Tom: No, no one bothers me.

Mandy: And does that upset you? That you don't get the same attention as someone like – Freddie Mercury?

Tom: No it doesn't bother me.

Mandy: But you'd like his level of fame?

Tom: I'm just happy being employed as a musician, if I can keep doing what I'm doing I'll be very happy.

Mandy: There's a lot of talk about your gigs being violent, is this something you condone? We know that there are some venues that won't book you in any more.

Tom: I don't condone violence and I've never asked for it. I'm not sure what I'm doing wrong, or if there's something I've said lyrically, I haven't meant to... I certainly don't want anyone to get hurt. I know a lot of gigs though, not just ours, are turning into massive fights. It's a sign of the times I think.

Mandy: Meaning?

Tom: There's a lot of angry people out there and maybe our music brings out that anger, or they feel they can express it in front of us. I'm pro freedom of expression, you know, but as I say I don't want anyone to get hurt. It's the same thing with football matches I think. There's just a lot of anger out there and people don't know how to express that anger, they don't have an outlet so it's expressed as violence. If people were happy, satisfied, it wouldn't happen.

Mandy: And then you'd be out of a job.

Tom: Well no, I might write happier songs and maybe people would sit and listen to them or dance without, you know, spitting at me and lobbing chairs at each other.

Mandy: What do you think would stop this anger?

Tom: I don't know, lots of things, get Thatcher out, give people jobs, give people decent places to live. Some sunshine wouldn't go amiss.

Mandy: Sunshine?

Tom: Yeah, there's a lot to be said for getting a bit of sun on your face. We don't get enough sun here, we really don't.

We Take What We Want including the hit singles We Rip Out The Phone and Corn Fed Me is now available from all good record shops.

***

For the attention of the sophisticated Tom Harding
Friends of Horsefly
PO BOX 113
London W2
15th July 1981

From Maud Harrison (not sophisticated, but impossible in this house)
22 Slater Street
Godforsaken
Hutton
Preston

Dear Tom,

Sarah wasn't in school today, I hope she's in tomorrow because we're breaking up soon and I won't get to see her very much. I decided to try and talk to Michael at dinnertime, the boy in my drama class who got shown a penis on the back of the bus. He quite often eats on his own. I sat with him and we both said 'hi' and then after a while I asked him if he wanted to talk about the penis on the back of the bus. He said no, so then we just ate our food. Then I asked him if he had read 1984 and he said no. Then I'd run out of things to ask him and he didn't ask me anything so then we just cleared our trays up and I went off on my own to sit in the library.

I'm not sure where he goes at dinnertime. I'm not sure if he has any friends. Sarah says he might be gay but I don't know why she thinks that. How can you tell? Do you have any gay friends? I will try and speak to him again because if he is gay then that's quite interesting. I'd like to know more about it. I can't just ask him that though can I. Maybe when Sarah is back in school we can both go and sit with him. She's a bit better at chatting with people than I am. Maybe I could ask him if he likes Ted Hughes and then look at his face to see if he blushes. If he blushes then maybe it's because he thinks Ted Hughes is really handsome and therefore he is gay and if he doesn't blush he's not gay. Unless he doesn't know what Ted Hughes looks like. I wonder if I can get hold of a small picture of Ted Hughes to show him. Although it's possible that Ted Hughes is not the sort of man he finds handsome, in which case he won't blush. Like if someone showed me a picture of Ken Dodd, I definitely wouldn't blush but that doesn't mean I'm not attracted to men (I am).

I've just spoken to Sarah on the phone. She won't be in school tomorrow either. She has a bad stomach. I asked if it was to do with eating all the toilet paper and she just said 'shut up'. I don't think she wants anyone to know about it. So it's just me again then tomorrow at school. I will try and talk to Michael again.

I'm going to go now because I want to look for some pictures of men to show Michael. Maybe you are his type. I will show him a picture of you too. If he does blush I won't feel jealous because he's a boy.

Love Maud

P.S. I know it would be a bit crazy of me to feel jealous of someone blushing when they look at a picture of you. I wish I hadn't written it now but it's too late and if I cross it out you'll wonder what it was that I crossed out, you might think it's something much worse than it is so I'll just leave it.

P.P.S. I have enclosed some tiny scissors. They are good for cutting cotton, the end is a bit bent, not because they are broken, it's so you can also cut your nails with them. I've wrapped them in tissue so they don't cut through the envelope. I've never seen anyone using them to cut their nails apart from my Grandma, and I just bite mine off. I think Simon does too. Simon has warts on his hands. Mum gets really angry about them but I don't think it's Simon's fault. How do you get them?

P.P.P.S. Here is the poem I wrote about Michael seeing the penis at the back of a bus, it's written from his point of view, I don't have a penis.

I Saw a Penis

I saw a penis at the back of the bus
A man had unzipped his flies
He waggled it around quite a lot
While I tried to avert my eyes.

I couldn't help but look
It didn't look like mine
Mine is quite a bit smaller
But I'm younger so that's fine.

I saw a penis at the back of the bus
I'll never forget it was there
The man that showed it was very rude
I hadn't asked him to share.

That penis haunts me every day
I wonder if I'll see it again
I wonder if he's shown it to anyone else
I bet he has. Amen.

Your Friend Forever

***

For dear Tom Harding
Friends of Horsefly
PO BOX 113
London W2
30th July 1981

Maud Harrison
22 Slater Street
Unfrequented
Hutton
Preston

Dear Tom,

I'm so upset, I tried to talk to Simon, I just said something like 'about the other day, Dad will come back because he has to because of us', something like that, I was only trying to start a conversation with him and he just went nuts at me, screamed in my face. I ran away, and then later on I went in my bedroom and there was all this black tape everywhere and then I realised he'd ripped up all my tapes. Pulled them all out of the cassettes. I've been trying to fix them, normally if they get a bit chewed up you just have to carefully get them out of the tape recorder and then wind them back up using a pencil. But he'd actually pulled them out at the ends, the only one I could fix was one that just has a few songs off the radio, they're all ruined. I told Mum and she just said 'for God's sake Maud I've got enough to worry about'.

I know they're only tapes but they mean everything to me. I can't even copy them off friends because I don't know anyone that's into the same music as I am. Not even Sarah. Well she likes a few of the things I like but she really likes jazz singers and people like Frank Sinatra. I think it's what her parents like but she says they don't listen to music apart from when they are getting semen on the navy sheets and they don't want her to hear.

I'll just have to listen to the radio, it'll be okay. But it was such a mean thing to do. He knows how much I like listening to music. I hope they play you lots on the radio. Mostly it's just Shandy Hand isn't it? I really like Shandy Hand but I like all your other songs too, maybe more, and they hardly ever get played. Sometimes you can listen to a song too many times. Do you ever get that? I can't write any more, I just feel like crying. I think I actually will. I've just realised I am already.

Bye, love Maud x

My brother has ripped up my tapes

My brother has ripped up my tapes.
He's taken away my comfort.
He's taken away the place I escaped to
And now I can't rhyme any more.

My brother has ripped up my tapes
Without thinking of me at all.
Rage swept through him
And now I can't rhyme any more.

My brother has ripped up my tapes.
Was he trying to break me?
Or did he just hate the songs?
Why ever he did it
Now I can't rhyme any more.

> My brother has ripped up my tapes
> So all the kind voices have gone.
> And now it's just me, standing alone.
> I can't rhyme any more
> So I'll just turn the radio on.

Sorry Tom, I could go on forever with this but it's making me a bit too sad. I just wish I knew how to give him a dead leg but I've never managed to do one properly.

   I'm going to go to bed now.
   Love Maud

P.S. I can't bear it.

P.P.S. Charles and Diana got married yesterday. I thought the dress was very frumpy and she could have at least crimped her hair or something, it seemed to me like a missed opportunity to really get noticed. I don't find Prince Charles handsome. My Dad told me once that Prince Charles looks like that because of generations of inbreeding. Then he said something else about farmers and bull semen (sperm) and something about mongrel dogs being stronger than thoroughbreds and then he started talking about horses and then I just went upstairs, I think I might miss him. It's been ages.

August 1981

For Tom Harding's eyes only
Friends of Horsefly
PO BOX 113
London W2
4th August 1981

Maud Harrison
22 Slater Street
Hutton
Some deserted street
Where the wind doth blow
Preston

Dear Tom (or do you prefer being called Thomas? Or did your Mum christen you just 'Tom'? I like both names, I would love to know how to address you properly, please tell me if I'm doing it wrong. Oh maybe you like being called Mister Harding, or Master Harding? There are so many options.)

Dear Tom,
  Last night I had a dream about Tony Hadley from Spandau Ballet. I don't even like Spandau Ballet very much. I mean,

they're okay but I prefer bands that are sort of, a bit edgier (like Horsefly). I hate Duran Duran. I would never believe anything Simon Le Bon said to me, he looks like a liar. Anyway I dreamt that Tony Hadley was my teacher. I had a lesson with him and it was the end of the day and everyone else was leaving and he grabbed my arm as I was going out of the door and said 'Maud can I have a word with you please?' I agreed and then after everyone left we closed the classroom door and then he picked me up and popped me on his knee like I was a little girl and he asked me if everything was okay at home and I said it was and he said 'it's not though is it?' and then I started crying on him and all my tears made his stripy cotton shirt stick to his chest. He held me and rocked me really tightly until I stopped crying. He was humming a song as he was holding me. I can still hear the tune in my head but I don't recognise what the song is. It's quite catchy though, actually I think it was Musclebound. Then he wiped my tears away and he has really really big hands and he said I was very pretty. I can still picture really clearly in my head his shirt buttons, because my head was just laid on his chest. At the end of the dream I think we were about to kiss but I woke up. Which I'm thankful for because I don't see Tony Hadley like that, although maybe my brain does. Or maybe I woke up because my brain didn't want to see me doing that. Anyway when I woke up I was crying, my pillow was all wet but I sort of felt quite good and quite happy. What do you think it means? I told Sarah about it. She thinks it means I secretly fancy Tony Hadley but I'd tell her if I did. It wouldn't be anything to be ashamed of. He's not Simon Le Bon is he? What do you think it means? I'm quite looking forward to going to bed tonight in case it happens again.

I read in a book that dreams are what is happening to you at the same time in another dimension. I think it means that on every planet you could be doing something different. So on one planet I live here and I write to you. And on another planet Tony Hadley is my teacher and he likes cradling me, and on another planet I'm supporting you on tour with my own band. I don't know what this band is called at the moment. Hmm what about one of these?

Hadley's Hands

Hadley's Tears

Tears for Hadley

Wet Cotton Shirt

Wet Buttons

Cradled by a Teacher (more of a song title than a band name)

Kiss the Teacher (again more of a song title, it might get banned though)

Hadley's Cradle

What do you think? I quite like a lot of them at the moment but then I often make lists like this and by the next day I've gone off all of it. I need a name that I'm going to be happy with for the next ten to thirty years depending on when the band splits up.

How did you come up with the name Horsefly? Do you like all different types of flies? Or do you like horses and flies or do you only like the horsefly, or do you hate them? Or is it to do with it being a fly that bites you, like music could bite you like a horsefly? Did you come up with the name or did you all decide it together? I have so many questions. I read that Spandau Ballet got their name from Nazi prisoners of war. I'm not sure why they wanted people to be reminded of the Second World War. I've heard it was really awful. Was your Dad in it? Mine wasn't. I never met either of my Grandads so I'm not sure if they were in it or not. I should ask my Dad really if I ever see him again. I don't think it's the best time to be asking Mum about anything let alone if her Dad was in the war. I don't really like any kind of fly but they are useful. There was a big pile of dog excrement outside our house on the pavement and I think it was entirely eaten by flies. Flies and worms are really important aren't they, and bees. I wonder if The Bee Gees like bees and horse racing?

I have to go now.
Yours
Maud

P.S. Ooh what about Harding's Hands? Or Harding's Tears?

P.P.S. Although you weren't in the dream at all, which is weird.

P.P.P.S. What about Maud Harrison and her Wet Cotton Backing Band. Or is it a bit showy offy to have your name in the title of the band? If I did would that mean I have to be the singer? I'm not sure I'd be suited to that. I've heard my voice on a tape player and it wasn't very good so I'm not sure how it would sound through a real microphone.

P.P.P.P.S. Although you don't really sing, do you? More a sort of a shout, you always sound quite cross but it's very effective.

***

Zena Barrie

For the attention of Mr T. Harding 1960–198? (A.D.)
Friends of Horsefly
PO BOX 113
London W2
16th August 1981

Maud Harrison 1968–198? (A.D.)
22 Slater Street
Hutton
Preston
The Town of Ashen Faces

Dear Tom,

I'm really tired, really really tired but I wanted to write to you before I go to bed so I can get things out of my head. I'll post it tomorrow. I had really achy legs last night and then cramp, do you ever get that? The muscle goes really tight and you can't relax it. You have to get out of bed in the middle of the night and then jump up and down for ages until it goes back to normal. It really hurts and then hurts most of the next day too. And your legs hurt but it's the bone inside that hurts, so you can't rub it or do anything to make the pain go away.

I went downstairs in the night and got some Disprin and my Mum was still up and on the phone and she was smoking a cigarette! I've never seen her smoking before, I had no idea. She was really angry with me and shouted 'Maud, get back up them stairs'. I did but I got my Disprin first. I've seen a picture of you smoking. Are you addicted? Which brand do you prefer? I've only ever tried Regal Kingsize so those are my favourites. How many do you smoke per day? It doesn't smell nice or taste nice does it but there's something about it I really like. It's been ages since I tried it, I might ask Sarah if she'll get some more, she's quite good at getting hold of stuff because of her childbearing hips. She's had booze out of her Mum's cupboard a few times, I'm not sure if she's actually bought any herself apart from once in a bar. I didn't even know my Mum smoked so I've no idea where I'd look for her cigarettes. I know smoking can make your hands go yellow. I know your hands aren't yellow though, I've seen a picture of them. Your hands are a bit hairy aren't they? When did you start getting hairy hands? My Dad has got hairy hands. I hope I don't get them too. It looks all right on men but it wouldn't look right on me. I'd have to shave it off, and then I'd get five o'clock shadow on my hands, that would be terrible. People always say I look like my Dad so I hope I don't get his hairy hands. I know some people rip out their leg hair with wax. Maybe I could wax my hands. With my Dad it's an 11am shadow. Well it was, I'm beginning to wonder if he's dead and no one's bothered to tell me. I wish the hair on my head would grow as fast as men's facial hair, then I could try out loads of different styles all the time and if it went wrong it wouldn't matter because it would just grow back straight away. I like your new hair. What was the thing at the back though? Is it some sort of animal tied on? A skunk? Or is it made out of wool? I can't tell, sorry. It looks good though, I wonder if they'll start selling them in Chelsea Girl.

Do you remember I wrote to you before about Lisa who looks like a hog? That's horrible isn't it? But she does, she looks like a hog and keeps telling us she has a nineteen–year–old boyfriend who she seems to have anal sex with incessantly if she is to be believed. Every morning I have to hear new details about what she's done in the park. Sarah says it's so he doesn't have to look at her face. That's pretty mean isn't it? But she told me I'm really ugly and look like Popeye's wife Olive Oyl. I think it's okay to look like Popeye's wife, I do a bit. It's okay, she wasn't known for being ugly was she? She was known for being a bit skinny and having two men after her all the time, two sailors. One of them quite butch and one of them an old man who smoked a lot. If I was Olive Oyl I wouldn't be interested in Popeye or Brutus, anyway at least I don't look like a hog. I don't know why I say hog instead of pig but hog just seems right. Have you ever seen the book Fungus the Bogeyman? She looks like Fungus the Bogeyman's wife. I haven't said this to her. She won't know who he is. None of them read anything. I'm going to go to sleep now. Thanks for listening. I'm so glad you're there.

Maud xx

P.S. If you were Olive Oyl would you go out with Popeye or Brutus or neither of them? I might make a list of pros and cons for each of them. I think in the end though you have to at least fancy a person a bit don't you? Popeye looks older than he probably is, don't you think? He looks about 70 years old but he's still working as a sailor, which would make him only about 30. Brutus is I think just much too big up top and yet he has a tiny waist. What do you think? Which one would you go out with?

P.P.S. Have you ever been attracted to a cartoon character? I expect you like Penelope Pitstop, I think everyone does though she'd be pretty annoying to go out with I think. She's not very independent.

P.P.P.S. I quite like Grover from The Muppet Show even though he is only a waiter.

P.P.P.P.S. Have you ever had anal sex? Was it because you didn't want to look at the woman's face? If I was going out with an ugly man I don't think I would want to have sex with him from behind. I think I'd just dump him. Is it always the man that takes the woman from behind or can a woman take a man from behind. I'm not sure how it would all work.

P.P.P.P.P.S. I've been reading the Dramatic Lyrics of Robert Browning. 'Neath our feet broke the brittle bright stubble like chaff. If he was my boyfriend and kept talking like that, I might have to take him from behind instead of face on. Although maybe I'd have to kiss him to make him properly shut up. Do you think Robert Browning was handsome? I've never seen a picture.

***

>Sergeant Tom Harding
>Friends of Horsefly
>PO BOX 113
>London W2
>19th August 1981

Inspector M. Harrison
22 Slater Street
Two streets back from the end of the earth
Hutton
Preston

Dear Tom,

It's still the summer holidays. Everything's really quiet. Sarah has gone on holiday but we're not going anywhere. Dad has been gone for a few weeks now and Mum keeps crying but I don't ask her why because she seems to get cross whenever I open my mouth, I think he's gone, properly gone.

Anyway I'm a bit worried about you. I read that article in Melody Maker where you said you hate yourself and all your songs are shit and you want to die. Please don't die. You can't hate yourself! You're brilliant and handsome and funny and your songs are moving, poetic and inspirational. I don't know what I'd do without them. I hope you were mis-quoted, I know that happens sometimes in the gutter press.

The one bit of good news is that Simon has stopped wearing his clicky brace, but his orthodontist has to stick on a metal one now. Why do teeth have to be exactly straight anyway? It's like you say in Hate Hate Hate, 'we're robots living in a robot world', why do we all have to be the same? I don't think I care what I look like, well I probably do a bit. There's not much point caring too much when you look like me. People should like me for my mind, they don't yet but I'm hopeful. You're really handsome anyway so you don't have to worry about your teeth being straight. Do you ever go to the dentist? My Dad never did but he's not got that many teeth left so there's no point really.

Sarah sent me a postcard from Rhyl. She says it's shit but she's bought a copy of the Communist Manifesto for me, she saw it in a charity shop and they let her have it for 5p. I can't wait to read it when she gets back. I really hope it changes my life. She also said she's been practising doing her makeup like Steve Strange from Visage. I hope she doesn't try and make me do it. I'm not really into wearing much makeup. A bit is okay, but it's smelly. Sarah has this stuff called pancake and it really stinks. It used to be her Mum's, I think it's from the 1960s. It makes her face orange and you can see a line around her neck. When Sarah wears makeup she looks older, I just look like a clown.

Preston is so boring, there's just nothing happening. I think even for the grown ups there's not much to see or do, no wonder everyone shouts so much. It's just full of old women eating pies pulling shopping trolleys full of more pies. Everyone looks like a pie and smells like a pie. Maybe I'll write a poem or a song about it. Do you eat many pies? I hate the jelly in them. What is it? It makes me feel sick. My Mum keeps telling me off for saying that everything makes me feel sick but it does. When I go back to school I'll be in third year. I need a new blazer because mine is really short in the sleeves but Mum says it can last me for another year. I can't even do it up. I really want a new skirt too. There is a slit up the back of mine and it was about two inches when I got it but because of running around and stuff it got bigger and bigger and I have to sew it up all the time, it looks really messy and Mum told me off for using red cotton but I think the red looks punk and the teachers haven't told me off for it.

I need something new to read, I hope Sarah comes back from Rhyl soon, I'm not sure how long they've gone for. What do you like reading? I want to read something that makes my head explode. I wish I could read whatever it is you're reading at the moment. If you ever have time to reply you could send me a book list. I'd love that. I'm not sure if our library will have any of them though and I would be too shy to take out anything that was very rude.

Yours
Maud Harrison

P.S. Please don't die.

P.P.S. I have enclosed some fabric chalk from the sewing box. No one uses it. I only use the needles and thread and Mum doesn't use any of it. I don't even know how to sew properly, I just sort of do loops and it seems to do the trick. I might write some more lyrics now. About the pie women, you've inspired me.

Zena Barrie

***

FAO Thomas (Tom Harding)
Friends of Horsefly
PO BOX 113
London W2
20th August 1981

Maud Harrison
22 Slater Street
Hutton-on-Excrement
Preston

Dear Tom,

Sorry for writing again so soon but I've written another song. Here it is. It's about Preston and also about a girl that left school last year.

Preston Town

Pie shop pie shop pie shop
Cardigans are £2.99
They are factory seconds
They're from Marks and Spencer
The market seller reckons

You're pulling a trolley with one hand
Eating a pie with the other
You only left school last year
You already look like your mother

Your waist line has expanded
The same can't be said for your mind
You trawl the town for trinkets
You'd probably test positively for rickets

You drink Bacardi and Coke

Your Friend Forever

Or sometimes half a lager
Within twelve months
You'll be married to someone exactly like your father

Your veins must be filled with meat and potato
Or straight from the freezer
Sarah Lee frozen gateau

Don't you worry about the day when you die?
Nobody is discovered
Coffin filled only with pie?

It seemed like you were born to rule
Only last year you were cock of the school
Now you're walking the streets like a fool
You and your mother in matching kagouls

So eat your pies
Enjoy your factory seconds
It's not for me
Something else brighter beckons

By Maud Harrison aged 13 1968–? (A.D.)

I haven't worked out the tune yet, or maybe it's just a poem. I know it's not very good because all the verses have different amounts of syllables in them even though I did try to do them in an AABB style (I prefer an ABAB style normally but it just didn't work out like that). I tried to work out if your songs had a pattern, I'm sure they do because you're a very good songwriter but I couldn't work out what it was. Maybe your songs are in iambic pentameter (lines with ten syllables), like Shakespeare. I'm going to go and count them again.

Love Maud Harrison

P.S. Please do a gig in Preston soon.

P.P.S. You could all stay in the garage, there's plenty of space since Dad took the car. That's what garage bands do isn't it? Does it get cold?

***

>For the one and only Mr Tom Harding
>Friends of Horsefly
>PO BOX 113
>London W2
>23rd August 1981

Maud Harrison
22 Slater Street
Hutton–on–Bastardo
Preston

Dear Tom,

It's just me, Maud Harrison. Not much has happened so I've not much to talk about. It's still the holidays, Sarah is still away. There's nothing to do. Mum is still sleeping all the time or shouting at us to be quiet. Either that or she sends us to the shop to buy her paracetamol. I've been trying to work out how many she has every day. There are twenty-four in each little tub and she seems to be sending us to the shop for them nearly every other day. I don't think she's trying to have an overdose or anything. But then I do think she's having too many of them. She says she has a headache all the time. I know she's not stocking them up anyway because I've seen her taking them. It just seems to be a lot of the time.

When I'm back in school I'll have a new form teacher called Miss Bailey. I like her, she sometimes gives me knowing smiles, she takes us for English and drama too which I like mostly. Do you have a friend that gives you knowing smiles? Well

I suppose she's not my friend, she's my teacher but from the looks she gives me sometimes I feel confident that she knows I have a greater understanding of the world than the other people in my class. I would love to be able to hang out with her after school sometimes. It's like what Anne of Green Gables used to say about kindred spirits, you don't have to talk about it, when you know someone is a kindred spirit, you just know.

I love Anne of Green Gables, Sarah and I got quite obsessed with the books for a while, with both of us loving Anne and being in love with Gilbert. I did find Anne frustrating at times though. If I was asked out by Gilbert Blythe I would say 'yes' immediately, I wouldn't hit him over the head with a slate. She was angry with him for years because he called her 'Carrot', she should try living in Preston, being called Carrot would be a good day. I know he's not real though. Unless it's based on a true story. In which case he might be real. Oh but it's an old book, about seventy years old, so that would make Gilbert about ninety which is too old for me. My cut off is thirty, Sarah doesn't have a cut off. So she'd probably let him still finger her if we can track him down. I wonder how much it would cost to get to Prince Edward Island in Canada (where the books are set). By the time we've saved up the fare he'll probably be dead if he isn't already. Or what if he lives in an old people's home and Sarah and I turn up and she really flirts with him and he's sat in one of those smelly chairs trying to watch television and drinking soup through a straw. Also he might still be in love with Anne, he probably would be, love like that doesn't falter over the years and Sarah isn't anything like Anne. I'm more like Anne than Sarah is but still, I wouldn't want to let Gilbert finger me, I am very fond of him but if my calculations are correct and he is about ninety now, that's just not something I want to experience. I'd rather sit with him and maybe feed him some mash on a spoon.

Sarah should be back from her holidays any day now, I hope her arms have healed up. They looked really sore at the end of term. She covered them in scratches from her compass. She said she was going to put ink into the scratches and that would turn them into tattoos, but I never saw her putting ink in them and loads of lines up her arm won't be a very good tattoo. She'll be better off waiting until she's old enough and going to a tattoo parlour and getting a picture of a rose, or a snake, or a rose with a snake on it.

Have you got any tattoos? I think I like them but I don't know what I would choose, not a rose or a snake. Maybe a giant horsefly right across my back or some of your lyrics tattooed down my arm so if I was feeling sad I could just roll up my sleeve and look at them and that would make me feel better. I'm not sure which lyric though. Do you have any ideas? I really like the song Get Ready, track three on the Pigs album.

> Get ready, that knock's gonna come
> Do you join them or do you run?
> Get ready, this peace don't last for long
> There's a place we could all belong

But I'm not sure it would work as a tattoo and it's probably more frightening than comforting. I think I'd have to join them because I'm not a good runner.

Anyway, thank you for being there, you always make me feel better.

Love Maud

P.S. This is quite a long letter isn't it? Sorry.

P.P.S. I haven't written any new songs for a while but I will do some more. Maybe about Gilbert Blythe and Anne.

P.P.P.S. Actually I'm going to role play that I'm Anne for a while, I always enjoy that until I forget to do it. It's like going into a little trance where you are someone else. Then you get shouted at and you fall back into your own body and your own head with a thud. I spend quite a lot of time being Anne, or an alien.

September 1981

A man called Tom Harding
Friends of Horsefly
PO BOX 113
London W2
14th September 1981

A teenager called Maud Harrison
22 Slater Street
A place called Hutton
In a town known simply as Preston

Dear Tom,

We had pancakes the other day because my Mum didn't have anything in except a couple of eggs and some flour that's been out of date for two years but she said it doesn't go off.

My brother told me if you mix sugar with lemon juice you get whisky. He was eating loads of it when my Mum wasn't looking. Is that true? Is that all it is? Is it the same when you use lemon juice out of a plastic squirty lemon? (Also out of date, I remember Dad sending Simon to the shop for it last year. It still tastes fine though.) I read that you like drinking whisky. I'd like to send you some as a present, I know how to make it now,

I could make some and send it to you. Would you like that? If I can find a bottle I might do that next time, though I'm not sure how that would go in the post and I'm not sure how much it would cost to send, also I wouldn't be able to make much whisky, the Jif lemons are only the size of a real lemon so I'm not sure how many I would need to fill up a two litre bottle. Quite a few I think, and they're quite expensive. I suppose I'd need almost a whole bag of sugar too to fill the bottle up. I could do it, let me know if you'd like some homemade whisky and I will do it for you. Or now you have the recipe you could give it a try.

Here is some lace trimming out of my Mum's sewing box. I was thinking of sewing it on something but I can't think what, so (sew) maybe you can use it for something instead. I can't quite work out your fashion at the moment, sometimes you look punk and sometimes you've got all your buttons done up like a prefect, I wish people would put dates on photographs so I could put them in order. I like both looks. I don't really have a look as I don't have many clothes and mostly it's school uniform. I wish I had some Dr Martens, Sarah has some with eight holes. I want some with at least twelve holes, maybe more. So I really look like I could kick someone's head in with them.

Dad hasn't been home for nine weeks now. He called but my brother answered the phone and he just asked to speak to Mum straight away. She was just crying and we couldn't really tell what the conversation was. I just kept hearing her saying 'No T, no T, I can't let you, no T. I'm not the one doing this T. Don't put it on me'. All that sort of thing. She always calls him T. His real name is Terry though. I wish someone would call me M. She never calls me M though and she never calls Simon S, although S and M don't have quite the same ring to them as T. I sort of wish my name began with a more interesting consonant, I think maybe K or T, or V or W are the best ones. Though they are in sounds, but not when you say the letter, like 'Doubleyou come and get your tea'. If you're going to say 'Doubleyou' you might as well just say Maud I suppose. Doubleyou would be a good name for identical twins. Actually it wouldn't. Maybe it would be an okay band name, if the band had twins in it. Doubleyou should really be Doublevee anyway. Who makes these things up? No one with half a brain.

Mum went up to her bedroom straight after she'd put the phone down with Dad. So it wasn't anything good. I picked up the receiver to check if he was still there but he wasn't. I don't miss him that much to be honest but he did stop Mum from being so shouty all the time and he did used to let me do more stuff. I feel a bit like a prisoner sometimes in a really weird prison.

Maybe they should get mums to run prisons and just tell the men off all the time for spitting and swearing and the mums could make them tidy up all their bunks and behave themselves and do the washing up and they'd never be allowed to go out ever or watch Grange Hill. At least Dad used to buy me Melody Maker sometimes. I can still read it at the library but I can't cut anything out of it.

Mum's shouting at me to go to the bloody shop again, probably more paracetamol or maybe a pair of tights.

Love Maud

P.S. Fuck Thatcher. (Do you still hate her?)

P.P.S. Bring back Guy Fawkes.

P.P.P.S. Please don't ever be sad.

P.P.P.P.S. American Tan tights, can you think of anything worse? Not including apartheid or pain and suffering, I just mean in the world of tights. You only have to look at her face to see she hasn't been anywhere to get a tan, especially not America.

***

MELODY MAKER

16th September 1981
Horsefly Doing What They Do Best... Drawing Blood

Snap up a ticket if you're feeling brave for the few remaining dates of the most chaotic rock tour since The Viper Studs played a tour of community centres and left almost all of them not just in a mess but in need of serious building work.

The seven remaining dates are listed below. Rumour has it that the band is unlikely to make it to the end so maybe don't bother booking for the last three or four.

Warren Hamble has been playing guitar with a plaster on his arm. Tom Harding had visibly bleeding knuckles on stage in Newcastle and Ed Nailer's face looked like it'd been slammed into a wall at high speed. Don't expect an encore either. Tom Harding has been leaving the stage the second he sings his last note and legging it from the venue on foot. People were still shouting for Shandy Hand ten minutes later but sadly they'll have to wait until they get home. Oh and if you don't want to get into a scrap, stand at the back and leave early, or better still don't bother.

- November 30th Coventry Apollo
- December 1st Derby Assembly Rooms
- December 2nd Manchester Free Trade Hall

- December 3rd Bradford St George's Hall
- December 4th Blackburn King George's Hall
- December 5th Poole Wessex Hall
- December 6th London Brixton Academy

October 1981

> For Tom
> Friends of Horsefly
> PO BOX 113
> London W2
> 1st October 1981

Maud Harrison
22 Slater Street
A boring little place called Hutton
Part of Preston, the town made from paving stones and chewing gum

Dear Tom,
    Sarah has read this book on sexual magnetism. It's called Sexual Magnetism. I'm not sure who wrote it. You probably won't want to read it anyway. She's gone a bit weird since reading it. She says to draw men in you have to look them directly in the eye and say 'good morning' and picture in your head that you have had sex with them the night before. She says you have to maintain eye contact for just one second longer than usual (which is enough to be creepy) and that's enough for them to start thinking about you in a sex way. She says it will usually give them a semi (a verpa in Latin). (When your

penis is neither up nor down.) What do you think? I think it's a bit weird, at our age we don't say good morning to anyone, maybe a teacher sometimes I suppose but I don't fancy any of my teachers. Well Mr Williamson our other science teacher is quite handsome (he looks as if he's wearing eyeliner all the time) but I don't think he would stand for any sexual nonsense transmitted through my eyes. Sarah has been doing it to everyone with a penis. She says she wants to be seen as a sexual being. I don't understand why she's doing it to people she doesn't even fancy but she is, everyone. She's just walking round school saying 'good morning' to everyone. She has had some funny looks that might be lustful, I'm not sure. The thing is once she's said 'good morning' and they're looking into her eyes I can't then do it as well to test the theory. It would be really strange if we both walked round saying 'good morning, good morning', people already think we're weird.

I have asked her what the other tips are as it's an entire book and it can't all just be about that. She said there is stuff to do with positioning your body towards people as if you're ready to have sex with them. I'm not sure how you do that without it being rude or someone noticing what you're doing. Also there is stuff about biting your lips and asking men for help. This all seems a bit old-fashioned to me. Also I don't know any men I'd ask for help with anything. She went a bit far the other day, we got our dinner and took our trays to sit down and she said 'let's go and sit with Mr Williamson', his bottom eyelashes are just really dark and thick like a giraffe or a cow. Anyway. She sat right across from him and did the eye thing and said 'good afternoon' as it was 12.15 and then she turned to me and said she'd had a Flake in the bath last night and then turned to look at Mr Williamson and asked him if he'd ever eaten a Flake in the bath. He went really red and said no and then just put his head down and wolfed his food and went as quickly as he could. He ate his cornflake tart in one go. Sarah said he was probably rushing away so he could go and 'finish himself off'. Is that what men have to do? Once you've got a semi do you have to finish it off before it will go down? What exactly does that entail? I hope Sarah doesn't end up getting pregnant by a teacher and then have to start pretending to be middle aged.

I do worry about Sarah sometimes, we both have lots of the same ideas about things but she is definitely wilder than me (and not as well read). Also her arms are really covered in tiny cuts and scars now, some of them white lines where they've healed up and some fresh ones, all the lines are at different stages of healing and she hasn't turned any of them into a tattoo like she said she was going to. And she still keeps eating toilet roll. All I can do is keep an eye on her and hope that 'good morning' doesn't turn into being fingered by the headmaster at the back of the school field or worse. It could happen easily you know, she said 'good morning' to Mr Ranson and she reckoned it gave him a semi almost instantly. She said she could see his trousers move at the front (the zipped or buttoned bit that the penis sits behind). And then he went in his science supply cupboard for a while where he normally eats his sandwiches.

Love Maud

P.S. Thanks for listening, you are good at that too.

P.P.S. What's it like having a penis? I wish I could have one for a day. I'd stand outside Tony Hadley's house and if he came out I'd say 'good morning' to him and then he'd say it back to me (I presume he has nice manners) and then see if I get a semi. Hopefully not a full on erection. That would be embarrassing. I would have to go and hide until it went down. Do they go down on their own? It must be really difficult for you.

Zena Barrie

***

STAR SECRETS WITH TOM HARDING

8th October 1981

Robot voice: What colour pants are you wearing?

Tom: Red.

Robot voice: What is your favourite colour?

Tom: Yellow.

Robot voice: How old were you when you first kissed a girl?

Tom: Seventeen.

Robot voice: What are your hobbies?

Tom: Reading, writing songs, playing my guitar, sleeping.

Robot voice: How much do you love your mum?

Tom: Erm, a lot?

Robot voice: Does she still do your washing?

Tom: No, she doesn't live anywhere near me.

Robot voice: What's your favourite Christmas song?

Tom: Little Donkey.

Robot voice: Duran Duran or Spandau Ballet?

Tom: Erm, Spandau Ballet I suppose. Or Duran Duran.

Your Friend Forever

Robot voice: You may leave now.

Tom: Right, thanks. Buy my record.

December 1981

To be opened only by the addressee Mr T. Harding (don't worry, it's not a gas bill)
Friends of Horsefly
PO BOX 113
London W2
3rd December 1981

Maud Harrison
22 Slater Street
Hutton ahhh ahhh
Is becoming like a Ghost Town which is
Preston

Dear Tom,

Sorry I haven't written for a while, I haven't had any money for stamps. It's not far off Christmas, I'm dreading it to be honest, I don't know what it will be like without Dad but I think worse than usual.

Christmas at our house is like every other day but with Mum shouting from about four in the morning instead of about eight in the morning. She gets up really early to put a turkey or a chicken in the oven and then cooks it for hours and hours and hours until it's dried up. Then we eat it. Then there's a row over the TV. Dad gets drunk, they have an argument then me and Simon just go to our rooms. Also when we eat the Christmas dinner it's over in about ten minutes. I'm sure families are supposed to sit round a beautiful Christmassy table and have conversations about what they've been doing and laugh and chink glasses and pass each other gravy and that sort of thing. That really doesn't happen round here. Does that happen at your house? Sarah's allowed to get drunk at her house at Christmas. I'm not, though I'm not sure I would want to. It just seems to make people sad or angry and I feel like that a lot of the time anyway.

Mum is bagging up all of Dad's clothes so I'm keeping out of the way of her, she has a really nasty temper sometimes. I'm not sure what she's going to do with them. I don't know if he's coming to collect them or if she's taking them to the charity shop, I hope she doesn't put them in the bin. It seems like a waste. I'm sure he'll want to at least come back for them or I could cut them up and make some cool clothes out of them. I could rip one of his shirts up and draw on the back and put safety pins in it. That is, if she's only going to throw them away she might as well let me have them.

Christmas is supposed to be religious but I don't believe in God, I sometimes wish I did but I can't make my mind do it, if it did turn out that he exists he would have a lot of explaining to do because he does some pretty horrible things to people.

Mum probably won't bother with Christmas this year unless Dad comes back. I'm going to just pretend it's not happening. I have found it's best to keep my expectations as low as possible at all times regarding all matters.

Why did Jesus not have any female disciples? Did he not let them? It sounds a bit like a golf club. Sarah's Dad used to belong to one and women aren't allowed. He isn't a member any more though, they sometimes have loads of money in that family and then none at all.

I know that people like religion because it gives them strength to get through their days, and it makes them think that life is really hard but not to worry, it will all be nice when they go to heaven so long as they behave themselves.

I can get strength from a nice song or a poem or something in a book. Books don't make me believe in heaven though. I believe when we die that is the end. So we should do something good with our lives while we have the chance. Like you do.

Why do they bother teaching us all these lies at school? We'd be so much better off having the spare time to go and read.

I can't wait until I can vote. I'm going to vote communist. Mum says there isn't the option to vote communist in Preston but I think she's feeding me lies too. They are all at it, luckily I am on to them. Question everything.

Love from Maud

P.S. Merry Christmas and a happy New Year.

P.P.S. Sorry I haven't made you any whisky yet. To be honest I don't see how I'm going to be able to afford to do it. Sorry if I got your hopes up and then dashed them.

P.P.P.S. I hope the tour is going well, I wish I could go but I'm just not old enough yet and I've no money for a ticket and I couldn't get to any of the places. It makes me sad but sometimes when I know you're playing somewhere at a particular time I imagine you on stage and know that that's what you are doing at the exact time I'm thinking about it. It feels nice. It feels like I'm connected to it somehow, without actually being there.

Your Friend Forever

P.P.P.P.S. Hello it's me. I'm in the school library. I've just looked up what the ten commandments are because I could only remember the one about not having sex with your neighbour's wife. It's quite surprising that there are only ten rules for life and three of them are about neighbours. No stealing from your neighbours, no having sex with your neighbours, and no being jealous of them. It's a lot of attention on neighbours. We rarely see ours.

***

MUSIC WEEKLY

3rd December 1981

This issue we talk to little Tommy H. from Horsefly to see if he's got what it takes to exist outside of this bubble we call POP.

MW: Tommy, how many 'O' levels have you got?

Tom: It's Tom, erm, eight I think.

MW: You think?

Tom: Yeah eight.

MW: What in?

Tom: Erm, English language, English literature, art, maths, biology, French, chemistry, geography.

MW: Did you know that's three more than Prince Charles?

Tom: Erm no, I didn't know that.

MW: So you're cleverer than royalty?

Tom: Well he must be pretty fucking thick then with all the opportunities he's had.

MW: Meaning?

Tom: Well he's not gone to the local comp has he? He's not had to freeze his bollocks off doing a paper round instead of doing his homework.

MW: Not a fan of the prince then?

Tom: From what I've seen of him, he's a c*nt.

MW: So you're not hoping to be knighted then?

Tom: I think there's about zero chance of that ever happening, have you read my lyrics?

MW: The one about wanking? Or the one about shagging a ghost? Yeah they're not very good are they? How many 'O' levels did you say you have?

Tom: Oh fuck off.

***

Your Friend Forever

> For Tom Harding
> Friends of Horsefly
> PO BOX 113
> London W2
> 7th December 1981

From Maud Harrison (a friend of Horsefly)
22 Slater Street
Hutton
Preston

Dear Tom,

Sarah has turned into a Christian, a born again one. It all happened really quickly. She said she'd been on her own on the swings in the park and smoking a fag because she's got addicted now so she likes to do it on her own and she keeps nicking her parents' fags and they're not bothered. Anyway she was on the swing and she said this really handsome boy came up to her and started chatting. He is called Stephen and he's seventeen years old. I haven't seen him so I don't know if she is telling the truth about how handsome he is but from what she said he sounds lovely and unlike most of the boys you see in Preston. He is tall with wavy black hair and a really nice smile and lovely olive skin with no spots. Every other boy in Preston has pasty skin and lots of spots and sort of red blotches. Basically all the boys look like pies with greasy little wigs on their heads. I've already decided not to go near any of them until they turn into men, when they'll hopefully have better skin. Also they spit a lot and I hate that. So she chatted with him for ages and he told her she shouldn't be smoking and he took the cigarette out of her hand and squashed it under his foot and said 'that's better' and she said it was really sexy. Then he invited her to go to his youth club. I didn't even know there were any youth clubs round here. It's in this really old building in the park near Sarah's house, like a one-storey house that looks like a mini church. He gave her a flyer and he said he'd love to see her there and he put his hand on her arm and smiled at her really nicely and then just walked away and then looked back at her and smiled again and she said it made her knees go weak so she sat back down on the swing. When he'd gone she picked up the cigarette and unsquashed it and lit it again. Then two days later she went to the youth club and Stephen was there and he went over to her straight away and said he was really glad she came and that she needed to talk to this other man first about becoming a member before she could do youth club things. I'm not sure what those things are. So she went into this little room with a man called Bryan who is bald with a white ponytail and John Lennon glasses and she said he was really nice and he told her that they were Christians and she could be one too, he made her feel really welcome and she chatted to him for ages and he made her hot chocolate with milk not hot water and gave her some biscuits too and told her about their community. I'm not sure what else was said but now she says she's a born again Christian and she's part of the youth club and she says I can go too if I like but I have to speak to Bryan first about being part of the community. She said he's a hippy that's really into peace and love and that he'd let me join too so long as he thought I was into being a Christian and wouldn't disrupt everything.

What do you think? Do you think it's possible to be born again? Sarah seems to think she is born again. I don't know how that happens. I'd quite like to go to a youth club but I'm not sure my Mum would let me anyway and I'm not sure about being born again. I wouldn't mind being born again if it was to a different family. I'd choose a family that was really nice and lived in a nice house where there was no shouting. It doesn't work like that though. I'd still have to be me but with different beliefs. I don't believe in God and neither did Sarah before she met Bryan. I wonder what he exactly said to her to suddenly make her believe. I've asked Sarah what the activities are but she just said 'youth club stuff' so I don't know if it's worth it or not. I suppose I could pretend to be born again and not really mean it. What if they brainwash me though. I don't want to become religious. Sarah said it's just about being kind. I think I'm kind anyway so maybe I would fit in. I'm a bit jealous too because Sarah has these new friends now and I don't know any of them. I wonder if my mind is strong enough to not get brainwashed. I don't know how good he is at doing it, but he did it to Sarah really quickly. Though Sarah changes her mind about stuff all the time, one week she likes jazz and then a week later she's into something else like country music and she does her hair differently. Then a week later it's all crimped again, with eyeliner. I like eyeliner. I wore it at home once though and my Mum spotted it straight away and made me go and wash my face. It's a shame as it made me look older and a bit cool and less gaunt.

I know what I like and what I don't like and I don't change my mind very often, though maybe I should be more open to change. It's not like my life is brilliant, maybe a change would be a good thing. Maybe I'll go down and see what it's like. I'm not sure if Stephen is her boyfriend now or not. I think I should go. What do you think I should do? There isn't anything else to do around here, there isn't a youth club for atheists.

Have you ever flirted with religion? That's what people say isn't it. Like flirted with religion or flirted with capitalism or flirted with communism. It's a bit weird isn't it? Who is it you're flirting with? God? And if God is all seeing and all knowing and all doing then he'd know that you were flirting. He'd probably have to say 'stop flirting, I'm not like that'.

Nuns are married to God aren't they? So he has loads and loads of wives. So actually maybe he doesn't mind teenage girls flirting with him, they could be future wives when the nuns die. Though if there is heaven then all the nun–wives would be in heaven with him. Probably doing all his cleaning and washing up and stuff. It just doesn't make sense does it? Any of it. I might go out of interest but I am not going to be born again, I've thought it through and it doesn't make sense. I won't tell Sarah it's rubbish though. I think she'd get angry with me because she seems quite happy with all of it. I will let you know how it goes.

Yours,
Maud

P.S. I would love to know what you think about religion.

P.P.S. I'm really hungry and there is no food in the house except half a bottle of ketchup and some vinegar. I hope the school dinner is good tomorrow. I hate it when it's this tomato sloppy stuff that doesn't even have a name.

January 1982

To Tom Harding
Friends of Horsefly
PO BOX 113
London W2
6th January 1982

Maud Harrison
22 Slater Street
Hutton–not–on–Sea
Preston–not–for–me

Dear Tom,

Happy New Year! I hope 1982 is a good year for you. Hopefully it will be for me too. I'm almost fourteen which is good, it means I'm almost an adult. Sorry I haven't written for a while. I've had no peace and quiet to write to you, no money for stamps, there's been a lot of shouting. Christmas basically didn't happen, I mean it did happen but in this house we just sort of pretended it was like any other day. Mum has been really on edge so I've been trying to help out as much as I can to keep the peace. I don't think she likes it when Simon and I are off school. I don't like being off school either. Dad didn't come back for Christmas and he didn't phone or send us a card or anything. I suppose he might have done and Mum might have chucked it away. I'll never know. I wish I could talk to Simon about it but he barely speaks. It's like living with a deaf mute (a man who can neither hear nor speak).

I told Sarah I would like to join her youth club to see what it was like and she said she didn't think it was a good idea. I don't know if she's worried about me meeting Stephen or meeting Bryan or if she thinks I'll embarrass her or what. I tried to ask her about it and she didn't want to talk about it. She's still eating lots of toilet roll and still cutting her arms so being born again hasn't sorted that out yet, maybe it will take longer. I think I just have to stop asking her about it and carry on being her friend. She's being a bit quiet in general. It feels as if she doesn't think she can laugh at things any more or something, maybe it's not Christian to laugh. As though she doesn't know what to think about things any more. If we talk about music or boys or teachers or anything really, it's sort of as if she's thinking about her answers before she says them, do you understand what I mean? And then she doesn't really answer much because she just seems a bit unsure of herself. She was never like that before. It's weird, she seems sad. I wish I could ask my Mum about it but she just doesn't listen, she doesn't listen to anything. I bet if you asked her she couldn't tell you a single thing that's happening in my life. I wish Dad would come back. Things were more normal when he was around, shouty but more normal. It feels like we've gone to rack and ruin since he's gone.

I have to go now. I've got bloody geography homework to do. It's about farming and precipitation. I don't know what that even has to do with maps and I don't ever want to be a farmer, ever, it's just not on my list of possible jobs, so why do I have to learn about it?

My possible jobs for when I grow up after I have been to university:

Songwriter.

Writer of books.

Cleaning out ears (I love cleaning out my ears).

Designer of comfy clothes like a boiler suit you can also sleep in like a sleeping bag with a built-in fan heater, I would never get out of it.

Designer of a new bald hairstyle so you don't have to think about doing your hair.

Writer of poems. I have so many poems in me. Actually I might be better at poems than songs. It sort of depends if I ever get to learn an instrument. I just look at something and I hear a poem in my head. Usually though I can't get it written down in time and then I forget it. (Don't worry though, I would never put my head in an oven. I can think of so many better ways to kill myself. I wouldn't want to be found covered in lard.)

Working in a charity shop.

Working in a bookshop.

Working at the library (although I don't like the Dewey decimal system, it's just boring, I much prefer how books are laid out in a charity shop or a secondhand bookshop, sort of all over the place and then you have to look at everything and then you might find something brilliant for 5p. If I ran a library I'd put in loads of comfy chairs and blankets and give people hot water bottles for their knees and all the books would be higgledy piggledy all over the place. They'd still have plastic covers on because I like that and you'd still be able to borrow them, you'd just always have to have a good rummage. Some people just go in, go to the exact book they want and then get it out and take it home. Where is the fun in that?)

I'm not sure when I can post this because I have no stamp

money at the moment. Hopefully next week. I will use my Clippercard money for stamps and just walk instead of getting the bus. It's pretty rubbish being poor but I know there are people worse off than us. Sometimes I watch the news and everything looks awful. It's not so bad round here really. Christian Youth Club has to be better than rioting doesn't it? Even if I'm not allowed to go. I hope Sarah starts being herself again soon. I miss her being stupid with me.

I think I will sign off now and put this letter in an envelope even if I can't post it today. I'll write the date on the envelope so I send them in order, because I might have written to you again before I post this one.

Thank you for being there, it means a lot to me.

Love Maud

P.S. Have you ever needed to know about precipitation in your work as a musician?

P.P.S. Have you ever had your ears cleaned by someone else? I would do it for you for free, and I would be really careful not to poke too hard and pop your eardrum. Maybe once I've cleaned your ears out you'll find you hear loads better, it might really help you with your music.

P.P.P.S. Sarah hasn't mentioned fancying people or sex for the last few weeks and it used to be all she went on about. Christian Youth Club has changed her.

P.P.P.P.S. I hope I can post this letter soon.

***

Your Friend Forever

Ground Control To Major Tom (Harding)
Friends of Horsefly
PO BOX 113
London W2
10th January 1982

Maud Harrison
22 Slater Street
Hutton
Preston, as desolate as space, and not as interesting

Dear Tom,

At lunchtime today I was eating with Sarah as usual and then after we'd finished she said she had something to do and when I asked her what it was she just shrugged and said she wanted to be quiet. She has never been quiet before. I finished off my dinner and then got some seconds of mash, they do that sometimes, you can go up and get an extra scoop. I always do if I can because Mum just doesn't bother making tea any more and there's never much in for me to make something. I might make some toast if there's bread but I don't eat it in front of her because she just seems to go mad at the sight of me. I don't actually know what Simon has been eating. Maybe he's been doing the same as me, just getting some extra mash, I hardly ever see him at school and if I do see him he pretends not to see me. Loads of people complain about the school dinners but I think they're okay. They fill you up and there's always a hot pudding. Who gets that at home? Especially at lunchtime. Maybe on Christmas day, not this year but it has happened, but not the rest of the year though.

I wasn't sure where Sarah had gone but I walked past the form room and looked through the little window in the door that the headmaster sometimes pokes his fat nose through. She was just sat at her desk staring into space. I thought about going in but I didn't. So I put my coat on and went outside for a bit. Michael was sitting on a wall on his own so I went and sat next to him. We watched the older boys playing football. I wondered if it was giving him an erection, or maybe a semi at least, but I didn't ask (or try and look at his trousers). I did ask him though if he had a favourite and he just looked me in the eye for about three seconds and then turned away. Then I asked him if he was thinking about the penis. He said 'what penis?' and I said 'you know, the one from the back of the bus'. Then he said 'no'. I thought 'what penis?' was an interesting thing to say, sort of a dead giveaway, that there were maybe several different penises that he could have been thinking about and he needed me to tell him which penis I was referring to.

An interesting thought though, if he is gay and I think he is. Would he really be thinking about penises? If he likes males, then that makes him kind of like me. I don't think about penises very much at all. I've seen some, men's ones, not little boys' ones. Sarah showed me some pictures from a magazine, they looked okay. But I don't think about them that much. I do think about nice eyes and talking to boys and I suppose I think about sex and what that would be like. But I don't think about an actual penis on its own. Like men, or boys anyway seem to think about ladies' breasts all the time. Boys constantly pinging bra straps (not mine) and going on about the girls in the class and how big everyone's breasts are (mine are small but have started to grow finally). There is one girl in my class called Carol who has really big breasts. She has to wear a bra that is a 36D. She is completely covered in acne but all the boys still want to go out with her and I think it must be entirely because of her breasts. It's like they never even notice her face and they are not one bit interested in her mind, which is good because she barely has one. Am I supposed to be like that with penises? Am I supposed to see a hunk and think he's handsome and then daydream about feeling up his penis? Because that's not what I do, could this mean that I'm a lesbian? A boy at school called Damian once grabbed me from behind at school and I jumped because I was surprised and he said I was frigid. Maybe that's because I'm really not into fancying boys. It's all a bit confusing. And when I look at girls I can see which ones are beautiful and which ones aren't, I can really tell the difference. But maybe that's because I fancy some of them and don't fancy the other ones. But I don't daydream about girls' breasts either. Maybe I'm not a sexy person at all. Maybe I'm destined to be on my own because I don't like breasts or penises. I suppose that would be okay. If I decide not to bother with men or women then I'll have more time to concentrate on my career. And I think maybe that should be poetry, or maybe writing obituaries and epitaphs, I've just learnt about them. It sounds like something I could do, I think.

> Here lies Lisa.
> She liked anal sex and writing her name on other people's property.
> She had thick legs and thin hair – an enigma!
> I am led to believe she could read and write and do very basic mathematics.
> We will remember her at the going down of the sun.

Maybe I will need some practice or to write them about more interesting people. We don't get to see the careers advisor until we're in the fifth year. I wish I could see them sooner to ask if I'd be more suited to being a poet or an epitaph / obituary writer or if it would be possible to do both.

I really wish I knew where my life was going and if I'm a lesbian or not. Is there a word for people that are neither one thing nor the other? I like you, but I have never wondered about your penis. I do think you're handsome though, so maybe I should stop worrying about it all for a while. Did you ever fancy a boy? Do you have a girlfriend? I bet you have lots of beautiful girlfriends all the time. Do you like them for their minds or do you like them for their breasts or their faces? I suppose I am still going through puberty so maybe I don't have the full array of feelings yet. I'm not sure though, how many more feelings I can cope with. The nurse came round and told us all about puberty last year. Maybe when I'm a bit further into puberty I will suddenly start thinking about penises. There's still time isn't there?

Sorry if this letter is a bit rude, I hope you don't find it offensive. It's just good to talk about these things isn't it. In one of your songs, Whistle as You Fall, I like these bits:

> You thought I was whistling, I was losing my breath.
> You think I'm lying down, I'm close, so close to death.
> You'll never see me, though I see you.
> For you, a smile is a smile is a smile.
> My concrete mind you will never break through.

I think this is about being misunderstood, by someone who can't see that you're having a hard time. Just because you can smile it doesn't mean you're happy does it. It makes me think you'll understand this letter even if it's a bit blue in parts. I hope I'm right. Please tell me if I'm wrong. 'Blue' is a bit of an old-fashioned word isn't it? My Grandma always said to my Dad, 'you don't hear Ken Dodd making blue remarks'.

Your friend forever,
Maud

P.S. I'm very tired, I might just go to bed nice and early. I'm fourteen in a couple of weeks. I wonder if my Mum will remember. I'm not too bothered if she does or she doesn't. I'll know I'm fourteen and I'll be very pleased about it.

P.P.S. I have just got some English homework back from Miss Bailey and she's written all over it in red pen. 'If you are going to cite quotes from people you must say who they are from.' I'm a bit embarrassed as all the quotes are from me, just my opinions on things. It's rubbish that I have to go and explain myself. I should be allowed an opinion at my age. If I could find any writers that agreed with me then I'd quote them but I haven't found any texts about Hamlet most likely being a hermaphrodite. They should be glad I know the word. At least I take an interest in the subject matter. Not like Lisa who is only interested in getting nineteen year olds to put their penises inside her bum hole. I don't know how she even got into it. What's wrong with just listening to pop music? Have you ever put anything into your bum hole? I could say ass but I don't want you to get confused and think I'm talking about a donkey.

P.P.P.S. When you get a mule, which is the child of a horse that's pro-created (had a baby) with a donkey, I wonder if it's usually the horse that's the father in this sort of situation. You'd think so wouldn't you. Typical. I hope for the donkey's sake it's never happened with a shire horse but it probably has knowing the state of this world.

***

Zena Barrie

> FAO T.H. Esq.
> Friends of Horsefly
> PO BOX 113
> London W2
> 11th January 1982

Sender Miss Maud Harrison Esq. who resides in a barren room at
22 Slater Street
Hutton
Preston

Dear Tom,

I'm tired, I'm hungry, I'm lonely. I know I shouldn't moan. I know it'll all be all right but just at this moment I feel awful. I feel really stupid for telling you all this. I'll be at school tomorrow and there will be people there and I can eat and I can sleep tonight. It's just all awful at this moment. When does it end? When do things start getting better? There's nobody I can talk to at home. My Mum just bangs around. Simon looks at me like he hates me and Sarah is still a Christian. I've got no one to talk to. At least I can write to you. I read something in Sounds though at the library that said Horsefly might be splitting up soon. I hope that's not true. It can't be true can it? Why would you split up when you're doing really well? I really hope you don't split up. If you did split up what would you do? I suppose you could do anything. Maybe you have a big list of possible jobs like I do and one of them was pop star and now you've crossed that off the list you can go on to the next one. I wonder what it would be. Surgeon? Or do you have to have really good eyesight to be a surgeon? Your lenses look quite thick so I think you must be shortsighted which wouldn't be good for surgery but you must at least be clever enough to be a surgeon and you have lovely hands (I've seen them on your guitar) which you need to have when you're a surgeon. I read about that in an old copy of The Lancet I found in a charity shop. It's actually a pretty good magazine but they don't sell it in our corner shop and they don't even have it at the library, I asked them because I liked it so much. Maybe you just want to retire. Maybe you've made enough money that you don't have to work for the rest of your life, you can just drink Bacardi and jump into swimming pools and eat prawn cocktail. Is that what you're planning to do? I wish I could retire with you. Well that's not true, there are things I'd like to do with my life, I'd just like to try prawn cocktail really, though I'd eat anything at the moment, what kind of alcohol goes into a prawn cocktail, is it cider? Or Bacardi?

I'm not sure when I can post this because I need to save my money in case I desperately need it for something. I just wish I was an adult and could go and get a job. I tried to get a paper round but the shop doesn't do them, not enough people want papers.

Sorry for moaning. I'm going to do my homework now. All I can do is try and learn everything I can and then get a job as soon as I'm old enough. It's English homework. I have to write an essay about The Crucible which is a play by Arthur Miller. I quite like it, it's about witches. There is a character in it that I know is handsome even though I know he's a fictional character. He is called John Proctor and he has an affair with a young girl who might be a witch called Abigail Williams. A few weeks ago Sarah would have fancied John Proctor too, she'd have said she wanted to be a witch and for him to have an affair with her and finger her but she hasn't said anything about it. She just said it was a boring play, which it really isn't. I don't know if she's even read it. They sometimes do different books in her English class (we're not in the same set). It's about affairs and witches, how can that be boring? I had thought that witches were just from fairytales and something that you dress up as at Halloween but in America they had real ones and men wanted to kill them. I'm not sure why, maybe because the men were jealous that they didn't have any special powers. Maybe the witches made them feel vulnerable. Men aren't usually scared of women but if a woman is a witch and can go home and make a potion, for example to make a penis fall off, the men would have good reason to want them dead. I don't know what spells they cast but I imagine it would be along those lines. I wish I was a witch. I wouldn't wear a stupid hat or anything. I'd just be a normal girl that was also a witch like Abigail Williams.

Spells I would cast:

1) Make Dad come home.

2) Make Mum how she used to be (or slightly nicer).

3) Make my brother nice.

4) Magic some food in, nice food including prawn cocktail.

5) Burn the Christian Youth Club down, or maybe just get Sarah out of it, I'm not sure.

6) Make Lisa at school have no mouth so she can't talk about anal sex any more (and she won't have the option to get into oral sex, though knowing her she'd stick it in her ear next).

7) Make Michael be my friend so we can talk about whether we think about penises or not.

8) Make me older so I'm not at school any more.

9) In fact put me straight into university. A degree in poetry and there is a gorgeous lecturer who wears tiny round glasses and he's in love with me and it's the 1950s. And it's Ted Hughes and my beauty surpasses that of Sylvia Plath, in fact he doesn't look at her twice.

10) Maybe you could be my brother or cousin and we'd get

on really well and you'd always stick up for me when I needed it. Or maybe you could just keep on being you but live round the corner and be my friend and teach me how to play guitar and give me one of your special plectrums (that you use for playing your guitar) I could use. I'd love that.

11) Make Mr Ranson's penis fall off. That'll teach him.

Too tired to keep writing now. Thanks, I feel a bit better now actually. I'll just go to sleep and try not to worry and tomorrow will be okay. Maybe I'll really try and confront Sarah. Maybe she wants me to. I might spend the day pretending I'm secretly a witch. That might make me feel quite powerful, I could do with that. Wish me luck. Sorry if this is the most moaning letter you've ever had in the world.

Your loving friend,
Maud

***

Thomas H
Friends of Horsefly
PO BOX 113
London W2
18th January 1982

Maud H
22 Slater Street
Hutton
Preston
Tired

Dear Tom,

It's raining here, what's the weather like in London? I've heard it's always warmer down south. I'd love to be warm all the time.

Sarah wanted me to go off with her after lunch, she hasn't done this for a while, she's just been going to the library on her own and sitting with her head in her hands. I was so pleased. We went and got some crisps from the ice cream van that parks just outside our school at lunchtime. The man in the ice cream van looks exactly like Brian May out of Queen. Then we went to the corned beef wall (you can still see where the corned beef was, it's like a black stain on the wall now) and we just sat on the floor and chatted like we always do. I thought everything was getting better but it's not, it's loads loads worse. I asked her if she was still going to Christian Youth Club and she said she was and then she started doing this secret smile sort of thing so I asked her why she was smiling and she said I mustn't tell anybody so I promised. And then she told me she'd finally lost her virginity. I just couldn't believe it at first because neither of us have ever even kissed anyone. I asked her what it was like, and I thought it must just have been with Stephen who is the seventeen-year-old boy that she met in the park with the lovely hair and nice eyes, the one who made her put her fag out in a sexy way and then gave her a leaflet for Christian Youth Club. But it wasn't him. I don't even want to write it down it's so horrible. It was with Bryan. Bryan is the man who runs the Christian Youth Club. Sarah just said he's really lovely and nice to her. But he's bald with a white ponytail. How old must he be? Forty? Fifty? Even sixty? That's not right is it? She's only fourteen and we're not even allowed to do it until we're sixteen even though loads of girls do do it but when they do it's with boys our own age or maybe a little bit older.

I asked her if she kissed him and she said no which is a shame because she's practised that loads on her arm so I know she'd know what she was doing there. I asked her if she had ejaculated and she said no and that girls can't ejaculate the first time, and Bryan told her this. I have read about this so this isn't a lie. A girl has a bit of skin like a door called a hymen that gets broken when the penis first goes inside you. Or a Tampax (that you use when you have a period but I haven't started yet). Or a finger (I haven't been fingered yet). Or from horse riding (I've never been horse riding, apparently I have been on a donkey but I can't remember it, I think I was only about five and I don't want to ask my Mum if the donkey broke my hymen, I can't talk to her about these things). So it's normal for it to hurt and bleed. I'm not sure if men have a similar thing where they start bleeding from their penis when they first have sex. Did that happen to you? What was your first time like? I hope that I do kissing before I do sex.

I asked her if she really likes Bryan and she just said yes and I asked her if he was her boyfriend and she said no, it's not like that, and then she wanted to change the subject. She has cystitis, I think that's how you spell it. It's when you get a stinging vagina. I told her that I'd read about it in a magazine and you're supposed to put cottage cheese in your knickers for a day and that sorts it all out. Sarah said she thought you were meant to put natural yoghurt in your knickers not cottage cheese. Anyway we weren't sure but she met me after English at the end of the day and we walked to the shops together and she bought a tub of cottage cheese and a pot of strawberry yoghurt. All yoghurt is natural isn't it? It's a bit of a waste though. And I've never even tried cottage cheese but anyway, hopefully that will fix the stinging. I will have to wait until tomorrow to find out, our phone has been cut off. We've been cut off before but this time I don't think Mum's in any hurry to get us connected again.

How could she fancy Bryan? Maybe he's not as old as I think he is. Some men go bald when they're quite young don't they. Phil Collins out of Genesis is quite bald isn't he and he's not that old. And how old is Errol Brown? He doesn't look very old and he has no hair on his head but he does have a moustache. And there's Buster Bloodvessel from Bad Manners. He's fat, but he's not old is he (I quite like their music but I prefer Horsefly). And then some men have way too much hair. They have it really long and greasy or really big and bouncy like Brian May. Brian May isn't that old either is he. Maybe I'm worrying too much. But she did say he was bald with white hair in a ponytail. Maybe he's an albino. That's when you have no pigment in your skin and you are really prone to sunburn and going blind. This girl called Tessa at school had an albino guinea pig that she brought into science once. It wasn't very interesting and it had long hair and round its bum the hair was all matted and full of faeces. I think you have just the right amount of hair, short but with various things going on. I sometimes wonder if I should cut my hair quite short but as I'm still quite flat chested, I might look too much like a boy. Especially when I'm not allowed to wear any eyeliner which is ridiculous.

Do you think Sarah is okay? She said she was okay, she said she likes him. I will try and find out more about it. If he's over fifty should I call the police? Or over sixty? I'm not sure how old he has to be to be a pervert. Everything is confusing isn't it.

Yours truly,
Maud

P.S. I hope you're okay. I keep reading things about your gigs being violent and also people saying that Horsefly are going to split up. I hope nobody punches you or throws bottles at you or spits at you or anything. If I was there and someone did that to you I would kick their stupid head in for you, I really would. I'd be so furious I'd kick in their hymen and burst mine.

Your Friend Forever

***

Tom Harding ONLY
Friends of Horsefly
PO BOX 113
London W2
19th January 1982

Just Maud Harrison
22 Slater Street
Hutton
Preston–le–Shitty

Dear Tom,

    I chatted to Sarah at breaktime a little bit more about her having sex with this man called Bryan. She said it was in the office at the youth club. That's not very nice is it? I don't imagine there is a bed in the office. Then I asked how old he was and I tried to ask really casually like I didn't care. She said she didn't know but she thinks about sixty-something, and that he's really young for his age. It made me feel a bit sick, but then she said she's thinking of not going any more because it's getting a bit boring. I told her we'd had a leaflet through the door at home saying that they want kids aged twelve to sixteen to join the St John Ambulance Brigade and maybe we could go to that instead. Sarah looked really happy about that. Now I really hope that my Mum will let me go. It's 5p a week to go and learn first aid. First aid is learning how to help people very quickly in their time of need, which will be a very useful skill to have. I don't mind blood and Sarah definitely likes it. I think Sarah is hoping there will be some handsome boys / young men there. I'm not too bothered about who will be there, I'm more interested in learning about how to save a life and I suppose getting out of the house. I wonder what a medical education will be like. I hope we learn in depth about how to treat the Four Humours, I have memorised them in case we get asked on our first day. They are: Blood, Yellow Bile, Black Bile and Phlegm. I know about blood, and phlegm is what we have in all the water jugs in the dinner hall. I still need to find out about black and yellow bile. I would like to try out wearing a plague mask but I'm not raising my hopes this high. I suppose there might be a handsome boy there that also has a keen interest in taking St John Ambulance seriously.

I had a weird experience in the library after school today, not the school library but the one in town, the school library is shit. It's just full of the books they make you read in class but hardly anything else. Unless you want to sit and read an Encyclopaedia Britannica, which I have done at my Grandma's but it's not something I want to do all the time because it makes you have weird dreams, all about things beginning with the letters A, B etc. One of my teachers once said the Encyclopaedia Britannica had everything in it about everything, all the world's knowledge in that one set of books. It's one of the first times I knew that grown ups are liars and also that they can be stupid, there's a real mix isn't there. Of clever people and stupid people. I wish I could spend more time with the clever people. I feel like I am capable of being a clever person but that there are lots of stupid people in the way all the time, trying to stop me from learning things.

I have made myself a hot water bottle. It's really nice. It's on my knee, slightly burning me a bit but I still really like it. I wish I could take it to school with me. School is freezing. How is anyone supposed to be able to concentrate when all you can think about is how cold you are? Sarah says she puts a hair dryer on under her covers to warm her bed up before she gets in it. It sounds brilliant. We don't have a hairdryer. Mum used to have one but the electrics went. She was really cross about it.

Anyway, when I was at the library I met this woman in there with a young baby, she said it was six months old. The baby fell asleep while I was talking to her. I was telling her about The Colossus by Sylvia Plath and about how weird it is and that I wondered what it was that Ted Hughes really liked about her. Then she said she was really desperately tired and asked me to push the baby round while she closed her eyes for a minute. She practically begged me to push the pram round the block and she said she'd come and find me when she woke up. She was in tears so I just took the baby off her and pushed it round the block but it woke up and was screaming its head off. It looked really surprised to see me when it woke up. It might have been okay if it had been facing the other way. I pushed the pram round with the screaming baby for absolutely ages and then the woman finally found me, she'd been woken up by the librarian because they were closing for the night. Luckily I still managed to make it home before Mum got back. It's made me realise that I never want children. Do you want children? I suppose if I had a loving husband that really wanted children I could maybe do it but I don't think I would leave the house with the baby. It was awful. A woman in the street told me to pick the baby up but I didn't want to, she gave me a disgusted look. I think she thought I was a teenage mum which is ridiculous (still no hips). I don't think I'm a natural with babies.

Love Maud.

P.S. Do you like me putting a full stop next to my name? I think it looks good. Quite grown up and a bit artistic. I wish I had some braces (to hold my trousers up not for my teeth) and could shave half my hair off or something like that, and wear eyeliner. I will be able to eventually, she won't be able to stop me (my Mum).

***

Documentation enclosed for Sire Harding
Friends of Horsefly
PO BOX 113
London W2
23rd January 1982

Maud Harrison (sender)
22 Slater Street
Hutton
Prestonian

Dear Tom,

I've been thinking loads about my Dad. I haven't seen him for seven months now. That's a really long time isn't it? All his post still keeps coming here though, there's tons of it. Mum keeps writing on them 'Not known at this address' and getting Simon to go and post them again. He is known though, we do know who he is. I don't know where he is, but he is known.

I think I look more like my Dad than my Mum. I've got his skin colour and hair and we have the same hands. Sometimes my Mum looks at me and says 'God, you're exactly like your Dad'. As if it's a bad thing. I think he'd got us into lots of debt so we have minus an amount of money. I'm not sure how much we are minus.

Dad used to work on the Ribble docks but him and all of his workmates got made redundant, that's when you lose your job because the boss can't afford to pay you any more, not because you've done something wrong. I liked it when Dad was working and sometimes we'd all go to one of his work dos as a family and that was quite good. There would be potato pie suppers. It wasn't even potato pie, it was the middle of the pie on a plate and then you'd also get given a piece of pastry. It looks weird but it still tastes the same. His friends were all quite funny and they were always nice to me. We don't see any of them any more. Dad was funny, him and Mum did used to laugh sometimes, it's just been a really really long time. He used to make a lot of jokes at the news while that was on and he used to say stuff about Mrs Thatcher. Some really bad stuff, stuff I wouldn't even like to write down. For example he said he'd like to 'shit down her throat' once. I don't even know how you'd do that. Mum didn't like it when he shouted at the telly. I found it quite exciting.

I hope the TV doesn't get cut off. We've only got a black and white TV so the licence isn't really expensive. If you've got a colour TV it costs loads. Do you have a colour TV? I expect you have, you've earned it. Dad used to always watch snooker on the TV and he said that all the balls were supposed to be different colours, that made him swear a bit too. But then there's a man's voice over the top saying stuff like 'he's going to go for the pink' so you'd know which colour the ball was supposed to be but you wouldn't know which one it was until it got hit. Snooker is quite relaxing isn't it. Do you play it? I think I would quite like it and you don't have to get out of breath playing it and you can stay indoors in the warm. You don't ever see any women playing in the matches though. Maybe that will change soon now we have Mrs Thatcher in charge. I bet she would be a formidable snooker player. Formidable is my new favourite word. I think I'd like to be formidable when I'm older. I keep imagining that I am for a moment and it feels quite good. I think you are formidable.

Sarah has started to get acne. I haven't got any. The other day I felt a bit glad about it, that she had acne and I don't.

That's horrible isn't it. I hope I get acne now just to spite myself for having mean thoughts about my very good friend. How long does acne last? Did you have acne? When did it clear up? My doctor is covered in acne scars. He must have had it really badly. Some of the boys at school look so horrible. You wouldn't want to touch their skin, it's all red and oozy. Again, I am being mean. I'm going to stop it. I will read some more Sylvia Plath and then get to sleep. She wouldn't have been mean about her best friend's acne. She was a good woman, who was married to a very handsome man. You are very handsome too but Ted Hughes is handsome in a very normal way and you're handsome in a more unusual way.

Yours.
Maud

P.S. I realise the full stop after 'Yours' doesn't really work but I thought I'd try it for a change.

P.P.S. Do you like potato pie? It's very filling. I'd like some of it now, my tummy is rumbling.

P.P.P.S. I hope you don't think badly of me even mentioning the acne. I don't think people can help it can they. I'm just so glad not to be someone that has it, although maybe it's because puberty hasn't kicked in properly yet. I might wake up in the morning absolutely oozing. I really hope not, on top of everything else I have to deal with, I don't think I deserve it.

P.P.P.P.S. Now that Prince Charles is married to Diana Spencer, she will be the Queen one day. What do you think of her? She has hair in lots of sort of flaps, and it doesn't move much. Sarah says 'there's still Andrew or Edward' as if there's a chance one of them will want to marry us. I wouldn't want to be in the royal family anyway and I'm surprised Sarah is interested. Dad said ages ago that Edward is a fairy (he meant gay) and no one ever mentions Anne much do they? It's as if she doesn't count at all because she's a woman. Maybe that's a relief for her. Or maybe she's sick with jealousy and wants to kill her brothers. If I was her I would be sick of my brothers getting all the attention. People forget she even exists. She's older than Andrew and Edward but she doesn't get to be in line for the throne in front of them because she has a vagina instead of a penis. They have decided how suited she is to be in charge based entirely on the contents of her knickers. I think she's more suitable than Charles. At least she can grow her hair to cover up her ears inherited from all the inbreeding they do.

***

Dame Harding
Friends of Horsefly
PO BOX 113
London W2
25th January 1982

Lowly Maud Harrison
22 Slater Street
Hutton
The Hamlet of Preston

Dear Tom,

Things are still rubbish at home but Mum gave me four quid on my birthday and said 'make it last'. She didn't say 'happy birthday' so I'm not entirely sure if it's birthday money but I suppose it is, so now I'm fourteen. I'm going to really make it last because I don't know when I might get another four quid. I bought some stamps. That's all I bought. Second class ones I'm afraid but best not to splash out. I haven't even paid for a bus fare or anything recently. I've hidden the money in my room so my brother can't find it. I won't even write it down in this letter in case he reads it and then looks for it. It's a very good place though. Here's a clue. C90.

We had RE today. It's one of the few classes me and Sarah are in together because we're in different groups for English and maths and science. I'd have thought she'd be really into the RE classes now she's a born again Christian but she's not. We were sat at the back and she was just looking bored and running her compass down her arm. It didn't bleed but she was doing it really hard. I reached over and took it out of her hands and put it in my pencil case. She looked annoyed but she couldn't say anything because you get done for talking. We've been learning about Judaism, Hinduism and Sikhism. We just have to learn it as if it's all facts and we're not allowed to question it or have any debates about it, when I questioned it the teacher just shut me down and told me to get on with copying off the board. After the class Lisa, the anal sex girl, pushed me against a wall and called me a stupid bitch and did an impression of me asking the teacher a question. I'm not going to let it bother me though. She's the stupid bitch. There's so much I don't know about the world but I at least know that. I asked Sarah what she thought about doing RE after the class and she just shrugged. Bertrand Russell said something good about religion. I will have to go back to the library though and look it up because I can't remember what it was. I wish I could have my own Bertrand Russell book that I could just keep referring back to constantly, it would be so useful.

In maths we've been doing Pythagoras's theorem (theory), it's awful but at least it adds up. At least it's not lies. I worked it out the long way with a ruler and it's definitely not lies. Why we have to learn it though I don't know. I'm sure I'll never use it in a poem or an obituary. Or maybe I should. A maths poem? No, actually that would be really really dull. It would only be worth doing if I wanted to try and have a romantic affair with a mathematician but I don't know any and I bet if I did know one he wouldn't be my type anyway. I'm still feeling sexless so there's no point in that. I'm quite good at maths though I suppose, the answers are either right or wrong. Pretty much all other subjects are open to debate aren't they. There is room for doubt. Like in history, there are two sides to everything. Al Capone was a baddie but he also seemed quite cool and probably was nice to all his friends. Sometimes I think I'd like to have lived in 1920s America and been a flapper and worked in a speakeasy which was an illegal pub where there were flapper girls doing the Charleston which was a kind of dance. They smoked really long cigarettes at the same time as dancing and they swung beads around a lot. Then I think, if I was in 1920s America I'd still be sat in my bedroom with shit hair and I wouldn't be allowed to go to a speakeasy and then even if I was allowed Sarah would still be a born again Christian so there's no way she would go with me, and I wouldn't have anything to wear anyway. I wonder if Michael is the type that would like going to a speakeasy. He might be, we could pretend to be boyfriend and girlfriend for the night. It must be really hard to meet someone else that's gay if you're gay. I'm going to try to keep getting to know Michael even though he just sort of grunts at me. He might be the only other interesting person in the entire school. Or he might just be really boring and I've got him entirely wrong. We're doing Hiroshima next week.

There's so much I'd like to ask you and so much I'd like to tell you. Mostly thank you so much for your brilliant songs. What would I do without them? I can't even begin to imagine. I'd be a completely different person without them. Without them I'd be much thicker, I'm not sure whether I'd have had sex or not, it's possible I would have by now. I don't blame you though.

Yours,
Maud

P.S. I'm reading Much Ado About Nothing for school work, well I don't have to but it's on our reading list and I like to read everything on it even though I think I might be the only person that bothers to do this. Do you like Shakespeare? I'd like to get to the stage where I can read it for pleasure. I still find it very difficult. I read each line at least three times and then have to sort of translate it in my head before moving onto the next line.

P.P.S. I'm so sleepy. Must try to read a few pages at least. Night night.

***

Baron Harding
Friends of Horsefly
PO BOX 113
London W2
26th January 1982

Baroness Harrison
22 Slater Street
Hutton
Preston

Dear Tom,

Last night I had a dream that was so real that for ages afterwards I sort of thought it had happened. I knew it hadn't, but it sort of felt like it had. I got trapped in a lift with you in the indoor market. Just you and me. You were stood up looking cool. You had on a little denim jacket and a black scarf and your glasses, and your hair was quite neat, how you used to have it a little while ago. I was carrying loads of bags and was wearing an old coat of my Mum's that's way too big for me. I was horrified. I looked like a wreck. The plastic bags were cutting through my fingers and you could see all my shopping bursting out and it was all toys and stuff. I had no eyeliner on (because even in my dreams I'm not allowed to wear it) and my hair was a mess. I hadn't been expecting to see you. Anyway the lift broke down. I was too shy to speak but you asked me if I was okay and I just said 'yes thank you' and then you suggested I put the bags down because it might be a while before they got us out. So I put the bags down and you gave me a warm smile. I wanted to ask you so many things but I didn't. We just stood there for ages and then eventually you sat down leaning against the wall and then I felt really awkward stood up but felt too awkward to sit down. You even asked me if I was okay standing up and I just nodded at you like I was okay, but I wasn't. Eventually someone came and got us out and off you went and I stood there feeling like the biggest idiot in the whole world.

I told Sarah about the dream. She asked me why I didn't flirt with you. I didn't want to flirt with you. I'm only fourteen. I wanted to ask you everything about your life and to learn stuff from you, but I couldn't speak. Even though it wasn't real I feel like the dream was a real missed opportunity. Maybe I didn't ask you any questions in my dream because I would have to be the person answering them (because the dream is coming only from my brain) and I don't have the wisdom to answer them. Maybe the only thing my brain could successfully predict was that you'd sit down and tell me to put the bags down, so I knew you'd be tired and also sensitive to other people's plights. You must know what it's like to have a plastic carrier bag digging into your hand. Cutting off the circulation in your fingers and then eventually snapping leaving you with shopping everywhere or trying to carry it with one handle, or carry your shopping like a baby which is even more unattractive. Even if I'd wanted to flirt with you how would I have done that in a lift with lank hair and a size sixteen peach coat with some bleach spots on it? How? I think, and I could be wrong, but I think peach might be the worst colour in the world. It's really a nothing colour. It's just basically the colour of skin. Not interesting skin, but just peachy bleaurgh kind of skin. The sort of skin you see in Preston when no one has seen the sun for about 700 years.

I've been trying to teach myself about men and women. Mostly by trying to work out what Ted Hughes and Sylvia Plath liked about each other and what might have eventually torn them apart. I find Ted Hughes's poems easier to understand than Sylvia Plath's. In one of his poems that I was reading earlier he says a parrot looks like a 'cheap tart'. I think this is really unfair on the parrot. The parrot can't help what colours it is and they can't help if the colours don't match or look a bit OTT (over the top). Also I don't think parrots would be slags. I just can't imagine it at all and they're not cheap. My Mum had a friend with a parrot once and apparently it had cost about £300. It was a white one, a bit bald. Do you even get slaggy animals or is it just humans that want to have sex with everyone? Not that I do, but I'm still waiting for my hormones to kick in. Ted Hughes also mentioned 'gentle pedigree dove'. So he thinks doves are gentle, because they are white, but parrots are slags. I think he's actually a bird racist, or at least sexist. I'd like to at least discuss this with him and point out to him the error of his ways. Sometimes people can be racist without even knowing they are doing it. A dove is more likely to be a slag than a parrot anyway. Sometimes you see big flocks of pigeons and a couple of them look like escaped doves that wanted to go and have a good time. I have to forgive Ted though for his views on parrots because I do just love him unconditionally, he's so handsome. I'd like to write to him but he doesn't have a PO Box, I wish he did. Of course I would still write to you (you're very different people).

My favourite Sylvia Plath poem so far is this one called Ouija. I think it's about a Ouija board. I expect her and Ted used to sit in the evening doing Ouija boards after they'd had sex with each other. Maybe it was an angry ghost that told Sylvia to put her head in the oven. Have you ever done a Ouija board? Is there anyone special in your life that has died and you'd like to contact them again? I might try and get Sarah to do one with me. It depends how Christian she's being, I think she might have slightly forgotten some of the Christian stuff so it should be okay. I just have to remember not to remind her about it. People don't like being reminded about things they are embarrassed about. I'm embarrassed about what happened with you in the lift in my dream and that didn't even happen.

I have to go now, I have so much more to talk about but I have to write an essay on a book called Cider With Rosie. It's not as exciting as you'd think. In fact it's possibly the dullest book I've ever read. I'd much rather read poetry and try and do a Ouija board and see if I can get a message to you from your Great Grandma who left you the thimbles in her will. I wonder if anyone will ever leave anything for me in their will. I don't think so. I hope I don't get given my Gran's horse brasses. They are probably not worth very much as a lot of people seem to have them in their houses even though no one round here is horsey. I can't understand people actually buying them in the first place. What made my Grandma pop out to the shops, buy a load of horse brasses and then nail them to her wall? Why would you want to sit and look at a horse brass? What pleasure do people get from them? I can understand looking at a beautiful painting. I can't understand looking at a horse brass.

Also, how embarrassing if someone came round who was a horse person and they'd say something like 'nice horse brasses, where do you keep your horses?' and then you'd just have to answer 'I don't have any horses. I've never even met a horse. I just like nailing horse brasses (whatever they are) into my front room wall. I like smoking fags and staring at them. I get an enormous amount of pleasure in sitting on my brown sofa and smoking Benson and Hedges or Regal Kingsize and staring at horse brasses. They fill my soul. My horse brasses are an inspiration.' I think they are the same people that also have pictures of dogs smoking fags and playing snooker. Horse brasses and dogs smoking fags. What a world.

Also what are fishermen's balls for? My Mum has some really dusty ones hanging up in the kitchen. I asked what they were once and she said 'fishermen's balls'. I have since seen them in a few other houses that I have been in and none of the houses have fishermen living in them. My Dad used to do dock work but there were never any fish involved. Why are they still there? No one is getting any pleasure from looking at them. No one uses them. I wouldn't know what to use them for. They can't be very valuable because we'd have pawned them by now.

Yours truly,
Forever and a day,
Maud.
Maud Harrison.
Maud B.H. (before hormones).
Maud A.D. (after death).
Maud Harrison Esquire.
The Reverend Maud.
Doctor Maud Harrison.
Maud Hughes.
Maud Dove Parrot.

P.S. I wish I hadn't written down all these names but there's no point scribbling it all out.

P.P.S. I am very tired all of a sudden. I'm going to fill a hot water bottle and go to bed.

P.P.P.S. I've got William Blake's Songs of Innocence and Experience out from the library. I think I'm going to love it.

***

Sir Tom Harding
Friends of Horsefly
PO BOX 113
London W2
27th January 1982

Lady Maud Harrison
22 Slater Street Manor
Hutton
Preston

Dear Tom,

Can you die from just eating Rice Krispies and school dinners? I hope not. It's not going to help me grow boobs though is it. Or pubic hairs. Or get hormones to turn me into a woman. I do have a few hairs in my armpits though, so it's a start. I found a rusty Bic razor in the bathroom and managed to get rid of them I think. I don't want anyone seeing them at PE. It's weird isn't it, hoping to get some hairs so that you can shave them off. Or hoping to get your period so you can bleed every month and moan about it like everyone else.

My Mum has some giant sanitary towels in the bathroom

cupboard so I know I'll be all right if that ever happens (my period) but not sure it will happen if I keep only eating Rice Krispies. Although on the box it says they have niacin in them which is a chemical that I think is supposed to be good for you so maybe that will help me to start releasing eggs every month. Maybe my body has decided there's no point releasing eggs until I have better hair and visible breasts. I don't look like someone who should be able to have children yet. I certainly don't want any so I'm not sure why I'm even bothered about having a period. Boys just have wet dreams instead, where they have a rude dream and then ejaculate in their sleep for the first time and then they know they are capable of fathering a child.

How old were you when you first had a wet dream? It sounds a bit better than getting blood all over everything every month. Especially when you don't have a washing machine. Did you have a washing machine when you grew up? So wet dreams weren't an issue for you? Do you still have them as an adult or is it just when you're a teenager? I might try and ask Michael. I bet he doesn't want to father any children though so I'm not sure if he's the right person to ask. Maybe if I make myself daydream about having babies my period will come. I'm not sure I can be bothered to do that though, or what if I start enjoying the daydreams and end up going out and becoming a teenage mum.

Did you know that when a girl is born she already has all her eggs inside her? That means my future baby (if I have one) was inside my mother for nine months. I hope that doesn't mean my baby will be like my mother. It also means I was inside my Grandma. So I've been on this earth since about 1937 (she had my Mum when she was quite old, forty-three). So that means I've been around since the Second World War. That means I've been through rationing before, and the Nazis. No wonder I sometimes feel as though I'm a lot older than everyone else

Your Friend Forever

that's the same age as me. I wonder if I think really really hard I can try and remember any of it. I don't think I've ever met a German person so I don't know if I'd have a bad reaction to them or not.

I'm going to try and remember now so I must finish this letter while I still have this idea in my head. I was here during the Second World War. We both were. I wonder if we knew each other.

It's different with men though isn't it? They are not entirely filled with semen when they are born.

Love Maud (an old woman trapped in the body of a girl with no pubic hair).

P.S. At least I can't get pubic lice. Have you ever had pubic lice? What are they like? I imagine they are a bit like nits. Or scabies. I've had both of those.

P.P.S. Sarah and I are going to St John Ambulance tomorrow. I hope it's interesting.

***

> The Right Reverend Mr Tom Harding
> Friends of Horsefly
> PO BOX 113
> London W2
> 28th January 1982

The Bishop Harrison (Maud)
22 Slater Street
Hutton
Preston

Dear Tom,

Sarah and I went to our first ever St John Ambulance meeting last night. It was not at all what I had expected. Everyone apart from me and Sarah were in uniform. They have given us a uniform each to wear next week. I'm not sure what I think about it. It's a plain grey dress that goes over the knee and zips up the front and you have to wear a nurse's cap with a St John cross on the front. I think I'll feel like a bit of a fake wearing it. Also the dress is really old. I think it's been worn by a lot of young nurses. I'm not even sure I want to be a nurse. Sarah seemed quite pleased with it. She thinks it's sexy, but she fills hers out a bit more than I do (with her breasts). Mine's a bit big. Also what if I wear it and then someone asks me to help them with some first aid? I wouldn't know what to do even though I would be dressed as a nurse. I'd be okay if it was just doing a triangular bandage, that's what we practised (there was absolutely no mention of phlegm or yellow bile). We got into pairs and put triangular bandages on each other. Then the boys stayed downstairs and we went upstairs with this woman who showed us how to make a bed properly. That bit was sort of boring but quite funny. They have loads of sheets and blankets and this big black rubber sheet that you have to put on first over the mattress so that urine doesn't all go everywhere as a lot of patients urinate in their beds. And it takes two people to make a bed because you have to do these special things called 'hospital corners' where you fold the sheets in really neatly. It all feels very Victorian at St John Ambulance which is nice. There were quite a few middle-aged men in uniform that Sarah was making eye contact with and then some boys who looked as if they could have been about nine or ten. No one was handsome. I don't know if handsome boys go to St John Ambulance. Anyway we both quite liked it in a weird way so we're going to go back next week and see how it goes. I'm a bit embarrassed about wearing the uniform. Maybe I can just put the hat on when I get there but you have to sort of pin it on your head so I might be better doing it before I leave. It's about a two-mile walk from my house, I was quite surprised Mum let me go. Maybe I'll be able to shove a bobble hat on over the top of it and then just take it off really carefully when I get there. Sarah says she might tie-dye her nurse's dress. I really hope she doesn't. I think she'll get in trouble for it and then I'd get in trouble too. Have you ever needed a triangular bandage for anything? Usually for a broken arm or a suspected fracture (that means broken). You have to basically tie the arm around the person's neck so they're not waving it around everywhere and making the fracture worse. It makes sense. I wonder if I'll be good at nursing. I think I'm quite kind, but also I worry a lot about myself and I had mean thoughts about Sarah's spots (which are slightly worse) so maybe I'm not the right sort of person because I think about myself too much. I do like those upside down watches though. You don't actually get them with St John Ambulance even though the woman who taught us how to make a bed was wearing one on her dress, but I think she might be a real nurse in real life. Maybe being a nurse would be a good job. I could look after people and then write poems about them at night time whilst watching them sleep. Nurse Maud sounds quite good. I like Carry on Matron. I can't imagine ever being a Matron though (I'm not fat) but I can't imagine being a sexy nurse either like Barbara Windsor. I can't ever imagine being sexy. How old were you before you felt sexy? Do you feel sexy once you have cool clothes and a good haircut? I've never even been to the hairdressers for a proper haircut. My Mum used to do it and now she doesn't bother any more. So it's just long and dark brown and does nothing. I wish it was blonde or black or bright red or all three. Or blue.

Sarah said she'd bleach my hair for me but I'm not sure I'd trust her and my Mum would go crazy at me. And what if all my hair fell out? Being bald would be loads worse. I do have some things to be thankful for. Sarah also said I could try ironing my hair. I might try that, but my hair is pretty straight anyway and I'm not sure how I'd do it. I don't know how close I'd dare put the iron to my head. I wouldn't want to burn myself or fry my hair. I might try it though, if Sarah will help me. Have you ever ironed your hair? You have lovely curls when you let it grow a bit, but I know people with curly hair normally want it to be straight.

I wish my Dad would come home soon, I didn't realise it before but I do now. I miss having someone around that loves me, I think he does or he did. But then if he did why hasn't he come back? Why haven't I seen him? How could he just abandon us? I suppose Sarah loves me, but she loves penises more. I think she's developed a taste for sex. Maybe once you've tried it you can never go back to not having it again. She hasn't done it with anyone else yet as far as I know but she's trying. She says 'good morning' and makes eye contact with practically everyone with a penis between the ages of thirteen and sixty. Sex must be amazing. Even in an office with an old man with a white ponytail. Though she hasn't mentioned Bryan for ages. I hope that's over. Do you love sex? I hope you don't meet Sarah. She would probably try and have sex with you. Have you ever had sex with a man? Some people like men and women. It wouldn't surprise me if that was Sarah's next thing. Her parents let her do anything. I wonder if she'd try it on me. I wonder if I'd let her. I suppose having an experience is better than having no experience at all, though I don't want to be put off. I best go now, I need to scrub my shirt collar in the sink, it's PE tomorrow.

Yours,
Nurse Maud. (Esquire.)

P.S. Forget the Esquire bit, I still don't know what that means.

P.P.S. I really like William Blake, I was going to start a scrapbook on him but then I realised there would be nothing to cut out. I can't cut his book up because it's a book and it's from the library. It's a shame Smash Hits don't branch out a bit and cover some poets. A nice double-page poster of Ted Hughes would be a good start.

***

Tom Harding
Friends of Horsefly
PO BOX 113
London W2
30th January 1982

Maud
22 Slater Street
Hutton
Preston

Dear Tom,

Simon's been in my room and drawn all over my posters with marker pens.

This is what he has done.

He's drawn big ears on you, like Big Ears from Noddy (the poster that was on the inside of Smash Hits last year where you're wearing tight jeans and your hair is slicked back apart from a bit dangling at the front and you're wearing red and white checkered pointy shoes and a silver belt buckle that has Chinese words on it, I wish I knew what it said).

Also he's drawn a small penis coming out of your jeans and

he's done a speech bubble coming out of your mouth that says 'I drink my own piss'.

I have a small poster of Sting which I'm not too bothered about but he's drawn a penis coming out of the top of his head and going into his mouth with stuff coming out of it. I'm not sure if it's supposed to be piss or semen.

I have a double-page poster of The Clash that was from ages ago, I remember my Dad buying me that Smash Hits. Simon has drawn hats on them all. They are either dunce's caps or Ku Klux Klan hats. I am not sure which.

I have a one-page-size poster of Elvis Costello (I really like him) and he's drawn a penis coming out of his ear going over the top of his head like headphones and then going into the other ear. Again either piss or semen going into his ear.

A picture of Siouxsie Sioux who always looks brilliant. He coloured her eyes in black and drew snot coming out of her nose and a speech bubble coming out of her mouth that says 'I can't sing'.

A double-page Stiff Little Fingers poster that Sarah gave me. He drew a penis coming out of Jake Burns's stomach and going round him like a snake and then going over his head and then showering down on him either piss or semen.

A one-page picture of Johnny Rotten. Simon drew Nazi swastikas over his eyes.

A double-page poster of The Clash. Mick Jones's penis going into Joe Strummer's mouth and Joe Strummer's penis going into Mick Jones's bum.

A one-page poster of Madness. A penis coming out of Suggs (the lead singer, I don't know what his real name is) and splitting into five parts and going into the mouths of the rest of the band. Again, I am not sure whether it is supposed to be piss or semen.

A one-page poster of The Specials, he has coloured in the

faces of Terry Hall, Roddy Radiation, Horace Panter, Jerry Dammers and John Bradbury to make them black. Lynval Golding and Neville Staple are already black. Also they all have little penises coming out of their heads.

A one-page poster of Kate Bush. He did speech bubbles coming out of her mouth. One that says 'Waaaah' and another one that says 'I'm president Reagan'. What do you think of him? He seems nice.

I'm just sat in here with the door closed. I don't know what to do. Do I take them all down and throw them away? My room will look really rubbish without them. But they are all ruined. I'll never be able to replace them. He must really hate me. I wouldn't dream of going in his disgusting bedroom. Maybe I should. Maybe I should give Darth Vader a big penis and make him put it in Luke Skywalker. But he will just hit me if I do that and I don't really want to get hit. I just want my posters back to how they were.

I'm too sad to talk about anything else. I hope your day is better than my day.

Love Maud x

P.S. What posters do you have up at your house?

February 1982

FAO Tom Harding Please Friends of Horsefly
PO BOX 113
London W2
1st February 1982

Maud Harrison
22 Slater Street
Hutton
Preston

Dear Tom,

Something really bad has happened. Really really bad.

    I got home from school and when I came in the house Mum was lying on the sofa and I thought she was asleep but then I realised she wasn't asleep because she wouldn't wake up and there was an empty bottle of vodka on the kitchen top (strong alcohol) and she just wouldn't move so I ran next door and asked them to call an ambulance because our phone is cut off. They came really quickly and they took her and they asked if I wanted to go with her in the ambulance and I said I would wait for my Dad and brother to get home so they just left with her. I'm not sure why I lied. I just panicked. I've got my bedroom door open. I'm just waiting for Simon to get home. Should I have gone in the ambulance? If I had done that then Simon would be home on his own and wouldn't know what was going on. I could have left a note. I didn't think of that. Why didn't I think of leaving a note? I'm not sure what to do now, hopefully Simon will know when he comes back from school. I'm still really angry with him though. We don't have any money to get a bus to the hospital, unless Simon has some secret money and I don't really want to use mine up yet. We'll have to walk and it's at least four miles away and then they'll wonder where our Dad is. I suppose I can just say I'm a bit older and that Dad is still at work or something. What if she dies? Why has she got really drunk during the day? The ambulance woman took something out of our bin too. I'm not sure what it was. Maybe she's got food poisoning from eating something bad. Maybe it's like when you get bitten by a snake and you have to know which snake has bitten you to get the right anti venom quickly before you die. I hope she doesn't die. I know I'm not very nice about her because she's really cross all the time and angry and just shouts at me but I don't want her to die. I think she's been having a horrible time too because of Dad and that's why she takes it out on us. I think things will get better at some point. Things do don't they? I hope she doesn't die. What will happen if she dies? What will happen to me and Simon? Would we just carry on living here? How would we get any money? I wish Dad was here. I wish I could phone him up but I don't even have his address. I can't think of anyone that might know his address. I wish there was a grown up here.

Simon's back.

Hi, we are setting off to the hospital together. I'm going to risk it and take you with me in my school bag. I don't know why I'm taking my school bag. I suppose I could read or something if we have to sit in a waiting room. The only trouble is we're still doing Hamlet and it's – sorry have to go now.

I'm in the toilet at the hospital. Simon shouted at me to hurry up so we had to set off. I will tell you about Hamlet another time (I think I love him). She's not dead. They haven't told us anything else yet. I best go.

I'm back in the toilet again, I don't even need to go. They have said they'll let us go in and see her soon. They don't seem bothered by us not having a grown up with us. I suppose Simon is quite tall these days. He isn't talking to me but we are sat next to each other in the waiting room. There is a magazine called The Lady. I thought I'd have a read of it but it's just adverts from ladies that want nannies. Maybe I could be a nanny and live in a lady's house. I bet I'd get a nice bedroom and a bed with bed posts, oh but I'd have to look after their children. I better go someone else needs the toilet.

Hello again from the toilet. We are setting off to walk home in a minute. We saw Mum but she was just sort of sleepy. She had a drip attached to her. I will tell you what that is later.

I am home now. It is 1.23am. I am so tired. I will write more tomorrow. Night night xxx

Hello, it's morning, I'm very very tired. Going to school now, Simon is speaking to me at least. We've both had some toast. He said he'll see me after school to go to the hospital again. Hopefully he'll be back a bit quicker tonight and we won't have to wait for ages when we get there. I've got a phone number for seeing how she is but our phone's still cut off. I have to go now. I'm taking you to school with me.

Hello, I'm just at a desk in the school library, trying not to fall asleep. It's dinnertime and classes start back in fifteen minutes. Sarah's off school anyway today. It would have been good to talk to her but at least I can write to you. Here's what

I know. A drip goes into your veins and puts extra liquid into you, so Mum must have been completely dried out.

Hamlet is just incredible and I think I could be falling in love with him. I am actually a bit jealous of Ophelia (his sort of girlfriend who falls in a river) which is bonkers because it happened almost 400 years ago and I don't even know if it's a true story and even if it was true Hamlet would definitely be dead by now and he was in a royal family (the Prince of Denmark) so I'd never get to meet him even if he was still alive, which obviously I know he can't be. It's not like Gilbert Blythe where there is a chance he might just still be alive but as an old man. He is very poetic and definitely a little bit mad. I can tell that he's handsome and has dark wavy hair and sparkly brown eyes and is very slim, a little bit like you I suppose. I can just tell. Have you ever thought of being an actor and playing the part of Hamlet? If you would like to do it you should do it soon before you're too old. Hamlet's Dad dies and his Mum just marries his brother really quickly. He's called Claudius, he's not a good person and not to be trusted, Hamlet definitely doesn't like him. I wonder if his Mum had always fancied the other brother. Or if they'd been at it for ages anyway. I wonder if my Dad has a girlfriend. I wonder if my Mum will ever get a boyfriend. Maybe a doctor will fall in love with her while she's in hospital. Doctors get paid well so maybe he could go to the Co-op and get some proper food in. Maybe he'll really like me and Simon and start helping us with our homework and he'll take us into work with him and he'll teach me how to use a stethoscope and he'll push me to follow in his footsteps and go to medical school. I'd really like that. I like knowing stuff about human bodies. We've been learning all the real names of the bones. My favourites are Cranium (your head), Mandible (your jaw), Atlas and Axis (where your head is attached to your backbone) and I like the word Scapula (your shoulder blade) and I already know Labia, Outer Labia and Hymen (these aren't bones). Lots of people laughed at the word Phalanges (the ends of your fingers and toes), why is that a funny word? Mr Williamson had to say 'come on now everybody settle down'. I have no idea why they thought it was so funny. Mr Williamson is so handsome. Although she is in a different science class Sarah still keeps saying 'good morning' to him every day and giving him her slightly too long stares that apparently mean 'sex, now'.

Time to go back into class. I'm not looking forward to that long walk again tonight. Hopefully Mum will be out soon.

Hello, it's me again.

Sorry this is such a long letter. I hope it doesn't bother you. We went all the way to see Mum, a nice nurse led us onto her ward and we sat on chairs next to her bed. There was a bag of light brown liquid attached to the bed and Simon pointed at it and started sniggering. It was Mum's urine in a bag. There was a tube coming out of the bag and under the covers. The other end must have gone up her urine hole. I don't know how that can be done but of course there must be a hole for urine that you don't really think about. I've been wondering about it and it definitely wasn't coming from her vagina, I might try and look properly for my urine hole later. Mum was sort of sat up in bed with her eyes shut. She looked quite old, she isn't though. She's only about forty-five or something. I'm not used to seeing her without any makeup on and her skin looked really dry and she was wearing a paper nightie. I should have thought to bring some of her stuff from home but I didn't and I felt really stupid. We didn't take her anything. There were visitors at other beds and they were all giving cards and presents and loads of magazines and fruit and things. I didn't even think to take her some knickers. We sat there for a few minutes and then I poked her to wake her up and Simon told me off for it, but she did wake up. She just looked really sad, she sort of looked at us and then rolled her eyes and looked at the ceiling and did lots of sighs. When she looked back down again her eyes were watering. So the drip must be working. That's good anyway. I asked her if she was okay and she said yes and that she'd be home as soon as she could. She said if she's not out by Friday she'll discharge herself. I didn't really know what to ask her after that and Simon didn't say anything. Then a woman came round asking all the patients if they wanted a cup of tea and she said she did want one. I wanted one too but didn't ask because I think it's only for patients. Then Mum told us to just get off home before it got too late and told us to put the chain on the door which I have done. Simon's just gone in his room. I'm going to go down in a minute and fill a hot water bottle so my bed is warm for when I've finished my homework. More Hamlet and biology so it's fine, I like it, though I wish it was warm. I can actually see my breath in the house. I feel like everything would be a lot easier if it was warm. I'm wearing my Mum's old coat to do my homework in, and to write this. I won't sleep in it though. I don't know if we will go to the hospital tomorrow. Mum said not to. I'm not sure if she was being brave or just doesn't want us visiting. Simon seems pretty keen on not going again. I don't really want to go all the way over there on my own. I'll see what the weather is like tomorrow and how guilty I feel about it. I should visit her shouldn't I? But I don't know what to say to her and I don't want to ask her about what happened because I think she'll be embarrassed so it will just be silence again. I suppose I could take her some clothes. That would be a good thing to do wouldn't it? And it can't be nice wearing a paper nightie. No one else on the ward was wearing a paper nightie. I don't want to get in trouble though for going in her bedroom. I'll just have a look and see if I can see a nightie and see where her knickers are but if I have to rummage around too much I won't do it.

I've just had a look in her bedroom, the bulb has gone though so couldn't see very well. It's a real mess, I don't think I should look for anything. I'd sort of like to go in and tidy everything up for her and do the washing but I've no money for the launderette and she'll just have a go at me, I'll leave it.

I've put a towel along the bottom of my window, it gets really wet with condensation. At least I keep my room clean and tidy. I'm going to take the posters down and cut out as best I can the bits Simon drew on and then stick them back up again. There are a few bits I can save. It will end up being a sort of collage.

I've finished my homework now. I hope I wasn't too over the top about Hamlet, Miss Bailey is very encouraging but I'm not allowed to quote myself any more and I have to not make my essays too long or 'run away with myself'. I've put my uniform on the chair ready for tomorrow and I've wrung out the towel in the bathroom and put it back under my window and my hot water bottle is in my bed and my homework is all in my school bag ready to hand in tomorrow. Everything is okay. I think Simon went to bed ages ago. I'll just check again that the chain is on the front door.

The chain is on and I've drawn the curtains downstairs and made sure everything is turned off. I'll get in bed now. Night night. Wish you were here. Not in a sex way. Just wish you were here.

Love Maud

P.S. When she comes home, do you think she'll be an invalid? Will I have to nurse her? Her bedroom doesn't look fit for convalescing in (convalescing is when you recover from illness, I think it's often done by the seaside, we are not too far from

Blackpool but Blackpool is not the right sort of place to convalesce in, I'm sure of it). Also I don't even know what's wrong with her and I've only been to one St John Ambulance meeting. I suppose I could give her bed hospital corners. I'd have to get Sarah to come and help me because it's a two person job. We have sheets and blankets here but no rubber one. I wonder if St John's would let me borrow the rubber sheet for my Mum. Maybe she can get to the toilet anyway. I hope so. I hope she doesn't still have that bag of brown urine attached to her. Though if she found out I'd borrowed a rubber sheet for her use I think she'd hit the roof. I wonder if Simon is worrying about any of this. I bet he's not.

P.P.S. Sorry for the long P.S., I didn't know it was going to be so long or I'd have put it in the main letter, which is now really really long. Sorry, I'll try not to make it any longer. Goodnight.

P.P.P.S. Hello, it's me again. It's the middle of the night. I've started my period. It's all over my bed. I went in the bathroom and there were no sanitary towels in the cupboard. Mum must have used them all. I have used some toilet roll but there isn't much of that and I don't want to use it all in case one of us needs to evacuate our bowel in the morning. I will try to evacuate mine at school. And I will remember to steal a toilet roll and put it in my school bag. I've put a towel over the wet patch on my bed for now. I'll have to wash everything in the bath tomorrow. It's very messy. To be honest the timing isn't very convenient.

P.P.P.P.S. I'm a woman now. A W.O.M.A.N. Woman. I will try and behave like one from now on.

P.P.P.P.P.S. But it's hard when you're cold and your thighs

are all covered in dry blood and there's no hot water. I'll just get up early and sort it out. I hope the toilet paper doesn't fall out of my knickers. I really hope I don't bleed all over my school uniform. If it's really bad I might call in sick. Oh but the phone's been cut off. It's hard being a woman. I wonder if I can ask one of my teachers for a tampon. Sarah says putting one in is a bit like having sex, so it really would be a day of firsts.

***

For the attention of Captain Tom Harding
Friends of Horsefly
PO BOX 113
London W2
4th February 1982

Maud Harrison
22 Slater Street
Hutton
Preston

Dear Tom,

You will not believe how awful today has been. It was a Duke of Edinburgh day and I had completely forgotten that I ever said I was interested in doing Duke of Edinburgh. I got to school and Mr Young was stood at the front with the school minibus and he shouted his head off at me and told me to get in, so I did. All the other kids were in hiking stuff, eight boys, three girls, I don't know any of them. I was in my school uniform, not even any tights, and my period is still going strong. I can't believe I've got any blood left.

We had to climb up Scafell Pike. It is the highest mountain in England. I had to climb it in my school uniform. It was freezing and it rained all day. My period kept running down my leg and I had to keep wiping it up with dock leaves. Luckily everyone was so muddy and wet no one noticed I was doing period on myself. We had to climb through a cloud, actually go into a cloud and through it and out the other side. I have never been so cold in my life. I didn't have a packed lunch with me, everyone else did. It was freezing and exhausting. I saw an aeroplane pass underneath us. That's how high up we climbed. It was awful. I can't tell you how awful it was. I never want to do anything like it again in my life. I just won't. If anyone ever suggests anything like it to me again I will murder them. And Simon has eaten the last of the bread so I have had some Rice Krispies for my tea again. At least the milkman has carried on delivering milk to us, I don't think he's been paid for ages as Mum makes us be quiet and keep away from the window when he knocks on the door. I've had three cups of tea as well to warm me up and I'm in bed with the hot water bottle under my feet, burning them a bit but they are still cold on the top. Mr Young had no sympathy for me whatsoever. He just blamed me for forgetting and not having any of the right stuff with me. I can't believe I actually got to the top, I was on my hands and knees by the end of it. I couldn't feel my feet they were so cold and wet. And I'm covered in scratches from gorse and brambles and nettles and so much dried period. I am half dead.

When we got to the top the others were cheering and jumping about and whacking each other on the back. I just wanted to cry, cry and come straight back down. Getting down was quite a bit quicker than going up. I had to go on my bum for some of it though and my uniform just looks wrecked. When I've warmed up I'm going to wash it in the bath and hopefully it'll be dry by the morning. I'll peg it out because it won't dry in the house. Please please don't let it rain tonight. I've heard the Lake District is really beautiful but we could barely see anything. I don't know how Mr Young knew where we were even going.

I best wash these clothes and put them out before I fall asleep. I'm so tired. My whole body hurts.

It's Friday tomorrow, hopefully Mum will be back.

Love M. Your exhausted friend.

P.S. What do you think of me calling myself just 'M'? My Mum used to call my Dad 'T' so it is a thing that people do, I quite like it. I might stick with it for a while and see how it goes. I wondered about calling Sarah 'S' as a way of getting her to call me 'M' but 'S' isn't very good to say on its own. It's like you're hissing at the person.

P.P.S. For our homework we have to start thinking about our curriculum vitae (Latin for C.V.) and what we would like to have on them. So far under skills I've got 'triangular bandaging' and 'nothing surprises me'. I'm not sure what else I can put down.

Your Friend Forever

***

JOCKEY RECORDS LTD

Minutes of meeting

Location:	Jockey Records, 23–28 Smith Street, London W2
Date:	8th Feb 1982 2pm
Attendees:	CEO – Clive Butler Secretary – Evelyn Lyons Tom Harding Warren Hamble Ed Nailer Martin O'Connell David Simpson – Accounts

Agenda

1. Financials from most recent tour – Pigs on Tour
2. Band dismantling
3. Contract with Jockey Records
4. Tom Harding solo project
5. Outstanding claims from last tour
6. James Sims – medical update
7. Book tie / gagging order
8. Merchandise storage and ongoing sales

1. Financials from Pigs tour

David Simpson provided a breakdown of the most recent tour incomings and outgoings. He explained that while there would have been profit there are many outstanding expenses due that must come out of the joint band account. The expenses include (these are just the main items):

- Payment to venues for short notice cancellation.
- Payment to sound / lighting engineers for cancelled shows. It was discussed that they are self–employed. However they were booked for the duration of the tour and we (Jockey Records) want to be able to use them in the future. While we had them in our diary they were unable to seek work elsewhere.

A few of the venues have put in claims for damages. Including but not limited to:

- Graffiti in dressing room
- Mirrors smashed in
- Rider smashed and left on the floor
- Toilet broken
- Faeces smeared on the toilet wall
- Fridges removed from dressing room
- Bin removed from dressing room
- Assault committed on venue staff (James Sims) (needs paying off)
- Sink pulled off wall
- Sound desk needs replacing after liquids spilt all over it
- Fire damage in dressing room

Tom and Martin made the point that they were not responsible for these items. However Jockey records maintains that the payments must come out of the main band account (INC PRS and Mechanical) and then if they want to make payments between themselves that is up to them.

2. Band dismantling

It was agreed that Martin, Ed and Warren will walk away taking no further payments. Paperwork to be sent to them next week.

Tom will release solo records at the rate of at least one per two years at minimum cost until the account is out of arrears. After that we can consider a new contract for Tom should he wish to have one. All recording costs must be run through accounts and kept to a bare minimum.

Ed Nailer punched a hole in the door before leaving the conference room. David Simpson in accounts says he will add this onto the arrears. Martin, Warren and Tom then left the meeting early. Tom will be sent any paperwork he needs to see.

Evelyn will draft a press release to go out next week.

Meeting closed.

***

Zena Barrie

Private and Confidential FAO Tom Harding
Friends of Horsefly
PO BOX 113
London W2
10th February 1982

Maud Harrison
22 Slater Street
Hutton
Preston

Dear Tom,

You won't believe this. Mr Young found me at school and gave me a letter saying I had to pay £12 for the trip to Scafell Pike. I didn't know it was £12. How am I going to get £12? My Mum will kill me if I tell her. That's if she's still alive. She might get home at any moment (it's Friday) but she isn't home yet, but she did say she would discharge herself if they didn't let her out today. But then would she have to walk home in a paper nightie? I should have gone to see her yesterday to find out what was happening. I was too tired after crawling up the tallest mountain in England. I don't remember them ever telling us it was £12 because I would never have gone on it. Mr Young said the letters had been sent home with us ages ago. How can I get £12? I don't have anything I could pawn. Simon ripped all my tapes up and I'm not sure you can pawn those anyway. I don't have anything. I suppose this is when a collection of horse brasses would come in handy. They are probably worth at least £12.

I thought the Duke of bloody Edinburgh was paying for it. I might write to him and complain actually and ask for him to pay the bloody £12 if he thinks it's so important for me to go up a mountain.

I'm glad I've got my uniform off. It didn't really dry on the line overnight, it just sort of froze. I thawed my skirt out this morning by using the steam from the kettle but it didn't dry it, it just made it not frozen. So I've been damp all day. The skirt is almost dry now anyway. It's on the chair in my room. I'm not going to put it out to dry ever again. I might not ever wash it again. I will just wipe it with a cloth if it gets mucky. You don't sweat in a skirt really do you. How often do you wash your trousers? I suppose so long as you're not rolling through mud you really don't need to wash them that often. I expect you have your own washing machine anyway. Or maybe you have a tumble dryer. That would be lovely.

I can hear someone trying to get in the front door. It might be Mum. I think I've left the chain on.

Hi, it's me again. It was her. She shouted at me. She said 'why've you got the bloody chain on?' She told me to put it on and it's extra protection isn't it from people breaking in and I've been a bit worried. There are a lot of burglaries round here. She had her own clothes on anyway. I forgot she was wearing clothes when they took her away in the ambulance.

I've tidied up downstairs loads and hoovered and the kitchen is clean but she hasn't mentioned any of it. I made her a cup of tea and put it next to her, she didn't say anything but she did look at it. I knocked on Simon's door and said 'Mum's back' but he just said 'go away'. So now I'm back in my room.

My uniform is tidy for tomorrow and I've done all my homework apart from some reading which I will do in bed soon. I have to read a short story by D. H. Lawrence and then we are going to talk about it in class. I'd rather read Lady Chatterley's Lover (also by him). I've been too shy to get it out of the library and was worried my Mum would see me reading it. Do you think she would know it's a sex book? Is it common knowledge? It's about a posh woman who has sex with her gardener. I'd like to read it, maybe I will pluck up the courage and if the librarian raises her eyebrows at me I can just say that we're doing it at school. The cover doesn't have naked people on it or anything, but the title does say 'lover' rather than 'love' and you can't really disguise the word lover as anything else can you? Unless I altered the cover to something like 'Lady Chatterley's a lover of animals'. That would work, but I can't deface a library book. Maybe I could read it while I was at the library but that would be a bit embarrassing too. I suppose I could hide it inside another book. I will do that. I'll let you know if it's any good. You might have already read it, you're probably not embarrassed about reading pornography in public.

I'm going to go downstairs and check on Mum before I get in bed to read.

I checked on her, she was asleep on the sofa. I touched her to check she was alive and she is. She opened her eyes. I asked her if she was okay and she said 'yeah I'm just going to sleep down here'. I asked her if she wanted her covers and she said yes so I got the quilt off her bed and took it down to her. It felt quite damp but that happens when you don't go in a room for a few days doesn't it? This means I am allowed in her bedroom. I might start cleaning some of it up tomorrow, maybe if I do a bit at a time she won't notice I've done any of it.

Very sleepy now so goodnight. Hopefully I can stay awake long enough to read the story.

Thanks for being there.

M. xxx

***

Your Friend Forever

Your Royal Highness Prince Philip (The Queen's Husband)
Buckingham Palace
London
10th February 1982

Maud Harrison
22 Slater Street
Hutton
Preston

Hello Your Royal Highness (Prince Philip),

I haven't said 'dear' because at the moment you don't feel dear to me at all, even though you are in our Royal Family. I'm sorry I didn't put a stamp on the letter but you can afford it, it's not going to make a huge difference to you is it? I feel like you have wronged me and it's not fair at all because I am really quite poor and you live in a massive palace and have servants and can afford to eat what you want and put the heating on when you want and your only job is cutting ribbon and smashing up champagne bottles which is all a massive waste but you don't seem to care about that. I've never even tasted champagne. I bet you had when you were fourteen.

I accidentally went up Scafell Pike with school on the Duke of Edinburgh's Award Scheme (run by you). Now the school want me to pay £12 for it. I don't have £12 and I had a horrible time. A truly horrible time. It was freezing and I didn't have a kagoul or any Kendal mint cake, I did have my period running down my leg though. Something you have never had to deal with I'm quite sure. I have no money and my Dad has disappeared and my Mum is very ill (she's just come out of hospital for drinking too much vodka, she had to have a bag for her urine (piss) and a drip) and we don't have £12.

I am very angry that you have seen fit to put me in this situation.

You are supposed to be a Prince and I am one of your loyal subjects! (Not that I believe in the monarchy, if I had my way you would all be sent out to work in factories like everyone else and I would move the homeless of the United Kingdom into your palace, I think they would all fit, they could probably all have their own room and their own horse). I don't know how you can live with yourself really, living in a palace and doing nothing all day apart from waving a bit off a balcony, you don't even wave properly, has no one ever taught you? Is there a reason you do it in slow motion? And as if you're not actually waving, or as if you're waving at someone you hate and you don't actually want them to see that you're waving in case they wave back at you and come running over for a chat about their scabies. Have you ever had scabies? We had an outbreak of it at school last year, everyone was scratching, even the teachers. It's when bugs go to live in your skin. They eat it and they shit in it too, leaving their faecal excrement wherever they go. Imagine having that and nits at the same time, and your period and nothing to plug it up with but school bog roll. That's what it's like for me living in Preston. I have this to deal with and now I have a Prince basically begging me for £12 that I don't have. I've never had £12 not even at Christmas.

How do you sleep at night? Does it bother you that you're so lazy? How does your wife (Her Majesty The Queen) sleep at night? Is it true that your wife doesn't go to the toilet? I don't see how that can be possible but it's great that people respect her so much that they can't imagine her going to the toilet. I can imagine you going to the toilet. You seem like a normal man to me who has just got very very lucky.

You can send me the £12 as cash (although the postman might nick it so if you're doing this wrap it up in some bog roll or something so Her Majesty The Queen's head (your wife) can't be seen through the envelope). Or you can send a postal order made out to me, Maud Harrison. I can then take it to the post office and swap it for cash which I can then take into school and give to Mr Young who is giving me a very hard time about all this and I really feel very strongly that I don't deserve this on top of everything else (Mother, Brother, Nits, Scabies, and another Period coming my way soon no doubt).

Yours in anticipation of a favourable reply
Your subject
Miss Maud Harrison Esquire

P.S. I hope this will make you think about your actions in future.

P.P.S. I know you resent not being the King, that doesn't mean you should take it out on teenage girls.

P.P.P.S. Maybe if you got a proper job then Her Majesty The Queen (your wife) would respect you more and decide to make you a King. Is it a bit embarrassing still being a Prince at your age? I'll be happy being a Miss until I'm about twenty-five and then after that I'll worry that people are judging me for not being married, so I do understand your predicament. Not that I necessarily want to get married, I feel fairly sexless at the moment so I'm not sure it will ever happen for me.

P.P.P.P.S. Is it hard trying to be Majestic all the time? I'm not sure you always succeed.

P.P.P.P.P.S. It is really embarrassing isn't it? That you're a Prince at your age. Do you think she'll ever make you King? I suppose if she was going to she'd have done it by now. Did she make any promises about this matter when you agreed to become man and wife?

P.P.P.P.P.P.S. Do you get a pension? Do you go to the post office with a book to pick it up every week? It's not very much is it. I know this because my Grandma only eats oxtail soup and two ounces of tongue. Though her budgies always seem to eat quite well.

P.P.P.P.P.P.P.S. Do you feel stupid in that driving uniform she makes you wear?

P.P.P.P.P.P.P.P.S. How tall are you? You're very thin aren't you?

***

To Duke Harding
Friends of Horsefly
PO BOX 113
London W2
12th February 1982

Duchess Harrison
22 Slater Street
Hutton
Preston

Dear Tom,

    I've written a letter to Prince Philip asking him to send me the £12 I need to pay Mr Young for the Duke of Edinburgh Award Scheme. Do you think that's a fair thing to do? I've been thinking about it a lot and I think it's fair. I imagined it was the other way around. For example.

I set up the Maud Harrison Award Scheme for Teenagers where people like me can share their feelings and write poems.

Prince Philip signs up for it thinking it's free because nowhere do I mention the fact that I want £12 for people to go to it (I wouldn't charge £12).

Prince Philip arrives on the day, he writes some poems but he doesn't really fit in with the rest of the group, in fact he hates it.

Then before he leaves I demand £12 from him.

He says, 'But I thought it was free.'

I tell him, it was not free, nothing in life is free Philip. Pay up or I will make your life a living hell until the end of the fifth year.

Hmm, on reading this back I still feel like I am the injured party and that Prince Philip should pay up. I think this means I'm wrong about asking him for the £12, or that I just hate him. I think I might just hate him. Fuck the royals! Seriously, how dare they? How dare they prance around in crowns and ball gowns when people are living off Rice Krispies because they were on special? Do they think it's funny? How bloody dare they? He should bloody pay to go on my teenagers' course. If he's so stupid to sign up for it he can bloody well pay for it.

I hope he sends the £12. Do you think he will?

I wonder if he'll send a letter apologising for his behaviour.

Have I committed treason? I read about treason, I think you can still go to the Tower of London for it. And you get guarded by Beefeaters who eat nothing except beef I suppose and are really good at guarding things. I think I'd get bored of just eating beef, I'm getting bored with just eating Rice Krispies.

Love

Maud

Zena Barrie

***

Viscount Tom Harding
Letter to Friends of Horsefly
PO BOX 113
London W2
14th February 1982

Maud Harrison
22 Slater Street
Hutton
Preston

Dear Tom,

I'm really upset and I can't pretend not to be.

Dad came to the front door. I could see him through the window but he didn't see me. He was shouting at Mum so much, I've never heard him that angry before, he called her a 'fucking bitch'. He obviously didn't realise it's Valentine's day.

Mum was crying and practically screaming at him. The neighbours came out telling Dad to 'sleep it off' and to 'go away'. Eventually he went. Mum is sat behind the front door crying. I asked her what was wrong but she just told me to go to my room. So I did, and I'm really hungry but she's still down there behind the front door crying, she's not moved. My school bag is in the front room and I need to do my homework but I don't want to go down there. If I don't do it I'm going to get in loads of trouble tomorrow. I don't know what to do. I wish you were here. You could go and get my school bag for me and maybe my Mum would stop crying because she'd be too embarrassed to do it in front of you. Once when she was being okay she said you had a nice voice. It really annoyed me at the time. I'm playing Corn Fed Me taped off the radio.

I have it on loud enough so I can hear your voice but quietly enough that she won't hear it and shout at me even more. It's like living in a library. A library where the librarian is possibly drunk and always crying and really angry at you if you want to take a book or a record out.

I read that you like Simon and Garfunkel. I've heard of them but I don't know their songs. I've put my name on a list to get any album of theirs out of the library. If I like it I'll try and copy it onto a blank tape. I don't have tape to tape but Sarah could bring her ghetto blaster round and I could play it on hers and record it onto mine. We'll just have to sit really quietly.

There is one bit of good news. I got some Freepost envelopes. Sarah got them for me, so I don't have to use my bus money on stamps or my birthday money that could be needed for an emergency. All I have to do is scribble out the address that's already on them and write your address underneath and get this, Skipton Building Society will be paying for it! I don't feel bad about it because all property is theft. I can hear Mum shouting at my brother now. I'm just going to get in bed and pretend to be asleep.

Goodnight Tom, sleep well.

Love Maud x

Hello again, it's the middle of the night. Just saying hello. I got up to do my homework. I'm so tired I can't stand it. I'm going to get a really rubbish mark for this but I can't keep my eyes open. Mum must have gone to bed because she's not behind the front door any more. She has chained it though and she's dragged the comfy chair behind it. I hope I can get out of the house tomorrow.

P.S. Night night Tom.

P.P.S. I don't know if Freepost is first class or second class or some other speed of service. Not sure how I can find out. I hope it doesn't take too long to get to you.

***

> To the most Right Honourable Viscount Lord Harding
> Letter to Friends of Horsefly
> PO BOX 113
> London W2
> 16th February 1982

Maud Harrison
22 Slater Street
Hutton
Preston

Dear Tom,

Something awful has happened, it's so awful I feel as if I can't move, I can't write properly, I can't breathe very well. Sarah's Dad has to go to prison. He's done something bad with money. I don't know what. He hasn't hurt anyone or anything like that but he's done something bad with money that wasn't his. That's all Sarah knows. Sarah and her Mum have to move in with Sarah's Grandma because they can't afford the mortgage so they have to rent their house out. Her Grandma lives in Gloucestershire so Sarah has to move school. I can't bear it. What am I going to do? It's all happening really quickly. Sarah isn't even coming into school again because her Mum is keeping her at home to help pack their things up. They have to pack their stuff up really quickly and then they're driving to Gloucestershire with it and that's it, I don't know if I will ever see her again, I don't know her Grandma's address or telephone number. She's really upset, she really likes her Dad and she doesn't know how long he has to go to prison for and her Grandma's house is really tiny and she doesn't even know where she's going to sleep. She says it smells and is full of ornaments and horse brasses even though her Grandma has never even been on a horse as far as she knows. It's like someone wearing a Horsefly T-shirt when they haven't even listened to one of your albums. I wouldn't want to wear a band T-shirt unless I knew every lyric of every song in case anyone tested me.

What am I going to do? I don't know how to get to Gloucestershire to visit and it will probably cost too much anyway and it will cost too much to phone her because it won't be a local call so my Mum probably won't let me call and even if she would let me the phone's still cut off. Sarah's Mum definitely won't let her call me because Sarah says they have no money any more. I was going to ask my Mum if she knows anything about Gloucestershire or how to get there but she just looks really angry whenever I speak to her and it just sets her off crying or shouting at me and I can't be bothered with either. I am going to get a map out of the library and see if I can do some photocopies. Maybe there are some buses I can get. Maybe I could get there using one or two Clippercards.

I can't bear this. School is going to be so rubbish now. I'm just going to be on my own the whole time, I'll have nobody.

Just two more years of awful school and then maybe I can go and live in Gloucestershire with Sarah and we'll get our band going. I can do whatever I want can't I when I'm sixteen? Did you just leave home when you were sixteen and start the band? I wish someone had written a book about you and your life so that I would know exactly what to do. Who else is there I could read about? I really need to go to the library and get out a road atlas of England, and some biographies of people that I like. I can't think who but I suppose when I look on the shelf I might get some inspiration. I really hope there is a map that fits Preston and Gloucestershire on one page of A4 so I only have to pay for one photocopy. Then all I have to do is colour in the roads and then look for buses that go down those roads.

Right, I am going to the library now. At least Mum has started letting me just go there without making a fuss. I need to take my other books back.

Bertrand Russell on God and Religion (one of the books you said you'd liked in Melody Maker), I liked it too, it's made me think but probably not as much as I would like because my head is too full up at the moment. Riders by Jilly Cooper (Sarah told me to read it), I didn't like it. Sarah said there's lots of sex in it and there is a lot of sex in it, mostly a man called Rupert but it's not very nice. It's put me off doing it. I suppose I might do it with Bertrand Russell. I really hated Rupert. If he was a real person I'd want to track him down and then, well I'm not sure. Maybe get a horse to eat him.

Thanks Tom, bye bye for now.
Maud

P.S. Do you know where Gloucestershire is?

P.P.S. Is there an actual place called double Gloucestershire? If there isn't a place called double Gloucestershire why is the cheese called double Gloucestershire? I've just got no one to ask. Except you.

P.P.P.S. Sorry I haven't asked about you. You must think I'm really selfish. I do hope that you are okay.

***

Your Friend Forever

Professor Thomas Harding
Letter to Friends of Horsefly
PO BOX 113
London W2
17th February 1982

Professor Maud Harrison
22 Slater Street
Hutton
Preston

Dear Tom,

I went to the library and got the atlas of Great Britain. I've worked out the scales and everything and it's 150 miles to Gloucestershire. Though it's a big place and I'm not sure if she's going to live at the top or the bottom. I have to wait until I get my first correspondence from Sarah and then I can mark her off on the map. I hope it's the top as that's nearer to Preston. It seems to be quite a straight line between here and there. Maybe I could hitch there in a lorry. I just need to find the right place to stand and stick my thumb out. I hope I look old enough to hitch or maybe no one will take me if I look too young. God it's rubbish being young and having no money and not being able to do anything. How long would it take to go to Gloucestershire in a truck do you think? I hope she writes to me soon. I'm worried I will never hear from her again but then I have to remind myself to have faith in our friendship being strong enough to bear this ungodly pain and suffering.

I would like to hitch to London too to visit you, it's 220 miles to W2 from here. I'm not sure where to go in W2 but I'm sure I'd find you eventually. I could just find the corner shop and they'll know. Or if you didn't want a visit from me I wouldn't mind. It would just be nice to see London and see where you go and everything. Also I would like to see where the plague happened and the Great Fire of London and I'd like to go to St Paul's Cathedral and see where the woman fed the birds in Mary Poppins. You're so lucky living near St Paul's Cathedral. If I lived there I would go every day and look at where the old lady fed the birds. Maybe I would also feed the birds. Have you ever fed the birds at St Paul's Cathedral? I really like history. Also there is a whispering gallery in St Paul's where you whisper and your whispers come back at you and possibly all the ghosts of the past whisper back to you at the same time. That would be amazing. I saw a photo in a book recently about a cathedral like St Paul's but it's in Italy and there is a painting in it of a devil putting a red-hot poker up someone's bottom. I was very shocked by it. I knew that hell is supposed to be on fire and all the bad people of the world live there together but I didn't know that the devil was supposed to be there actually putting burning rods up people's bums. Anyway I think hell might not be that bad. Years ago they sent all the bad people from England over to Australia to live in a sort of hell together but instead of it being fires and red-hot pokers they all just got a nice tan and wore shorts and hats with corks on them and had bbqs at Christmas. It seems like a really nice place. Maybe in hell right at this very moment Hitler is having a bbq with, who started World War One? Hmm I can't think of anyone else as bad as Hitler, well I can but they are still alive. Well maybe when Thatcher dies she will have a bbq with Hitler and Rupert from Riders and hopefully they'll just relax and have a nice time and try not to start a new political party because it wouldn't be good.

I'd also like to go to the Tower of London and see where the two princes were locked up. Maybe I could steal the crown jewels while I was there so I could buy a coach ticket to Gloucestershire.

I really hope Sarah contacts me soon because not having her address or her phone number is making me feel very anxious. I won't be able to sleep properly until I have them. I need to be able to write to her. I've now got two full Clippercards for emergencies that Mum doesn't know about. I'm not sure though if every town uses the same Clippercard system which means I might get to the outskirts of Preston and find that my Clippercards won't get me any further. So I suppose I'll have to be prepared to hitch. Have you ever hitched? I always imagine people in bands must hitch all the time with their instruments. I just imagined that I was sticking my thumb out and a big truck pulled up and it was you that was driving it. That would be brilliant. I don't even know if you can drive. Can you drive? I will be old enough to do lessons in three years but I don't think I'll have any money to pay for the lessons. Maybe I should steal the crown jewels after all and then I can get my coach ticket and some driving lessons. I could probably get some new shoes too. These ones are flapping at the heel when I walk. I don't want to mention it to Mum though, it'll only upset her. I'm trying to just keep my head down, I can't wait to get out of here.

I was falling asleep in class today. I half hoped Mr Young would ask me if there was anything wrong but he didn't, he just told me to sit up and listen and was sarcastic about if he was boring me or not. Very rude considering how boring he actually always is. He never attempts to make the maths relatable so with that in mind he shouldn't be surprised to see people nodding off. Teachers never seem worried that it's them that's the problem rather than us the willing pupils. I didn't say anything of course. I just sat up a bit straighter and tried to keep my eyes open.

I've got to go, my brother's shouting about something, it'll be to have a go at me as usual and then I have to do my homework. There's loads of it, absolutely loads.

I can't believe I have to carry on every day as if nothing's changed, what am I going to do without Sarah? I'm just going to be on my own every day without anyone to talk to. I try to get Michael to talk to me and tell me about all the penises he's been thinking about, but he hasn't done so far, and Sarah used to let me eat some of her dinner sometimes, because she just wanted toilet roll, that sounds greedy doesn't it?

Yours forever
Maud

P.S. I hope yours forever isn't a bit much, I just like it, and I am your friend forever. I hope you know that.

P.P.S. Thank you, I don't know what I'd do without you.

P.P.P.S. Really I don't.

P.P.P.P.S. I don't believe in heaven or hell. But if they did exist, Thatcher, Hitler and Rupert from Riders would absolutely spend all their time together horse riding. Hitler would probably have to have a Shetland pony because he was very short wasn't he?

***

TOM HARDING AND JOCKEY RECORDS

Telephone conversation, 19th February 1982

Evelyn: Jockey Records, Evelyn speaking, how may I help you?

Tom: Evie, it's Tom.

Evelyn: Tom, how are you babe? When are you coming in to see me?

Tom: Probably not for a while sweetheart, after last time. Listen, do you know what will be happening with the post?

Evelyn: Did you not get your statement this quarter? I'm sure I sent it out, let me have a look. There wasn't a cheque.

Tom: No I get that, there won't be a cheque for a long time. I mean the PO Box stuff.

Evelyn: All the loony stuff?

Tom: Yeah, whatever, the loony stuff.

Evelyn: Hold the line, babe, let me check with Rita, she deals with all the post stuff for everyone. Rita babe, did you close the Horsefly PO Box?

Rita: Yes babe, I gave notice on it last week, hardly got used anyway. Why you asking?

Evelyn: Tom's wondering what's happening with the post.

Rita: Can you tell Tom that we've got fourteen crates of

Horsefly T-shirts in the store room. If he doesn't pick them up Clive says they're going in a skip and he'll have to pay for the skip.

Evelyn: Okay babe, see you later.

Evelyn: Tom babe, are you still there?

Tom: Yep.

Evelyn: The PO Box address has been shut down, my love, now that Horsefly are no more.

Tom: So if anyone writes to me?

Evelyn: It'll just get returned to the sender my love.

Tom: Returned to sender?

Evelyn: Yes babe.

Tom: That's the last fucking thing she needs. Why did nobody ask me? Can you get it reopened?

Evelyn: Last thing who needs, babe? I can't reopen it m'lovely, Horsefly aren't on our roster any more, so I can send out your statements but that's it really, until you've got your own record on the go. Oh and Clive says you need to pick up all your unsold merch or he's binning it.

Tom: Great service as fucking ever. Evie, do you know how I get the PO Box reopened?

Evelyn: I don't know Tom, you'd have to call the Post Office.

Your Friend Forever

***

TOM HARDING AND THE POST OFFICE

Telephone conversation, 19th February 1982

Maria: Royal Mail, Maria here, how can I help you?

Tom: Hello, I need to reopen a PO Box address. It's number 113.

Maria: That number's taken I'm afraid. You can open PO Box 2599.

Tom: No, I already have 113, I just need to reopen it.

Maria: Let me check that for you.

Tom: Thanks.

Maria: Hello, thanks for holding. 113 has been closed down. I can't reissue that number.

Tom: It was my PO Box number, can I not just pay you to keep using it?

Maria: No, but I can open you a new PO Box account.

Tom: I don't want a new one, I just want to keep using the old one.

Maria: What's your address please?

Tom: Thanks, it's 19 Hawthorn Lane, E9 7PT.

Maria: I'm sorry, PO Box number 113 is not registered to that address.

Tom: No I know, it was registered to my record company's address.

Maria: That's right, so it's not your PO Box account, I'm afraid. Do you want me to set up 2599?

Tom: Forget it, just forget it.

***

               19 HAWTHORN LANE, LONDON E9 7TP
                               26TH FEBRUARY 1982

MAUD,

HERE'S SOME MONEY TO HELP YOU OUT A BIT

IF YOU NEED ME YOU CAN CALL ME ON 01 985 8745.

THINGS WILL GET BETTER, YOU ARE GREAT, HANG ON IN THERE.

Tx

***

Your Friend Forever

> For the attention of Mr Tom Harding
> Letter to Friends of Horsefly
> PO BOX 113
> London W2
> 28th February 1982

Maud Harrison
22 Slater Street
Hutton
Preston

Dear Tom,

I got a letter from my Dad today, he sent me his number and it was from a London address. He said to call him if I need him. I don't need him. I ripped it up. He said 'you are great'. How would he even know if I'm great or not? I haven't spoken to him for months and months. Even when he lived here he didn't really talk to me. How would he know anything about me? It's not as though he's been asking Mum how I am and she wouldn't know either. I sometimes think if I ran away she wouldn't even notice that I was gone.

I can't believe he's gone to live in London without telling me. He even signed the letter 'T' instead of Dad, like he's not even my Dad any more. He put sixty quid in the letter too. I didn't rip that up. I've hidden it for now but I might have to give it to Mum because I know she hasn't got any money. At least, I don't think he's sent her any cash. Though if I give it to Mum she'll be cross that Dad wrote to me and then she'll probably shout at me again so I can't win. Maybe it's best if I keep hold of it for emergencies. She might buy vodka with it if I give it to her. I might spend some of the money on stamps. Oh I hope Sarah writes to me soon and I hope she remembers to put her address on the letter so I can reply.

I came on my period again at school today. I plucked up the courage to ask my teacher Miss Bailey if I could borrow a tampon (for some reason I didn't want to say sanitary towel), well you don't borrow do you because you could never give it back. I don't know why I said borrow. Anyway, I didn't know how to use it and it dropped in the toilet. I was going to fish it out and try again but then I realised I had already urinated and I thought it would be bad to put urine into my womb. Also I could see that the tampon was already expanding. The tampon was probably thinking I had a very roomy vagina. If I ever get a baby in there I want it to be welcoming, I don't want the baby to smell her Mum's old piss. That's not the sort of mother I want to be. I made a kind of pad of folded toilet paper and then I had to go back to class and soon I could feel it all leaking out. I took my jumper off even though it was really cold and tied it around my waist. At breaktime I went to the toilets again and got some wet toilet paper to clean the blood off my legs and thighs. It had all soaked through my skirt. I am going to wait until my Mum is in bed and then get up and try and wash it. I'm not sure I will be able to go to school tomorrow. I can't go with a wet skirt covered in blood. In fact I will just go in the bathroom now and try and sort it out, the sooner I do it the longer it will have to dry. I suppose I will have to use some of the money to buy sanitary towels, though it feels wasteful to spend money on something I'm just going to bleed on and then throw away, it would be better to spend some money on a loaf of bread. I will have to think about it carefully.

Thank God I have you to write to. I really need to hear from Sarah, I'm worried about her. She'll be in touch soon won't she? Maybe she's already made a new best friend at whatever school she's going to now. New kids are either really popular straight away or shunned (ignored). I hope she's not shunned but I don't want to be replaced. Though I would prefer Sarah to be happy, I don't want her to have nobody.

   Yours,
   Maud

P.S. Do you have a best friend? I hope you do. I bet they are wonderful, Sarah is wonderful.

***

Zena Barrie

For the Attention of Tom Harding
Letter to Friends of Horsefly
PO BOX 113
London W2

RETURN TO SENDER

This PO Box is no longer available

***

Your Friend Forever

For the Urgent Attention of Tom Harding
Letter to Friends of Horsefly
PO BOX 113
London W2

RETURN TO SENDER

This PO Box is no longer available

***

Zena Barrie

> For the Attention of Tom Harding
> Letter to Friends of Horsefly
> PO BOX 113
> London W2

RETURN TO SENDER

This PO Box is no longer available

***

Your Friend Forever

Tom Harding
From Horsefly
London
United Kingdom
Great Britain
The World

RETURN TO SENDER

Not sufficiently addressed

Part Two

January 2011

MAUD AND SARAH

Facebook Messenger conversation, 2 January 2011 21:36

Maud: Are you there? Happy New Year! Did you go out in the end?

Sarah: Happy New Year! We didn't. Couldn't get a sitter and couldn't be bothered. Where would we even go? Plus I'd have to talk to Ian all night and we don't do that. We watch things, separately.

Maud: Fair enough, we stayed in too. Well, I stayed up with the kids and Colin ate all the crisps and then went to bed.

Sarah: Sounds amazing.

Maud: It was nice. We watched Thelma and Louise and Amy cried. I was so proud. Leo took the piss out of her though but I think it was just to distract us from his eyes that were a bit shiny.

Sarah: Ahh so that girl has a soul after all?

Maud: Yeah she's got soul, she's just, I don't know, controlled or something, not like me.

Sarah: She's an ice maiden.

Maud: She's not, she's a little dream, you should have seen her face when they drove off the cliff at the end, it was very sweet.

Sarah: I hate the ending to that film.

Maud: Yeah I know, it always feels very unfinished.

Sarah: Well they killed themselves, that's pretty final.

Maud: Not necessarily, I'd like to see them do Thelma and Louise 2 where they've recovered from their catastrophic injuries and they're living it up in Mexico.

Sarah: What would they be doing in Mexico?

Maud: I don't know – eating refried beans and stuff.

Sarah: Right. Can't wait to watch that, let me know when it's coming out won't you? Anyway, I've got you something and you will never fucking guess what. You're going to go fucking mental.

Maud: What is it? I thought we weren't doing Christmas presents any more? I haven't got you anything, not even a nice candle. I could give you one, would you like one? I've got loads people have given me. I never use them because I'm scared they'll burn the house down.

Sarah: Love, I don't want a fucking candle.

Maud: Ok, good.

Sarah: Right, hang on a sec, I'm just going to get some wine and I need my handbag, I don't know where the fuck I've put it. Hold on, don't switch off.

Maud: Ok, I'll get some wine too, hang on.

Sarah: I couldn't find any wine so I've got half a pint of Kahlua.

Maud: I'm back. I'm on red.

Sarah: Right, you know Ian's mate Will? The carpet fitter?

Maud: I think I've met him, lanky with blonde hair? Haunted face? Tiny wife?

Sarah: Yeah that's him, except he's not really lanky any more, he's sort of morbidly obese now. Anyway, he's moved down south.

Maud: Does he still look haunted? Has his wife grown? Ooh I suppose I could buy you 20 fags, would you like that?

Sarah: Yeah, yeah, fags, that'll make up for all the ones you nick from me when you're drunk. Anyway, Will, he still looks haunted and he's morbidly obese.

Maud: Menthol?

Sarah: Yes, but shut up.

Maud: And his wife?

Sarah: I have no idea but she's not going to have got any taller is she?

Maud: Ok, and what about him? Is this going to be another one of your stories that's basically a porno?

Sarah: No no no, just stop typing. READ.

Right, so, fat haunted Will has started fitting carpets down south, Carpet fucking World or Carpet Land or something about fucking carpets.

Maud: Ok, and what? You've got me an offcut of carpet?

Sarah: No, you dick.

Maud: What then?

Sarah: You will NEVER GUESS whose house he's just put in a new stair carpet.

Maud: You want me to do guessing?

Sarah: Yeah guess, come on.

Maud: I don't know. Tony Blair?

Sarah: Fuck no.

Maud: David Cameron.

Sarah: Why would that be exciting? Anyway, I think he lives in the Cotswolds doesn't he? Near Kate Moss and Rebekah Brooks, they all go hunting together or some fucking bollocks.

Maud: I don't know then – Nick Clegg?

Sarah: Seriously, Tony Blair, David Cameron and Nick Clegg

are the only three names of people you can think of in the entire fucking world?

Maud: I don't know! Lembit Opik? You know, that Lib Dem MP with the battered nose who went out with a Cheeky girl.

Sarah: The one who looks like Stephen Fry's parasitic twin?

Maud: Well, a parasitic twin wouldn't be so fully formed, they're normally inside the body of the other twin. Not outside it working as an MP. But if they were Siamese twins and they were being separated, Stephen Fry would be twin A and Lembit Opik would be twin B – the surgeons would put all the resources into saving twin A.

Sarah: So they'd leave Lembit Opik to die? Are the NHS allowed to do that?

Maud: Only if they had to, if they got them open and found they shared a heart or shared an important blood vessel or only had one functioning kidney or something like that they would give it to twin A and then twin B would die.

Sarah: You're saying he's the runt?

Maud: Sort of. Except Lembit Opik and Stephen Fry aren't actually from you know, the same litter.

Sarah: And he's an MP?

Maud: Yeah, how can you not know that?

Sarah: Ok got it, he's an MP, I saw him on some programme or other and it wasn't Question Time. I suppose I might have seen him on the news, or Bargain Hunt. Anyway, you're supposed to be guessing.

Maud: Is it Sting?

Sarah: Warmer – but someone YOU FUCKING LOVE.

Maud: It can't be. Not Tom, not Tom Harding?

Sarah: Yes, Tom. Fucking. Harding.

Maud: Ahhhhhh.

Sarah: I know.

Maud: Did he get me his autograph?

Sarah: Better than that.

Maud: He's not in your house is he? Please tell me you haven't shagged him. I'll never speak to you again if you've done that. Well I would, but it's going to take me some time. Oh God please, if you have I don't think I want to know.

Sarah: I've told you before, not really my fucking type. Look here it is: wiggleitalittlebit@fpl.co.uk

Maud: And that is?

Sarah: It's his fucking email address.

Maud: The obese carpet fitter? Why would I need that?

Sarah: Tom Harding's email address. It's Tom Harding's fucking email address.

Maud: Oh my God, thankyou thankyou thankyou. Are you sure?

Sarah: Totally fucking sure, his personal email address.

Maud: Let me find a pen and I'll write it down.

Sarah: It's in your messages. You can copy and paste it.

Maud: I know but it might get deleted.

Sarah: I'll text it to you, now when can we go out for a drink and work out what the fuck you're going to say to him?

Maud: Oh God yes we need to meet up soon, Colin's away all the bloody time. There's no one to babysit ever, can you come over here do you think?

Sarah: I'm in the same boat, though at least Colin is working, Ian just fucks off out whenever he wants without telling me. Anyway are yours not old enough to leave on their own yet?

Maud: No love, not unless I want them taken off me.

Sarah: Fair enough.

Maud: At least Ian doesn't spend all his money on plastic figures. You should see our bloody credit card bill. Petrol petrol Forbidden Planet petrol Forbidden Planet petrol.

Sarah: Stop it, you're turning me on.

Maud: Really?

Sarah: No. Remind me. Why did you marry him?

Maud: There was something I liked about him. His hair and shoes or something.

Sarah: Ahh yes, I remember the hair. It was good hair. Nice and thick.

Maud: It was, shame it didn't stick around (on his head) for a bit longer.

Sarah: Bollocks, one of mine is shouting at me, is it too much to ask that they go to bed and just bloody go to sleep?

Maud: Try lacing their dinner with a sleeping tablet?

Sarah: Don't tempt me. Best go and see what it is.

Bye. Love you bye xxxx

Maud: Don't forget to text me that email address.

Sarah: It is literally there in front of you.

Maud: Please. And are you completely 100 per cent sure?

Sarah: It deffo is.

Maud: And Tom replied to him, about his carpet?

Sarah: He must have done because Will has definitely fitted his carpet.

Maud: How did it go?

Sarah: How did what go?

Maud: The carpet fitting, how did it go?

Sarah: I don't know, I just know that he did it. I mean they usually go ok don't they? It's a carpet fitting not a date.

Maud: Ah well never mind. Do you know anything about the pattern?

Sarah: What pattern?

Maud: The carpet pattern! What carpet did he go for? What was his house like? Does he live with anyone? Did he take any photos? Was it plain or stripy or what? I'd have thought he'd have a parquet floor by now.

Sarah: What the fuck do you mean?

Maud: Everyone eventually gets a parquet floor, if they can afford it.

Sarah: Maybe he can't afford it.

Maud: He should be able to, after all these years, he should be able to afford a nice parquet floor. At least he's got his own stairs. I suppose people don't have parquet stairs.

Sarah: Shall I text Will and get some details?

Maud No! That's really embarrassing.

Sarah: Ok, I won't, I don't know why people want to pretend to live in their old school hall though. It's not like it was that good.

Maud: Do you think that's why people get parquet floors? Maybe you could ask really casually next time you see him?

Sarah: Right, I'll do that. Are you going to send him a picture of your tits?

Maud: No! Why would I do that?

Sarah: There must be loads of women sending him pictures of their fanny every day.

Maud: Do you think so?

Sarah: NO, how fucking old is he anyway? Oh shit she's still shouting me I have to go up.

Maud: Not really that much older than us actually. He got successful very young because he's extremely talented.

Sarah: Aww bless you, you're so defensive about him, it's really cute. Gotta go xxx

Maud: I'm not cute!

Sarah: 🙂

Maud: And stop using those faces

Sarah: It's an emoji!

Maud: You're a child.

Sarah: Get with the programme! Love you xxxx

Maud: Love you too xxxxx

Maud: Sarah? Are you still there? I've just remembered Lembit Opik lost his seat last year.

Maud: Bye then xxx

***

Sender: maudcampbell@bluemoon.com
Recipient: wiggleitalittlebit@fpl.co.uk

13 January 2011 20:45

Dear Tom,
    I hope you don't mind this unsolicited email.
    My friend has a friend, who is a friend of yours, sort of, well I'm not sure if you made friends with him, that might be pushing it a bit. He's definitely an acquaintance of yours anyway, I'm sure you'd have been very polite with him and possibly made him a cup of tea. He fitted your carpet a few weeks ago. On your stairs I believe? I hope there's not too much fluff coming up off it? That's how I got your email address. I'm sorry I know I shouldn't have it. I don't want to invade your privacy and I don't expect a reply.
    I just wanted to say, THANKYOU.
    I've loved your music for years and years, I was about eleven I think when I first heard you on the radio in the kitchen and it was just love, straight away.
    It took me ages to find out what band I had heard or what the song was (it was Shandy Hand) but I never stopped thinking about it, once I had heard it, it was the best thing I had ever heard, I can't imagine what my life would be like if I hadn't heard it. It didn't really change my life exactly but it changed my outlook, it sort of rewired my brain. I started

looking at things differently. It improved my mind. Or at least it made me want to improve my mind.

I probably only heard half of it that first time, ninety seconds. I can picture exactly where I was in the kitchen because I was looking at the chip pan. It was full of dirty oil and bits of black chip. My Mum used the same oil for – well you won't believe me but I don't think she EVER changed the oil in the chip pan. It was the same with the one she used for Christmas dinner. The same oven dish that she pulled out with the same congealed lard in it every year. If I went round now I could probably still dig it out. Is that normal? I don't think it's normal. I don't do it anyway. People don't really use lard any more do they? Sorry I don't know why I'm talking about lard. Goose fat is fashionable again though so maybe lard will come back into its own. Someone told me once that lip balm is just coloured lard. Not sure if that's true or not. I've never tried to cook a potato in Chapstick. I would need quite a few. It wouldn't be economical.

I suppose lots of people have told you over the years that they love your music and, well, I'm sure they do, but for me it's more than that. Your songs are my family, the family I chose. You kept me going through everything. I've always had this thing to hold onto that no one could touch, I didn't feel alone. It's been so important to me. More than I can ever describe. I just don't know how I would have coped without it, it opened up so many doors in my brain, it gave me so much secret superhero strength, not strength you could see but strength inside my brain, just where I needed it.

So, thankyou thankyou thankyou. If there's anything I can ever do for you in return just ask. I don't know what that would be, but just ask anyway.

Anything at all. (Though I'm squeamish about white-head spots and I'm a bit scared of large dogs so if you wanted me to squeeze your spots and look after your pet Alsatian for example I'm not sure I'd be the best candidate. Though I would force myself to try and do it to help out.)

Yours

Maud Campbell (formerly Maud Harrison, I sent you one or two letters when I was young, not sure if you ever got them?)

P.S. I hope your life is going well at the moment, I know you've been through a lot over the years. I hope that you're happy, and treating yourself nicely and eating well, that would make me happy, if you were. Sarah (my best friend of thirty odd years) says I'm the only person that puts P.S.s in an email. She says I'm Victorian. The Victorians were excellent at building sewage systems, there are worst things to be compared to.

***

Sender: maudcampbell@bluemoon.com
Recipient: wiggleitalittlebit@fpl.co.uk

16 January 2011 22:13

Dear Tom,

I hope you don't mind me writing to you again. My kids Amy (middle name Sylvia) and Leo (middle name Ted) are asleep and Colin (my husband, no middle name) is upstairs in the box room playing with his figures. Actually playing with figures, a fully grown (bald) man (apart from his lower back). Well, not playing with them exactly but rearranging them on little shelves. I just ignore it, I know everyone has to have some sort of outlet outside of their work, but plastic figures? I don't get it, I've tried to get it, but I can't. When I first met him he was really into old black and white films and I found that quite romantic, that was so much easier to support. He said I looked like a film noir character because I was so pale and slight. He used to say I looked like I could disappear.

If I question the figures, and to be honest I've given up, he says Leo really likes them, but Leo isn't interested, not even slightly. Lots of them are still in their packaging anyway and he won't let anyone open them. What's the point? Leo is somehow much too cool for plastic figures, I don't know how I've managed to have a cool son. He's always been so self-assured. He just gets on with everything.

Recently, I've been reading Aesop's Fables and loads of Brothers Grimm and Hans Christian Andersen but I can't seem to concentrate on them tonight. (I've been reading the New Testament stories too because they're all just moral tales – I'm not at all religious but I do think it's nice to have some moral standards.) I know they're for kids but I'm rereading them because I had this idea about writing a book of modern moral tales for adults.

It's hard to think of ideas though. Sarah suggested I write a story about a woman who votes Tory and then gets run over straight away.

I think it needs to be more complex than that though.

I've been trying to pick apart the fables to see if there's a magic formula to writing them but when I start reading them I get completely drawn in and then forget I was supposed to be focusing on their structure. Last night I read The Constant Tin Soldier. If you haven't read it, it's basically about a one-legged man (ex military) who stalks a dancer who quite clearly isn't interested and she ends up burning to death. I'm not entirely sure what the moral message of that one is, maybe avoid going out with ex soldiers who are possibly unstable due to PTSD? I should probably read it again.

Do you research your songs before you write them? Some of your songs could be seen as moral stories (especially the one about foie gras). Not all of them though, some of them are quite abstract aren't they. I have no idea what some of them really mean. Sarah always said it's because some songs just don't mean anything, no thought has gone into them. Like Club Tropicana, it's just about a free bar, or Russ Abbot's song Atmosphere, it's just about a party with a nice atmosphere. It's enough, isn't it?

Not everything has to be Proust does it. But it's hard for me to imagine that anyone gets to be a songwriter without having deep thoughts. If I wrote Agadoo for example, I wouldn't show it to anyone. Let alone insist that someone records it. I'd pop it in the bin. Maybe it's because I'm not a man. A man who just churns out any old shit and happily and confidently hands it over to someone and says 'I scribbled this down last night while I was watching Top Gear, please turn it into a hit song.' I'm not saying that's what you do (you're a master of the craft in my opinion). I'm over thinking everything again – apologies.

Where do you find inspiration? I suppose a lot of your songs are about your life. If I wrote songs about my life they'd be so dull. Washing, putting clothes away, cleaning, ironing, homework, cooking, reading, driving the kids about. Listening to Radio 2, trying and failing to ever get on PopMaster, reading. There isn't much else at the moment. I have so many ideas I want to write down but I never quite put pen to paper, I'm not sure what's stopping me. So I've only myself to blame really, that I'm not a modern–day Sylvia Plath (minus the depression, but with the shiny hair and alarmingly beautiful husband).

Do you ever do a thing where you decide to entirely reinvent yourself and you end up sitting straight or using a teapot and a cup and saucer instead of a mug for maybe an hour or so until you completely forget that you've reinvented yourself? I do that all the time.

It's daft isn't it? I don't think we're very good at changing.

Anyway, that really is enough from me for now. Sorry for waffling on, I don't even really know what I'm talking about tonight. Everything and nothing.

I'm going to go and throw away all the tangerines left over from Christmas that have now turned into hard pale orange balls. I don't know why I always buy them, I'm sure I'm the only one that eats them and even then it's only when I'm pretending to be someone else – who eats tangerines. When I've thrown them away I'm going to be a woman who uses her teapot to drink camomile tea (have you ever drunk it? It's like wee, and sort of tastes like nothing but helps you to sleep apparently). Then bed.

Night night.

Love Maud

P.S. Do you ever wish you knew how many days you had left on the planet? I think it would really make me jump into action. Unless of course it said three days, in which case I would tie myself to my children and never let go of them, for three days. Oh but then I'd be dead and they'd be tied to me which would be awful for them. Better if I die in hospital so they don't have to deal with my body. Also I wouldn't want them always thinking 'that's the room Mum died in' and I wouldn't want them to have to throw the bed away because I'd died in it, or keep it but feel haunted by it. It's best not knowing isn't it? When you die (although obviously I would prefer to die first so I don't have to witness your death. Not that I would witness it, why would I be there as a witness to your death? That would only happen if you were killed in front of me and I wouldn't let that happen. You are older than me though, and a man, and you were a heavy smoker and I have to face up to the fact that you'll most likely die before me) I would go to your funeral. Not that I would be allowed in (though I've never seen a bouncer at a funeral), but I would go, I would stand outside the church. I would visit your grave and always take a scrubbing brush with me in case someone spray paints 'wanker' on your gravestone. Even if that meant going to London all the time to do it. Maybe I could buy a plot in the same graveyard as you. Actually no, Mark in the office was moaning the other day about how much it cost to bury his Mum. Burials are not cheap. Also, I realise now that it would be a very odd thing to do. I'm not the constant tin soldier.

P.P.S. Do you believe in molecular memory? I read somewhere that particles have memory. That we live with inherited memories from where the particles that make us have been before. So your songs might actually be coming from Elvis – well not Elvis, he was still alive when you were born. Hitler maybe. Fascinating isn't it?

P.P.P.S. I sometimes wish I didn't have a memory. Sarah told me the other day she watched Last of the Summer Wine and she said when she had finished watching it she masturbated thinking about Clegg and Compo. She fancies Clegg (which is fair enough), but Compo? She said something about him just turns her on because he's such a pervert. She's the pervert unfortunately.

***

Your Friend Forever

Sender: maudcampbell@bluemoon.com
Recipient: wiggleitalittlebit@fpl.co.uk

19 January 2011 23:27

Dear Tom,

I can't concentrate properly on reading tonight, I've read the same page so many times and I still don't know what I've read. My mind is racing but I can't put my finger on what's bothering me, but something is.

I should just go to bed really, it's getting so late but I know I won't be able to sleep. I keep thinking about my wedding. I played some of your music at the party afterwards.

> So turn me up loud, hear my voice in your ears,
> Drown out the sound as your spade hits the ground.
> I've had enough, I've had enough, I've had enough.

I know, it's not really weddingy is it. More the sort of thing you might play if you were burying someone you've just killed or at least hit on the back of the head with a paperweight. I do love that song though and it meant something to me to feel your presence at my wedding, like you were a little part of it, a secret bit just for me, like you were there cheering me on or something. Though if you knew Colin I'm not sure you'd be cheering me on. I sometimes wish the ghost of Christmas future could have visited me at the wedding and whispered in my ear 'he's going to lose all his hair really quickly.' Though I can't regret everything. I wouldn't be without Amy and Leo.

You were there when I had Amy too, on a cassette, well for the first eighteen hours, after that everyone voted not to turn the 'bloody tape' over again so I ended up pushing out Amy to Steve Wright doing his factoids.

Leo came out in a huge rush a week early so there was no

time to choose songs. It was a bit of a shame really. I think giving birth to Amy was probably the most attention I've ever had.

The wedding was seventeen years ago, how did that happen. Have YOU ever felt like a grown up? Or do you feel exactly the same as you always did but in an older body? I always thought somehow that my brain would morph into something or somebody else that would think differently to me, but it hasn't happened yet. I suppose it's a relief in some ways, I'm still me, but trapped in the life of a middle-aged woman who is much more boring than I feel I am.

I've just got myself about an inch of sherry, maybe it'll help my mind to stop racing. Colin thinks sherry is disgusting but I like sipping it, even when it's not Christmas. There's something quite comforting about the smell and the taste. I liked the idea of getting into brandy but it's foul. I bet Sylvia Plath could manage to drink it.

I adore my kids, and I love being a mum. I do have a lot to be thankful for but I'm still in Preston and it hasn't got any more interesting, I live in a three-bed semi that looks like all the others on the street, married to a man that collects plastic figures and that I can't really talk to about anything, and my colleagues are so pedestrian they sometimes make me want to die.

I've known for ages things don't feel right but for some reason recently it's felt more urgent. Something needs to shift or something is on the verge of shifting. I don't think I should give up on myself.

How can I flourish if I don't ever go anywhere? I feel like I did the caterpillar bit for an extended period of time, then got into a cocoon and stayed in it.

Did you know Lord Byron died when he was just thirty-six? I'm forty-two and if I died now I'd have done nothing of any note. You achieved so much in your twenties, how did you manage that? You must be so brave to put yourself out there like you do. Proust said we always end up doing the thing we are second best at. Something to do with being scared of failing at the thing we know we should be doing. The people that are successful must be the ones that are brave enough to try their first best thing. Unless you think being a singer / songwriter is your second best thing? Maybe you're brilliant at something else too. I'm sure working in the business rates section at the town hall can't possibly be my first best or my second best thing. I really hope not.

Amy and Leo are happy and settled and clean and well fed and warm with good trainers so they don't get put through hell at school, and they have friends. I wanted that for them and I don't want to do anything to ruin that. I just wish – that when I was at school one of the teachers had given us a class and said, 'You know that person stuck in your head, the one that's you? Well that same person is in your head until you die, you better start liking them and getting to know them, and be nice to them, and try and make their dreams come true, make them use moisturiser and pay them some compliments. That should be your life's work (unless your dream is to be Hitler or a rapist. In which case you should commit suicide immediately).' I think that would have really helped.

Sarah (that's my best friend of forever) asked me the other day why I married Colin and I couldn't think of a reason. That's terrible isn't it. I think a lot of people around me were getting married and it seemed like a reasonable thing to do. Like if you hang around with fat people you end up getting fat too, or if you hang around with women that wear boot cut trousers and carry massive handbags you end up wearing boot cut trousers and buying a massive handbag. I hung around with a lot of girls that got married. Though they married their uni boyfriends, and mine turned out to be gay, so I married the next person I got involved with. I probably didn't wait anywhere near as long as I should have to get to know him. I'd have probably had a happier time if I'd stuck with Louis the gay boyfriend. At least we had things in common, he was so much fun, I miss him often.

Amy is fourteen and Leo is twelve. Amy is quite creative but not very alternative, I keep hoping she'll suddenly start wearing some eyeliner she's nicked from a chemist or decide she wants to dress in my old clothes but she's quite strait-laced at the moment, she draws a lot of wolves, a few years ago that would have been cool but it's not any more. They all bloody love vampires and wolves. It's mainstream. There's still time though. Leo is very normal too, he likes football and skateboarding. I had quite hoped he might be gay. Alas I don't think so. I showed him a picture of John Barrowman and he didn't blush so I'm stuck with a straight son who lets his bum almost entirely stick out of his trousers. Why is it a fashion? I've seen middle-aged men doing it too. I'm glad you don't do it.

It can't be very easy to walk knowing at any point your trousers might be round your knees, it's the sort of thing that people have nightmares about, isn't it? So why would you go out of your way to turn a nightmare into a reality? Maybe this is a sign I'm getting old. I don't feel old though, I feel the same. Well I suppose I'm a bit wiser. Do you feel wiser? Have you had to work hard at it?

I'm so sorry I've written loads again. I do it every time. I can't seem to stop once I've started.

Well good night, my brain feels a bit clearer now, I might be able to sleep, I'm going to try.

Yours faithfully

Maud x

P.S. Tomorrow I'll write a list of all the things I don't like about my life and then I can work out how to change them to be more like Sylvia Plath. I think it'll really help.

P.P.S. I don't think I could get my hair like hers though, and I'm not blonde. I suppose I could go blonde. I don't think I'd suit it though. Anyway the changes I need to make are more serious than hair. Though having significantly better hair would certainly do wonders to help my mood and self-esteem. Do you find having a good haircut brightens your mood and sense of self-worth? It must have been terrible for you in the 1990s when you had curtains. No wonder you had all those drink and drug issues back then.

P.P.P.S. Don't worry, there's no chance of me sticking my head in the oven. I don't think I've cleaned it since we moved in. Not that I think you're sitting around worrying about me.

***

Sender: maudcampbell@bluemoon.com
Recipient: wiggleitalittlebit@fpl.co.uk

20 January 2011 23:22

Dear Tom,

I really hope you don't mind me writing to you again. It feels so good to write down my thoughts and get everything out. I forgot how much I like writing letters (or emails that are like letters). People don't do it much any more do they? My best friend Sarah and I used to write to each other a lot. A couple of times a week at least. Her Dad got put in prison (he'd been laundering money for someone, I still don't exactly know what this entails but it's nothing to do with actual laundry). She and her Mum had to move away while he was in there.

I used to hang out behind the front door hoping for a letter addressed to me, she used to make her own envelopes from folded paper and draw stupid pictures on them. Mostly penises either pissing or ejaculating semen, I'm not sure which.

She moved back to Preston eventually but not until after I'd left school and we went to different sixth forms, and then to uni, then nothing was ever the same again. I did English literature and English language and classical languages. I messed up the classical languages 'A' level because it wasn't what I thought it would be. Sarah did a BTEC in art. She wasn't very good at art really but the teacher looked like a young Dustin Hoffman so her class was full of seventeen year olds that weren't that great at art but did want to have sex with their teacher. It must be dreadful being a good-looking teacher. Though at least he'd have had a good attendance record.

Things just change don't they. Whether you want them to or not. You never know when the last time you do something is going to be the last time do you? Well I suppose you do sometimes.

I know you know what I mean. You couldn't write the songs you do without having a good understanding of humans, even if you're not big on writing letters yourself.

I sometimes think the only thing that changes as you get older is that you want to use picture frames instead of blu tack.

Sarah has a theory about people that buy art from IKEA, it's not very nice. I kind of agree with her though, every time I go in someone's house and see a black and white picture of men sat on a piece of scaffolding on top of a skyscraper with their legs dangling eating sandwiches my heart sinks.

I tried pretending to be Sylvia Plath the other day. It was

going really well until I got into work and someone had put up another dispiriting note in the staffroom about the milk and not leaving teaspoons on the side. I read it, and all the Sylvianess I had built up in the car just vanished. I hate people putting shitty little notes up. Once, John who works on the same floor as me put up a note that said 'If you notice this notice you will notice that this notice is not worth noticing.' I wanted to stab him to death.

Well I was going to write a short email and I've done my usual thing of writing too much, I always do, and about nothing in particular. My lecturers at uni were always giving me my essays back and saying stuff like 'we said 2,000 words, this is at least 8,000.' Sometimes though, you just need more words, don't you? Well I do. I need to learn to be more succinct. Your songs are succinct and yet you still get so much across. I need to remind myself to use fewer words but to greater effect. I'll start, at some point – I'm not entirely sure when. I suppose I could start by deleting 'I'm not entirely sure when.' And now I've said it twice.

Yours Maud

P.S. I'm really sorry if you buy art from IKEA or use blu tack. Blu tack is very handy and IKEA sell a lot of nice things. I take Amy there sometimes, she loves it and the café is really excellent too. Have you been to the café? If you have been then my guess is that you've tried jam with gravy – isn't it the best? Even though it shouldn't be. I tried making it at home using lime marmalade and Bisto and to be honest it made everything it touched inedible.

Zena Barrie

***

INDIEPLANET FM

The Ian Purvil Show, 21st January 2011 11am

Ian Purvil meets Tom Harding

IP: And coming up next on the show we have a visit from Tim Harding, formerly of The Horseflies, to find out what he's up to at the moment and a little bird tells me he's brought with him a copy of his new single so we'll be giving that a spin, first though here's Pulp and Babies.

IP: And that was Babies from Pulp's 1994 album His 'n' Hers. I think my favourite album they ever did actually. Tim Harding, it's nice to have you here, were you a fan of Pulp?

TH: It's Tom. Hello, thanks for having me. Erm no not really, I was never that into Pulp.

IP: You must have had a favourite song though?

TH: A favourite Pulp song?

IP: Yeah.

TH: Erm I don't know, I hated that year 2000 song and I hated that other one, what's it called, Common People?

IP: You hated that? Ah, to many that's an anthem of the nineties.

TH: Yeah well I wasn't a fan.

Your Friend Forever

IP: So what did you listen to in the nineties?

TH: Well I listen to a lot of stuff, I really like Americana and actually a lot of classical music, it keeps me calm.

IP: Ah okay, and do you like musicals?

TH: Erm no not really, sorry. Do *you* like musicals?

IP: We love 'em here on this show. You must like Annie Get Your Gun?

TH: Never heard of it I'm afraid.

IP: You *must* have heard of it! 'Anything you can do I can do better, I can do anything better than you.'

TH: Oh right, I have heard of that yeah.

IP: Can you make a pie?

TH: I'm not that into cooking but I could probably manage a pie, yeah.

IP: No no no no, you're supposed to say 'No'! And I say... Neither can I!

TH: Pardon me?

IP: From the song.

TH: Which song? Common People?

IP: Annie Get Your Gun.

TH: Sorry you've lost me a bit.

IP: Right, well I'll explain it to you while we play a song, does that sound okay?

TH: Not more Pulp?

IP: No we're going to play one of yours. The last song off your first album Pigs, the unforgettable Shandy Hand...

Music plays 3 mins 5 secs

IP: And that was Shandy Hand from The Horseflies and their now classic album Pigs, originally released in 1980, a slow burner at the time but has now made it into Rolling Stone's list of the top 500 Indie albums ever released, apparently. How do you feel Tom when you listen back to Shandy Hand? It's thirty-one years since you released it.

TH: Bit embarrassing really.

IP: Can you remember writing that song?

TH: Yeah kind of, I was I think nineteen or something, living with my mate John. I just thought it was funny, you know? You think stuff like that's funny when you're young. I didn't spend ages on it, it was just one idea, I wrote it down and then worked out the chords. It was simple, it's a very simple tune, if you look at it structurally there's not much to it.

IP: And you don't find it funny any more? Are you not proud of your hit song?

TH: Well how can I be proud of... Shandy Hand... Well it's just embarrassing really, there's nothing funny about wanking. It's a bit sad isn't it?

IP: Woops, watch your language please Tim, it's only early! Shandy Hand must pay your bills though?

TH: Well I suppose in part yes, but I have had nine albums out, it'll be my tenth soon, plus two lots of greatest hits, so Shandy Hand isn't the only thing buying the bog roll.

IP: Two lots of greatest hits? What's on them then? Apart from Shandy Hand? What else have you done?

TH: Well you know, loads of my other songs, from my nine albums...

IP: And you never made it in America did you? Not even Shandy Hand.

TH: Well thanks for being so thorough with your research.

IP: Things have been pretty bad for you at times it says here on your press release. 'Not every record has been a success' and 'none of your singles have troubled the top forty for several years.'

TH: My press release says that?

IP: Yes, and it also says you had hard times with 'drink and substance abuse'.

TH: Does it. Right.

IP I think I remember you now.

TH: Oh you do? Well that's great.

IP: Thanks! So, tell us, are you healthy now and over all the dark stuff?

TH: Yeah, the fame stuff was all a bit too much for a while and I was very young and had a lot of money in the early days, I made some poor decisions but now…

IP: Not that famous though.

TH: Right, thanks, yeah, not that famous.

IP: You say you had money 'in the early days' – does that mean it's all gone?

TH: It's not all gone, no, but there just used to be more money in this industry. People don't buy so many records any more, bands make their money from touring and I don't tour. There was no internet when I started out so you know things have changed a lot.

IP: And why's that then?

TH: Well, like I just said, the internet has changed everything with music. I think the industry is still catching up with it.

IP: Weird. And why don't you tour?

TH: Well I wasn't interested in doing it for ages. I had some really bad experiences with Horsefly, and now I've no band, I suppose I could put one together at some point. I wouldn't rule it out.

IP: And what would you call the band?

TH: You mean if I went on tour now?

IP: Yeah. What would you call yourselves?

TH: Erm, I'd probably still just go by my own name.

IP: Is that not a bit self-centred? What about calling the band The Horseflies?

TH: Right... well I've been solo for a long time, people know me as Tom Harding, and Horsefly split up a long time ago.

IP: You think people know who you are?

TH: Not everyone, but the people who buy my records do.

IP: Talking of selling records let's play the new song. It says in the press release it's a departure from your usual stuff.

TH: Yeah well I like to keep moving on, I don't want to get stuck in a rut musically.

IP: And is it true you had to have singing lessons for this album?

TH: Yeah that's true, some of the songs I wrote turned out to be a bit more singy than some of my other stuff so I thought I'd do well to get some lessons.

IP: So you've gone all Celine Dion on us have you?

TH: Not quite.

IP: You'll be starring in Annie Get Your Gun before we know it!

TH: I don't think so.

IP: You'd need to smarten yourself up first of course, and get rid of that beard.

TH: Right, thanks for the advice.

IP: Well here it is, the first single from your new album, White Blobs, why've you called it that?

TH: You know when you stare at the sun?

IP: Yeah.

TH: Well, you know, that.

IP: Okay… here goes! Thanks for joining us today Tim and all the best with the new single, out February first on iTunes.

TH: It's Tom…

***

Sender: maudcampbell@bluemoon.com
Recipient: wiggleitalittlebit@fpl.co.uk

25 January 2011 23:02

Dear Tom,

I'm sat at the kitchen table with my laptop, having a glass of wine. I was going to do some writing, I started a poem but once I had written a few lines I couldn't work out what it was about, and then I started playing solitaire so now I'm emailing you instead. I hope you don't mind.

Colin got home from a long driving job today and just fell asleep on the sofa with his bag all strewn across the front room. He stinks and he's dribbling onto my nice cushion (Sarah bought it for me years ago), it's really bright colours, it's not something I'd ever really buy for myself. A fancy cushion. It seems a bit frivolous. I always worry about not having enough money. Sarah thinks I worry too much, I don't think she worries enough. Whenever she comes round she goes through my kitchen opening and closing the cupboard doors and laughing at all the food I've got. I never waste food though. I just don't want to run out.

A couple of months ago she spent £100 on a pedometer you strap to your wrist, she's always trying to lose weight. She says she has to take 10,000 steps in a day which is not that far really. But after two days she couldn't be bothered to do it and I Skyped her and she was in bed (drinking wine and eating peanuts) waving her arms backwards and forwards to get the pedometer up to 10,000. She hasn't said much about it for a while. I imagine it ran out of batteries (or she's smashed it).

I sort of wish Colin was still away. I know that's a horrible thing to say, he does work hard, but he doesn't add much to our family life. He pays his bit, but I mean he doesn't add much to the children's lives, or my life. When he's here they're not jumping all over him. He doesn't take them out, do homework with them, ask them how they are, ask them about the million and one things happening with their friends at school. He never has done, he never seems that interested in them, he's just not really involved with us. It makes me sad, I wanted them to have a doting mother and father. At least they've got me. I'm definitely a doter.

I married a man with thick dark curly hair who used to use eyeliner to draw on a 1920s style moustache when we went out. That was his way of smartening himself up, to draw on a moustache. I loved it, I know it sounds stupid but that moustache was everything. I was seduced by it. It made him look rakish. He definitely doesn't look rakish now. I was disappointed that he didn't draw one on for our wedding day. I remember the feeling of disappointment when I saw that he hadn't, it felt like a cop out. Or surrender or something. It was just really sad.

After we married his hair fell out in what felt like weeks but was probably about three years. Still that's pretty quick isn't it? Not that hair should matter – it wouldn't with the right person. Is it too much to ask that once in a while your husband puts on a bit of eyeliner or draws on a moustache? Although I suppose if Colin started asking me to wear more makeup I'd get very cross with him. The last thing I would do would be to put any on. I think I'm being probably being sexist – to my husband.

The problem isn't that he looks so normal, I don't really care about that. We just don't have anything to talk about, we don't do anything together. He's not interested in me and, well, I already know everything about him. I think couples are supposed to grow together and we haven't, we've drifted apart and we're just not playing for the same team any more. He can't possibly be happy either. He is making me become normal, middle of the road, boring, unadventurous. My creativity is at Zero. I shouldn't be blaming him I know, I shouldn't need another person cheering me on to get anything done. It would help though.

I go through phases of trying to make an effort with him, to see if there's something still there, but it's just impossible, he doesn't engage. He doesn't notice. I'm the invisible woman.

He's never hit me, which is something, but not the best review of a marriage.

'Here lies Colin Campbell, he never hit us.'

I try and think back to when we were just going out with each other, but it feels like that was someone else, it's such a long time ago. My Mum was really mentally unstable, Simon my brother had moved away and I was on my own with it all. I really needed someone I suppose. You can't always do everything on your own.

My Mum is bi-polar, but we didn't know that for a really long time, she tried to kill herself three times before she got that diagnosis and started getting the right help and medicine.

It should have been caught sooner – though it's no one's fault really.

There was no psychiatric follow up after the first suicide attempt, which I hadn't even realised was that because I was about fourteen at the time. Anyway she was really erratic, really up and down and self-medicated a lot with alcohol, it was horrible to be around, and frightening a lot of the time.

She still is completely self-absorbed but at least I know why, so it doesn't hurt like it used to. Now I just try not to take any of it personally, but it's hard, even when you know why, it's still hard, she is my mother after all, it's hard to love someone and for them to be incapable of loving you back the way you need them to. Anyway, I'm a grown up now.

She takes medication for her head these days which works pretty well I think, and she sees a doctor quite regularly, so there's a lid on it, and the lid comes off sometimes but mostly it's on, she simmers away underneath it. Occasionally she'll call me and she talks really fast and enthusiastically about things and I know she's on her uppers.

At one point I found out she'd racked up loads of debt on a credit card buying crap off QVC. The stuff was all still in boxes. We sent back what we could and got it refunded and then me and Colin spent ages listing stuff on eBay and selling it to pay the cards off. He did help me with that stuff, he was pretty good then really. That was a few years ago now.

I think the medication makes her quite foggy and tired so when it's working she's neither up nor down, just foggy. I get jealous of other people that have helpful mums or kind mums or mums they go shopping with or mums that call them up and ask how they're doing or mums that can actually give really good useful advice. My Mum hasn't ever been any of those things. It's not her fault, it's not, but sometimes I feel like I got a really short straw. Then I feel like I should stop being a baby.

Zena Barrie

My Dad went off when I was thirteen and apart from sending me a note and some cash just once I never saw him again until I was twenty-five when he turned up on my doorstep – that was a shock (to say the very least). He came in and I made him a cup of tea but neither of us had anything to say to each other. I mean, there was so much to say that in a way there was no way of saying it, I didn't know where to even begin and he looked so awkward and scared – and old actually. So we didn't. We had a cup of tea like two polite strangers and then we swapped numbers and he left. He had wet eyes and shook my hand really vigorously as he was leaving. He doesn't live that far away, only about an hour's drive, I have his number and he has mine but we don't use them. I can see it must have been really difficult for him, to be married to someone so volatile. But it was harder for us because we were kids, we couldn't just up and leave. I can't forgive him for abandoning us and leaving us to deal with it all. I don't want to punish him for it, but I don't think I could ever get past it enough to have any kind of relationship with him again. How could I ever trust him?

Best go now.
I'm getting a bit Maud...lin.
Love Maud

P.S. You've never mentioned your parents in interviews. Are they still around? Are / were they nice? I hope so. If I was going to guess I'd imagine they were nice, and supportive, because in nine albums you've never written a song slagging them off and if I were you I don't think I could have resisted it.

P.P.S. I've been having another problem completely unrelated to my parents. Amy had these two male guinea pigs and they were lovely but one of them died and we got another male to replace him but it turned out it was a girl and she had babies. I took the adult male to have his penis tied but he'd already got her pregnant again. Anyway this has gone on and on, more and more babies all the time. I've been trying to re-home them and have got rid of a few but they still keep multiplying. Just when you think it's sorted and I'm back to two females or two males one of them gives birth. They hide their penises away really well. All the babies are inbred so they keep dying or because they've given birth too young they die or can't walk. It's horrible. We have to keep having burials for them. We only have a small back garden and it's turned into a mass grave for disfigured baby guinea pigs. It's like a catholic orphanage. I think I need to convince Amy that we should have NO guinea pigs. That might be the only way to stop it. I will run that idea past her, she might be fed up with the sadness of it all. If I'd been skinning them I'd have enough for a coat now I'm sure. People are very funny about fur aren't they? I can see it's cruel but is it any worse than eating meat? Or wearing leather shoes? Or eating tripe? (Which Sarah used to think was vegetarian because it's not made of meat. It's not meaty, but it's not lettuce is it?)

P.P.P.S. Sarah just called me (she calls or texts me a few times a day) to tell me about a dream she had about Gordon Brown. Well she said it was a daydream so basically she's just being filthy again. She said she was working in his wood-panelled office in the House of Commons. He came into the office in a really foul mood, something to do with David Cameron or something and then she said he grabbed her and pushed her against the wood panelling. He kissed her passionately and then put his hand up her skirt. I won't tell you the rest except to say Gordon Brown is far more sexually adventurous than you might imagine. I can't believe David Cameron won over

Gordon Brown, can you? I'm quite sure no woman fantasises about David Cameron being brooding and adventurous with them sexually while working out how to give a better life to young disadvantaged kids and helping out single mothers. I asked her if the one-eyed thing made a difference to her and she said she didn't know Gordon Brown only had one eye. If I had a dream about him he'd probably get me against the wall and then his glass eye would pop out and I'd spend the rest of the dream looking for it and wake up exhausted.

***

Sender: maudcampbell@bluemoon.com
Recipient: wiggleitalittlebit@fpl.co.uk

27 January 2011 21:17

Dear Tom,

I'm having a cup of tea and listening to Drinking Games while the house is quiet. Just waiting for Amy to come back from her friend's house (who lives two doors away) and Leo is in the bath, he's always in there for a long time and comes out smelling like Superdrug. I imagine he's been playing with himself. That's what boys do in the bathroom isn't it? I haven't asked him. Do you think I should or just leave it? I suppose there's not much to say so long as he cleans up after himself. I haven't found anything grotty so far. Maybe I'll check under his bed when I can get in there. Actually, I don't need to know do I?

I think Drinking Games is my favourite album of yours, except the first Horsefly album but I can't really listen to that at the moment. I've overplayed it, have you ever done that with an album? Played it so much that you suddenly realise you can't listen to it again. There isn't a bit of it you don't know, every lyric, every riff, every breath on it. Isn't it weird how entire albums can stay in your head in complete detail for decades, to be plucked out at will at any point. Whereas I never know where I've put my phone, or my keys, or my bag that I had five minutes ago. The brain is a weird thing isn't it. Do you find that you know songs from your childhood really well but new songs don't really stay in your brain? Or they just don't hit the same spots do they? Maybe there is something particular about how the teenage brain is wired, that it takes in all this stuff endlessly and then you hit twenty and your capacity to retain it all stops. Or maybe that's just me.

Sometimes I really can't stop listening to Numb though that makes me a bit emotional and sometimes I'm emotional enough without adding to it, in fact I usually listen to it about three days before my period starts. I don't know why it's called premenstrual tension, it doesn't make me tense. It just hurts and makes me want to kill everyone on the telly, and everyone at work, and everyone driving, and then finally myself. Tension doesn't seem like the right word for all of that. At least it's only once a month. I suppose I won't have that to worry about for too much longer. Sarah is already peri menopausal. Well she says she is anyway, but they won't put her on HRT yet. She's dying for it. She says it makes your skin look loads younger and increases your sex drive. I don't think hers needs increasing. If she's got enough drive that she's willing to do it with the entire cast of Last of the Summer Wine I'd say she has no problems in that area.

I'm not really worried about my skin ageing or not wanting to have sex. It's natural isn't it? I've had my kids. My vagina doesn't need tampering with any further. I don't want to be eighty and still going to clubs hoping to get fingered in a toilet.

Anyway I don't think I look that old, maybe it's because I still feel like a kid, in my head. Though I suspect everyone else does too. Even people in really important jobs. Like judges. They are all going around looking like old men in wigs but inside there's a boy who wants to climb trees and wank into a sock in a tree house.

I love your song on the Drinking Games album called Turn to Page 7, all about the crap people have written about you. It must be hard being in the public eye, I hope it doesn't make you feel awful all the time. The papers can be so cruel, especially when they get a whiff of someone not doing well. They seem to love it. I've seen some awful things written about you. It makes me sad, I know you're a good person, I've always instinctively known that.

Time for another cup of tea I think and maybe I'll find something good to watch. Have you watched any good films recently? I seem to watch the same handful over and over again, maybe it's comforting or something, and it means I don't have to concentrate on anything.

I just went upstairs to use the bathroom, my bedroom door is open and Colin is asleep in the middle of the bed, with only his boxers on, snoring like a train. I went in and covered him up, I don't want the kids seeing that. I don't want Amy to see that. She shouldn't be subjected to seeing her Dad's flaccid penis hanging out of his shorts.

This is not what I imagined for myself.

I suppose Colin didn't think he'd end up spending all his time driving a truck up and down the motorway. He wanted to make modern day silent movies, I quite like the idea of it really. Unfortunately he was all talk. He had a camcorder and tripod and made a few short films that weren't really very good. I was in one of them. I was 'girl at bus stop'. Then he worked in a video shop for a while which he enjoyed but really, if you want to be a fashion designer you don't go and work on the tills in Primark. The video shop went bust. I thought it would have been a chance for him to get back into filmmaking but he just went and got a driving job, then got his HGV licence. I can't talk anyway, I've worked for the council all these years. The thing is, when you've nothing to fall back on you really worry about taking risks. Because what if it all goes wrong? I see other people taking risks though. Maybe when the kids are older and have got jobs I can start taking risks. Well not huge risks, doing some creative writing night classes probably isn't really that high up on the scale of risk taking is it? I quite fancy doing a bit of pottery too, or maybe sculpture. I'm so glad line dancing isn't a thing any more. That was a horrible blot on our country's collective history wasn't it?

When I was young and imagined myself as an adult I was married to Ted Hughes surrounded by ceiling-high shelves of books in a big airy room with no TV in it, we just sat and read and made love and sometimes I would listen to him talk about Sylvia and I wouldn't be a bitch about her because she was dead so I wouldn't need to be jealous.

Actually I think I'm going to go to bed, Amy has bunks in her room so I'll sleep in there. Her room is so nice. Lots of pictures of wolves and sexy vampires, bless her.

Yours faithfully
Maud xxx

February 2011

Sender: maudcampbell@bluemoon.com
Recipient: wiggleitalittlebit@fpl.co.uk

12 February 2011 23:04

Dear Tom,
    I popped into my friend Michael's homosexual coffee shop on the way home from work. It's just like a heterosexual coffee shop really but with loads of rainbow flags in the window, and inside there are nicely framed pictures of Andy Bell, Jimmy Somerville, Holly Johnson, Freddie Mercury, George Michael, Pete Burns and Marc Almond. Oh and a young Rod Stewart just wearing his pants. It's mostly full of old women with their shopping trolleys. I think Michael was hoping it would be full of handsome gays with their laptops but he forgot that this is Preston. Anyone who was a potential handsome gay with a laptop has moved to London, or Manchester or somewhere else. Preston is full of old people. He says he serves more tea than coffee, which really annoys him because he spent loads of money on fancy barista equipment. He went on a barista training weekend too (which seems quite OTT, how hard is it

to make a cup of coffee?). But now he can make little patterns on the froth, for if a gay with a laptop ever comes in his shop. He says old ladies go in, buy tea and then take out their pasties they've bought next door and happily eat them in front of him. I told him he could stop them, or just stock pies himself, but he's worried if he stops them eating their own they won't come back in for their cups of tea and anyway he couldn't do pies as cheaply as Greggs. He's trying to get a late licence to attract late-night handsome gays but I just don't think there are enough of them about. He does have a boyfriend but he's just turned sixty-five. I think he was hoping the shop might widen his boyfriend prospects but not so far. Still, I'm very impressed with him for giving it a go. I hope he doesn't go bust, but he says there is a very wide profit margin on tea so he's ok for now so long as the rent doesn't go up.

Colin's gone to bed. He has to be up first thing to drive a truck to France, I'm not sure what's in the truck, hopefully not loads of thirsty women and children. He always has your greatest hits in the lorry, it annoys me. He borrowed my CD and then I had to keep asking for it back. When he finally handed it over the case was all broken and covered in melted Snickers and the lyrics booklet was missing. I told him to keep it and got myself another copy. So disrespectful.

Sarah has just sent me a picture of Des O'Connor. We have an ongoing joke about his pubic hair. Just that he must have a lot of it. Sarah imagines him having the thickest pubic hair any man has ever had. She spends too much time thinking about pubic hair because she thinks she has male pattern baldness with hers. She says there is a patch that just doesn't grow any more. I suppose it's better than it going grey.

Des O'Connor always has a really good tan doesn't he? It must be strange being his wife, waking up every day and finding yourself in bed with Des O'Connor, I'm not sure I could ever get used to that. Do you think he frequents nudist beaches in order to get that tan? Probably not – I think they're mostly for gays to hang out on aren't they? And naturalists. Or is it naturists? I don't expect David Attenborough is big on nudist beaches. William Blake was a nudist, he wasn't gay. At least I don't think he was. Although the title Songs of Innocence and of Experience does sound like it could be a Marc Almond album, maybe he was gay. I haven't really thought about it before.

Men I would prefer to be married to or at least in a romantic relationship with:

Ted Hughes (from the 1950s)

Vincent van Gogh (before he cut his ear off ideally)

William Blake (so long as he's not gay, if he is I would like to be his friend)

Michael Palin (ideally from the 1970s but now would be more than acceptable)

Ranulph Fiennes (with his fingers intact ideally)

Ranulph Fiennes's son (I think he still has all his fingers)

Ranulph Fiennes's grandson (if he has one. If so how old is he? Must look that up)

Sir Ernest Shackleton (I would enjoy writing to him while he was away at the South Pole)

all of the McGann brothers (but not individually)

the Kemp brothers (not individually, and pre-court case and pre-head injury)

the Attenborough brothers (younger and individually would be fine)

Hmmm, Colin is nothing like any of these people. Although neither am I. Who am I trying to kid?

I saw an article in the paper years ago about William Blake having a blue plaque in London. I'd love to go and see it one day. I should just bunk a day off work and go really, shouldn't

I? There's nothing stopping me. Why does it always feel so hard to get round to doing things that I would actually like to do?

Urgh, I just went to make a cup of tea, and there's a copy of The Sun on the kitchen counter. How can I be married to someone that reads The Sun? It's so unlike me, it doesn't fit. Maybe it did at one point, but it doesn't any more. I can't imagine what Colin sees in me either. He'd be much happier with an Anthea Turner type of woman, well she's a bit of a one off isn't she. He'd be happier with Anthea Turner but he's probably too mucky for her, she's very clean isn't she. I bet her house is very shiny, with white carpets, no guinea pig hair or mucky skirting boards or mass (guinea pig) graves in her back yard. To be honest I think I'd be happier with Anthea Turner.

You wouldn't see Ted Hughes, bald, reading The Sun, while knocking back cans of lager would you? He would never let himself go, he was a very dignified and powerful man. Ted Hughes wouldn't have a lorry full of Snickers wrappers. He'd listen to Classic FM and certainly wouldn't borrow CDs and give them back with the lyrics insert missing. He would appreciate a nice book of lyrics. If Ted Hughes was a lorry driver his glove box would be full of volumes of poetry and maybe a tobacco tin. He'd just read a book and smoke a couple of very thin cigarettes as a break in the layby. I can imagine him licking the cigarette paper in a very cool way. He would also drink wine and not be scared of that being effeminate, that's how much of a man he was. I am not suggesting he would drink wine while driving a lorry. He would wait until after his shift.

Anthea Turner has quite strange hair doesn't she. Almost like a swan or a duck, feathery hair on each side of her head, and she never changes it. I bet she'd look great with a nice bob. I wonder if anyone's ever told her.

I'm drinking Tia Maria. I don't even like Tia Maria but it just somehow looked really Christmassy in Asda and now I have a litre of it to get through. I need to put a note in my diary that pops up every year to remind me that I don't like Tia Maria. Port's nice isn't it? A bit strong (you have to remember it's not wine), but it warms you up nicely, it's almost like drinking medicine. I'm listening to Pigs, I haven't listened to it for so long, you must have been really young when you wrote this album, about twenty-one or twenty-two I think. I like it a lot, it's more raw than some of your other records, it feels gritty and real, it reminds me of being young, not that being young was great but I did have an optimism and a wonder at the world that I don't have now. Well I do have wonder, but it's in a box at the moment, to be opened at some point. I said that to Sarah once and she said I should open my box more often. She has a filthy mind. You can hear the instruments properly in Pigs. With some albums it's hard to know what could be making the sound you hear. It's all sort of vague and orchestral / electronic sounding.

I didn't do anything clever when I was twenty-two – I mean, I got a degree but anyone can get a degree these days can't they. And it's what you do with it. I haven't really put my English lit degree (specialism in English Romanticism) to any use at all, I have books and books of notebooks full of half-written poems but I've never shown them to anyone. Does a poem exist if no one ever reads it?

When I left uni I just took the first full-time job I managed to get. It was the right thing to do because I needed some stability. I should never have stayed in the job though. I should have kept looking for something more interesting, more suited to me. I feel like I've missed the boat now.

I never had a plan for after university, I think that's where I went wrong, I should have had a plan. No one told me I needed a plan. The kids that came from wealthy families all went home and then spent ages looking for the right job or doing unpaid work. They knew they needed a plan, although about half the people who did the same degree as me have ended up teaching English literature and English in a high school. I always knew I couldn't teach. I'm scared of all teenagers that aren't my own.

No one has gone on to become an English Romantic, I think I'd still like to do that. That's what the aim should be I think, with that sort of a degree. If everyone just teaches it and no one ever does it, that would be very sad. I'm already English, I just need to become a Romantic. I'm not sure how to approach it.

I really should stop writing now, so bye, good night.

Maud x

P.S. Why do I make myself drink the Tia Maria instead of just pouring it down the sink? I hate waste but that doesn't mean I should force myself to drink it. I suppose I could top the bottle up with a bit of cough medicine and then hand it in for the school raffle. But then people would be suspicious at such a good prize. Hmmm. I wish I didn't waste my time thinking about what to do with it. Maybe this is why women get less of the top jobs, because we are worrying about leftovers too much. A man would just chuck it away without thinking about it, or just down it. I wonder if there's a recipe I could use it in? Do you like Tia Maria? If you do I'll post you some. I promise not to put Benylin in it.

P.P.S. I realise if you wanted Tia Maria you could just buy your own, it's a tenner a bottle in Asda. I'd be delighted to post you mine but the postage would cost more than buying a new bottle. You know what, I'm going to just pour it away.

I've poured it away. I feel a little bit elated. I might find some old knickers to throw away next. Maybe I need to have a good clear out. I'm not sure how to become a Romantic but I know wearing old knickers is not part of it.

***

Sender: maudcampbell@bluemoon.com
Recipient: wiggleitalittlebit@fpl.co.uk

14 February 2011 07:05

Dear Tom,

Just getting ready to go into work. Happy Valentine's day!

Colin's still away in France, so no card for me this year. He does usually chuck one at me and I pop it in a drawer followed by the bin and that's about the extent of our Valentine's celebrations.

That's fine with me. I am a romantic but I find Valentine's day excruciating. The hearts, the bears, the tacky cards, the snogging, the people holding hands, the underwear, yuck.

Romance to me is looking for a cigarette and suddenly Ted Hughes is beside me and asks me if I want a rolly and I say 'yes' and he rolls one for me with his very nimble hands, as he licks the paper he makes eye contact with me for a little bit too long. Then he leans provocatively against the wall and looks at me inquisitively. I put the rolly to my mouth, it's still damp from his tongue. He whips out his lighter (a real one that you have to put fuel in, not a plastic one with a cannabis leaf on it). He holds the lighter up to me and I light my cigarette, I take a puff and lean against the wall, he is already in a good position to kiss me, hard, against the wall, but that doesn't happen yet, he is a gentleman. He says something to me like 'so, who are you?'

and looks me up and down with a wry smile. By this point my knees have gone and I'm powerless. I reply with a cool 'who are you?' even though I know he is Poet Laureate Ted Hughes. He asks me if he can buy me a drink, I reply that I'm on a date. He says something like 'ditch him, come with me,' I give him a look, he stubs out his rolly and takes my hand. I let him. And then probably some kissing against the wall happens and then my date comes out of the pub to look for me and calls me a slag and Ted Hughes punches him in the face and knocks him unconscious. We leave together. THAT is romance. It's a shame that can't ever happen. Because he is dead.

I remember the day he died. I was at work when they said it on the radio. I picked up my bag, left work ill, went home and Sarah came over. We drank ourselves stupid. Sarah was incredibly patient with me. I kept reading poems to her from The Hawk in the Rain and crying and she asked me a lot about my fantasies about him. Mostly about him reciting poems to me and drinking red wine.

I woke up on my couch covered in a blanket with a bucket of vomit next to me. It's what I needed. Though I suppose it sounds very disrespectful to have mourned him by vomiting into a bucket.

Anyway I'm looking forward to a nice quiet evening with the kids. Usually I try and make them watch a film from the 1980s that they're not interested in. I will let them choose, but they each like different things. When they start arguing over things like that I just leave the room and tell them to find me when they've made a decision. I can't get involved in those types of disputes. I think it's because my school never taught public speaking and there was no debating society. There was no society of any kind. I mean, there is always 'society' but not societies I could join. Only the society I was already a part of.

I'm actually glad Colin isn't here which is a bad sign isn't it? I just don't feel like, you know – I mean, I can shut my eyes and it's no worse than having a smear test. No worse than a smear test isn't a great review though is it? The thing is, he might as well just do it on his own really, it would be more polite. How would you feel if a woman described sex with you as 'no worse than a smear test'?

I know I should be more involved. I just don't want to be, not with him. I did used to have interesting sex that involved a lot of dressing up. Not in sexy underwear but in costumes from the drama department. Victorian role play, bustles and pantomime costumes, a pantomime horse, burglar role play, French role play, peasants, everything. But that was at university with gay Louis, before he came out – all the signs were there.

We had so much fun together, I wish we were still in touch, I should try and track him down. I think I thought I was supposed to be really cross with him about it all and I wasn't really. I think I knew. I think we always know. It's more about when we choose to believe what we know, to bring it to the front of our brains and address it. I'm sure you know what I mean. I was happy for him really.

I wouldn't mind being married to a gay man to be honest. So long as he was respectful and tidied up after himself which I am sure he would. I don't think you really get slobby gay men. Or maybe that's a massive generalisation. Do you know any slobby gay men? I will ask Michael. He's always immaculately turned out. Though I think the makeup he wears to cover his acne scars is a shade or three too dark for his skin colour. He always has a tide mark on his jawline. I would never mention it to him though. His shirt collars must always be brown. I'm glad I don't have to wash them.

Are you married? I've never read that you've been married, but I think you've always been a pretty private person, or at least you've tried to be. If you are married I'm sure it's to an exotic woman with lovely long legs who enjoys having sex with you very much and would never dream of rolling over so she didn't have to look at you and I'm sure having sex with you would be much better than having a smear test.

Oh gosh, look at the time, I should go to work now, sorry I know I go on a lot about absolutely nothing.

Have a lovely day.

Yours Maud x

P.S. Did I say happy Valentine's day? Happy Valentine's day! I hope you have someone very special in your life. Maybe I will too one day.

***

Sender: maudcampbell@bluemoon.com
Recipient: wiggleitalittlebit@fpl.co.uk

23 February 2011 22:15

Dear Tom,

I had the radio on but they just seem to play the same three songs over and over again, I know I'm supposed to listen to 6 Music, that's what the cool people listen to, but I like Radio 2, I'm set in my ways, I like the routine of Ken Bruce, Jeremy Vine, Steve Wright and Simon Mayo. They're so soothing. I'd marry any of them, except Steve Wright of course.

I am eating some fruity cheese, some people really get on their high horse about fruit being in cheese don't they? It's the same people that act like they're going to be sick at the thought of pineapple on a pizza.

Idiots.

I like pineapple on a pizza, it's a fruit portion at least, like chocolate raisins. Sarah got me into eating them. She says they give her the runs so badly it's like going on a crash diet. Though I know that emptying out your colon really quickly isn't the same thing at all as actually burning off actual fat through exercise. And when you have the runs, you just lose loads of body fluid, so then you have to drink loads of water and then you end up weighing the same as you did before the chocolate raisins – apparently.

We're supposed to have five lots of fruit and vegetables a day. Who manages to do that? And eight glasses of water. You'd have to spend all day either drinking water or going to the toilet. My pelvic floor couldn't take it. I'd have to replace my office chair with a toilet or have a urine bag attached to me if I drank that much water.

I watched a documentary once about some special rare cheese that's put out in the sun so that flies lay their eggs on it and then the cheese gets wrapped up and put away for a couple of days and then when they go back for the cheese it's completely crawling with maggots, but guess what. The maggots are entirely made of cheese. Then people spread the maggoty cheese on some bread or a cracker and eat it. It's illegal so men have to meet up secretly on a mountain to do it. They must really love it. I'd like to try it. I suppose I could try making it myself by shaking a milk bottle up and putting the curd on top of the bird table for a couple of days and then I could wrap it up and put it in the airing cupboard. Yeah I might try it. I'll get the kids involved. It's good to do science with them isn't it?

I love how in the song Port in a Storm (it's just come on) port is the drink and also somewhere you can park a boat. Do you park a boat? There's probably a nautical word for it. It's such clever word play, it must be great to have such a talent with words. Where did you learn to write or is it all self-taught? Who inspired you? You've never really talked about it in interviews. They always seem to ask you the same thing, about thimbles and about what Shandy Hand is about. Are you really that interested in thimbles? I think I might have sent you one when I was a kid. Do you get fed up with people asking you the same questions all the time?

I'd love to hear all about your inspirations, it would be great to find some new things to read or to listen to, I love having my mind opened up. Colin doesn't read at all. That must be why his soul is so undernourished. Can you feed your soul if you don't read? Pizza isn't going to help. I wonder if you can fix anyone by making them read. Or if with some people it's just too late. If the pathways in the brain have never been opened can you open them as an adult? I suppose it depends on the person.

Well, I suppose I must sign off now and attend to the ironing. I didn't used to bother with ironing but the kids are at that age now where they're quite particular about how they look at school. Hopefully they'll be able to iron their uniforms themselves soon, they're getting big enough really. I just worry about them leaving it plugged in or burning themselves. I'm sure I fuss too much.

Sometimes I put one of your CDs on while I'm doing it (the ironing) and sing along, I've been told I have quite a nice voice (by my neighbour who heard me through the wall once). He may well have been making fun of me, he has one of those faces though that's really hard to read. Hmmm. I wish I was hard to read. Even if my face was hard to read though, I'd just tell the person exactly what I was thinking. Sarah says I have verbal diarrhoea. Thank goodness for spell check, 'verbal runs' just doesn't sound the same.

Love always,
Maud

P.S. I'm actually going to turn the music off now and do the ironing in front of the telly. There's a new series of Masterchef on. I'm not that interested in cooking but I like watching people cook. It's relaxing I suppose. I don't like it when they make foam though. It just looks like someone has spat on the plate. I also hate it when they talk about chocolate soil or emulsion. These are not words that I feel should be associated with food. Have you ever been asked to go on Celebrity Masterchef? Or Celebrity Big Brother? Or into the jungle? Would you ever do it? If you did, I'm not sure I could watch. I think I'd find it really difficult. I'm not sure why. I'd still vote for you though, if you decided to do it. Not that you'd need my vote, you'd win anyway.

March 2011

Sender: maudcampbell@bluemoon.com
Recipient: wiggleitalittlebit@fpl.co.uk

2 March 2011 23:04

Hello,
 I'm so fidgety tonight. I keep wandering around and picking things up and then putting them down. My front room is so beige. Why do we all have mantelpieces with objects on and carpets and rugs? All front rooms are pretty much the same aren't they? Sometimes I want to write all over the walls and throw paint on them. I don't feel like I'm allowed to though, even though it's my house. Somehow I feel like I'd get into trouble. I suppose Colin might not like it.
 I have to take my youngest (Leo) to the hospital tomorrow for physio. He's got curvature of the spine, not really badly but he does look a bit bent to one side when he walks. I think maybe if he'd just try and walk straight it would sort itself out. He doesn't seem to understand the importance of decent posture. No one wants to look at a stooping man do they?

Maybe I should make him watch The Hunchback of Notre Dame with me.

Can you think of one attractive well-respected man with a hunchback? Apart from Stephen Hawking who is so respected that everyone is attracted to him because they want to hear what he has to say. Although for someone who is so into science I don't see why he won't embrace it a bit more and get a new more modern voice.

He could have the voice of either Top Cat or Tramp from Lady and The Tramp, the two sexiest voices in history. I pointed out to Sarah once about how sexy Tramp's voice is, and later that night she sent me a text saying she'd masturbated to the film. She found a bit where Tramp has a sort of monologue and kept her eyes shut apparently because the cartoon dog thing would have spoiled the moment.

Top Cat has probably spoken enough words that Stephen Hawking could use pre-recorded bits of them to make up his entire vocabulary. Although Top Cat didn't have much to do with science and space, most of his days are spent around a bin, so if Stephen Hawking still wanted to continue working in the field of science (which he absolutely should) he'd have to use someone else's voice for those bits or he could use his old voice, otherwise he'd have to refer to everyone as either Officer Dibble or Benny. And every time he discovered a new star he'd have to call it Benny 1, Benny 2, Benny 3, and so forth. Perhaps he could be Top Cat when he's with his wife (I'm sure she would enjoy that) and continue with the more robotic voice everyone knows for his lecturing. At least it's clear and easy to understand. If I could buy an off the shelf accent I definitely wouldn't choose the Preston one I've been lumped with. It's not as harsh as some voices you hear around this area but I'm a long way off sounding like Angela Rippon.

I wonder how Stephen Hawking sounds when he's angry

or upset. Does he have a volume button do you think? So he can shout when he's angry or whisper when he's being passive aggressive or sarcastic. I've only ever heard him talk about space. He is brilliant, isn't he?

I suppose even scientists get stuck in their ways. Unless he's been asking for a new voice and everyone has just ignored him. I suppose his wife can just unplug him if he's bugging her. Not everyone has that luxury. I would like to unplug Colin, and some of the men in my office.

Best,
Maud C x

P.S. I feel like I've been rude about Stephen Hawking. I'm sorry if you're a fan of his. He is a great man isn't he? I just think, you know, that he could have a more interesting voice.

***

Sender: maudcampbell@bluemoon.com
Recipient: wiggleitalittlebit@fpl.co.uk

6 March 2011 22:35

Dear Tom,

I've been feeling a bit unsettled and anxious for a little while, a few months at least and tonight, I've been watching Colin. I had a feeling, just a feeling that I couldn't shake that something wasn't right but I couldn't work out what the feeling was linked to. I just knew that something felt a little off. I thought it was just me. Do you ever get that? Where you sort of have a knotted feeling in your stomach and everything sort of feels wrong but you can't put your finger on what's making you feel that way? On the surface everything seems normal.

I got home from work as usual, the kids are fine and I'm getting on with the tea. They're doing homework, or at least they're supposed to be. Then Colin came home. And there's something off kilter. I talked to him as I normally would but there's this funny look in his eye, except it's not funny. There's a look in his eye and I couldn't place it but I know something is wrong. We all give away so much on our faces don't we? I think I've always been quite good at reading people. Knowing when they're feeling more than they're letting on. This look is something new though. I'm trying to think how to explain it without sounding like a crazy paranoid person, because I'm sure that's what people would say to me. Or if I confronted Colin I would have absolutely no evidence to back up what I'm thinking, none at all. But I know it. I know he's having an affair, and I know because of a look in his eyes. He is in the room with us but not in the room with us. He is speaking to us, but he is processing his thoughts before he speaks. He has removed himself from us. Does any of this make sense? It's so hard to explain. He is now a character actor playing the role of husband and father but mentally, he is a few steps back from us, in another house, with another woman. There is a distance. Does any of this make sense? I know it in my bones. I don't know what to do about it yet, it's making me feel very tired. When bad things happen I have to sleep a lot. It's the only way my brain can work out what to do.

Fuck.

When Sarah and I were young she would often have a few boys on the go at the same time. I could never do that. Not because I didn't have the chance to behave that way. I could have done, I had the chance, but I couldn't. My face would give it away, but more than that. If I loved someone I would be there, mentally, in the moment with them. I just don't have it in me to be able to two-time someone.

Sarah still does it even though she's married, have I ever told you that before? I know that makes her sound terrible, but we all have different circumstances don't we. Sarah uses this website where married people hook up and mostly get pissed in hotel rooms and then have sex. It always sounds pretty horrible to me. It just doesn't appeal. I'm not completely sure Sarah likes it either but she has this need to be wanted or something. I don't think it's the right way to go about it. I don't think it makes her feel better. I don't think the men treat her very well or vice versa but I can't stop her doing it so I just make sure she's safe. She lets me know when and where she is going and with who and she tells me when she's arrived and when she's leaving, stuff like that. She's always been ok so far. Colin won't be doing anything like this. Colin has met someone and fallen for them. I can tell from his eyes, he's just gone. He was looking at my face as I was looking at his. He was trying to act normally. He doesn't usually look at me, not in the eye, not about the tea anyway. He's gone.

I've suggested to Sarah that maybe she should have therapy instead of the men but she said she can't be fixed. She thinks she's too old to be fixed and thinks that sometimes it's just best to get on with life rather than dragging up a load of things you can't change. I agree with her in part, but if your past is making you do stupid things in your present then it's damaging and it's not something you can just leave in the past because it's right there with you every day.

Anyway, I have to go now, I'm feeling sad, the feeling of sadness has sort of replaced the anxious feeling. I feel weighed down with it. The stupid thing is, Colin's gone to bed and I'm feeling so sad I want to go and get in with him and curl up behind him and put my arms round him, hold on and cry into his back. I'm not going to though. I think I'll just put on some music and get a blanket and sleep down here. I don't feel angry at all but the sadness feels overwhelming. It's times like this when you really remember how much you're just a lone person on the planet trying to make your way through it and it's just you and it's always been just you but you put these people around you to try and pretend it's not just you but it is.

Anyway, I'm ok, I'm ok. Just need to sleep off some of this.
Night Tom, thank you for being a person in the world too.
xMaud

P.S. I'm glad I've said it out loud, well written it down. I know you'll understand. I know I'm absolutely right about it. What I don't know is what to do. Oh God, I just heard some squealing and went into the back room and we have another bloody litter of guinea pigs. They are very sweet but the mum looked up at me with really sad guinea pig eyes. I think if she could speak it would be to say 'why am I stuck in this cage having kids that I'm both mother and grandmother of?' I really need to get her out of this situation. Maybe she and I will run away together. (Not practical.)

***

Sender: maudcampbell@bluemoon.com
Recipient: wiggleitalittlebit@fpl.co.uk

8 March 2011 01:03

Hi Tom,

Just back from a works do, someone's fiftieth, it was so boring. Bit drunk. Actually I feel very drunk. I'm going to have some water. I should go to bed but I can't lie down because I'll start spinning. Do you ever start spinning? It's awful. And then you don't stop spinning until you sit up in bed and puke on the floor and then you fall asleep and then when you wake up you have to deal with the sick which is absolutely the last thing you feel like doing. I hardly ever get like this. I think I didn't eat enough before I went out. There was hardly any food, I have a boss like Jabba the Hutt and he got to it all first. He's so boring. He goes on and on about the fact he once met the actor that plays Ken Barlow. 'He was surprisingly down to earth.' Really? Was he? What surprised you about that exactly? What do you mean by down to earth? People just say things for the sake of talking sometimes. It makes me want to rip my own head off. Why can't people just be quiet? And listen? You must think I'm a wordy person but I'm not really. All the words are in my head or I write them down. I don't speak them. This is why I have such an affinity with Vincent van Gogh. (I don't for one second believe he shot himself though, they should reopen that case, if indeed a case was ever opened.)

There is a vague chance of redundancy in my department, I'm going to try and go for it, though I've been there so long I don't think they can afford to get rid of me. Just imagine, I could take a year off work and do all the things I want to do. I could sit on a hill and write poems. I could sleep. I'm so tired all the time.

I am not thinking about Colin at the moment. It's too much. It can wait. I have to rely on my brain to just quietly work things out in the background and it will let me know when it's come up with a plan, it's good like that.

Love you
Bye
Maud x

Zena Barrie

***

Sender: maudcampbell@bluemoon.com
Recipient: wiggleitalittlebit@fpl.co.uk

10 March 2011 12:15

Hi Tom,

I've been having a look at your new website. It's very informative isn't it? But it doesn't look very modern. Is that a look you've gone for on purpose? I suppose it might be quite fashionable now to have retro websites that look like the ones we had at the council back in 1997. I do love that we have the internet. But sometimes I wish that it would go away and we could all go back to the days of the Encyclopaedia Britannica and the People's Friend Annual. We didn't have them but my Gran did. Though mostly we just looked at sexual reproduction and Elephantitis disease over and over again. I did at one point decide to read them from start to finish but I only got as far as Amphibians... I suppose we didn't go over very often. I think most of them went unopened. I know my Gran wasn't sitting around in the evening reading them, what a shame. I bet that was the same for every house in Britain. They could have saved a lot of paper and money and space by just selling people a pamphlet about reproduction and Elephantitis.

I listened to your interview on Indie Planet Radio, will you be putting links to all your new interviews on there? I hope so. I always miss things like this. I wouldn't really think to listen to Indie Planet. I must say I think the interviewer was very rude, do you think he was a volunteer? They really should know who the person they're going to interview is before speaking to them. It may not be Radio 2 but they should have some standards. He seemed to think it was his job to humiliate you. He should go and work with MPs. They like that kind of treatment don't they? At least that's what Sarah's told me. Anyway, here is the most important thing to say today, I **REALLY LIKE YOUR NEW SINGLE**. Your voice sounds so strong on it, those lessons you've had have clearly paid off. And your voice sounds wonderfully deep and tranquil. I absolutely love it.

I am really excited to buy your new record, it's been ages and it's always such a treat. Do you really think you might put a band together? That would be so exciting, I'd love to come and watch you on tour. I know you haven't toured since Horsefly. I think it would be ok now, it's not like it was years ago, I think people are better behaved. People don't smash chairs up and spit any more or throw bottles. It's all a bit more sit down and have a glass of wine and listen. Although some people just take pictures and film all the way through now. Maybe that's worse than people having a fight. I'm not sure which would annoy me more if I was the one up there singing. All of it I suppose. The whole mobile phone thing at a gig makes me want to puke to be honest. A sea of people holding up mobile phones instead of lighters, it's just not very rock and roll is it? And holding up a phone just makes people look like idiots, whereas a lighter, a lighter meant solidarity, and romance, and it was sort of religious. You did get burnt fingers though. Some people now watch the entire gig through their phones. What's the point in even going? I've actually seen people looking through photos and videos they've just taken as the gig is happening. Why would anyone do that? Why can't they at least wait until they get home? We used to take so few photos. Only really if you were going on a day trip and then you'd have a twenty-four film and no flash and then you'd have to wait until you could afford to have them developed and then wait a week for them and you'd get eighteen pictures of your thumb and maybe a picture of the sky that looked good at the time but just looks shit in a photo. Urgh just realised I must sound really old. I will shut up.

I haven't been to a gig for ages, I think the last one was when Sarah and I went to see Paul Weller in Margate, that was at least four years ago. We were sat down all the way through drinking wine. He wasn't that great really, he's not got much personality has he? Maybe he's really posh so he just keeps his mouth shut. Sarah said to me that he'd been using Nice 'n' Easy hair dye and we got the giggles and spent most of the gig actually crying with laughter until it hurt. We hadn't seen each other in ages and I think we were a bit giddy and emotional. He sang Changing Man and Sarah whispered 'that's the name of his hair dye' in my ear and I almost wet myself. Then he sang You Do Something to Me and she said 'yeah, I dye your hair for you,' she did that with every song. I really wish he'd get a different haircut, don't you? Just to confuse all the men that have been copying his hair all their lives, they wouldn't know what to do with themselves. Has anyone ever copied your hair? I suppose it would be quite hard to copy, your hair is just sort of there isn't it, without doing anything in particular (in a nice way). Mine doesn't do much either.

I've been thinking about getting one of those nutribullets and trying to get super healthy. Actually who am I kidding – it's not for me. I don't know what I'd put in it. Pasta? Anyway, why am I talking about that? I'd best go, I'm at work.

Maud x

P.S. I'm still mulling over everything to do with Colin. I feel like my brain is calmly doing all the work in the background and I'm just looking after it really well and getting lots of sleep and one day very soon I will wake up and know just what to do. It will involve divorcing him. I know that. And actually it is exciting, scary but exciting. There's an expression isn't there? Getting your ducks in a row. I don't have any ducks but I'm getting myself strong and gathering myself together, it's the same sort of thing. Maybe I will splash out on a nutribullet. If I'm going to go through a divorce I don't want people judging me and thinking it's because I've let myself go. I haven't, but there's always room for improvement isn't there?

***

MAUD AND SARAH

Facebook Messenger conversation, 11 March 2011 23:15

Maud: Hello?

Sarah: Hiiiiii, you ok love?

Maud: Yeah sort of, I think so. Not really but I will be.

Sarah: Well what's that supposed to mean?

Maud: Ok, don't freak out.

Sarah: What is it? What's happened?

Maud: Ok, well I have no evidence and there's no need to panic but I'm sure Colin's having an affair with someone. I just know it.

Sarah: Holy shit, really?

Maud: Really, I know it.

Sarah: Ok, ok, how do you know it?

Maud: It's hard to explain.

Sarah: ???

Maud: Ok, it's just a look in his eyes.

Sarah: A look in his eyes?

Maud: I've known him a really long time, I can read his face like a book. I'm one hundred per cent not wrong about this.

Sarah: Ok ok. I believe you.

Maud: He's analysing everything, every conversation, I think he's analysing things and then changing them into stories about me.

Sarah: What stories?

Maud: He probably tells her I'm a horrible person. He probably tells her that I'm some dumpy boring horrible person that doesn't understand him. That doesn't let him live his life. I bet he's told her really personal things about me, slagging me off so that she doesn't feel bad about it so she can go and tell her friends that she's seeing this fucking fucking great new guy and yes, he's married but 'honestly if you knew what his wife was like you'd feel really sorry for him.' I know it, I know that's what he's doing. He will make me out to be some complete bitch and she'll feel sorry for him and like what she's doing isn't that bad.

Sarah: Well you won't want to hear this.

Maud: What?

Sarah: Well that's exactly what men having affairs do. The ones

I've met through that website. I'm sorry you must think I'm a cunt. I always tell them I'm not fucking interested but some of them feel so guilty they feel the need to paint their wives as some sort of wicked witch to make them feel better about what they're doing. I've never taken any notice of it but, they do do that. It's not like I want to know, I don't ask them, they feel they have to tell me. It's not sexy, it makes them look like fucking whining babies.

Maud: So they feel really guilty, and to be able to deal with feeling really guilty they make their wife into the baddy? The wife who's at home looking after their kids, cleaning their house and probably making their tea and probably washing the spunk off their clothes. AHHHHHHH I'm so FUCKING FUCKING ANGRY.

Sarah: It's ok it's ok. I'm going to just have a quick word with Ian to make sure he can look after the kids and I'll jump in the car and come over. Ok? I won't be long.

Maud: What if Colin gets back?

Sarah: If he gets back he can look after the kids and we'll go to the pub. Don't say anything yet. Ok? Hang on a sec. Ok, Ian's in charge, I'm on my way. Have you got supplies?

Maud: Half a bottle of red.

Sarah: I'll pick up supplies on the way then, won't be long.

Maud: Ok. Love you, get fags.

Sarah: I will. Love you too xxx

Sender: maudcampbell@bluemoon.com
Recipient: wiggleitalittlebit@fpl.co.uk

12 March 2011 21:45

Dear Tom,

I've told Sarah all about my suspicions about Colin, she believes me and I'm still convinced about it. We went to the pub, it was good to see her. I got quite drunk but I wasn't sick.

It's a very strange thing, the feelings I've been having about Colin. I've been trying to break the whole thing down into lists of facts to help keep my thoughts clear. Like this sort of thing.

A Colin is having an affair

B I am not in love with Colin so it's not too sad

C I don't want to live with Colin any more

D I want to get my life back

E I want to leave my job

F I want to do a job that I enjoy

G I want to change my front room around (get rid of ornaments etc)

H I want to stop feeling the drudgery (of routine)

I I want to write poetry and drink tea and look out of a window and wear nice dresses that show off my waist (26 inches) (I know)

J I want to paint the walls different colours

K I don't want to get to the end of my life and suddenly realise I haven't lived it

L that means taking a few risks

M and that's ok

I feel weirdly powerful about it all. Which you wouldn't

maybe expect except that I have a reason to leave him now, or a reason to get him to leave me. I feel like things can finally change. I feel energised by it. I know this must sound very strange. It's like I've been handed a ticket to get things to change without me being the baddy. I suppose that's it. I didn't want to be the bad one, and now I'm not. Except maybe I am. I should have sat down and talked with him about this a long time ago but I didn't. I am to blame for this too. I am. I know I am. Anyway, I'm not going to do anything until I have some concrete evidence to hand over to a solicitor. So I am being a detective. But so far there's very little to detect. He carries his phone with him everywhere. Even when he goes to the toilet. So I need to take that off him and make him think he's just lost it. Unless I can get into his emails or get his phone bill. Do I sound like a psycho? I'm sure I must sound unhinged. I just have to be careful with all of this. I have to think about the kids and I want things to stay nice and stable for them. I think in a strange way my mind feels clearer than ever. I suppose humans have some animal instincts they can use, when they're under attack, and that's how I feel now. My body is probably pumping out a lot of adrenaline. I hope I don't run out of it. Where is it stored?

Very excited to see you're on The Wright Stuff tomorrow, I wonder what you'll be talking about. I hope it's nothing too embarrassing. Sometimes people go on there and then have to have an opinion about something they wouldn't really know anything about. Like you might have to have an opinion on smear tests or something.

Just in case that happens – imagine a big metal prodder pushed up the inside of your penis and then prised apart, it's EXACTLY like that.

You have to just lie there and drop your knees down and open up your vagina in front of a stranger. Can you imagine how horrible that is? Maybe you can, at your age you might have had a colonoscopy, have you had one? I think you might have to have one after you turn fifty to check for polyps. Colin had some polyps. They burnt them out and froze off his piles all within the same appointment. That's the NHS for you. He was really scared to go to the toilet for weeks afterwards. I suppose I was the same after I had Amy, too scared to go for a poo in case all my stitches broke (from the episiotomy). I'm sort of annoyed by my episiotomy, I'm sure I'd have squeezed her out eventually without having my vagina sliced open by an eager man. I suppose I will never know now. I didn't have one with Leo but he basically just fell out.

Will you be doing any other TV appearances to promote White Blobs? Loose Women maybe? I bet they'd be all over you, it's pretty embarrassing to watch sometimes. You should have seen them with Enrique Iglesias. Coleen Nolan looked like she was going to dive under the desk to give him a blow job. Goodness knows what they'd have done if Julio himself had been on. That reminds me, have you ever met Chris de Burgh? He seems a bit odd to me. Like someone who could lose their temper and kill at any given moment. Do you know what I mean? You always look very patient. Are you?

I won't be able to watch you live on The Wright Stuff because I'll be at work and I've run out of holiday allowance for this year. I've not even had any holidays. I've had to take loads of days off to take Leo to the hospital for his physio.

My new allowance doesn't start until 5th April, so I'll just have to watch on catch up (having the day off to watch The Wright Stuff probably isn't the best use of my holiday time, though to be honest more relaxing than going on an actual holiday, I could actually watch a programme, put my feet up and have some wine and garlic prawns without anyone distracting me. Maybe that's the perfect way to take a holiday).

It's good that we can watch stuff on catch up now isn't it? What do you think of Matthew Wright? I quite like him, he's intelligent and empathetic. Sarah HATES him. Don't know why, she's never met him, as far as I know. Hate is such a strong word isn't it? I don't hate many people.

I can hear Leo banging about upstairs, I'd better go and see what he's up to before Amy starts shouting at him. I wish they'd come downstairs sometimes and actually speak to me.

Anyway.

Night, thanks so much for being there. It really helps me more than you could know.

Maud x

***

Sender: maudcampbell@bluemoon.com
Recipient: wiggleitalittlebit@fpl.co.uk

14 March 2011 01:21

Hi Tom,

I've just finished watching The Wright Stuff. It's really late, I had to wait until Colin had gone up to bed, he would have been funny about me watching it and not in a funny way. I know it shouldn't matter what he thinks but I'm not ready to get into a row with him just yet. I read once that you can only keep seven thoughts in your consciousness at any one time and the rest is in your subconscious. This worried me because I'm always thinking about everything all the time (I think probably more than seven things at once but I've never been able to count all the things). Colin only uses up three of the seven things he could be thinking about, Lorry, Penis, Plastic Figures. What a waste. I haven't got hold of his phone yet. There's no point getting it until I know what his password is because I won't be able to open it and look at anything.

I thought you did really well on The Wright Stuff, you picked good news stories and you came across really well. I could tell you were a bit nervous but you did great. Everyone likes stories about animals, those baby pandas were adorable and it was a good idea not to get too bogged down in politics. You look very well at the moment, it's heartening to see.

I think even though Matthew Wright seems quite left wing, he gets a lot of people phoning in who are right wing. Like Jeremy Vine. They'd be a nice pair to get trapped in a lift with. They'd have to talk to me wouldn't they? If we three were trapped in a lift? Or do you think they'd just talk to each other and ignore me? I think they'd talk to me. They seem very down to earth. If they ignored me for three hours while I was trapped in a lift with them I would consider that to be the height of rudeness. I wouldn't want to be on a desert island with them though, and forced to start a new race of humans. Matthew Wright and Jeremy Vine would have to have a fight to see who was going to procreate with me. And what if neither of them wanted to? Or if they were both firing blanks? Or what if they've both had a vasectomy? We'd have to try and reverse it on the island using only a fishing hook and a bit of fishing wire. I have no idea how you reverse a vasectomy. I suppose I could look on my phone if I had any battery left.

Also I'm a bit too old to have more kids now, it's not impossible but there would be a high risk of Downs. And then I'd be stuck on an island with a Downs baby that would need specialised care and Matthew Wright and Jeremy Vine, and we wouldn't know who was the father and we'd have no medical care and I'd have to feed the Downs baby coconuts and rain water filtered through one of Jeremy Vine's socks. I hope it's a warm island at least. Oh God and Jeremy Vine would constantly be going on about Eggheads and humming Werewolves of London.

Sorry – I'm sure none of this will ever happen so I'll try to put it out of my head. Gosh look at the time. I have to be up in four hours.

Night

Maud x

P.S. I like the beard! It really really suits you, and the salt and pepper hair, very distinguished.

***

MANAGER GARY BARNES AND TOM HARDING

Telephone conversation, 20th March 2011 2.30pm

Tom: Hello?

Gary: Mate! How are you?

Tom: What do you want?

Gary: Nothing! Nothing at all, just checking in with you.

Tom: Right, thanks, I'm fine.

Gary: All good my end too.

Tom: Okay great, well I'm in the middle of something so unless there's anything you need to tell me?

Gary: No, nothing I need to tell you. Oh except I've been in touch with your publishers this morning.

Tom: Right, and?

Gary: They're putting out another greatest hits.

Tom: They're what?

Gary: Another greatest hits. Nothing for you to worry about, you don't need to get involved.

Tom: Right, right, and would I be right in thinking I've got no choice in any of this?

Gary: Mate, it's up to them. Don't worry, just a low key release.

Tom: It's a fucking rip off.

Gary: No, it won't be, I knew you wouldn't like it being the same so we're adding in some B sides and rare interviews and stuff so people get something new for their twenty quid.

Tom: Twenty pounds, you are fucking kidding?

Gary: It'll be really nice, in a box.

Tom: A box set?

Gary: Yeah, with a postcard in it of the Horsefly album cover.

Tom: What else?

Gary: That interview you and Ed did after the Warrington gig in 1980.

Tom: The one where they recorded us having a row?

Gary: Yeah, that's going to be a bonus track.

Tom: No.

Gary: It's not up to you.

Tom: What else? So far, me having a row and a postcard.

Gary: That version you and Martin recorded of Jolene.

Tom: Me and Martin stoned... singing Jolene?

Gary: Yeah people will love it.

Tom: It's private, that was never meant for anyone to hear. How do they even have it? I don't understand.

Gary: Look they just needed a few extra bits to make it sellable to people who already have your greatest hits.

Tom: So, me having a row, me stoned, and a postcard.

Gary: And they're all going to be signed.

Tom: By?

Gary: You. Who else?

Tom: How many? How many do I have to sign?

Gary: They think they'll shift about 5k, don't worry they'll deliver them to you and you'll have about a week to do it, I'll pop round and drop you off some Sharpies.

Tom: If I say no?

Gary: I'll sign them, or Samantha will but then people will probably know it's fake and then complain so you might as well just do it.

Tom: You're a cunt.

Gary: You're cute when you're angry.

Tom: Oh fuck off.

Gary: It's been a pleasure, as always.

Tom: Wait, I've been emailed some bollocks from PRS. Can you have a look at it and let me know if I need to do anything?

Gary: Fire it over. Oh and I need you to sign a cheque for the carpet man, apparently you didn't pay for the foot treads or something. I'll bring it over with the Sharpies.

Tom: What email are you on these days?

Gary: Same as always – wiggleitalittlebit@fpl.co.uk.

Tom: You're a daft bastard.

Gary: You'd be adrift without me.

Tom: Yeah yeah leave me alone now please.

***

RICHER SOUNDS MAGAZINE

March 2011 issue
In Conference with Tom Harding

Q: Is it true your new album is called I Didn't Have Sex With a Ghost?

TH: Yeah, that's what the album is going to be called. It won't be out for a while yet though, it's not quite ready.

Q: And why's it called that then?

TH: You don't know?

Q: I have no idea.

TH: Okay, there are these things we call urban myths. Utter crap stories that somehow do the rounds. For example that Lisa Stansfield likes something called space docking and that Marc Almond had to have his stomach pumped and it was full of fifty different kinds of sperm, and that I have had sex with a ghost, sometimes I hear it's been multiple ghosts. I thought it was time to acknowledge that I have heard all about this rumour and whilst it's very funny, it's complete bollocks.

Q: And what's space docking?

TH: You'd have to ask Lisa Stansfield about that.

Q: Have you got her number?

TH: No, weirdly we don't all know each other.

Q: And this record then, it's being released on iTunes, will we be able to get physical copies of the album?

TH: No, no, not at the moment. I like the immediacy of iTunes you know. You can just put an album together and then get it straight out there, no messing about with production and distribution and record companies. I hate all that shit.

Q: Do you still have a record deal?

TH: Well you know I have a deal with myself, I still have

management but I wanted to put this one out on my own, it's just much easier.

Q: I've given White Blobs a couple of plays. Musically it's a bit of a departure from your other work.

TH: Yeah well I wanted to do something different.

Q: Don't take this the wrong way but there's actual singing on this record. I didn't know you had it in you.

TH: Yeah well I can sing you know, now I've knocked the fags on the head and I had some actual singing lessons because I just wasn't breathing right, it was really helpful. Wish I'd done it years ago to be honest, but I think I was too proud when I was younger, I don't care any more.

Q: The first single is called White Blobs. What are the White Blobs?

TH: You know when you stare at the sun for too long?

Q: Yep, oh yeah you get those floaty shapes in front of your eyes.

TH: Yeah well it's that.

Q: Right... tell me, is it true that you collect thimbles?

TH: Yeah I do sort of, well people send me them, I don't go looking for them.

Q: Why thimbles? Not very rock and roll.

TH: Well my great grandma left me her collection of like fifty thimbles, I liked playing with them when I was a kid and then

I mentioned it in a Smash Hits interview years ago and then people started sending me them...

Q: Do you have them on display like an old lady?

TH: A few, just a few, the original ones.

Q: Great stuff, thanks for your time.

Tom Harding's new single White Blobs is available to download from 1st April at the bargain price of 79p.

***

Sender: maudcampbell@bluemoon.com
wiggleitalittlebit@fpl.co.uk

29 March 2011 23:07

Hi Tom,
   I'm downloading iTunes, well I'm trying to. I don't have a Mac computer but Nigel at work says I can use iTunes on a PC, I didn't know that so I'd never even tried. My laptop is pretty old and clunky but I think it's going to work. It says it's downloading anyway, it's at twenty-three per cent. Then I'll be able to buy White Blobs when it comes out. I had to delete a load of crap off it first to make enough room to download it, I don't need seven hundred wedding photos do I?
   I was looking at them and doing that thing you can do, you know when you look at a picture of someone smiling and then cover up most of their face and just look at their eyes and you can see how they are really feeling. I did that with my wedding photos. Colin looked quite happy, I looked like I had just seen every person and animal that had ever died in the history of the universe, in their various stages of decomposition. I've kept

about twenty pictures. Not for me but Amy and Leo might be interested at some point.

I suppose I have this creeping feeling, that everything is borrowed. I keep thinking my stuff may be mine now but when I'm dead it will just be dumped in a bin or taken to a charity shop. My kids aren't going to want seven hundred pictures of their Mum and Dad getting married. They might want one of them to pop in a drawer but that's it. I don't even think they'd want to look at it, it would just be a thing to keep, out of duty. Did you know that people are only actually remembered for two generations? So my kids will remember me, and if they have kids they will remember me, but that's it, after that you're just a face in a photograph, but that's it. No one is alive any more that might have ever cared about you.

It's just made me think, you know, that if I want to eat a not insignificant lump of cheese for lunch then I might as well. And it's made me think that it's time for a big change – I suppose this is a midlife crisis isn't it? But I think it could be a good thing. There is a reason I suppose why midlife crisis is a thing people talk about and you don't understand it until you get here. I still need to tackle things with Colin but I'm taking my time. It's almost funny, watching him have the affair. It's all so obvious now. The sneaking about, the going out at odd times, the multiple trips to the shop when we don't need anything. It's funny to just make him keep doing it. Not forever but for a while at least.

It's at seventy-three per cent now. White Blobs is going to be my first ever mp3.

I'm also going to buy Love and Pride by King if it will let me because it's not played on the radio nearly enough is it? And we all need a bit of Love and Pride and the song makes me happy. I just thought though, will it mean I'll only be able to play it on my computer? I love listening to music in my car. Will the album come out as a CD? I hope so, otherwise I'm not sure when I'll get to play it. Maybe they'll play it loads on the radio. Do you think you might do some gigs this time round? Your website has a big list of interviews on it but no tour dates.

Anyway, I'm going to be doing my first download soon, wish me luck!

Maud x

P.S. I might download Chain Reaction too (a song completely about fingering), that was sung by Diana Ross but written by The Bee Gees. Have you ever met The Bee Gees? I know it's not cool, but they're SO brilliant. The world would be a much shitter place without them ever existing, and Barry Manilow for that matter. Imagine a world without Copacabana. It doesn't bear thinking about. I'm going to see if I can burn the mp3s onto a CD to play in my car. Then I could drive to work singing to White Blobs, Love and Pride, Copacabana and Chain Reaction. Then I'll get into the office in a really great mood and there will be my boss, Neil, stood there looking miserable waiting to tell me about the photocopier needing a repair and my good mood will be shattered. Really starting to resent that place. I'm keeping everything crossed that I get made redundant.

***

GARY BARNES AND TOM HARDING

Telephone conversation, 30th March 2011 1pm

Gary: Tom mate, it's Gary.

Tom: Ah right, I've been trying to call you.

Gary: Been super busy mate, got loads of great stuff lined up for you.

Tom: Is the single all set to go at the right time?

Gary: Yes mate, listen I've got a load of phoners lined up for you.

Tom: How many?

Gary: Quite a lot... lots of local stations, they've all agreed to play the single if you do the interview.

Tom: How many?

Gary: Listen I'll email you over the list. Just make sure you're by your phone at the right time.

Tom: Is it going to be people asking me if I collect thimbles over and over again?

Gary: Well just tell them you don't, tell them you've chucked them all out or just say you don't want to talk about them.

Tom: Are they going to play White Blobs or are they going to play fucking Shandy Hand?

Gary: Listen, some of them might play Shandy Hand but that's good, people will remember who you are and then be interested in your new song.

Tom: I fucking doubt it. When you listen to Slade at Christmas you don't start wondering if Noddy Holder's put out any solo stuff recently.

Gary: Trust me mate, it's all looking good.

Tom: Is there anything else lined up? Have you asked about me going on Andrew Marr, I could play acoustically at the end?

Gary: Mate you don't want to go on that, honestly. You'd have to actually play.

Tom: That's what I do. I sing and I play.

Gary: Mate it's booked up years in advance.

Tom: Jools Holland?

Gary: Mate, I wish I could, I really wish I could, they have proper musicians on there. We just have to do some leg work to get you back up and running, okay?

Tom: I am a fucking musician... I am a fucking proper musician.

Gary: Right, whatever, it's just we've not seen you ever play anything so, you know, forgive us for being ignorant of your talents.

Tom: You are supposed to be my fucking manager!

Gary: I am, and I've arranged you loads of interviews so just say thank you.

Tom: Any word on if it's been playlisted?

Gary: Still waiting to hear on that one, there's a chance at the C list on Radio 2.

Tom: How much of a chance? Have they said that to you?

Gary: They haven't said no yet.

Tom: Right, so you think they'll say no?

Gary: Well they only pick about five songs a week. There's a lot coming out at the moment.

Tom: Yeah but I thought you said March was the best time to release something and get it charting on about three sales.

Gary: Yeah mate, but I think lots of people have had the same idea.

Tom: Right, so it's going to get played on a handful of local stations and that's it?

Gary: There's more than a handful, some of them are digital, there's a podcast with about 5,000 followers… Listen mate, Friday's just the start of it okay?

Tom: You know I hate you, right?

Gary: You love me really.

Tom: No, I actually hate you and I think you're bad at your job.

Gary: Stay by your phone.

***

SMITHFIELD COMMUNITY COLLEGE

The Danni Leighton Show: Every Breath You Take (I'll be Watching You)

Podcast, 31st March 2011 8.30am

DL: Hello, is that Tom Harding?

TH: Yes it is, hello.

DL: Oh my God hello!

TH: Hello.

DL: Thanks for being on my show.

TH: That's no problem.

DL: I'm going to start recording now, is that all right? It's just that I have to go out soon.

TH: Yes no problem.

DL: Hang on a sec. Right. Hello you're listening to the Every Breath You Take podcast from Smithfield Community College and this is The Danni Leighton Show. Today we have a very special guest on the phone. Tom, are you still there?

TH: Yes, I'm still here.

DL: Tom Harding is on the phone, Tom Harding from Horsefly! If you haven't heard of him, he was in a band years ago.

TH: Hello.

DL: How are you Tom Harding?

TH: I'm fine thanks, how are you?

DL: Oh not bad thanks. Got loads of coursework to do which I really can't be bothered with but I've got to get on with it because the deadline is like really soon.

TH: Oh right... What kind of coursework?

DL: Digital Media BTEC, this is part of my practical. Really I just want to vlog and get free stuff.

TH: This podcast is part of your BTEC coursework?

DL: Yeah, I have to record it and edit it and then upload it to the college channel. No one listens to it, it's full of crap.

TH: Great...

DL: It's not bad, the main lecturer is really boring though, he's completely past it.

TH: Right... Did you want to ask me anything in particular?

DL: Oh yes, what was it like being in Horsefly?

TH: What was it like being in Horsefly?

DL: Hello? Are you still there?

TH: Yes, erm, being in Horsefly was exciting but difficult too in many ways, it was a very long time ago. More than thirty years ago.

DL: Really? Kin'ell.

TH: Yes... Really. And now I have a new record out called White Blobs.

DL: Brilliant.

TH: Did you want to play it?

DL: We can't play music because we don't have a PRS licence

Your Friend Forever

or something. You can't put other people's music on your blogs because you have to pay them or something like that. I don't know why.

TH: Right... do you have any more questions?

DL: Er... do you write your own songs?

TH: Yes, I do.

DL: That's brilliant.

TH: Yes it is, well good luck with your course, I best get off now.

DL: Can I have your autograph for my Gran?

TH: Yeah no problem, you'll need to email my manager though to arrange it.

DL: What's his email?

TH: wiggleitalittlebit@fpl.co.uk.

DL: Wiggle it a little bit?

TH: Yeah he's a twat...

DL: Ok, bye.

April 2011

SMILE COMMUNITY DIGITAL RADIO

Breakfast Show with Graham Smith, 1st April 2011
9.30am

GS: Hello this is Graham Smith at Smile Community Digital. Coming up we have Tom Hardy phoning in for a chat from legendary Indie band The Horseflies. Before that, a few adverts from our sponsors.

Sausage advert (30 secs)

Advert for local reform church (60 secs)

Advert for Citizens Advice (30 secs)

How to advertise on Smile Community Digital (30 secs)

Advert for Pete's Driving School (30 secs)

GS: Hello, this is Graham Smith here for Smile Community Digital. I'm delighted to have Tom Hardy on the phone.

TH: Tom Harding.

GS: Oh sorry, it says Tom Hardy on your press release.

TH: I'm definitely called Tom Harding.

GS: Right you are Tom. That's great.

TH: Yep.

GS: And a little bird tells me you have a new single out, is that right?

TH: Yes, that's right.

GS: And I've just heard it's gone to number one, congratulations Tom!

TH: Eh?

GS: APRIL FOOOOL. Haaa haaaa that was a good un wasn't it, we got you good and proper there didn't we?

TH: Yep, well done...

GS: Can't wait to tell the missus that one! And tell me Tom, how is the single going?

TH: I'm not sure yet, it's only being released today so who knows?

GS: Fabulous. Can you tell us a little bit about your time with The Horseflies?

TH: Well, it's a long time ago, more than thirty years.

GS: All a bit of a blur then?

TH: Not really no, but I've done a lot since then, I've released nine albums since Horsefly split up.

GS: And why did you split up? Pigs is a classic album.

TH: Yeah well it is now I suppose, but at the time it didn't do that brilliantly.

GS: Shandy Hand always gets people on the dance floor though.

TH: Well that's nice of course. Drinking Games and Numb sold a lot more copies though than Pigs has ever done.

GS: And how did you get the idea for Shandy Hand?

TH: I was really young when I wrote that... I think it's pretty obvious where I got the idea from.

GS: Okay great, well we're going to be playing it shortly.

TH: Are you going to play White Blobs?

GS: Well, Karen who does another show on here is a massive fan, she's actually taken your promo CD home with her. She thinks you're brilliant, she's a big big fan.

TH: Nice... so you don't have a copy of the song then?

GS: Karen was so excited to get her hands on it.

TH: Right...

GS: So what was it like being in The Horseflies? TVs out of the window? That sort of stuff?

TH: Horsefly... No not at all, we never saw much money or many hotel rooms in those days. Just lots of travelling round in small vans and doing lots and lots of gigs.

GS: Drinks, drugs, girls?

TH: Not really in those days, I saved all that for the 90s.

GS: Did you re-form in the 90s as well?

TH: No we never re-formed. I've been solo since Horsefly split up.

GS: Right so the 90s were pretty crazy days then?

TH: Pretty terrible.

GS: Thanks for your time Tom, really great to speak to you today. And the new single from The Horseflies, White Blobs, is now available from all good record shops.

TH: Just iTunes, just under my name.

GS: And here are The Horseflies with Shandy Hand.

***

RADIO LEICESTER

Miles Bradley on the phone to Tom Harding, 1st April 2011 10.30am

MB: And that was the new single from Tom Harding, White Blobs, and we have him on the phone now! Hello Tom!

TH: Hello.

MB: Thanks for taking some time out to speak to us today.

TH: That's no problem, thanks for having me on.

MB: Before we start I have to say I'm a big fan, Horsefly was one of the first gigs I ever went to.

TH: Oh right.

MB: I remember a stage invasion and you jumped into the crowd. It was a bit of a rough night.

TH: Yeah it would have been, they were all rough nights.

MB: Yeah it's all middle-aged people in couples now isn't it? Sitting down.

TH: Well I don't know about that, I don't tour any more, I haven't for years.

MB: Don't you miss the old days when everyone was spitting and fighting?

TH: Not really, it would be okay if I could just play music without having stuff thrown at me… I wouldn't mind that.

MB: Yeah I miss those days.

TH: Right.

MB: And I hear you have a thimble collection. What made you start collecting thimbles? Do you do a bit of quilting on the side? Ha ha ha.

TH: No, I've just got all my great grandma's thimbles, she

left them to me. Then in like, 1980 or something, I did an interview with Smash Hits.

MB: Ahh yes I miss Smash Hits.

TH: Yeah, anyway they asked me like what colour my socks were, my favourite colour and if I collect anything so I mentioned the thimble collection.

MB: What is your favourite colour?

TH: I don't know.

MB: Black?

TH: I don't know.

MB: Okay what colour are your socks?

TH: Erm black.

MB: I knew it!

TH: Yeah anyway once it was in Smash Hits loads of people started sending me thimbles so the collection just sort of got quite big.

MB: And do you have them displayed all around your house?

TH: No, just the ones my Great Gran gave me.

MB: Have you ever bought a thimble yourself?

TH: I did once, I bought this red one. It's just shiny and red. Most of them have flowers on or something. This one seemed like a man's thimble.

MB: How many do you have?

TH: I don't know. Lots.

MB: A few hundred?

TH: Probably about a thousand.

MB: Wow, a thousand thimbles. Have you ever thought of taking them on Antiques Roadshow? Are they worth a lot of money?

TH: I haven't thought of going on Antiques Roadshow.

MB: Not worth much then?

TH: I really don't know.

MB: Have you thought about exhibiting them somewhere?

TH: No I haven't.

MB: Well maybe you could do that.

TH: That wouldn't really interest me.

MB: Where do people send them to you now?

TH: People send them to my manager and then sometimes when I see him he gives me a load of jiffy bags with thimbles in.

MB: That's great, so if you'd like to send Tom a thimble, maybe you'd like to design your own? Maybe you could paint Tom on a thimble? Send them into his management – we'll pop the address on our blog for you.

TH: Ah right, I've probably got enough you know, to be honest...

MB: Let's see if we can double his collection with our listeners!

TH: ... great, thanks.

MB: Well thanks for your time today Tom, next up we're going to play Shandy Hand from Horsefly's 1980 album Pigs.

***

SALFORD CITY RADIO

The BIG SHOW with Danny Hassan and studio engineer Beth, 1st April 2011 11am

Shandy Hand plays

DH: And that was Tom Harding from The Horse Flies and he's here next in the studio.

Beth: He's not on the phone yet, I'm dialling now.

DH: Ah he's not here yet. He is a little bit late in so we have another record and that record is Boys Boys Boys from Sinitta. Are you looking for a good time in Salford?

Boys Boys Boys plays

DH: Hello is that Tom Harding from The Horse Flies?

TH: Horsefly.

DH: You're a little bit late so we will need to cut the interview down a little bit, so give me quick answers. Okay?

TH: I've been sat here waiting for you to call…

DH: Stay on the phone please, the song is ending.

TH: Yep.

DH: And that was Sinitta with Boys Boys Boys. Now I'm delighted to welcome Tom Harding into the studio, welcome Tom, you're looking well.

TH: I'm on the phone!

DH: Tom, do you like the summer?

TH: Erm yes I do.

DH: And on holiday do you wear long shorts or budgie smugglers?

TH: Eh?

DH: What kind of shorts do you wear on holiday? You know, round the pool.

TH: I haven't been on that sort of a holiday since I was a kid.

DH: Oh do you prefer a city break? Prague?

TH: Prague's nice, yes.

DH: Thanks for that Tom, and now we have Tom's choice for the next record. Voulez-Vous from Erasure's number one Abba-esque EP.

Voulez-Vous begins to play

TH: What the fuck?

DH: We only have a few records.

TH: Why did you say I chose it?

DH: Do you not like it?

TH: I don't not like it, I wouldn't have chosen it.

DH: Why not?

TH: Of all the songs in all the fucking world I wouldn't have chosen Voulez Fucking Vous being done by Erasure.

DH: No need to swear, what's the problem? Is it Andy Bell?

TH: Is that the end of the interview?

DH: We have a bit of time once the record has finished.

TH: Right, could you ask me about my new record then?

DH: Will do... Back on air three, two, one... Aaaand that was Erasure with Voulez-Vous, originally of course an Abba song. Tell me Tom, who was your favourite Abba babe?

TH: I don't have one.

DH: Oh come on, everybody, everybody has a favourite Abba babe. I like Agnetha of course... God what I wouldn't do with her isn't worth knowing about. Come on Tom, who's your favourite Abba babe? Don't tell me you liked Anni-Frid.

TH: I liked Benny.

DH: Benny?

TH: Yes, I liked Benny.

DH: You can't choose Benny.

TH: Why not?

DH: He wasn't one of the babes.

TH: My new single is out tomorrow. It's called White Blobs… You can get it on iTunes. Thanks, bye.

***

OLDHAM FM

Melanie Gladwell talks to Tom Harding, 1st April 2011 11.45am

MG: And that was Bryan Adams with Melanie C… I love that song, do you love that song? Text in if you do! I now have a very special caller on the line. It says here Tom Harding from 1980s band Horsefly, hello Tom!

TH: Hello.

MG We're very glad to have you on today Tom. Some of our listeners may not have heard of you, and I know I haven't, so would you like to give us all a bit of a background on who you are?

TH: Well, I was in a band in the early 1980s called Horsefly, we did two albums and then I went solo after that and throughout the last three decades I've put out another seven albums under my own name, and I've had two lots of greatest hits out.

MG: Oh great, and what band was that with then?

TH: Under my own name.

MG: Oh great so you're a solo artist now?

TH: Yes, for almost thirty years...

MG: Wonderful, and have you had any successes as a solo artist?

TH: Yeah, well I've sold a lot of records.

MG: Really? How many?

TH: A few million.

MG: Wow! I'm just Googling you here...

TH: Good timing...

MG: Oh yeah it says on your Wiki page that you've had a few albums out.

TH: Yes I have...

MG: That's superb Tom.

TH: Yep...

MG: Ooh I've just seen a picture of you, you were pretty fit way back when... ooh you've aged!

TH: Hmm.

MG: And what's your life been like since Horsefly then?

TH: Well you know, that was thirty years ago, I've been writing and recording for the past thirty years.

MG: Right.

TH: And I have a new record out.

MG: Oh that's good. I'm just still looking at your Facebook page, someone on here really doesn't like you.

TH: No, probably not.

MG: Why's that then?

TH: It's just the internet isn't it. I don't pay any attention.

MG: Oh go on give us the goss.

TH: There is no goss.

MG: Shame, you might be able to get some publicity out of it, you know for your new book.

TH: It's not a book, it's a record.

MG: Well for your new record.

TH: That's not really how I like to do things.

MG: Yeah well times have changed since you last had a record out in the seventies.

TH: I've had seven albums out since the seventies. Nine if you count the greatest hits.

MG: Not that I've read about though.

TH: They've done all right though.

MG: Just all right?

TH: I've sold millions of records.

MG And yet here you are on Oldham FM.

TH: Do you have a copy of the single?

MG Yes, it's here in a white sleeve with your press release.

TH: That's great, would you like to play it?

MG: It hasn't been programmed into the desk, but I'm told we do have a couple of Horsefly tracks programmed in so I'll play one of those. Let's see, Youth Spit or Shandy Hand? You choose.

TH: You know what, don't bother, can I pick a song instead?

MG: All right Tom, if we have it I'll play it for you.

TH: Do you have Voulez-Vous sung by Erasure?

MG: Hang on... We have it sung by Abba, will that do?

TH: Of course you do. Great.

MG: Thanks for coming in today Tom.

TH: I didn't, I'm on the phone, I'm hanging up now.

MG: And next up it's Voulez-Vous from Abba.

Zena Barrie

***

99.4 FM TALK RADIO

Neil Climes with Tom Harding, 1st April 2011 10pm

NC: Hello, you're listening to 99.4 FM Talk Radio and we have Tom on the line. Tom, first time caller?

TH: Hello, erm yes, first time caller.

NC: Great, well welcome, it's nice to hear a new voice on the phone.

TH: Oh right.

NC: What would you like to talk with us about tonight then Tom?

TH: Well I've phoned up to talk about my new single.

NC: Ahh we have a musician on the phone, good stuff, what sort of songs do you play Tom?

TH: Well I play my own stuff.

NC: Aha, a songwriter as well. So do you write your own songs and play them yourself? Guitar?

TH: Yes, I write my own songs and I play them on a guitar.

NC: And is it just you or do you have a band you practise with Tom?

TH: It's just me at the moment.

Your Friend Forever

NC: That's great and does your wife like your music?

TH: Pardon me?

NC: Does your wife enjoy you sitting around singing and playing your guitar all day long?

TH: I don't have a wife.

NC: HAAA *you do* surprise me! So tell me Tom, what are these songs about then? Are they all about being alone?

TH: Erm, well my new single is called White Blobs.

NC: HAAAA White Blobs? *White Blobs?* Tell us about these White Blobs then Tom, this is going to be fun.

TH: Right, well you know when you stare at the sun and—

NC: No I don't know about that Tom, how often do you stare at the sun? Do you wear glasses? Are they dark by any chance?

TH: Well what I mean is—

NC: Yeah go on then. What you mean is?

TH: You know when you look at the sun, just for a second.

NC: I would never do that as I'm not an idiot, but go on.

TH: Well if you look at the sun and then look away from it you get like, these white blobs floating around in front of your eyes.

NC: And have you seen an optician about this? Do you have cataracts?

TH: I don't have cataracts, no.

NC: Go on then, tell us more about these white blobs of yours. We're loving this aren't we listeners? Great to have a new caller.

TH: Well the song's sort of about those blobs.

NC: Ha!

TH: And about how seeing them makes you feel sort of ethereal and like you're on another planet.

NC: Will I be able to pop out to HMV and buy this then?

TH: No, it's on iTunes.

NC: Free I hope?

TH: No, it's not free, it's just 79p though, so much cheaper than a CD single or a seven inch.

NC: And I guess I can delete it straight away and never have to think of it again can't I. After I've heard it.

TH: Well you could delete it if you didn't like it I suppose.

NC: Yeah, I think we can safely say I can live without White Blobs popping up on random play.

TH: Have you heard it?

NC: I haven't yet had that pleasure Tom, perhaps you'd like to play it for us now.

TH: That would be great, do you have the promo CD?

NC: You sent us a promo disc? Ha! Well that will have been filed in the bin I'm afraid, sorry you wasted a stamp. Do you want to play it down the phone for us?

TH: I don't think that would sound very good.

NC: Can you not sing live Tom?

TH: I can, but I don't usually do it down the phone.

NC: Well perhaps you've got a gig coming up and we could all come and see you.

TH: Well I don't have a band together at the moment.

NC: Okay, so maybe an open mic night or something?

TH: Ha, that's funny.

NC: Why's that funny?

TH: Well, you know, I have sold quite a few records.

NC: So you've got some friends then?

TH: I'm going to put the phone down now, you think you're funny, but you're actually not.

NC: Bye Tom, good luck with your blobs, do call in again. What a saddo hey? Now for the news and then we have Martin from Surrey on the line to talk about his psoriasis.

Zena Barrie

***

GARY AND TOM

Telephone conversation, 1st April 2011 10.35pm

Gary: That didn't go too well did it?

Tom: They were fucking rude. Who did you organise that interview with?

Gary: What do you mean?

Tom: Who did you organise that interview with?

Gary: It's Talk Radio mate.

Tom: Yes I know that, but who did you book the interview with? Because they need bollocking, that was too much.

Gary: I didn't book it with anyone, it's Talk Radio, you phone up and you talk.

Tom: Say that again so I'm clear on what I think you're saying.

Gary: It's Talk Radio, you phone up, and you talk.

Tom: So they weren't expecting my call?

Gary: No, you just phone up, and you talk. You should have said who you were.

Tom: So I've just phoned up Talk Radio as a normal caller?

Gary: Yeah. You should have introduced yourself.

Tom: Why, why was this on my list of interviews?

Gary: They have a lot of listeners mate, it's a good way to advertise what you're doing.

Tom: And you don't think... You don't think that it might have been useful to tell me that I was blindly calling Talk Radio?

Gary: Well it says it's fucking Talk Radio on the list, what the fuck do you expect?

Tom: On Talk Radio, they sometimes have interviews, with people, with proper people.

Gary: Oh well if you're too important to just say who you are.

Tom: Are you fucking kidding me?

Gary: Look, it said Talk Radio, the idea is that you phone up and talk. No need to be a knob about it.

Tom: You're fucking terrible at this job, you know that don't you? You're really shit at it.

Gary: I'm shit at it? You're the one who just made a twat of yourself.

Tom: And why's that then? Why did I make a twat of myself?

Gary: Because you didn't say who you are and your song does sound kind of...

Tom: This list... this list... Are there any more on this list that are just Talk Radio? Tell me now and I'll cross them off.

Gary: I think that's the only one, I can't remember.

Tom: Right, that's just fucking fantastic isn't it.

Gary: Stop having a go at me, try and do better on the next one. Maybe try saying who the fuck you are next time. The idea is that we sell some of your pissing records. My mortgage won't just pay itself you know.

Tom: Fucking fucking fucking hell.

***

Sender: maudcampbell@bluemoon.com
Recipient: wiggleitalittlebit@fpl.co.uk

2 April 2011 01:56

Hi Tom,

   It's so late, but I just can't go to bed, I keep listening to your new song. Those singing lessons have really done the trick haven't they? Not that you couldn't sing before, you could, it just sounds much more – singy than you've sounded before. It's just lovely, you sound all sort of grown up as well. I mean, I know your voice broke years ago but maybe there's another time a man's voice breaks and it becomes something else again. Like Rod Stewart (though not so raspy) or Bob Dylan (who can't sing but does have the voice of an old man) or you know, Tom Jones who isn't very cool but he can sing can't he. And he's got a senior voice too.

   The lyrics are really beautiful. It's made me want to look at the sun in the morning to feel it happen, and it's made me want to just go outside more in general. Though not into my garden. The only thing to look at is a broken fence, a mass guinea pig graveyard, some tarpaulin covered in dirty rain water and the washing, which has been rained on at least three times now, it probably needs washing again. I really should try and get a tumble dryer. If I swapped out the washing machine for a washer dryer I could do it. I think it might be life changing. What do you think? I bet you have a tumble dryer don't you. I should just go for it shouldn't I. I best not look at the sun though or I'll send myself blind. Are you going to put a warning label on the album? I suppose you can't put a warning label on an mp3 can you.

I'm still thinking what to do about Colin, how to approach it, it needs to come to a head somehow and I suppose I'm avoiding it.

I have been having some fun with him though. I told him my phone was broken and asked if I could borrow his to text Sarah. He almost shat himself. Also the kids are both out on Friday night at their mates' houses and I said I'd make us a nice dinner and get a bottle of wine in, then I gave him a wink. He just stared at me, like a rabbit in headlights. I could see his brain spinning. I know me doing this doesn't help matters but it's helping me, it's helping me to feel in control of the situation. I wonder if he'd be unfaithful to her with me. He probably would. I'm not going to find out though. That wouldn't make me feel better.

Night. Maud x

***

SARAH AND MAUD

Telephone conversation, 5th April 2011 9.45pm

Maud: Hello?

Sarah: That you Maud?

Maud: Yep, it's me, you okay?

Sarah: No. To be fucking honest. To be fucking honest with you I am not fucking okay.

Maud: Okay, I'm here, I'm here, okay.

Sarah: I know, I fucking love you, you're always fucking here. You're always fucking here.

Maud: Right, first thing, while I'm on the phone, can you get up?

Sarah: Course I can fucking get up who the fuck do you think I am?

Maud: Okay, go into the kitchen for me and get a glass. Okay?

Sarah: I'm getting up, I'm fucking getting up. Oww.

Maud: You okay?

Sarah: Stood on some cunting Lego motherfucking Lego.

Maud: Okay, you're in the kitchen now?

Sarah: Yes, I'm in the kitchen, the cunt's kitchen.

Maud: Yes yes, you're in the cunt's kitchen, have you got a glass?

Sarah: Yep, I've got a glass, I've got a fucking glass from my cunt's kitchen, I've got a cunt's glass.

Maud: Fill the glass with water.

Sarah: I'm filling the glass with cunt's water.

Maud: Okay, have you filled it up?

Sarah: Yuuuurp.

Maud: Now drink all of it.

Sarah: The cunt's water? You want me to drink the cunt's water?

Maud: Yes Sarah, I want you to drink all of the cunt's water right now. Have you drunk it? Sarah? Have you drunk it?

Sarah: Giz a fucking chance.

Maud: Have you drunk it?

Sarah: Yep.

Maud: Okay, fill the glass up again.

Sarah: Filling the glass again.

Maud: Okay, now take this glass with you into the lounge and sit down on the sofa. Okay?

Sarah: Yes sir. Yes sir! I am going into the cunt's lounge with my cunt's water.

Maud: Brilliant, let me know once you've sat down.

Sarah: I'm sat, I'm fucking sat.

Maud: Good, well done, now have a drink of the water.

Sarah: I'm drinking it. Fuck I need a piss.

Maud: Okay, take your glass upstairs and get on the toilet.

Sarah: I'm getting up, I'm getting up, I'm taking you upstairs with me to my cunt's toilet. The toilet that I actually pop my cunt on every day.

Maud: Great, careful going up the stairs.

Sarah: I'm being fucking careful Maud. Fucking careful. Fucking fucking careful.

Maud: Are you still there? Sarah? Sarah are you still there?

Sarah: Just having a shit mate.

Maud: Well, I'm so delighted to be sharing it with you.

Sarah: I fucking love you, you cunt.

Maud: I know you do, I love you too.

Sarah: You know what it is don't you? You know why I fucking do this don't you? That cunt. That old bastard was in the fucking paper. Fucking smiling in the paper.

Maud: He was? Okay, you can tell me about that tomorrow. Have you wiped your arse?

Sarah: Need to put my glass down hang on.

Your Friend Forever

Maud: Are you there? Have you wiped?

Sarah: I'm not a fucking baby I've wiped my cunting arse okay?

Maud: Okay, have you got your water?

Sarah: Got my water.

Maud: Okay, fill it up again, take it through to your bedroom. Pop the water down and get in bed.

Sarah: Getting in bed.

Maud: Have you taken your shoes off?

Sarah: Taking my shoes off.

Maud: Okay love, are you in bed now?

Sarah: In bed, it's because of that cunt, you know that, that cunt.

Maud: I know love, drink some more water.

Sarah: I drunk it all.

Maud: Okay love, put your head down now, I'll speak to you in the morning.

Sarah: Love you you know.

Maud: Love you too, sleep well.

***

Sender: maudcampbell@bluemoon.com
Recipient: wiggleitalittlebit@fpl.co.uk

5 April 2011 22:22

Hi Tom,

I'm feeling so sad.

I spoke on the phone last night with Sarah, we've been friends forever and she's in such a mess, I don't know what to do to help her.

Most of the time she seems really ok and she always gives me good advice about things and she's so funny… We've been through so much together, she's a bit nuts but I wouldn't swap her for the world, not even if Sylvia Plath was begging me to be her best friend, I'd have to say NO, Sarah is my best friend until I die. That's how much she means to me. I would still become friends with Sylvia though and I'm sure I would really value her company and friendship. I think I'd be too shy to show her my poems though.

Anyway sometimes, not very often but sometimes Sarah gets really drunk and starts talking about this man that she had a sort of relationship with when she was a teenager, well it wasn't really a relationship, she was fourteen, I don't know how old he was but I think he's about ninety now, so he must have been about sixty. It was fucked up. And I knew about it, at the time it was going on. It's something that always makes me feel sick when I think about it, that I didn't do anything. We didn't know it was abuse then, I suppose he was a paedophile. Just writing that down makes me feel very uncomfortable. I remember thinking he was too old for her and that it was weird but I didn't tell anyone about it and I should have done. Sarah is so messed up about it. She gets on with her life but she does weird fucked up things sometimes and it must all be because of him. What he did to her. She's not really a creative person so she can't let it out like I would, I'd probably write a hundred shitty poems and then throw them all in the bin or something, I'd find some way of getting it out of my head without breaking myself. She doesn't have any outlets like that, apart from getting drunk or meeting up for mad sex with some married man. None of which helps matters, it makes her sad and guilty and anxious. She doesn't know that she's a brilliant person. I could tell her a thousand times and she'd still never believe it, not really.

It's all come to a head because she's found out that Bryan Crawley, the man that did it, has been awarded an MBE. For all the good work he's done in the community. He used to run the youth club and he's done loads of fundraising and stuff. He was a councillor for a while and a school governor. People think he's fucking great. The youth club building is still there (where it all happened), it's right near where she lives and she has to walk past it every day. It must have been closed down for at least twenty years but no one has ever taken it over so it just looks like it always did. There's still a glass cabinet on the outside of the building with a list of all the different activities you could do inside it. It's all faded but you can still read it. Sarah is sort of drawn to it and repulsed by it at the same time. I know it really does her head in. I think it's made her really weird about relationships and sex. She goes from one extreme to another... and then sometimes she just won't talk at all and just shuts everyone out. She's married but she's been really unfaithful to him, really a lot. I don't think she can help it... it's not out of enjoyment, I'm not sure why it is really, I think it's to do with power. Her needing to feel like she has some. I wish she'd get some proper counselling, I wish she would report him and I wish someone would burn that fucking shitty building down. It's so wrecked it's only fit for demolition.

I also think a lot about, you know, we don't know if there are other people he did things to, he was there for years, it can't just have been Sarah can it? When people abuse power like that, I think they probably do it all the time. He moved in on Sarah so quickly, it wasn't like he spent months building up to it. She thinks he'd done it to other kids. She remembers him being weird with lots of the girls, he was always having one on one sessions with them in his office. It was supposed to be Christian guidance, helping teenagers with any problems they might be having. Christianity is supposed to be about kindness and tolerance isn't it. It shouldn't have been a bad thing. I mean, you can be kind and tolerant without being religious but it shouldn't have been a bad thing.

When I talked to Sarah, she was having a bad night. And it makes me feel very sad because it's never got any better, she will always have bad nights because of him. She will probably still think about it when she's eighty. And now he's all over the local news because he gets to go to Buckingham Palace and meet the Queen and get a fucking medal for being so fucking good.

It makes me feel sick, really sick and guilty, really fucking guilty because I was the one person she told and I knew it didn't sound right and I should have done something about it. I did encourage her to go with me to St John Ambulance instead of the youth club, and she did eventually.

There's not many things I regret in life really, not even marrying Colin because you know without him I wouldn't have Amy and Leo and they are perfect, but the one thing, the one thing I regret and hate myself for is not doing something about Sarah going to that youth club. I should have told her parents. I didn't want her to fall out with me…

She's so fucked up and I don't think she'll ever be happy, not really, she will always have it hanging over her, shrouding her.

I'm sorry for telling you all this but – my poor lovely friend. It makes me very sad. Really very sad indeed.

I need a good sleep. I'm ok though, I'm ok.

Sorry if you've read all this.

Just delete it and ignore me.

xMaud

***

Sender: maudcampbell@bluemoon.com
Recipient: wiggleitalittlebit@fpl.co.uk

7 April 2011 04:00

It's 4am. I can't sleep. I keep thinking about Colin, away somewhere with another woman, he says he's in Belgium, the lorry's gone, but I'm not so sure. I'm thinking about where it went wrong. I was trying to remember the last thing we did as a couple and I can't remember it and that's making me a bit sad and also guilty. I know he's the one having the affair but I'm half of the marriage, it shouldn't all be up to him. I've happily ploughed on. Never doing anything with him. Literally nothing, we do nothing together, ever. I go to all the parents' evenings on my own because whenever I've asked he's just looked at me like he wanted to top himself and I've just rolled my eyes and said fine, forget it. We've not been on holiday since the kids were little. Sex is something that happens rarely, in the dark, quickly without a word. Am I to blame too? I feel like I probably am. I let things slip this far. I haven't made the effort to rescue this. It's him having the affair, but I haven't done anything to stop it and now it's all too far away for us to claw back. I'm going to try not to feel too angry with him. I'm going to try. I'm so tired, I should go to bed. I did before but I got up because it's horrible just lying awake in the dark and your mind starts going at a hundred miles an hour. Do you ever get like that? And then in the morning, if you remember your crazy thoughts, you wonder what the hell you were doing having them. I never trust my mind in the night. Especially when you can so easily get confused between your dream and being awake. I thought I was married to a baby giraffe once and I felt very strange the whole of the next day. I need a good night's sleep so badly but I just can't seem to switch my mind off. Do you ever get like this?

Sleeping is like hoovering up your mind and tidying away all the crap and putting some stuff out for the bin men and then waiting for the bin men to come because you really need that stuff to be gone and then you can wake up and feel less bonkers. I will feel bonkers tomorrow.

I always think Sarah should get more sleep and then she wouldn't feel so nuts all the time. You can't tidy thoughts away on your own. You HAVE to get your brain to do it. It's so clever isn't it?

Night night, I'm going to try and go back to bed.

Love Maud

P.S. I'm sorry if this makes so little sense. It's the middle of the night so I can't be held responsible. I'm not blaming myself for Colin's affair, I'm not making myself the baddy in all this. I'm just trying to acknowledge to myself that it's not entirely his fault, but it mostly is. Sarah would be so cross with me for even thinking any of this could be my fault. I should never have married him to begin with. He's not the one for me. Not that I think there is a one. I think I should be on my own really, for a good long time at least. And then maybe one day, start having gentlemen friends, if I feel like it. Actually, anyone who classed themselves as a gentleman would really irritate me. I like nice manners but I don't need to replace Colin with someone who wears a top hat. I'm rambling. I will go to bed. I don't want to go out with Softy Walter xxx

I feel like painting on the walls.

I'm going to paint on the walls.

Oh, I don't have any paint. Will get some tomorrow.

I think I might be able to sleep now xxxxx

***

Sender: maudcampbell@bluemoon.com
Recipient: wiggleitalittlebit@fpl.co.uk

12 April 2011 19:22

Hi Tom,

I'm shaking I'm so angry. Colin's come back from that long haul job and now he's saying he's going on fucking holiday for ten days. With his mates! He doesn't have any mates. He must be going away with this woman whoever she is, he must be. I mean, he really doesn't have any mates at all. He had a handful when I met him and they've all sort of drifted away. I used to tell him to call them and go out. I never wanted him to be friendless but he just could never be bothered to. That's crap isn't it. You have to make an effort don't you? I don't really know what the point of life is if you don't have friends. No one to share anything with. What would be the point if I ever got a book of poems published, it wouldn't really feel like anything if I didn't have any friends to be pleased for me. The only person he ever goes to see is his Dad and all they do is drink cans of beer and stare at the TV. What is the problem with men?

Do you have friends? I'm sure you do. Everyone should have a couple at least.

Anyway, the point is, the point is – that he is going away with a woman. He's going on holiday with her. It must be serious. I have to stop burying my head in the sand. Another thing. The job he's just done was in Bruges hanging out for a week until his lorry was ready to bring back so he's basically just had a week's holiday on his own (?) in Belgium, and now he wants to go again.

I can't imagine how amazing it would be if I got to go away for a week on my own. I could sit outside pretty cafés and write poems. I can't think of anything I would enjoy more. I never get to do it. The kids are old enough now that it would be fine for me to do it so long as Colin was around to look after them, but he just doesn't. He wouldn't know where to start with them. I might as well be a single parent. It would be easier actually.

Amy just shuts herself in her room when he's home. She thinks he's really lazy and just doesn't seem to like him much, I can't blame her. He's away for so much of the time and then comes back and sort of plonks himself in the middle of us and expects us all to sway to whatever he wants. He never does a scrap of housework, he never fucking sticks anything in the wash. He has no bloody idea what's going on. He never asks about Leo's hospital appointments – sorry sorry, you don't need to know all this. I'm just raging. I'm so bloody angry. I'm pretty sure we'd all be better off without him. Scrap that. We WILL be better off without him. He must be planning to leave us. He must be. He can't think it's ok to have an affair endlessly. Do I need to do something before he does it? Do I let him leave me or do I leave him first? I don't want to leave. I want to stay. I want him to just fuck off.

I'm sorry. But it's just so so good to vent. Ok, I'm going to take a deep breath and get a very large glass of wine and put one of your records on. Let's see if that will help with the red mist. I'm not sure anything will tonight.

x Maud

P.S. Is red mist the right expression for anger? I'm not sure, I think it might be what happens when a bomb goes off and a person's body gets turned into a sort of red mist. That would be horrible wouldn't it. Though I imagine it would be so quick you wouldn't feel it. It would be awful if you could feel it and you were aware of turning into rain. I read once that when people got their heads chopped off in the olden days their eyes and mouths still moved for a while afterwards. Imagine that – seeing your body lying on the chopping block while your head rolled around and there's nothing you can do about it. We're quite lucky really aren't we. Has there ever been a better time to be alive? I mean, I know we've got this stupid bloody government but Nick Clegg is all right isn't he? Sarah thinks him and David Cameron do it with each other. She's thought about it quite a lot. I suppose I have too.

***

COLIN AND DENISE

Text conversation, 12 April 2011 19:32

19:32 Colin: We're on. X

19:32 Denise: Really?! Xxxxxxxxxx

19:33 Colin: Yes really. I can't wait to have a whole ten days with u. X

19:33 Denise: Shall I book the flights now? Xxxxxxxxx

19:36 Colin: Yes book them from Liverpool, I've got a mate that's letting me park the lorry at his work. It's a big industrial estate so it's no bother. X

19:36 Denise:10 days with u, it's like a dream come true. Oh baby how will I ever give u back? Xxxxxxxx

19:42 Colin: All in good time. Let's just think of our 10 days, let's make the most of them. God I can't wait to fuck you again. X

19:42 Denise: I can't wait to have my arms around u, I want to run my fingers through ur bit of hair and smell u. Xxxxxxx

19:51 Colin: I'm going to fuck u so hard x

19:51 Denise: I miss the smell of u so much. What is it u use? I'd like to buy some so I can smell u when ur not here. Xxxxxxxxx

19:52 Colin: Dunno, it's the missus's. Going in the house now so cool it. X

19:56 Denise: Is she making u ur dinner? I hate that you have to put up with her moodiness. It's not fair on u when u work so hard. If you were mine I'd always have a nice meal ready for u. We could sit down together and talk about our days. Xxxxxxxx

19:57 Denise: Are you going to sleep in the same bed as her tonight or the spare room? Please say the spare room. Baby I can't bear you sharing a bed with her. Xxxxxx

19:58 Denise: I get so jealous. It's just because I love you and

I want you here with me. I'd look after you so beautifully. Xxxxxx

19:59 Denise: Please reply to me! When you don't reply I just think you're fucking her over and over again. Xxxxxxx

20:01 Denise: Please Col? Say you've not left me again? Xxxxxxxx

20:07 Colin: Cool it. I've got the kids here. Speak later. X

20:07 Denise: I'm sorry, I'm just crazy about u. I'm gonna leave Jason u know. I want us to be together. I don't care any more. Xxxxxx

20:21 Colin: Book the flights. We can talk on holiday. When you're not bouncing on my cock. X

20:21 Denise: I love u. Xxxxxxxxxxxxxxxxxxxxxxxxxxxxxxx

20:22 Denise: Do u love me too? Xxxx

20:22 Denise: Do u love me too? Xxxxxxx

20:22 Denise: Sorry I know u must be with ur kids. I just hate u being with her. She sounds like a sicko.

20:23 Denise: I hate the way she controls u.

20:23 Denise: I can't believe u married her how could she bully u like that? I would never do that.

20:45 Denise: I'm just watching some telly.

20:53 Denise: What are u doing?

20:54 Denise: I can't stop thinking about u.

20:55 Denise: Hope u luv me like I luv u?????

20:55 Denise: What did u have 4 tea????

20:55 DeniseI miss u. Do u miss me?????

20:55 Denise: Have u left me???? Xxxxxxxx

21:05 Colin: Have u booked the flights?

21:08 Denise: Hi baby, booked them. Can we join the mile high club???? I want 2.

21:09 Colin: Turning my phone off now. Will call u tomorrow.

21:09 Denise: I luv u sleep well dream of me I will dream about u. Xxxxxxxx

***

MAUD AND SARAH

Facebook Messenger conversation, 14 April 2011 10:45

Maud: Hi, are you there?

Sarah: Yeah.

Maud: Oh there you are, you okay?

Sarah: Not bad, Ian is pissing me off. I'm just too fucking tired to argue with him any more.

Maud: Anything in particular or just everything?

Sarah: Everything. He's a knob. Once the kids can make their own sodding toast I'll kick him out.

Maud: I know how you feel. Colin's back from Bruges and has just told me he's going on holiday with some mates for ten days.

Sarah: I didn't think he had any mates.

Maud: Apparently he has now. He's just told me he's going, like me and the kids have fuck all to do with him and he can just do whatever he likes. He takes no responsibility at all for anything. I'm sick of it.

Sarah: Fuck, you seem really angry.

Maud: I am, I really am. I'm certain he's going away with the woman. I don't know who she is, I don't know why she wants to go on holiday with him. But I know that it's happening.

Sarah: Really? You still think that's happening?

Maud: He is, I know he is. I just need to find some proof. There's no way he's not. He's been really weird. I keep looking him in the eye and he's got this weird look about him, like he's being hunted or something. And he's looking me straight back in the eye because he thinks that's what'll make him look less guilty. But he looks guilty as can be.

Sarah: And that's all you've got to go on? You've still not got hold of his phone?

Maud: I know it doesn't sound like much but I just know.

When you know you know. His pockets are always full of half packets of mints. That's new.

Sarah: Mints?

Maud: Yep, mints, and he's always saying he has to pop to the shop for something and I've watched him out of the window and the second he's out the door he's straight on his phone.

Sarah: And what does he come back from the shop with?

Maud: Nothing.

Sarah: That is a bit weird. Don't you ask him what he went for?

Maud: No, it's sort of funnier to just watch him being crap at covering his tracks.

Sarah: If it was me I'd say I needed tampons.

Maud: I thought of that! Although he might start wondering why I'm on my period all the bloody time.

Sarah: Menopause. Just say menopause.

Maud: I'm not there yet.

Sarah: He doesn't know that.

Maud: I wonder who she is. I wonder if she's got kids and where she lives and if I know her.

Sarah: Have you thought about just following him?

Maud: I can't because I'm always looking after the kids.

Sarah: Could you hire someone?

Maud: That would be just nuts, I need to keep my head together. I know it anyway.

Sarah: I know, I believe you. Have you got a plan yet?

Maud: I think I know what I need to do. It's just doing it. I might just need to vent a bit more. If that's okay.

Sarah: Of course, you don't need to ask.

Maud: Okay, I'll try and come over soon.

Sarah: Do it! Just speak to someone first though, before you do anything, okay?

Maud: I will, I will. I know, I've got to be so careful.

Sarah: You do but I think you'll be okay, it's not like he would want custody of the kids is it?

Maud: That's true. He'd have to actually live in Preston and pay some attention.

Sarah: Exactly. You'll be okay, just get some proper advice though because I don't know what I'm talking about.

Maud: Okay I will I will.

Sarah: You'll be okay you know? You're always okay.

Maud: I know. It's just not what I wanted. It's not what I wanted for me and the kids. How did it end up like this? Why is everything so fucking hard all the time?

Sarah: Because life can be shit but at least we don't live in you know Ethiopia in the 80s.

Maud: That's true. I just feel really really tired. I've hardly done anything. It's my brain, tiring me out. I wonder how many calories you burn from thinking hard.

Sarah: I don't know – that is a good question though.

Maud: Could be a new diet?

Sarah: Look, just remember divorce can be an excellent thing, I know it's not what you'd have chosen but fuck it, you only get one fucking life, don't spend it being a miserable cunt.

Maud: I just don't want to mess things up for the kids.

Sarah: Yeah but you know, they'd understand, they're quite big now. Plus they're going to be messed up whatever you do in some way or another. It might just be better in the long run. In fact it definitely will be. You know you don't want to grow old with him, so what the fuck are you waiting for? In fact, ask your lawyer if he'll do you a two-for-one and I'll get rid of Ian too.

Maud: You're kidding?

Sarah: Sort of. I'm fifty per cent joking.

Maud: But you'd never do that.

Sarah: I fucking hope to God I will do it, just not yet. I will though, eventually. There's no fucking way I'm going to grow old with him. I'd much rather grow old with you.

Maud: Okay love, look I'm really tired. Bed for me. I need to sleep some of this off.

Sarah: Let's get together soon, I can drive over, while cunt face is on his hols.

Maud: Yes please. Night love.

Sarah: Love you. And I'm sorry about the other night.

Maud: It's okay, that's what I'm here for.

Sarah: Night love you xxxx

Maud: Night, love xxxx

Sarah: Oh, I meant to ask did you ever use that email address?

Maud: What email address?

Sarah: Tom Harding.

Maud: No, I couldn't think what to say.

Sarah: That's not like you!

Maud: Feck off.

Sarah: Night xxxx

Maud: Night xxxx

***

Sender: maudcampbell@bluemoon.com
Recipient: wiggleitalittlebit@fpl.co.uk

20 April 2011 21:15

Hi Tom,

He's gone, he packed his bag and set off to Spain this morning, clean shaven and drenched in aftershave. We've all breathed a sigh of relief. The light has come back in at the windows. We don't get much light in the house when he's here, mostly because of his sodding truck parked outside, he's left it at some industrial estate. I hope he bloody leaves it there, it doesn't belong on a cul-de-sac. The neighbours must hate us, it goes across three houses. I'm amazed they haven't complained, I would. I must look really unapproachable. Actually come to think of it Amy's asked me a few times if I'm angry when I'm not, I think I must have a naturally angry face. I'm going to go and have a look in the mirror to check.

I had a look, I look a bit angry I suppose, my natural state isn't to smile, but then how many people walk about smiling? And at least I don't have lines round my face from loads of bloody smiling.

I feel very relieved he's gone. Everything is better when he's not here. I've got ten days to sort out everything. This has to be it. I can't have another day of him. I can't have another day of pretending everything is normal. It's not. I'm not sure what to do first. Actually I do know what to do first. A good night's sleep. I need it, I really really need it, at least I'll have the bed to myself and I'm so tired I feel like I will sleep soundly tonight.

Do you ever wake up with the answers to your problems right at the front of your head? I feel like that will happen tomorrow. I love my brain, it's been good to me, it's a very resilient little thing. Once I've got all this mess dealt with I'm going to be really kind to it.

Thanks for being there. I do feel better already. I'm going to be me again.

Maud: x

***

Sender: maudcampbell@bluemoon.com
Recipient: wiggleitalittlebit@fpl.com

22 April 2011 15:22

Hi Tom,

I'm shaking. I've started divorce proceedings. I've hired a solicitor, Sharon Parker, she's an old friend from uni, we've not much in common, she's very proper, but very kind. God I couldn't do a job like that, I wouldn't trust myself. She specialises in family law so she's been really helpful, and she agrees with me that Colin is having an affair. It was quite shocking to hear that from someone else, I don't know why.

Sharon says that all the stuff I told her sounds like completely classic symptoms of an affair. He's pulled away from us as a family, he doesn't engage, he eats separately, often sleeps separately, comes and goes as he pleases, carries his phone everywhere with him. He's just completely disconnected from us. She says it looks too obvious because it is obvious. It's just that simple. Men are that simple. Sorry to generalise about men but you must know what I mean, you must have some male friends and I bet at least eighty-five per cent of them are arseholes. Well hopefully your real friends are the fifteen per cent, the nice men. You know what I mean, I hope.

She told me to stay in the house and not to move out even if we have a big row. He's going to get papers through the post. I haven't even said anything to him yet. She said when he comes back to just give him the papers and get him to go and stay somewhere else.

Oh and I'm changing the locks.

Oh and I went in the little box room where he has all his figures set out and packaged them all up in boxes. I'm going to put them in the loft and pretend I've given them to charity.

I'm going to text him a picture of the empty room and tell him I've given them to the children's hospice.

I know it sounds like a mean joke but he'll get them back eventually, well maybe. I'm going to turn the room into a little study for the kids. I just don't want him coming back here, not even for one night. I've saved him a job with the boxing up.

Do you think I've done the right thing? I suppose it must seem pretty terrible to lock someone out of their home while they're away. I wouldn't like it if he did it to me. It would be horrendous. Oh God.

I know it seems extreme. I just can't do it any longer. I won't ask him for anything. I'm going to cancel the bloody Sky TV now. He hardly ever watches any sport on it anyway. I don't think he even likes sport. I think he just wanted to be able to say we have Sky. I wonder what else there is I can cancel. I'm going to have to go through every bit of paper and try and cut all our outgoings right down, if I'm going to be paying for everything from now on. God my mind is absolutely racing. This must be what it's like to take speed. I've never dabbled with drugs because I always just presumed I'm too nuts to handle anything like that.

It's not too bad though. At least there's only four and a bit years left on the mortgage, it's really small. It's all going to be ok. Sorry I know you don't need all this information. It just helps to write it down and to think about what I need to do. I just have to be very very practical and try not to get too upset about any of it.

I'm going to buy a washer dryer.

Right now.

And get it fitted.

And then Amy and Leo will have lovely hot clean soft towels.

Oh and me too. I need to remember me.

I don't know if I should tell them before or after I've told Colin.

Probably after?

I'll have to get them new keys cut though and tell them not to let their Dad borrow them.

Hmm maybe I should try and sit them down tonight and talk about it.

It's really happening isn't it?

But it won't feel real until Colin knows about it. I feel like I'm playing at it. I will do it though. Maybe I should call him and tell him while he's away so I can avoid having to do that face to face? That's going to stop him in his tracks isn't it? He won't be able to focus on having sex with her if he knows I know.

I suppose if I look at the facts, he's not going to be that upset. He IS having an affair, so he doesn't love me any more and he isn't interested in the kids. Maybe he'll be glad about it. I'm probably doing him a favour, he probably has some vague plan about moving out anyway. He won't be happy about me packing up his figures (and locking him out of the house). I think I have to though, I won't feel safe unless I do that.

I'm going to pack up his bits and bobs from the front room. His bloody dvds and that sort of thing. I will pack it nicely and pop it in the loft. I'm going to put some music on. Not your music, I need something a bit more upbeat to stop me feeling sad, my brain is all over the place up and then down. Betrayed and then I suddenly feel like a winner. I might need a couple of days off work.

xxMaud

**

TOM AND GARY

Telephone conversation, 24th April 2011 2.35pm

Tom: Hi it's Tom.

Gary: Tom hi, good timing, I'm just checking your sales.

Tom: Hit me with it then, how's it going?

Gary: Ninety-three.

Tom: Ninety-three in the singles charts? In the UK charts? That's not as bad as I thought actually, I'm pleased with that.

Gary: No mate, you've sold ninety-three, hang on it's just gone down to ninety-two.

Tom: How can it go down? Can you return an mp3? You can't return an mp3 can you?

Gary: I think you have a tiny window of time where you can say it was a mistake.

Tom: So someone's listened, and then wanted their fucking 79p back?

Gary: They might have just not meant to download it.

Tom: Ninety-two sales. Fuck me.

Gary: It's a start mate, give it a chance to build.

Tom: Build from where? What's next? Have you got anything else lined up?

Gary: Listen mate, I know you said you don't want to but if we can just get a couple of gigs loaded up for you. As soon as possible really then we might be able to pull this back.

Tom: So it's fucking hopeless.

Gary: No mate it's not hopeless, we just need to get you on the road, just a few gigs, small venues.

Tom: I don't even have a band!

Gary: I thought about that and I've actually had a chat with Ed Nailer and he's completely up for it.

Tom: Ed Nailer? You're fucking kidding me! Did you have to dig him up? This is not fucking happening.

Gary: It wouldn't be re-forming, it's just that he's a drummer and he's around at the moment and he could do it.

Tom: Under my name?

Gary: We'd have to have a chat about that. It would be easier to get the venues we want if we use Horsefly. I've also spoken to Warren and he can be available if we give him the dates soon.

Tom: I'm not getting on stage with those cunts. Well Martin was always okay but not the other two.

Gary: Listen mate, it's what people want. Bang out a few old tunes and the band will learn your new stuff. You'll shift some records.

Tom: I can't go on stage with that lot again, you weren't there, you don't know what it was fucking like. I can't do it.

Gary: Well if you're happy to throw your career down the pan for the sake of a few low key gigs.

Tom: Are you saying these are my choices? Gig with them or career down the toilet?

Gary: Pretty much.

Tom: Give me some time and don't speak to anyone else until I've thought about this.

***

GARY AND TOM

Telephone conversation, 25th April 2011 6.45pm

Tom: Hello?

Gary: It's me.

Tom: Brilliant.

Gary: Are you ready for this?

Tom: Ready for what?

Gary: I've got a brilliant idea.

Tom: I thought as much, what is it?

Gary: Two words. Eurovision.

Tom: What's the other word?

Gary: Euro Vision.

Tom: Yep.

Gary: The song contest, the Eurovision song contest.

Tom: Right, and what about it?

Gary: You're a songwriter. Write a fucking song for it. Write them a song!

Tom: You are joking?

Gary: You're always telling me that you're a songwriter.

Tom: I'm not 'always telling you that', but do go on.

Gary: So write a song, it's your job, it's supposedly what you're good at.

Tom: What do you mean, *supposedly*?

Gary: Well it's never been my cup of tea has it, we both know that.

Tom: Great, just great.

Gary: It's a songwriting competition. You are a songwriter or you were when I last checked. Write us a fucking song.

Tom: Sure thing, I'll just pull one out of my arse. What do you want it to be about?

Gary: Make it upbeat, lively, put a key change in there. More keyboard, less guitar.

Tom: Right, well I don't play keyboard but...

Gary: And you should call it Euro Vision, as in *your* vision of Europe.

Tom: And what is my vision of Europe?

Gary: You know, shagging and bikinis, cheap beer, fake tits, ye olde English pubs, that sort of shit.

Tom: Right... Yep... Because Europe is nothing more than a beach is it.

Gary: Just make it fun, and no more than three minutes.

Tom: Right...

Gary: Oh and you need to update your look.

Tom: My look?

Gary: Yeah, can you lose a few pounds and shave off that ginger nest growing out of your chin.

Tom: It's not fucking ginger!

Gary: It's not brown either.

Tom: Fuck you.

Gary: Just hurry up with it so we can enter.

Your Friend Forever

Tom: How are you going to do that? Do you know someone?

Gary: Just through the website, you can upload sound files.

Tom: Oh great... an open competition?

Gary: Yeah, just a demo.

Tom: I'm going to kill myself.

Gary: Write the song first. It could make us millions.

Tom: You're really not joking are you?

Gary: I'm not, no.

Tom: You're a fucking idiot. Just so you know.

Gary: Well you don't want to re-form Horsefly, we're running out of options here.

Tom: And these are my options? Re-forming a band or—

Gary: Or Euro Vision.

Tom: Please get off the phone, I need to think.

***

GARY AND TOM

Telephone conversation, 26th April 2011 9am

Tom: Hello?

Gary: It's me.

Tom: Yep, and what can I help you with? I said I'd call you, remember.

Gary: Look, what are you doing right now?

Tom: I'm watching a rerun of Location Location Location.

Gary: So you're free?

Tom: I'm not free, this is a really good one... it helps me think.

Gary: If you like houses so much why don't you do yours up a bit? It looks like a squat.

Tom: No it fucking doesn't.

Gary: Listen, if I picked you up in say one hour, could you be ready?

Tom: It depends what for really. What is it?

Gary: It's this TV show thingy.

Tom: TV show thingy? What sort of TV show thingy?

Gary: It's singing so make sure your throat's clear. Have a couple of fags and a good cough up before I get you.

Tom: I don't smoke any more.

Gary: Really?

Tom: Yes really.

Gary: Some pop star you are. Look, can you be ready in an hour or not?

Tom: You're being cagey and I'm not an idiot. What do you mean singing TV show thingy?

Gary: It's up to you but probably something that shows off your range a bit more than some of your own songs. Do you know any Aretha?

Tom: Gary, I'm not sure you've noticed, you probably haven't as you are about as dense as a person can be. Are you listening? I cannot really sing very well. I cannot sing Aretha. I can barely sing my own songs. I only get away with it because they are meant to sound rough round the edges, and I'm fine with that.

Gary: I know, it's just that—

Tom: Just that what?

Gary: There is this opportunity for you to sing in front of twelve million viewers on Saturday night prime time.

Tom: Is it The X Factor?

Gary: Yes.

Tom: Why didn't you just tell me?

Gary: I wasn't sure what you thought of it.

Tom: I think it's a pile of shit but I'm not an idiot, I've got a record to promote.

Gary: Great, glad you're being positive for a change, I'll pick you up in an hour.

Tom: I need to prepare. Is it a man or a woman? Do they have an idea of which song they'd like to do? Will I be mentoring or just singing with them?

Gary: Well there's Simon Cowell, Cheryl Cole, and the other two, so men and women.

Tom: No, I mean the contestant that wants to sing with me, male or female? Do we know which song they want to do?

Gary: You've lost me Tom. Can I just get in the car and we'll talk about it on the way?

Tom: No, can you just call the production team and find out a bit about the voice of the contestant so I can choose something suitable? If you don't understand me give me their number and I'll make the call.

Gary: I don't have the producer's number Tom.

Tom: Well, who have you been speaking to?

Gary: I've not been speaking to anyone.

Tom: For fuck's sake. *Who called you and asked me to go on to sing with one of the finalists?*

Gary: No one has asked that.

Tom: Then what the fuck am I doing?

Gary: Auditioning.

Tom: Pardon me?

Gary: Auditioning.

Tom: You want me to… let me get this completely clear in my head. You want me to audition to be on The X Factor?

Gary: Yes, you've a good chance of getting into the over twenty-fives category.

Tom: I'm fucking fifty!

Gary: It's twenty-five and over so you'd still be allowed in that category.

Tom: I've sold twelve million records.

Gary: Exactly.

Tom: You really are a complete moron aren't you? You really are as thick as I tell everyone you are, aren't you?

Gary: If you do the audition, they are bound to give you five minutes of back story. That's *free advertising* for your new album. You can't buy advertising like that.

Tom: It wouldn't be an advert though would it? It would be me looking like a desperate sad sack. Which I'm not. You clearly think I am. But I can assure you, please get it into your thick skull, I am not some sad desperate old has-been.

Gary: I've had a brainwave.

Tom: Really? So you do have a brain.

Gary: I audition and you come along as my friend. That way, you get to promote your album and I get to look at Cheryl Cole's knockers.

Tom: Fuck off fuck off fuck off fuck off fuck off.

Gary: Oh go on it's a day out isn't it?

Tom: I don't want a fucking day out with you stood in a queue of ten thousand kids murdering power ballads.

Gary: Okay, well I'll see when the auditions for Britain's Got Talent are on.

Tom: What for?

Gary: Maybe we could do that instead.

Tom: 'We' are not ever doing anything. Please God do some proper fucking work for me. PROPER WORK. NOT FUCKING TALENT SHOW AUDITIONS. NOT FUCKING EUROVISION. PROPER WORK.

Gary: So ungrateful.

Tom: I'm putting the phone down. Don't call me again today.

***

TOM AND GARY

Telephone conversation, 27th April 2011 9.45pm

Gary: Word up.

Tom: For fuck's sake… don't answer the phone like that… It's me.

Gary: And?

Tom: I'll do it. Horsefly. No more than ten dates though. No more than one thousand capacity. Then it's done, it's over, never again, and at least fifty per cent of the set has to be from my new album.

Gary: So long as you do Shandy Hand as the encore I couldn't give a fuck about the set list.

Tom: Well that's just lovely to hear. Thanks for caring, thanks for being so invested.

Gary: I'll get you all in a room asap.

Tom: And I don't want to hear another word about fucking X Factor or Eurovision or anything. Have you got that?

Gary: All right all right, but you make it very difficult for me to manage you.

Tom: You make it difficult for me not to rip my own head off.

Gary: Fine, fine. I'm on it.

***

GARY AND THE EVENING STANDARD

Telephone conversation, 28th April 2011 9.45am

Voice: Hello London Evening Standard, how may I help you?

Gary: Hi, can I speak to someone on the news desk please?

Voice: Anyone in particular?

Gary: I have a BIG story, a music story.

Voice: I'll put you through to Helen Smart, please hold the line.

Helen: Helen Smart speaking, how can I help you?

Gary: Hi, this is Gary Barnes, Chief Exec of Gary Barnes Management PLC.

Helen: And?

Gary: I have a BIG music story for you.

Helen: What's the story?

Gary: Let's talk about my fee first.

Helen: What's the story?

Gary: I'll give you the scoop for two grand or one grand for cash.

Helen: It doesn't work like that. What's your story?

Gary: Are you going to pay me anything?

Helen: Do you work here? Are you a reporter?

Gary: No.

Helen: Well then no.

Gary: Fuck you then, I'll phone someone who's interested in the biggest music scoop of this decade.

Helen: Go for it, best of luck.

Gary: I will do.

Helen: Bye then.

Gary: Shall I just tell you?

Helen: If you must.

Gary: Horsefly are getting back together, they're doing a tour. Dates coming out soon.

Helen: Original line-up?

Gary: Yep.

Helen: And you know this because?

Gary: I'm their manager.

Helen: Poor buggers... Okay, well if I can find space I'll stick it in somewhere.

Gary: Will I get paid for that?

Helen: Again, no.

**

Sender: maudcampbell@bluemoon.com
Recipient: wiggleitalittlebit@fpl.co.uk

28 April 2011 11:15

Hi Tom,

I'm sorry for writing all this to you. I just need to tell someone and I feel like you understand, I'm not sure why, but I feel you do. Feel free not to read any of it. You probably just delete my emails anyway, or maybe they go into your spam. I just need for someone to know, well you don't even need to know, I just need to tell, it helps me to process things. I can and I will tell Sarah but she's going to be so angry and upset about it that I'm not quite ready to do that. I don't want to manage her feelings while I can barely manage my own.

I did what Sharon (my solicitor) suggested and looked for evidence of an affair. I thought I might need a detective, she laughed and told me to just have a good poke around. It turned out to be so easy. I took me less than five minutes. I just logged into his email on the laptop, his password was saved. I searched in his email for his phone bill and that came up straight away and then I just opened it up and there are hundreds of texts to this same number. Sometimes fifty to sixty texts in one day, and lots of long late night phone calls, lots of phone calls from abroad and that wasn't him calling the kids because he never bothers calling us when he's away.

I downloaded the bill and just emailed it straight over to Sharon my solicitor. Then I called the number that comes up all the time from the landline, I did 141 first so she wouldn't be able to trace it. I don't want him to know I'm on to him until I'm ready. A woman answered, I just said 'Hi is that Alex?' She said 'No, it's Denise.' I said 'Sorry wrong number' and hung up. Denise. 'Denise'. She sounds rough doesn't she? She sounded rough. She has a smoker's voice. A northern smoker's voice. I think she might be older than me. Denise isn't very modern is it? I mean neither is Maud but I'm named after an old aunt of my Dad's.

This isn't very feminist of me. It's not her fault. It's not her fault. It's his. But still. It's easier to hate someone you don't know than to hate someone you love. Than to hate your children's father. It's a difficult thing. Because they look like him, so there's so much love tied up in my feelings about him. Denise might not even know about me and the kids. Men can just lie and lie and lie can't they? Who knows what he's told her? She won't really know about us, she won't know our history. She won't know about how we loved each other.

Sorry, but men are fucking lying shitbags aren't they? Not all... but most of them. Fucking hell (sorry for swearing and sorry for the generalisations) but they really are. The stories my friends tell me. You wouldn't believe half of the awful things that have been done to just my small group of friends. It's absolutely outrageous what they get away with. And there's some sort of conspiracy of silence around their bad behaviour. For some reason we're supposed to keep quiet about it. Or take the blame for it. Sarah blames herself for so many shit things that men have done to her. And we keep quiet because we think we're to blame or that it reflects on us. I don't want people to think I'm the sort of woman that has a husband that has an affair because it must mean I'm a shit wife. I'm not. I'm a good person and I don't deserve to have been treated this way. It's such a cliché. I just can't really believe it. I'm not so upset, it's more anger I think, anger and also relief. I don't have to have a difficult conversation with him and tell him I don't think we should be together any more and it's over. He's already finished it. He's already moved on, he just didn't bother to tell me. I'm not the shit person in this scenario. Do you know what I mean? Can you understand why that's a relief?

I suppose I should try and find out how long it's been going on for, look for more stuff, but I feel a bit sick. Maybe knowing is enough. Maybe I don't need to know all the details. What a cunt. (Actually why should he get to be a cunt? What is wrong with a cunt? Nothing.) God I'm so angry. I need to work out what to do now, I don't want to wait until he's home, I hate confrontation. Maybe I'll just text him, he's clearly a fan of texts. This other woman, God help her if she thinks he's a catch.

Ok, I'm going to do it, I'm going to end our marriage. I'm going to make a cup of tea and end our marriage.

Are you going to watch the royal wedding? I'm not really interested but it's hard to completely ignore isn't it? There's a few street parties happening round here, we're not going to any. I'm not a royalist but it was sad for the two boys when Diana died, she was their mother after all, even though she seemed to spend a lot of time away from them on yachts getting her toes sucked, or was that the other one? I can't understand all the people that come here from America to wave flags. Why would you get obsessed with the royal family from another country? It's such a strange thing to do.

Fuck the cup of tea, it's only early but I'm having a glass of wine. Sometimes, needs must.

It's such a weird feeling knowing that I was right about the affair. I knew, but now I have evidence. I feel like my mind was on a long leash and has now sprung back into my head. I'm so completely on my own now. Before I was part of a team, a rubbish team but part of a team. Now I'm just completely back in my own head. Having to think and make decisions. It's so strange. I didn't realise how much being married changed how I felt. I feel like a wild dog now that's being chased. I hope my brain calms down. I can do this. I'm not fourteen. It will be ok. At least he's not here, I don't like confrontation, I'm just not good at it. Some women are good at rows. I never think of come backs quickly enough. If Denise was here I'd probably accidentally offer her a cup of tea and say something derogatory about myself to try and make her feel better.

You should see the text Sarah has just sent me about David Cameron and Nick Clegg. It's absolutely filthy and I'm not sure it's even physically possible. Have you heard of a three-way wheelbarrow? I'm too scared to Google it. Anyway apparently in her head it's happened in the rose gardens at the back of 10 Downing Street near the plinth after a press conference got them all hot under the collar. I suppose when you work at their level there must be a lot of adrenaline pumping around your body so I suppose anything is possible. I'm glad Sarah's taken an interest in politics finally. I would like to see her taking more of an interest in the Labour politicians though. Although I can't imagine Ed Miliband and Ed Balls doing a three-way wheelbarrow. I think they'd be quite tender with each other. Not that I've really noticed a frisson between them. It's different with public school boys isn't it. And prisoners.

Wish me luck
Love and thanks
Maud: x

***

MAUD AND COLIN

Text conversation, 28 April 2011 13:20

Maud: Hello, I know you've been having an affair with a woman called Denise. When you come back from Spain you'll need to find your own place to stay.

Maud: Let me know when you have an address and I will send divorce papers there. Try and find somewhere nearby so the kids can see you. I'm going to speak to them tonight.

Maud: I am going to tell them we have separated because we've grown apart. I'm not going to tell them about the affair. I don't want them to hate you.

Maud: I can't believe you would do this to me. I deserve some honesty from you. You should be ashamed of yourself. Why couldn't you just tell me you'd met someone else? You think it's better to lie? To me? Your wife? Your partner? The person you live with? The mother of your children? You didn't think I deserved one tiny little bit of respect? You've treated me with contempt. Like I am your worst enemy. I have been sharing my bed with someone that views me as the enemy.

Colin: All I can say is I'm sorry. I don't know what else to say.

Maud: I'm dropping all your figures off in the morning, half at the hospice and half at the Sure Start Centre.

Colin: Please don't drop off the Futurama figures. They're worth a lot of money but only if they are still in their boxes. Can you leave it for me to sort out?

Maud: Too late. I've already sorted them all out, they're in my car ready to go first thing tomorrow.

Colin: Please don't do that. I've spent years collecting them. They're worth a lot of money.

Maud: I've spent years being married. I've dedicated a lot of time to it.

Colin: Look I'm sorry.

Maud: You said.

Colin: Well, there's not much point in me coming back. I'm going to stay out here in Spain with Denise.

Maud: How long for? What about the kids?

Colin: They can visit or I can visit. I can get work here.

Maud: Send me your address when you have one. My solicitor will be in touch.

Colin: I will, I'm sorry. I'll come and collect my things in a few weeks. When you've calmed down.

Maud: I am calm, I thought I wouldn't be but I am.

Colin: I'm sorry Maud.

Maud: I wish I believed that. I don't think you are.

Colin: I am sorry. I fucked up.

Maud: But you didn't. If you thought you'd fucked up you'd be coming home to try and sort it out but you're not. So you haven't fucked up, you've done exactly what you wanted to do. You stay in Spain with your girlfriend. I'll carry on working and looking after the kids. You didn't fuck up. You're a fucking baby who's walked away from his family.

Colin: There's no need for name calling.

Maud: Oh right, I'm the baddy now. You were sorry for all of 3 seconds. Well fuck you. And fuck fucking Denise.

Colin: There's no need for that. She's done nothing wrong.

Maud: Did she know you were married? Does she know you have children?

Colin: Yes she knows. She likes kids and thinks you sound really interesting actually.

Maud: Oh does she? Well that's just great. I'm sure we'll end up being best mates.

Colin: I'd like that.

Maud: Fucking hell you're actually stupid aren't you? It's just occurred to me. Jesus. Right. Bye. Stop texting. Go away.

***

Sender: maudcampbell@bluemoon.com
Recipient: wiggleitalittlebit@fpl.co.uk

29 April 2011 14:35

Dear Tom,

Something really upsetting and awful has happened. I'm at the hospital. Sarah took an overdose. She is going to be ok though. That fucking man. Bryan Crawley that abused Sarah at the youth club was on the front of the Gazette being awarded his MBE. He's really fat and almost entirely bald but still has this bit of hair at the back in a ponytail. Ian, Sarah's husband, called me from the hospital. He knows a bit about it but I don't know how much he knows. He's gone home to look after the kids, the neighbour had been watching them. I'm not allowed to see her at the moment but I'm just in the waiting room, I'm so upset. I want to do something about it but it's not up to me to do it. I think it has to be Sarah. I want to kill him. If I saw him right now I think I would. I would actually just attack him. I keep imagining holding him down and ripping his hair out and smashing his face into a pavement. Over and over again until he has no face left.

It's all too sad. He's getting all this praise for his work with kids. He did youth club, and Sunday school and was a school governor too. I just feel sick about it. If I tell someone though they might want to speak to Sarah about it and she doesn't feel she can. But she's so sad it's made her want to die. I don't know what to do. I'm going to get a cup of tea and call Amy and Leo. I've left them both at home, they said they were fine. I know they will be. I'm so lucky with them. Leo looked really worried, he loves his Auntie Sarah. He thinks she's nuts but he really loves her. I didn't tell them what had happened, just that she was in hospital. Right I'd better go. I don't want my battery to run out.

xMaud

***

Sender: maudcampbell@bluemoon.com
Recipient: wiggleitalittlebit@fpl.co.uk

30 April 2011 16:45

Hi Tom,

I was just about to set off to the hospital to sit with Sarah and the Evening News got pushed through the door. 'School governor accused of indecent assault'.

It's him. A woman has come forward. Not Sarah, someone else. They haven't given her name.

Do I show it to Sarah? Will it make things better or worse? I don't want to make her more ill, but then she will find out when she comes out of hospital anyway, there's no way she won't. They are keeping her in at the moment to check her liver function.

Ok, let me think.

She will find out anyway, it could send her under.

Better she hears it from me.

In hospital.

Where she can't hurt herself.

Ok, I'm going to go to the hospital now.

I hope you're ok, I read something online about a Horsefly reunion. I presume that can't possibly be true?

Ok, I am going.

Thanks

xMaud

May 2011

Sender: maudcampbell@bluemoon.com
Recipient: wiggleitalittlebit@fpl.co.uk
1 May 2011 01.19

Hi Tom,
   It's very late. I've been backwards and forwards to the hospital all day.
   I took Sarah the paper and when I got there she was sat up and having a cup of tea. I just sat beside her and handed it to her. She just stared at it for ages and I could see she was shaking and her eyes were brimming with tears. She read all of it and the tears fell out of her eyes and rolled down her cheeks but she wasn't crying, it was more of a leakage than a cry. She just said 'Can I use your phone, mine's run out.' I passed it to her and she said could she have a few minutes on her own. I tucked her in a bit and then pulled the curtain round her and went back out to the waiting room for a few minutes. I didn't really know how long to leave her so I gave her about ten minutes and then went back in. She called the reporter at the Evening News and spoke to her and told her what happened to her and she's going to meet Sarah tomorrow. She's going

to the hospital to interview her. I asked her if she wants me to be there but she said no, she said it would be too hard to say it in front of someone that loves her. She said I'd get too upset and it would make it harder. I understand it. She said she just called up and asked to speak to the woman who had written the article. She said she felt like she was on automatic pilot. Like her brain had had this all planned out ages ago but she just needed something to happen before she could do it. She says she thinks there will be more people that come forward about him. It's amazing isn't it? How your subconscious mind can know things before your conscious mind does. It's like your brain protects you until you're ready to face up to things. The reporter is called Gina and she's said she'll bring Sarah a meal deal from Boots which is really kind of her. Sarah told her she doesn't want 'fucking apple slices' as her pudding. It's good. It means she's feeling better. She's going to be able to go home soon. Her liver is functioning ok, she's been lucky. She could have really killed herself or made herself so ill she would never get better. I just don't know what I'd do without her. I can't think about it without crying.

She seemed so much brighter after she'd spoken to Gina. She was really animated. Still shaking quite a lot but animated, energised (she was probably full of adrenaline). I think there could be difficult times ahead but it's a positive thing. There is a crime number. She will have to speak to the police. Bryan Crawley is under investigation and his reputation is ruined. I'm so glad this has happened before he died. It would be awful not having the chance to get some sort of justice. Well there will never be real justice but it will be good to see his name dragged through the mud.

It will be a shame for his wife but then you never know how much she knew. I think if you were married to an abuser for many years you'd have some inkling about it. Maybe not, but I think you might have an idea about them. I don't know, what do you think? Do you think you'd know? I think my subconscious would know and I would hope it would tell me.

I should really go to bed but my head is spinning, I am very tired though.

Maybe I'll sleep. Maybe.

This has put my problems with Colin into perspective and also sort of on the back burner. He's decided to stay in Spain and I'm relieved. It's going to be a strange time for both of us. I still need to tell the kids but I'm not too worried. Sarah's problems have dwarfed mine. It's all fine, it's all manageable, I feel hopeful.

I Googled three-way wheelbarrow because I really wanted to know what it is and it just came up with an advert for Homebase. So it must be something that only happens in Sarah's dreams.

Lots of love, Maud x

***

GARY AND TOM

Telephone conversation, 1st May 2011 2.30pm

Tom: Hello?

Gary: It's me.

Tom: What do you want?

Gary: Why don't you ever get invited to the BRIT Awards?

Tom: You what?

Gary: Or the Moby Awards or the Ivor Novellos or the fucking BAFTAs. You never get invited.

Tom: I'm not interested in going to them.

Gary: Yeah but I am.

Tom: And?

Gary: Will you get me an invite?

Tom: To what?

Gary: Any of them.

Tom: As my manager, it's your job to sort out that sort of shit, have you got no contacts with anyone?

Gary: Not with the fucking BRIT Awards.

Tom: Well you know it shouldn't be that hard, you're my manager, I'm a Brit, I've been in the industry for over thirty years, it wouldn't be that hard to get a pair of fucking tickets. Use your head.

Gary: So who do you think I should email?

Tom: I don't know. But there's this thing called Google which knows fucking everything. It probably knows when I last had a dump so you can probably find out who's in charge of the guest list for the BRIT Awards.

Gary: Right.

Tom: Is that all you wanted?

Gary: Hang on, I'm writing that down.

Tom: Writing what down? I told you to Google it.

Gary: The bit about you being a Brit and being in the industry for thirty years, that's a long time isn't it?

Tom: Are you fucking kidding me? Do you even know my name? Do you know any of my music? I bet you've not even got all my records, have you?

Gary: Samantha has, she loves you.

Tom: Thank fuck for Samantha, I should be paying her though really.

Gary: For what?

Tom: If I ever want anything done, she does it. It's not you. Don't think I haven't noticed it.

Gary: She's my assistant.

Tom: Does she get paid?

Gary: She's my wife!

Tom: Yeah, but does she get paid?

Gary: For helping me? That's what wives do.

Tom: And do you help her with her work?

Gary: No, she's in publishing isn't she, what do I know about books?

Tom: What do you know about fucking anything?

Gary: Do I say the same thing for the Moby Awards?

Tom: Is Moby doing awards now? Cos he's not been around for a while.

Gary: Not Moby that did that song, the Moby Awards.

Tom: I've never heard of Moby doing awards, I will Google it, you should too.

Gary: I will.

Tom: Anything else I can help you with this evening Gary?

Gary: Have you been practising?

Tom: I have played my guitar every single day since I first got one when I was twelve. Is that enough practice for you?

Gary: So you can play well then?

Tom: Just get off the phone.

Gary: Okay okay, Warren and Ed and Martin can meet Wednesday for the Horsefly chat, is that okay for you?

Tom: Cannot fucking wait.

Gary: That's the spirit.

***

Your Friend Forever

GARY AND TOM

Telephone conversation, 1st May 2011 3.15pm

Tom: Hello?

Gary: It's just me.

Tom: What now?

Gary: I've looked into the BAFTAs and you have to become a member to get invited to anything, it's £230 a year. Can I put you down for a membership?

Tom: If you want to pay for it you can.

Gary: Well, I can pay for it upfront. It would have to come out of your money though, you'd be the member, I'd just use your invite.

Tom: Well no in that case, I'm not interested. Why don't *you* become a member?

Gary: It's £230 a year!

Tom: Okay great, so we're neither of us joining then. Is that all you wanted?

Gary: Can I enter one of your songs in for the Ivor Novellos?

Tom: How much?

Gary: £66.

Tom: No thanks.

Gary: I won't get invited to the awards unless we enter something... go on, you must have one decent one.

Tom: One decent one?

Gary: Yeah.

Tom: You think I must have 'one decent' song?

Gary: Yeah you must have.

Tom: Can you think of any?

Gary: No... but there must be one.

Tom: I'll leave you to ponder it.

Gary: Yes right, okay. I'll ask Samantha.

Tom: You do that... but if you do find a song you like, under no circumstances are you to approach the Ivor Novello people. They will think you are a village idiot and that will make them think that I am a village idiot.

Gary: Some fucking pop star you are.

Tom: I'm a musician. A *musician* not a pop star.

Gary: Don't get yer knickers in a twist.

Tom: Is that all you wanted?

Gary: Yeah I suppose so. Do you know any up and coming bands I could manage? I could do with earning a bit more.

Tom: I'm putting the phone down now.

Your Friend Forever

GARY BARNES'S OFFICE

**Horsefly reunion, 5th May 2011 2pm
Tom, Gary, Ed, Warren and Martin present**

Gary: Okay, so you lot aren't saying anything?

That's cool, that's cool, I get it. That's super cool.

The fact is, you are all here, sat in this room, legends of a sort, but only when you're together.

On your own you're nothing.

You want money.

I'm going to help you make it.

Then you can all fuck off again… except Tom.

Any questions so far?

First things first. Let me just get Samantha's notes, she's made me a list.

Right, here we go. Make yourselves available October to mid-December. You all got that?

Good, Samantha is going to book a ten-date mid-scale tour eight hundred to a thousand capacity.

Any questions?

I want you all to get fit, get healthy, you look a mess, you too Tom.

Get yourselves to the gym.

NOBODY and I mean NOBODY wants to see fat bald ugly men in skinny jeans holding a guitar.

The photo shoot is booked for the end of May, this gives you fuck all time. You cannot come back in this office looking like you do now for the photo shoot. We'll replace you. Nod if you are still listening.

I presume you all still want to get laid? Think of your gym memberships as a pussy pass.

Got it? Just nod. Ed, get that ponytail cut off. No one wants to see that.

Samantha has booked a rehearsal room for the whole of September.

You will be there every day from 10am until 10pm. You will not get drunk and disappear at lunchtime. You will not take drugs. If you do, you will be replaced. Are you all still with me?

Good.

Now I've seen some hazy footage from your last tour. It was shit. You got away with it but it was shit, you know that don't you? You can't get away with that any more. We need you to look good, we need you to be able to play. You're all going to have to get in the attic, blow the dust off your instruments and remember how to play them. This happens before September.

Any questions so far?

Tom, we need talking between songs, we need personality, we

need pit walks, we need high fives with the crowd, we need some decent outfits, you can't just play your songs and then fuck straight off, it's not enough.

Do you understand?

I saw some guy on YouTube running over his crowd in a blow up plastic bubble, Samantha's going to look into getting you one of them.

Any questions?

I'm going to email you all these details as well as logins for your Facebook page and your Twitter account. You all need to start tweeting. You have about four thousand followers just from existing. It's a good start but you need to start tweeting, teasing your old fans, hint at a gig, hint at a meet up, hint at making friends again. *Hint* but don't announce. For God's sake don't post any pictures of what you look like now.

We're not ready for that, no one is ready for that and no one wants to see that. I want to see you with at least 10k followers by the end of this week and 20k by the next, we've got a lot of tickets to sell and you need to do some of the leg work.

Comprende?

Samantha will email you all these notes later today. If any of you set a foot out of place you're out.

Now come on, there must be a question, somebody speak for fuck's sake.

Ed: I've written this song called Major Vadge, it sort of goes to the tune of Major Tom, can we stick that in the set?

Tom: Can I go now?

Gary: Any questions just email me wiggleitalittlebit@fpl.co.uk, oh and I want merch ideas, unusual merch ideas. Remember bands don't sell records any more. They go on tour, they sell shit. Think of some shit we can sell. Look out for the email and I'll see you chatty fuckers next month.

***

GARY AND TOM

Telephone conversation, 9th May 2011 11.05am

Tom: I didn't offer to send the girl at Metro a picture of my cock!

Gary: I know that, but nobody else does.

Tom: How do you know that?

Gary: We used to have a bet that you don't even have a cock. Samantha used to say you're completely asexual.

Tom: Can we sue them? I would never *never* speak to anyone like that. The interview wasn't great but I would never *never* speak to someone like that!

Gary: Mate it's not worth it, it's your word against hers and before you know it you're looking at a prison sentence.

Tom: Prison? What the fuck for? I've not done anything!!!

Gary: Indecent exposure, paedophilia… anything really…

Tom: What the fuck are you on about?

Gary: I'm just saying, even if you've not done it, it's your word against hers.

Tom: What the FUCK ARE YOU SAYING? I haven't met her. I spoke to her on the phone for less than a minute. How can that make me a paedophile? How old is she? She's not a child is she? She's a music journalist.

Gary: I'm not saying anything mate, I'm just saying it's not worth pursuing… and if you did (and I'm not saying you did) but if you did happen to have sent her a picture of Little Tom, you don't want it going any further do you?

Tom: But I haven't sent her a picture of anything!

Gary: But it's your word against hers and she's the one with a proper job.

Tom: I've got a proper job!

Gary: Well some won't see it that way.

Tom: Oh fucking hell… all I did was hang up on her.

Gary: Did you send her a little picture? Of your cock?

Tom: NO! I've never sent anyone a picture of my cock. Why would I?

Gary: Really?

Tom: Why would I do that?

Gary: You mean to say you've never sent anyone a picture of Tiny Tommy?

Tom: Again… why would I do that? Who would want to see it?

Gary: Why? Is there something wrong with it? Is it horrible?

Tom: There's nothing wrong with it, I just don't think anyone needs to have it hanging on their wall.

Gary: Dude you need to get with the programme.

Tom: What?

Gary: That's what *everyone* does now.

Tom: You mean you?

Gary: Women expect it.

Tom: I'm sure you're wrong about that.

Gary: You're very stuffy for a pop star.

Tom: I'm a MUSICIAN.

Gary: Don't shout at me, I didn't get you into this mess. Look, what you have to realise is she could use a picture of anyone's cock and say it was yours.

Tom: But it wouldn't be true… and why would she?

Gary: Listen, I can make a few phone calls if you like. If this is all going to come out we can make sure you're at least really well hung. We can get someone in and take some decent pictures.

Tom: What the FUCKKKK?

Gary: Calm down, I've got it under control. I'll get Samantha to ring round some porno agencies to see who's got the biggest. We'll get some snaps done, nice and tasteful, Photoshop them onto your body and send *them* to the Metro. Does that solve your problem?

Tom: NO NO NO NO NO NO NO NO NO FUCKING HELL NO. ARE YOU KIDDING NO NO NO NO NO.

Gary: Mate, I'm trying to problem-solve here.

Tom: I haven't done anything.

Gary: Do you want Tiny Tom all over the papers?

Tom: My cock isn't tiny!

Gary: Are you sure of that Tom? Are you really sure of that? Compared it to anyone else's recently have you Tom? I just hope you're completely sure because if you're not *everyone* will know. If you've never sent anyone a picture of it, how would you know if it's tiny or not?

Tom: I haven't got a tiny cock. I don't want a cock double. Don't do anything. I haven't done anything. Fucking hell.

Gary: Your choice Tom, you're the boss mate, you're the boss… Tom? Are you there Tom? Tom?

***

Sender: maudcampbell@bluemoon.com
Recipient: wiggleitalittlebit@fpl.com

11 May 2011 18:45

Dear Tom,

I can't quite believe it. I'm sat here with a letter that says I've been made redundant. Well, I applied for voluntary redundancy but didn't think I'd get it because I've been here for so long, I thought they wouldn't want to pay out to me. But there's so many cuts happening, in every office. Almost everyone that asked for it has got it. There'll be no one left. But it won't be my problem, someone else will have to worry about it. I can just go in, sign the papers and go. I don't need to give notice. They want me out as soon as possible. I can just take my mug and leave. Or maybe I'll leave my mug there. I'm not sure if it's something I'll want to look back on and smile at or not. Have you ever left anywhere? Did you take your mug? I don't want it to become something that I hate because it reminds me of terrible things. Well it's not the worst job in the world but it is so incredibly dull. It would be weird to leave my mug though. I suppose once you've owned an object for a long time it feels like it's part of you. Maybe it will just break before my last day and I won't have to think about it. It's nice and big though. (And yellow with a smiley face on it.) When I have a cup of tea I want a LOT of tea. Not just a small amount of lukewarm tea.

An actual bucket of tea would suit me best. I wonder if there's a competition for downing yards of hot tea? I bet I'd be quite good at that, so long as the tea was just the right temperature. I suppose these are things I can find out about once I've left my job. Oh my God. I can get up on Monday morning, put on a pair of jeans and then walk into work in my own time. Get my mug, sign the papers and then walk home again. In my own time! I could go to the library, I could go to Preston Art Gallery. I could go and see Michael and have a fancy coffee. Maybe Michael could give me a couple of shifts a week so my money doesn't just disappear really quickly. I am so excited!

I feel like I've won the lottery. They're paying me nearly £17,000. Oh my God. This could not have come at a better time. My hands are shaking. I need to sign the form and get it back to them before it dissolves or I wake up.

I can make some actual choices about what I want to do with myself. I can have a rest. I can take the kids away. Choices, I've never really had many before, at least I don't feel like I have. I'm so happy. I didn't have to hand my notice in. I just get to leave. Things are going right for me.

I'm going to have a drink. I can't stop shaking.

Love

Maud. Redundant Divorcée. (Exciting.)

Oh by the way, I saw that terrible story in the Metro about you know what (sending a picture of your penis to the work experience girl).

I don't believe it for a second. I mean, I believe she got sent a picture that she thinks is from you but I know it wouldn't have been you. Does someone else have access to your phone? Someone cleverer than me should be able to find out quite a bit of information from the photo, you will be exonerated I'm certain.

I know you wouldn't do that. If you ever need someone to talk to my number's at the bottom of the email. You can use it any time.

I'm a friend and I'm always here to help. I'm sorry you are

having a horrible time. It WILL pass. Your graphic images will be tomorrow's chip wrappers. Not that I think you sent any images and not that you're allowed to wrap chips in newspaper any more. Also if you worked in a chip shop I like to think you'd avoid putting a picture of a penis next to someone's battered sausage. I'd certainly remove page three because really, I think it would be disrespectful to the model to eat mushy peas or curry sauce off her breasts without her express permission.

I can't believe I've been made redundant. Maybe I'll sign up to a creative writing class! In fact, I definitely will. Oh gosh, I'm SO excited! Oh and Sarah's back home now. She's busy as a bee and really cheerful whenever I speak to her. I wish I could bottle this.

Sorry, I know you're having an awful time. I'd like it if you and I and Sarah were all happy at the same time. That would be wonderful.

Things will get better for you soon, I know it.

xMaud

***

HORSEFLY

@HorseFlyHQ, Joined May 2011
The latest tweets from HorseFly HQ

Tweets from the band
HorseFly news coming soon
#Shandyhand #Reunion #80's #WhenWeWereYoung
#TomHarding #fuckaghost #NailedbyNailer

Tweets 82 Following 140 Followers 3987

HorseFly@HorseFlyHQ 34m
Is this fucking working?

HorseFly@HorseFlyHQ 37m
You're a sexy little bitch aren't you? Where are you? Come to Daddy

HorseFly@HorseFlyHQ 38m
Ed, all your messages are public. Stop it

HorseFly@HorseFlyHQ39m
You like Shandy Hand do you? Wanna give me one? Call me baby you've got a sweet ass

HorseFly@HorseFlyHQ 41m
Remember HorseFly? Share your memories or post your pictures, we'll retweet them Love Martin

HorseFly@HorseFlyHQ 42m
Yeah you want some? You want Nailing by Nailer? I'm a fucking legend darling u couldn't take it

HorseFly@HorseFlyHQ 43m
Remember HorseFly? Exciting news coming up. Follow us to get the news first

HorseFly@HorseFlyHQ 44m
Big tits

HorseFly@HorseFlyHQ 57m
Pussy

HorseFly@HorseFlyHQ 2h
Is anyone fucking there? What does it do?

HorseFly@HorseFlyHQ 3h
Now where did I put that guitar? Answers on a postcard xMartin

***

Sender: wiggleitalittlebit@fpl.co.uk
Recipients: TomHarding59@fsmail.com, WarrenOhHamble@shotmail.com, EdNailsher@fsmail.com, Martinconny@bacup.co.uk

11 May 2011 20:45

Guys! Good work on the Twitter stream but stop following porn sites, apparently it doesn't look good. Samantha has gone through and deleted them, she doesn't want to have to do it again.

A lot of come-back bands now do a meet and greet gold package for their super fans so this will be happening at each gig. We will start off selling ten per gig but if there's call for it we'll just keep adding more at that price level. It's gonna be £240 for a gold ticket so they'll get a laminate and they'll get to meet you lot and get their shit signed so be nice, don't be off your faces, don't fist them unless they ask for it.

Merch wise so far we've got all sizes of Ts. Sam's put in a bigger order for **XXL** because she reckons most of your fans will be obese – fucking great. Also we've got babygrows and tote bags. I don't know what they are but Sam says she knows what she's doing.

We've also got Shandy Hand mugs and keyrings, baseball hats and hoodies.

Tickets go on sale Monday so keep on with the Twitter.
Gary

Your Friend Forever

***

Sender: maudcampbell@bluemoon.com
Recipient: wiggleitalittlebit@fpl.co.uk

13 May 2011 21:22

Dear Tom,

I couldn't help but notice that there is a lot of shit about you in the papers today, a lot. It must be so stressful for you, I thought this stupid story would go away. I just wanted to say, really, that I know none of it's true. The stuff about calling some girl at the Metro and sending her a picture of your private area, I know you wouldn't do that. I know you're a decent person and I'm sure it will all just blow over soon, it's just nonsense. Sad times though, I'm sorry you're going through this.

I also read that you're re-forming Horsefly. Something popped up about it on the internet, that there will be a tour soon. Is that true? Surely it can't be. It's exciting, I think – if that's what you want. I'm surprised though. I thought maybe you might do some gigs to promote your new album when it comes out, but I didn't expect this. Are they making you do it? I remember in an interview years ago you said that you weren't in touch with the other members of Horsefly and that you hated them and that Ed and Warren were just violent thugs. So this move surprises me, I hope you've not been bullied into it. I should be pleased being a Horsefly fan but really it makes me worry about you, stupid I know.

I have no idea if I'll be able to go to one of your gigs, if they happen, if it's really true. I have such a lot going on at the moment, I've had Colin's mother on the phone screaming at me, calling me a cunt and blaming me for him taking off to live in Spain. Colin actually called me the other day, it was civil at first. He's renting somewhere in northern Spain which is not near any of the main airports so it's going to be quite tricky for the kids to visit. They can't just jump on a plane and get met at the other side, it's a long train journey. He said they could do it, I said he would have to meet them. He seemed annoyed with me about this but I think he was just annoyed that he hadn't thought about it in the first place. Then he started asking when they could go over and I said I'd have to ask them if they wanted to go at May half term. He did get mad about that but it has to be their decision doesn't it? They might want to, they might want to hang out in town with their mates skateboarding and eating sausage rolls. They're pretty cross with him. I think, if he wants to see them, to start off with he's going to have to come and visit them, get back in their good books and maybe eventually they'll want to go over there. Things have been good since he left. No one is missing him. I bought a new mattress and a washer dryer. I'm not going crazy though. I don't want to be rushed into going back to work. It feels good to have a bit of time to think about everything. It's been quite a year so far.

I seem to keep having naps, needing them. Sarah says that's normal, to sleep a lot when you're going through a trauma. I'm not sure I can call getting divorced a trauma. I suppose it is, sort of. Anyway I am ok and I hope you are too.

Best go now, I'm here though, if you ever need a friend. All this stuff in the papers, it's so awful and so untruthful. If it gets you down and you need someone to talk to you can call me, ok? I'm sure you have plenty of friends but I'm here if you need one more.

After what Sarah did, I just worry about everyone. I don't want anyone feeling so sad they have to do something stupid.

Your friend
xMaud

Your Friend Forever

***

GARY AND MAUD

Text conversation, 14 May 2011 22:45

22:45 Gary: Hi there, is that Maud?

22:47 Maud: Hello, yes it is, who is this?

22:48 Gary: This is Tom Harding. U sent me ur number.

22:49 Maud: Really? Hello, are you ok?

22:49 Gary: I've been feeling really down about everything. My single didn't go very well.

22:52 Maud: I can't think why, it's brilliant. Maybe adults don't buy that many singles these days and kids just seem to listen to things online. I'm not sure they're bothered about owning copies. My two never seem to buy any music.

22:52 Gary: Ur so kind to me Maud, really kind and gentle.

22:53 Maud: I've been a fan of yours for a long time. I'll always buy your singles.

22:53 Gary: It's so nice to have a friend like u who believes in me.

22:55 Maud: Maybe it will be a slow burner like some of your other records. Please don't think it's because it's not good because really, it's excellent.

22:55 Gary: Ur so wise, I knew u would be.

22:57 Maud: Just try and be kind to yourself. Have some good food, get some good rest.

22:57 Gary: Yeah, I'm being kind to myself now.

22:57 Maud: I'm glad to hear it.

22:59 Gary: Do u want to be kind with me Maud?

23:02 Maud: I would always be kind to you.

23.02 Gary: U would? How would u be kind to me?

23:04 Maud: By being your friend.

23:04 Gary: What kind of a friend?

23:04 Maud: A good and loyal one.

23:04 Gary: Oh Maud I wish u were here now.

23:05 Maud: So do I.

23:05 Gary: Really? What would u do if u were here?

23:05 Maud: Give you a big hug.

23:06 Gary: That's nice, we could lie down together.

23:08 Gary: Are u still there Maud?

23:08 Maud: Yes I'm here.

23:08 Gary: Would u lie down with me Maud? I'd like that.

23:08 Maud: Yes.

23:09 Gary: What are u wearing?

23:10 Maud: Why?

23:10 Gary: I just want to picture u in my head and imagine u lying down here with me.

23:11 Maud: Jeans and a top.

23:11 Gary: Nice, I'm just lying here in my shorts.

23:13 Gary: What do u think about that Maud, me lying here in my shorts?

23:14 Maud: It sounds like you're very relaxed. That's good.

23:14 Gary: Why don't u lie down too Maud? Lie down and relax with me.

23:14 Maud: I'll just sit down on the sofa.

23:15 Gary: Are u on ur own? I hope so.

23:17 Maud: Well the kids are in bed, I've just been clearing up downstairs.

23:17 Gary: Just stop all that and lie down.

23:18 Maud: I'm just getting a glass of wine.

23:18 Gary: That's nice Maud, u get a nice big drink and then lie down with me. I'm waiting for u.

23:19 Gary: Are u relaxing now? If I was there I'd be rubbing ur feet. Have u got anything on them?

23:20 Maud: Just a pair of socks.

23:21 Gary: Take ur socks off, I want to rub ur feet.

23:21 Maud: I've taken them off. God they're a mess.

23:21 Gary: I bet u've got beautiful feet, I'm rubbing some cream on them now. Lie back and close ur eyes. I want u to imagine it. My hands are all over ur feet.

23:22 Maud: That's nice.

23:23 Gary: I'm pushing my fingers in between ur toes, they're all slippery.

23:24 Gary: Do u like that?

23:25 Maud: Yes. I suppose so.

23:26 Gary: U like me pushing my fingers between ur toes?

23:28 Gary: U do don't u? U love my fingers pushing in and out of ur slippery toes.

23:28 Maud: I can't remember the last time I had a foot rub. I think it might have been from Sarah when I was pregnant with Leo.

23:29 Gary: U deserve it Maud, close ur eyes and relax. I'm going to rub ur ankles now. I'm putting some more cream on my hands so ur ankles get good and slippery.

23:30 Maud: My heels are all cracked.

23:31 Gary: Shhh. I'm rubbing ur ankles now, they're smooth and bony. I love doing it.

Your Friend Forever

23:31 Gary: Can I rub ur calves now? Calves get very tired. I think they need a good rub too.

23:31 Maud: Ok.

23:31 Gary: I'll have to take ur jeans off Maud, I can't reach ur calves properly.

23:32 Gary: Is that ok Maud, me taking ur jeans off?

23:33 Gary: I have to unbutton u first. I'm undoing ur button and pulling down ur zip, nice and slowly.

23:34 Gary: And now I'm peeling ur jeans down, they're very tight.

23:35 Maud: Right.

23:37 Gary: Oh god Maud ur driving me crazy. Do you want me to rub ur calves nice and hard?

23:38 Gary: I've put more cream on my hands, they're really slippery, and I'm rubbing ur calves and u want it don't u?

23:40 Gary: U like it don't u? I'm up to ur knees now, I can feel u quivering Maud, but u have to wait.

23:41 Maud: How do you know I'm quivering? I should put the heating on but I don't normally bother at this time of night. I just fill a hot water bottle.

23:41 Gary: Shhh, shhh. Ok Maud, I can't wait any more. I have to rub ur thighs. U want it don't u? Ask me for it! Ask me for it!

23:41 Gary: Please, ask me for it.

23:42 Maud: Will you rub my thighs?

23:43 Gary: Oh fucking hell yes, my hands are all creamy and I'm rubbing them up ur inner thigh. I can feel you trembling. I can smell u. I can smell u Maud. U want it don't u?

23:43 Maud: I don't know what to say.

23:44 Gary: Say u want to take hold of my big hard dick. U can't hold back any longer. U need to feel my dick in ur hand.

23:44 Gary: U can't have it yet, u want it but u can't have it. I'm going to massage u now until u beg me to put my dick in u.

23:44 Gary: God u want it so badly don't u? U really want me to fuck u.

23:45 Gary: I'm turning u over Maud. I'm going to fuck u from behind. I want to grab hold of ur big fleshy arse. I can feel u pushing back, god ur desperate for it aren't u?

23:46 Maud: I don't have a big fleshy arse.

23:46 Gary: Ok Maud, here goes, I'm pushing inside u. I'm grabbing ur tits and fucking and fucking u.

23:47 Gary: Can I call you?

23:48 Gary: I'd really love to talk to u I want u to hear me cum.

23:49 Gary: Oh god Maud, I'm going to cum, I'm going to come inside u. You fucking love it don't u?

23:49 Gary: You love it don't u?

23:50 Gary: Oh god that was good.

23:51 Gary: Maud, are you still there?

23:52 Gary: Maud?

23:54 Gary: U were great. I'll text u tomorrow. Hope u enjoyed ur foot rub u minx X

***

Sender: maudcampbell@bluemoon.com
Recipient: wiggleitalittlebit@fpl.co.uk

15 May 2011 21:15

Dear Tom,

Thanks for texting last night, it was nice to hear from you. I do hope you are feeling a bit better. Have you got a hangover? I'm guessing you were quite drunk. I'd probably drink quite a lot too if I had to get back together with a band I hated. Do you have to do it? I can't believe you'd want to do that. After everything you've said about it over the years. It doesn't add up. I'm here as a friend if you need me any time. But no more foot rubs, I wasn't hugely comfortable with that. Not at all in fact.

Don't worry, I won't tell anyone about last night and I've deleted all the messages. I wouldn't dream of showing them to anyone so you don't need to worry about that, if you were worried.

Sarah came round at tea time. Her eyes were really bright, full of tears but not in a sad way, I've never seen her like it before. Two more women have come forward about Bryan after seeing the news story in the paper. Gina who's leading the story thinks there's going to be loads more. They've all lodged their complaints with the police now. It's awful, really awful but this has to be a positive step doesn't it? For everyone. I think. Unless it makes things worse for people, dragging up old buried feelings. But my guess is, and it's just a guess because thankfully it didn't happen to me, but my guess is it's all still there not buried at all.

I think you carry trauma round with you. In your cheeks and your hands and your shoulders and in everything you do. You don't want it to be one of your building bricks or something underpinning you, but that's what it becomes. Something heavy, something that digs in, holding you down, stopping you from moving on. I hope more come forward, there must be more and it's true that there's strength in numbers.

I'm doing a shift for Michael in the coffee shop tomorrow. His partner's going for a colonoscopy. It's very sweet that he's gone to hold his hand. They must be very close.

Warmest wishes
Your friend
Maud x

***

TOM AND GARY

Telephone conversation, 17th May 2011 2.46pm

Gary: Hello?

Tom: It's me.

Gary: What can I do you for?

Tom: I am going to change the password for the Horsefly Twitter account and I am going to be in charge of it.

Gary: But we're doing so well!

Tom: Have you seen it? It's absolutely disgusting. Ed is on there trawling for women. Someone is just following porn sites, again. It's full of filthy and abusive messages.

Gary: It's the twenty-first century!

Tom: You either let me change the password and let me do it entirely on my own or the whole fucking Horsefly tour is off. I am not being associated with this shit. Do you understand? I don't want you on there.

Gary: It's not very fair but whatever, change it.

***

GARY AND MAUD

Text conversation, 17 May 2011 23:45

23:45 Gary: Maud are u there? It's Tom.

23:46 Maud: Hi, how are you feeling? A bit better I hope?

23:46 Gary: Am I ur favourite pop star?

23:47 Maud: Ha, yes you've always been my favourite Tom, since I was about 12!

23:47 Gary: How much do u like me Maud?

23:48 Maud: Very much Tom, I think you are hugely talented.

23:49 Gary: I certainly am HUGE Maud. I'm HUGE right now.

23:49 Maud: Right.

23:49 Gary: Would u like to see how HUGE?

23:50 Maud: That's ok thanks.

23:50 Gary: I'm thinking about u Maud.

23:52 Maud: That's very nice.

23:52 Gary: I'm thinking u'd really like to see how huge I am.

23:52 Maud: No, that's not what I'm thinking about. I'm wondering if you are ok and I'd like to say I am here for you if you need me.

23:52 Gary: That's very nice Maud, very nice indeed. I DO need u. I need u here, sat on my XXXL cock. I need to feel ur tits.

23:52 Gary: I bet u'd like that wouldn't u? My hands all over ur tits while u ride me?

23:53 Gary: Ur absolutely DYING to ride me aren't u Maud? U want me like u've never wanted anything else. U can have me, u can have me right now.

23:54 Gary: Do u want me to sing to u Maud? I can sing to u while u ride my big fat cock. Would u like that?

11:55 Gary: That's it Maud, keep bouncing on my cock, I'm singing for u. Whichever song u want me to sing, I'm singing it, I'm whispering lyrics in ur ear and licking ur XXXL tits.

11:55 Gary: Oh god Maud u can't get enough of my cock can u? I'm going to have to cum.

11:56 Gary: Oh Maud u really are the best, u know that don't u? U know I can't resist u don't u? Ur SUCH a naughty minx.

11:58 Maud: I don't think you are really Tom.

11:58 Gary: Of course I am.

11:58 Maud: I don't think you are.

11:59 Gary: I am Tom my darling, Tom that you email all the time, Tom that you tell all your secrets too. I am Tom.

00:01 Maud: I don't think you are.

00:01 Gary: I am Tom and ur my little minx. Isn't this what u wanted?

00:02 Maud: You are not Tom, I am not a minx and this is not what I have ever wanted.

00:03 Gary: What makes u think I'm not Tom?

00:04 Maud: Tom would never say these things to me. I know he wouldn't. He wouldn't say them to anyone. He wouldn't say 'u'.

00:05 Gary: U don't even know me, how would u know what I would say?

00:05 Maud: You're right. I don't know you, but I do know Tom.

00:06 Gary: Ur deranged.

00:07 Maud: You're a sick pervert. DO NOT TEXT ME AGAIN.

00:07 Gary: I am Tom!

00:07 Maud: Tom would not text a stranger to say he was licking her tits.

00:08 Gary: So u admit u don't know him?

00:08 Maud: Him? Don't you mean you?

00:09 Gary: Oh fuck off u psycho bitch.

00:09 Maud: I will find out who you are.

00:09 Gary: I'm going to block u, u mad slag.

***

GARY AND TOM

Telephone conversation, 18th May 2011 3pm

Gary: Tom mate it's me.

Tom: I'm not your mate.

Gary: Any news for me?

Tom: No, have you got any news for me?

Gary: No news.

Tom: Why are you calling?

Gary: Just to see if you've got any work lined up I should know about.

Tom: No I haven't, have you lined me up any work?

Gary: No, not at the moment, just the ten Horsefly dates.

Tom: Right, well then, why don't you fuck off until you've got something to tell me?

Gary: I saw your DMs with Miley Cyrus.

Tom: How?

Gary: I've still got your login.

Tom: I thought I told you not to do Twitter any more.

Gary: It was me that told you to go on Twitter.

Tom: Yeah and it was you that made me follow loads of women with their tits out. I looked like some sort of sicko porn addict.

Gary: Says the songwriter of Shandy Hand.

Tom: I was about fucking twelve when I wrote that.

Gary: You clearly love wanking, people know you as a wanker. Wanking has put a roof over your head.

Tom: Yeah and a much bigger roof over your head for some fucking inexplicable reason.

Gary: Well I saw what she wants anyway so I'm going in for the kill.

Tom: What the fuck do you mean?

Gary: If she wants to use that bit of your song, she needs to give you a songwriting credit.

Tom: Yeah and I'm sure she will, standard. What's your fucking problem?

Gary: My problem is that this is my money.

Tom: Yeah, you'll get your twenty per cent like you always fucking do.

Gary: No, this deal is a bit different.

Tom: In what way?

Gary: Well you'll only get a twenty per cent songwriting credit for her song because there seems to be four others involved.

Tom: Yeah what of it? Twenty per cent is great. She sells more fucking records than I ever do.

Gary: Yes but my cut is twenty per cent, so it's my money.

Tom: What do you mean your money?

Gary: It's twenty per cent, so it's all mine, and this is the big time, it's Miley Fucking Cyrus.

Tom: You don't get all of it.

Gary: I do.

Tom: No you don't.

Gary: My cut is twenty per cent.

Tom: Agreed.

Gary: And your writing credit is twenty per cent. Yes?

Tom: Yes.

Gary: So it's all mine.

Tom: No, twenty per cent of it is yours.

Gary: Yes, the twenty per cent is mine.

Tom: FUCKING HELL.

Gary: Now don't start trying to twist this. It's all fair and square in your contract, I take twenty per cent.

Tom: Twenty per cent of my earnings.

Gary: Yes, but you normally get a hundred per cent of the songwriting, in this case, it's just twenty per cent so I take all of it.

Tom: You're FIRED.

Gary: Good! Once this song comes out I won't need to work again anyway.

Tom: You won't get anything. Over my dead fucking festering body.

Gary: I've told you before Tom, you don't want to fuck with me. I know people.

Tom: You don't know fucking ANYONE.

Gary: I do, I know people.

Tom: Who Gary? Who do you know?

Gary: Samantha's brother is well dodgy.

Tom: Graham is one of my closest friends you fucking village idiot. I am putting the phone down now. Don't you fucking dare call me back.

***

GARY AND TOM

Telephone conversation, 19th May 2011 9.45am

Tom: Hello?

Gary: Mate, it's me.

Tom: I'm putting the phone down.

Gary: Don't don't! Listen.

Tom: What?

Gary: Samantha explained it to me.

Tom: Explained what?

Gary: All the Miley Cyrus money isn't mine.

Tom: None of it is yours.

Gary: Twenty per cent is mine.

Tom: None of it is yours.

Gary: It is.

Tom: No it's not. I said it last night and I've never felt better about a decision in my life, *you are fired.*

Gary: Yeah but even still, I still get twenty per cent of everything.

Tom: No you fucking don't you idiot.

Gary: I do!

Tom: You don't!

Gary: The Miley Cyrus deal, at least give me that.

Tom: There is no deal yet, there is only a conversation and you only know about it because you broke into my messages.

Gary: Well prove it.

Tom: Gary, I can prove this very easily, and am happy to do so.

Gary: Well it's not fair.

Tom: It's fucking fair. What's not fucking fair is me having put up with you for so bloody long. Why did I? Sacking you felt so good. It's like an actual weight has lifted off me. It's the best thing that's ever happened to me. We are DONE. No more Gary on the phone. No more fucking Horsefly tour. I'm not doing ANY of it.

Gary: Yeah yeah, listen mate, I'll call you later when you've seen sense.

Tom: I've seen sense already 'mate' finally. I really have. It's great.

Gary: Nobody will work with you, word gets around.

Tom: Word gets around yes, but not from you, you don't know fucking *anyone*.

Gary: I know Vince Clarke from Erasure.

Tom: No you don't.

Gary: Yes I fucking do.

Tom: You've met him, you don't know him.

Gary: We spoke on the phone.

Tom: What the fuck about?

Gary: I was thinking of getting you into keyboards.

Tom: Jesus this gets worse… what did he say?

Gary: It didn't sound very good so I left it.

Tom: He must have thought you were a prank caller. You're a fucking idiot.

Gary: You'll see sense. I'll speak to you later.

Tom: I'm going to rip my phone out of the wall and pop it in the bin.

Gary: You're so fucking ungrateful, there's a lot I do for you, you know, that you don't see. A fuck of a lot. And you don't see it because I'm so fucking good at it that I take away your workload. I protect you from the outside world. I make it easy for you so that you can just sit about and write your shitty songs and strum your expensive guitar and choose what to wear for hours on end. Without me, you'd be a mess.

Tom: Seriously? Are you fucking serious? You do *nothing* for me. Tell me, tell me. What was the last thing you did for me? Hmm? Fucking tell me one thing, because as far as I'm concerned you phone me up, you insult me, you've got me no deals of any kind where I can make any money. I had to release my song on iTunes and do you know who else can do that? *Fucking everybody*! And you didn't even set it up, Samantha did, and I know this because I talked her through it over the phone, so basically it would have been quicker to do it my fucking self!

Gary: I sorted out your new carpet, that's not exactly my job is it?

Tom: You got your mate to come round and do a frankly shit job of fitting a new stair carpet and then you let him massively overcharge me. I didn't even need a new fucking carpet!

Gary: Overcharge?

Tom: Don't act the fucking innocent with me. A stair carpet for a terraced house should not cost four fucking grand. I saw it come out of my account. I bet you took half didn't you? All this time I let you get away with stuff because I don't want the fucking aggro. One half of it looks a different shade to the other. My guess is the ends of two separate rolls.

Gary: Well I got it sorted for you didn't I, it doesn't really fall under my job description does it? Yet I did it for you anyway. Do I get twenty per cent of it? No I don't.

Tom: No, I reckon you got about fifty per cent of it didn't you? You greedy bastard.

Gary: If I happen to do a deal with a carpet man that's not really any of your business is it?

Tom: I think it is Gary, I really think it is. So tell me, apart from ripping me off for a piece of carpet, what else have you done for me?

Gary: I deal with all your fan mail.

Tom: No you don't, you give it to me to deal with, you don't deal with it. You hand me a bag of letters and thimbles once a month, a child could do that.

Gary: That's not all of it, I deal with all the crazy fan mail that gets emailed. That's a bloody job in itself.

Tom: What do you mean? Fan mail that gets emailed?

Gary: You get loads of emails from fans, I deal with all of it.

Tom: Since when? How many? Who?

Gary: Oh loads and loads, there's this one woman, Maud, that emails you almost every fucking day. She can't get enough of you. I have to hose her down.

Tom: Maud? Maud who?

Gary: I can't remember her last name, she emails you all the bloody time and it's muggins here that has to deal with her.

Tom: What do you mean, *deal with her*?

Gary: Well last night for example, I basically had to help her, you know, polish herself off.

Tom: You what?

Gary: EXACTLY, all these things that I do for you that you know nothing about.

Tom: Polish her off?

Gary: Phone sex, just to, you know, cool her down. The emails were getting out of control.

Tom: You had phone sex with someone who emails me called Maud?

Gary: Yep, and frankly I don't have the time to keep doing it.

Tom: And who, who, answer me honestly, who did she think was on the other end of the phone?

Gary: Well you of course, she doesn't know who I am. Tom… Tom… Are you still there?

Tom: Send me every email, every single last email that poor girl has sent. Do it now and if you don't I will report you to the police. Right now. Go to your desk. Find every email. Send them to me. Have you got that?

Gary: Phone sex wasn't illegal when I last checked Tom… the police will just laugh at you.

Tom: Every single email. Right now.

Gary: Okay okay, I'll forward them, you're welcome to her. Keep your fucking hair on.

Tom: And you're fired. As fired as it's possible to be and if those emails are not with me in the next hour I'm calling the police.

Gary: Okay okay calm down it's only some emails.

Tom: That picture of a cock sent to the Metro. That was you wasn't it?

Gary: What? No...

Tom: It fucking was wasn't it?

Gary: No.

Tom: You're a liar. Emails. Now. THEN NEVER EVER CALL ME AGAIN.

Gary: Okay okay okay fucking hell.

***

Sender: TomHarding59@fsmail.com
Recipient: maudcampbell@fsmail.com

19 May 2011 22:08

Dear Maud,
   Hi, it's Tom, Tom Harding that you've been writing to.
   I just wanted to say how utterly sorry I am for what Gary, my bloody awful manager did to you.
   I found out yesterday a little of what's been going on. He's been pretending to be me and your emails have been going to him and I hadn't seen any of them until yesterday.
   It was crass and thoughtless and you must feel terrible about it. I am so so sorry, I feel sick about it.
   He's been sacked with immediate effect. I should have done

it a long long time ago. I honestly can't think why I put up with him for so long.

You wouldn't believe half of the stunts he played on me. He tried to get me to audition for The X Factor! Only a few weeks ago, as a normal contestant...

What was he thinking? What was I thinking putting up with him?

Maud I am so so deeply sorry about what he did to you.

I'd love to meet you and apologise in person if you can bear to give me the time of day? Can we meet up and have tea and cake or I'll buy you lunch?

Do you still live in Preston? I'll happily come to Preston and see you, just let me know.

Yours in anticipation of a favourable reply.

T

x

***

Sender: TomHarding59@fsmail.com

Recipient: maudcampbell@fsmail.com

20 May 2011 20:14

Dear Maud,

I haven't heard back from you but I'm pretty sure this is your email address so I'm going to write again and hope that you'll be able to reply eventually.

I remember you writing to me years ago, I used to really enjoy your letters. I never got much fan mail, and most of it was just people asking me to sign stuff, they never asked me anything or told me anything. Your letters were different, I really enjoyed them.

It's the same now, if people recognise me they want an autograph or a picture, and I don't get it. The selfie is like a picture that pretends we were hanging out, but we weren't hanging out. And they take the picture and say ta and then just walk off, and then they probably share it with all their mates but they didn't actually speak to me. They didn't ask me anything. They didn't even ask how I am. So it's like they're not interested at all.

You though, you always were, you always asked about me, asked me what I thought about things, told me about what was happening in your life, they were lovely letters. I missed them when they stopped. I couldn't write back to you, I wanted to but you were very young and I worried that they'd be taken the wrong way. Not by you because I think you were always quite wise, you had an old head on your shoulders, but maybe if you showed them to anyone else I could have got in trouble for it. You will have seen all this recent nonsense about me and some girl from the Metro, that's entirely made up but no one seems to care, well I'm pretty sure now my bloody manager did it. I'll have to give them a call.

Yours faithfully

T

x

P.S. I always loved your P.S.s, they made me laugh.

***

Sender: TomHarding59@fsmail.com
Recipient: maudcampbell@fsmail.com

22 May 2011 19:43

Dear Maud,

Your Friend Forever

It really is me, Tom.

Upsetting you is the very last thing I want to do, but I do want you to know it's me, it wasn't before but it's me now.

Please believe it's me.

Yours,

T

x

***

Sender: maudcampbell@fsmail.com
Recipient: TomHarding59@fsmail.com

22 May 2011 21:00

Please delete my email address.

Do not contact me again.

I've been humiliated enough.

***

Sender: TomHarding59@fsmail.com
Recipient: maudcampbell@fsmail.com

22 May 2011 21:27

Dear Maud,

I'm so very sorry, I understand you're very upset.

I am Tom, really I am.

Tom: that you used to write to when you were young. I remember all about you and your friend Sarah and her moving away, how upset you were, and I remember you saving up your Clippercards so you could visit her. You were very sweet.

And the corned beef wall! I really remember that. It made me laugh.

My record company closed down the PO Box account for Horsefly when the band split up so I sent you my number and address and some cash, I was worried about you, I remember you were having a really hard time with your Mum. Did you ever get it? I did wonder why I'd never heard from you, I thought maybe you were too shy to phone me. I've always wondered how you got on with everything. I'm really pleased to be in touch with you.

I hope you believe it's me. If you don't, don't worry, I won't email again unless I hear from you, the absolute last thing I want to do is upset you.

Yours

T

x

***

Sender: maudcampbell@fsmail.com
Recipient: TomHarding59@fsmail.com

22 May 2011 23:53

Is it really you?

I'm starting to believe it but I'm really uncertain after everything. I'm scared someone is playing a very cruel trick on me. If you are someone playing a cruel trick on me please stop it immediately. I am having a hard enough time as it is without having this extra upset.

I will be in Sunshine Valley Wine Bar, Market Road, Preston, from 7pm on Thursday night, 26th May.

If you really are Tom, you can come along. If you're not Tom, please please just leave me alone. I have had a really hard year, things were just starting to get better and this is the last thing I need and I don't have any patience for it and if it is some stupid prank just stop it now, it's CRUEL.

If you are Tom, I'll be very glad to meet you of course, and I hope you understand my trepidation.

Maud

P.S. If you are Tom, and you come and meet me, don't be surprised if I can't speak, or I faint, shake, cry uncontrollably or even vomit.

P.P.S. I will of course try not to vomit but as it would be from nerves rather than the unfortunate consequences of food poisoning I'm 99.9 per cent sure it wouldn't be projectile so you don't need to worry about that at least.

P.P.P.S. I just had a phone call from my friend Michael asking me to go to the police station and get him. He's been arrested for indecent exposure!

***

Sender: TomHarding59@fsmail.com
Recipient: maudcampbell@fsmail.com

23 May 2011 00:09

Hi, I will be there.

See you on Thursday.

I won't mind at all if you're sick though I hope for your sake that doesn't happen.

Looking forward to meeting you finally.

Yours

xT

Part Three

Zena Barrie

Your Friend Forever

CORNED BEEF WALL AND OTHER POEMS

BY MAUD HARRISON

To my beautiful friends
Sarah & Tom

© 2013

Acknowledgements

BIG thanks to Tiffany Murray who suggested at Arvon that I try writing something in young Maud's voice.

Thank you to Tim Shearer who made me get a draft finished.

Thanks to everyone at Unbound, particularly Xander Cansell who took the book on and Mary Chesshyre my brilliant editor. Plus all the Unbound Social Club.

Thank you to Reece de Ville for so kindly making me a trailer and to Robin Ince, Lizzie Roper and Alex Lowe for being my first readers.

Thank you to Natalie Haynes for Verpa and Craige Barker for his photography skills.

Thank you to all the lovely spoken word community in Manchester who have listened to bits of this book over and over and over again... and to Michelle Flower who babysat for me whilst I did this.

Thank you my brilliant supportive friends who always spur me on. I was going to list all your names but I'm too scared of missing someone out.

Thank you to Meredith, my brilliant funny daughter and the best person I know.

Oh and Charlie Hartill, long gone now but forever a supportive voice in my ear.

Unbound is the world's first crowdfunding publisher, established in 2011.

We believe that wonderful things can happen when you clear a path for people who share a passion. That's why we've built a platform that brings together readers and authors to crowdfund books they believe in – and give fresh ideas that don't fit the traditional mould the chance they deserve.

This book is in your hands because readers made it possible. Everyone who pledged their support is listed at the front of the book and below. Join them by visiting unbound.com and supporting a book today.

Sarah Allchurch
Polly Andrews
Bennett Arron
Shona Barker
Helen Bass
David Benson
Schirin Boudny
Torso Boy
Katy Brand
Margaret Cabourn-Smith

Gemma Cammidge
Richy Campbell
Blaized Carmey
Nicholas Chadwick
Louise Chantal
Jason Cobley
Jude Cook
Alison Cooke
Debbie Cooper
Billy Cowan

Ruth Cutting
James Delargy
Andrew Dempster
Samuel Dodson
Chas. Early
Justin Edwards
Stephen Edwards
Carolyne Ekong
Adam Evans
Stephen Evans
Jon Ewing
Judith Faultless
Kate Feld
Marisa Ferguson
Julieanna Fierro
Janis Finigan
Christiane Fischer
Sue Fleeshman
Jane Flynn
Tim Fountain
Ashley Frieze
Naomi Frisby
Richard Fry
Merryl Futerman
Rosie Garland
Alan Gillespie
Mary Gleeson
Chris Grady
Emma Grae
Josephine Greenland
Lucy Haken
Fiona HallenanBarker
Naomi Hart
David Hartley
Mike Heath
Gemma Hepworth
Stephanie Hewson
Guille Ibanez
Tom Jenks
Dan Johnson
Gaynor Jones
Ali Kahn
Simon Kane
Lisa Keddie
Steven Kedie
Malcolm Keen

Robbie Kennedy
Dan Kieran
Claire Knight
Darren Lea-grime
Holly Lombardo
Steph Lonsdale
Alex Lowe
Ewen Macintosh
Emily Macklesworth
Ava Macpherson
Joanne Mann
Sue McGeorge
Karl McIntyre
Oriane Messina
John Mitchinson
Ben Moor
Jakki Moore
DH Morgan
Pegeen Murphy
Ali Murray
David Murray
Susan Murray
Sarah Myers
Carlo Navato
Jo Neary
Claire Nightingale
Lisa O'Hare
Owen O'Leary
Jen Pang
Alexia Pepper de Caires
Rebecca Peppiette
Justin Pollard
Michael Powis
Janet Pretty
Sobia Quazi
Cameron Robertson
Danny Robins
Kate Rodwell
Dan Rothschild
Shay Rowan
Geoff Rowe
Lee Rowland
Fay Rusling
Karl Sedgwick
Delea Shand
Carly Sheen

Thomas Shepherd
Gary Sigley
Davie Simmons
David Skinner
Adrian Slatcher
Stephen Smythe
Paul Stanley
Emma Taylor
Frances Taylor
Matt Thomas

Jessica Toomey
Alys Torrance
Serina Wain
Tom Ward
Phil Whelans
Gavin White
Louise Wilkin
Jez Wingham
Dotty Winters
Anne Wynne